Moon of Desire

D0977790

Moon of Desire

SOPHIE DANSON

First published in 1994 by
Black Lace
332 Ladbroke Grove
London
W10 5AH

Copyright © Sophie Danson 1994

Typeset by TW Typesetting, Plymouth, Devon
Printed and bound by
Cox & Wyman Ltd, Reading, Berks

ISBN 0 352 32911 4

Black Lace novels are sexual fantasies.
In real life, make sure you practise safe sex.

Prologue

Ragzburg, 1880

The moon emerged from behind a cloud, its cold, pallid light casting eerie shadows in the darkness. Shadows that moved in a secret synchronicity, shapes darting between the trees as the branches swished and swayed in the night-wind.

It was a cold night, the wind a searing gust that tore at naked flesh, whipping the women's waist-length hair into ragged tails that streamed behind them as they ran. Their nipples were stiff, but not with cold. An unearthly passion drove them on, warming their bellies and moistening their love-lips with honeydew. The hunger was especially sharp tonight.

They had left their prey behind them, drained of its usefulness and half-covered now with the drifting leaves. The young man had served to slake their desire for a few brief moments, his firm, muscular body and long, hard cock engines of sweet pleasure that had lasted, alas, too short a time. Little fool; did he not understand how dangerous it was to go walking alone in the forest on nights of the full moon? Spent now, he lay sleeping among the larch and fir, the women's passion still wet and sticky on his flesh.

Sleeping or dead? There was no way of knowing, and in any case, why should they care? They had already

1

forgotten him. There would be others tonight – many others – and all would be forgotten by morning. Reaching the edge of the forest, they gathered together in a close-knit pack, their breathing a hoarse harmony of longing. Their bodies glistened white in the moonlight as they huddled together and raised their faces to the night sky in a thin, keening cry of longing.

The house on the hill had seemed deserted. But now a lamp was burning at an upstairs window, its flickering flame a warm, orange glow in the darkness.

Come to us. Come to us.

The wind sang through the trees, shrieked around the low eaves of the old stone cottage as a face appeared at the window.

Now is the time. You are one of us. Come to us, come . . .

The casement window opened and the girl leaned out, her white cotton shift blown hard against her body by the chill night wind, moulding the outline of two firm, stiff-nippled breasts. Her eyes were bright stars in a pale face, her lips full and crimson, moistened constantly by the tip of a darting pink tongue.

As she lowered herself slowly from the window, her long rope of black hair swung behind her, reaching past her waist and tied loosely with a green ribbon.

She hung for a few seconds by her fingertips, then let go and fell the last few feet to the ground, landing barefoot on the soft, springy turf.

Voices and shapes encircled her and she smiled, her eyes filling with a deep, dark intensity.

Naked, you must come to us naked . . .

Hands pulled at her cotton shift, clawed at it with long, sharp nails that tore the thin fabric from her young body. Fingers slid the emerald silk ribbon from her hair so that the next gust of wind caught it and sent it flying out behind her like a banner.

Their touch aroused her, made her laugh with a mad joy as her vulva throbbed with the anticipation of ultimate pleasure. Tonight, for the first time, she was giving in to the dark hunger. Tonight, that hunger would be satisfied at last.

2

Now you are one with us. Come . . .

And now she was running with them, along the edge of the forest and towards the isolated upland farmstead, redolent with the scent of sweet, fresh meat.

Chapter One

The mud-spattered taxi careered recklessly through the
streets of Ragzburg, its driver talking animatedly as he
rested one bronzed hand lightly on the steering wheel.

'There are so many mysteries, so many stories to tell.
They have been passed down from generation to generation in my family. Only we Romany people truly know
the secrets of our ancient city.'

In the back of the taxi sat Lukas Mankiewicz of the
Ministry of Mines and Public Works, only half listening
as they bumped over the cobbles of the old town on
their way to the airport. He had heard it all a dozen
times before. Janos had a typical gypsy's love of the fan-
tastical and the grotesque; and loved to bore his passengers with tales of the strange chimerical beasts said to
live in the mountains above Ragzburg.

Carried away by his story, the dark-eyed man craned
his head back to look at Mankiewicz, and the car swerved alarmingly, narrowly avoiding a collision with a
tractor.

'For God's sake, man, keep your eyes on the road!'
snapped Lukas, glancing at his watch. If he hadn't been
so pressed for time, he'd have walked the two miles to
the airport. Anything rather than entrust his safety to
Janos and his filthy taxi. He brushed traces of mud off

the sleeve of his Armani suit. 'And it's all rubbish anyway. Werewolves? Demons? There's nothing strange living in those mountains – I've skied up there hundreds of times, and I should know. Even the wolves died out years ago, any fool knows that. Save your quaint folktales for the tourists, Janos. Maybe they'll fall for them.'

Janos shrugged and swung the car round a sharp bend and out through the city gates onto the main road.

'As you wish, Mr Mankiewicz,' he replied cheerfully. 'But Janos knows what is truth and what is fantasy. Janos knows what he has seen.'

He scratched his ear then rested both hands on the steering wheel, the sleeves of his coarse peasant shirt pushed up to the elbows. Deep white scars made a striking contrast with the sun-bronzed flesh of his forearms, livid furrows emerging from beneath the cream-coloured linen and ending just short of his wrists.

He glanced over his shoulder at Mankiewicz as the taxi bumped into the airport car-park.

'I do not expect you to believe my little stories. Everyone thinks Janos is a little crazed, no? But you would do well to heed Janos's words, Mr Mankiewicz: there are some things that it is wise to be afraid of.'

Don Emilio de la Costa Arañuez had the biggest, hardest, most beautiful cock Soraya had seen in a long time. That alone was enough to make this afternoon a memorable one. And the best thing about it all was that the whole damn thing was on expenses.

She cradled Don Emilio's balls in her perfectly-manicured hands and felt him tremble with desire. Excellent. This afternoon must also be a memorable one for the Brazilian Justice Minister if Soraya was to return to the Embassy with her mission accomplished.

'You're a witch, Soraya Chilton,' groaned the Minister, bracing his back against the bedroom wall as Soraya manipulated him with gentle skill. 'And I ought to tell you and your British Government to go to hell.'

'That's your prerogative,' smiled Soraya, giving his

glans a playful pinch. 'But I thought we had an arrangement. Of course, if you'd rather I *didn't* suck you off . . .'

'Stop playing games with me, Soraya. Just let me put my cock between those divine lips of yours, before I change my mind about our little deal.'

Suppressing a smile, Soraya parted her glossy scarlet lips and curled them around Don Emilio's impressive shaft. She always took a great deal of trouble over her make-up whenever the Foreign Office sent her out on one of these special assignments. After all, you never knew when you might be called upon to use your initiative . . . Experience had taught her that there was nothing that turned a man on more than a pair of luscious red lips fastening round his shaft. And Soraya Chilton had an unshakable rule: never to disappoint her contacts.

This trip to Rio had come as a very pleasant surprise. After several unspeakably boring months in the Department's London offices, Soraya was beginning to crave a touch of tropical sunshine. So she was more than eager when her boss James, the Assistant Under Secretary, had told her she was off to Brazil to corrupt a few trade officials.

'This job's definitely got your name on it,' he'd told her, handing over the briefing documents. 'Seems the secret gay lover of one of the Princes has got himself thrown into a Brazilian jail for diamond smuggling; and he's threatening to blow the whistle on the entire British Royal Family if we don't get him out. He's a nasty piece of work, but if we can get him back over here, we have ways of persuading him to keep his mouth shut. Jeremy's already over there, arranging for a little financial sweetener. All you need to do is, well . . .'

'What I do best?' suggested Soraya sweetly, opening the envelope and scanning the contents.

'Precisely. Just be nice to the main man, and for pity's sake don't come back without the signature and the photographs, or the Foreign Secretary will have my balls for cuff-links.'

'Don't worry, James, I won't let you down. You know how nice I can be when I want to. In fact, I think I'm really going to enjoy this assignment. It'll make a welcome change from vetting applications for export licences.'

And so here she was in Brazil, at the culmination of a rather successful fortnight in the sun. She'd tried to spin it out as long as she could, but the time had come to conclude the deal and get out. The hidden camera was whirring quietly to itself inside the hotel wardrobe, and the Minister had absolutely no idea that his little indiscretions were being recorded for posterity. Should he decide to renegue on their little deal, Soraya would have ample evidence to persuade him back to the path of righteousness . . .

'Oh yes, do it to me . . . harder now, I want to feel your teeth.'

Don Emilio's eyes were closing in ecstasy as Soraya worked on him, sucking hard on the tip of his cock.

'Take it all into your mouth. I want to see you take it in, right up to the balls.'

He was big; so big that it almost choked her to let his shaft slide back over her tongue until it touched the back of her mouth. She felt incredibly aroused to be here, now, kneeling on the floor of a Rio de Janeiro hotel room, with her tongue curled about the Brazilian Justice Minister's cock. Under her smart but sexy business suit, her nipples were iron-hard and her erect clitoris was throbbing against the gusset of her white satin panties.

With a natural and practised skill, Soraya continued sucking and biting at his shaft whilst her fingers stroked and squeezed the heavy fruit of his balls. There was something so irresistibly sexy about sucking off a man when he was fully clothed; and Don Emilio's manly organs were such a delightful golden-brown against the light grey fabric of his summer suit. It was plain to see that Don Emilio's golden tan extended to every point of his muscular body.

He was gripping her shoulders now, beads of sweat

7

gathering on his handsome brow as he felt pleasure approaching and urged her on, thrusting hard into the depths of her.

His semen came in a series of hot, powerful spurts onto the back of her throat, and she swallowed down the salty tide with relish as it flooded her mouth, a few stray droplets escaping from the corners of her scarlet lips. Bliss.

For a few moments Don Emilio stood motionless, his eyes closed and his still-erect shaft rammed up to the hilt into his lover's mouth. Soraya made no attempt to push him away, savouring the taste and the feel of him on her tongue. Then he opened his eyes and laughed dismissively as he withdrew from her.

'You're a born slut, did you know that, my dear Miss Chilton?'

'I shall take that as a compliment.'

'As indeed you should. You've a wicked skill with those pretty lips and hands of yours. But perhaps . . .'

'Perhaps what?'

'Perhaps we should see what other skills you have. As you can see, my cock is far from spent – already he is ready to crow for you again. Maybe we should see what little tricks you know how to play with your quim . . .'

Soraya needed no second bidding. Almost before he had spoken she was slipping seductively out of her jacket and skirt to reveal the lacy bra and panties beneath, the white satin suspender belt holding up sheer seamed stockings.

With a grunt of approval, Don Emilio pulled her towards him, crushing her soft white skin against the rough fabric of his suit. His huge rod pressed against her belly like a battering ram, demanding entrance to the inner sanctum of her womanhood.

'Do you know what I'm going to do to you now, my gorgeous English filly?'

Soraya giggled, the champagne she'd had earlier making her even randier and more uninhibited than usual.

'Tell me.'

8

'I'm going to throw you on that bed right now and have you, that's what!'

'Oh, you are, are you?' She teased him with butterfly-soft caresses on his hardening prick.

And suddenly – without even taking his jacket and tie off – Don Emilio gathered her up in his arms, striding across the room towards the bed. Lying there across his strong arms, Soraya presented the very picture of frail womanhood, a sweet confection of frills and vulnerability. It was better that Don Emilio did not know about his 'conquest's' second-Dan black belt in Karate. She could easily have resisted his amorous intentions if she'd wanted, but of course – she didn't. Soraya Chilton was the consummate professional; and she truly loved her work.

He dropped her onto the bed and she lay there, gasping and giggling, as he ripped off her bra and panties, as impatiently as a child unwrapping presents on Christmas Day. The screwed-up tatters of satin and lace he flung onto the floor, the discarded wrapping paper of this, his very best present in a long, long time.

'Aren't you even going to undress?' laughed Soraya as he straddled her with his strong thighs.

'Undress? Why the hell should I want to undress? You've already driven me to the point of distraction, you little temptress. I am aching to get inside you right now.'

Paradoxically, the brutal suddenness of his love-making was massively erotic for Soraya. There was something irresistibly sexy about coupling with a man who wanted her so desperately that he simply unzipped his pants and took her. As his cock drove into the well-lubricated furrow between her thighs, she felt hot shivers of excitement running through her whole body. The fabric of Don Emilio's suit was a coarse linen, and as he pressed home the tip of his manhood, the roughness ground against her naked pelvis, exciting her clitoris to peak after peak of frenzied pleasure.

It felt so, so good. The air was warm and scented with

9

frangipani blossom; and Soraya's head was spinning with the intoxication of sensual enjoyment and champagne. What other job could take you half-way across the globe to confront the handsomest, most powerful men in the world – and seduce them into glorious submission?

They thrust together, moving hungrily on the sunlit bed. It didn't matter if this time it didn't last more than a few minutes. They had all afternoon to explore every position in the book – and there was a three-hour tape in the video camera.

Yes, Soraya was enjoying this assignment. And when Don Emilio had glutted his desire, and they had shared half-a-dozen orgasms, she would ply him with more champagne and remind him of their bargain.

And if he refused to put his signature to the deal? Why, she would simply resort to other, less subtle techniques. She did not particularly enjoy blackmail, but it was certainly a useful method of persuasion. She was sure that, once he'd viewed his indiscretions on film, Don Emilio would quickly see the merits of the British Government's point of view.

The rain seemed to be falling from the sky in a single continuous sheet; and Soraya hugged her raincoat about her tightly. She was sure she could feel a cold coming on.

Bloody London. Why did it always seem to be raining whenever she came back from a foreign assignment, no matter what time of the year it was? She looked down at her bare, tanned legs and realised how out of place they must look on a grotty February day in dismal London.

Still, never mind. The Rio assignment couldn't have gone better, and the Foreign Secretary had thanked her personally for her efforts in getting the Prince's lover out of jail and back to Britain. Why they'd been so keen to protect the Prince's reputation, was completely beyond her; but it wasn't her job to question Foreign Office policy, just to do what she was instructed to do.

10

She pushed work out of her mind. This morning, she had promised herself that she would shop till she dropped, and spend every last penny of the bonus she'd been awarded for 'smoothing things over' so neatly in Rio. It was nice to be appreciated.

The sky seemed unnaturally dark on this depressing February morning, and Soraya shivered, suddenly aware of a bone-deep chill, even in the midst of the West End rush. She took a short-cut down a side street and the air seemed to close in on her. It felt as if there were shadows within shadows, eyes watching her from dark doorways. Ugh. Horrible. That was the trouble with London. One minute you'd be walking down a completely respectable street lined with exclusive dress-shops; the next, you'd find yourself wandering into the middle of a seedy underworld with grotesque buildings and gruesome people straight out of a Hogarth etching.

Soraya disliked weirdness in all its forms; she much preferred things to be ordered and neat and comprehensible. She was widely respected in the Department as a down-to-earth, common-sensical young woman who got things done and brooked no nonsense from anyone. Head down, she walked quickly through the shadowy street and was relieved to emerge at the other end into a busy thoroughfare. She breathed more easily. Even the rain seemed to have eased off a little.

A cappuccino and a slice of sticky *sachertorte*, that's what she needed to cheer her up. And she was due to meet Rosa at the Café Vienna in half an hour's time, for one of their regular tell-all girlie chats. Rosa always had the best gossip in London. Soraya glanced at her watch. If she was going to make the rendezvous in time, she had better get a move on.

Bags bundled under her arms, she hurried along, keeping close under the shop fronts to take advantage of the shelter, and avoid the drips from the awnings. As she passed a travel agency, the bright lights caught her eye and she paused, her mind momentarily a thousand miles away, on a Caribbean beach.

11

A holiday. Yeah, that would be great. She had some leave coming, too – James was always nagging that if she didn't take it before the end of the financial year, she'd lose the entitlement. How about ten blissful days under blue St Lucian skies, making love in the warm ocean with some exquisite young man; or two; or more . . .

She scanned the travel agent's window, looking for the perfect bargain break. Jamaica . . . oh yes. Or maybe the Bahamas, Mexico, the Gambia . . . there was so much to choose from. So why did her eyes keep snapping back to that crumpled card in the bottom left-hand corner of the window, offering a three-day package tour to the ancient central European city of Ragzburg?

Ragzburg? Oh come on, it was hardly St Tropez. Despite a distant family connection with the city, Soraya had never been there; in fact, she'd never felt more than a passing curiosity towards the place. In photographs it always looked rather cold and grim, like the set for a low-budget horror flick. So why did she feel so peculiarly drawn to it now?

No, no, that wasn't her cup of tea at all. Tearing her eyes away, Soraya noted down the details of a two-week break in the Bahamas, and pushed open the door of the travel agency. A trip to Ragzburg? Some other time, maybe.

'All leave suspended until further notice, Soraya, you know the rules. The Permanent Secretary's word is law.'

'Bollocks to that!' Soraya slammed her fist into the desk in a fit of pique. 'I've got a fortnight's holiday to get in before April, and I'm damn-well taking it.'

James Delauney sighed. Soraya was a good friend and a terrific worker, but even he had to admit she could be difficult at times.

'Look, sweetie . . .'

'Don't you "sweetie" me! I want to see Sir Adrian.'

'You can't. He's not here.'

'Well when will he be back?'

'He's not coming back.' Delauney sat down wearily behind his desk. God, he fancied Soraya. It was a damn shame she'd never returned the compliment. He wondered if now, just for old times' sake . . .

'What do you mean?'

'He's not coming back because he's been . . . relocated. Look Soraya, you're not supposed to know this, so keep your mouth shut, but there's been a bit of a scandal. Sir Adrian and a couple of call-girls, you know the sort of thing. He's very kindly agreed to tender his resignation to keep the whole thing quiet, and they're moving him up north somewhere. It's all very hush-hush. The thing is, it means that the Department is being reorganised – it's a complete shambles. That's why all leave has been cancelled right now. I don't even know where I'm going to be this time next week. They could transfer me anywhere they like.'

'Bloody hell.' A slow smile spread over Soraya's face, and she sank down on James's office sofa. Sir Adrian, hoist by his own petard? She remembered all the times he'd tried to get into her pants. It was almost funny. 'The old goat!'

James gazed longingly at Soraya's endless thighs, so teasingly revealed by her split skirt as she lolled back on the sofa. He imagined lying on top of her, crushing her slender body into the soft leather cushions, getting out his shaft and pushing aside the gusset of her little white panties . . .

'Are you OK, James? You've gone all red.'

He shook himself back to reality. Who was he kidding? Soraya was well out of his reach. He took a quick drink of water from the glass on his desk.

'OK? Oh yes, fine. Anyhow, Soraya, the fact is that if you want to argue the toss about this holiday of yours, you're going to have to complain to Gavin.'

'Gavin? Who the hell's Gavin?'

'The new Assistant Under Secretary, he is taking my place. Tricia's been posted to Cyprus and they're talking about sending me to Overseas Trade.'

'I see, and what's this Gavin like?'

James hesitated, twiddling his pencil, trying to frame the words. It wasn't easy finding the right way to tell a colleague that her new boss was a little shit.

'Hmm. Well, he's a bit of a ... Look, you'll find out for yourself soon enough. He's over there, in the outer office.'

Soraya peered through the glass partition at the scene in the open-plan office beyond. A rather insignificant young man with the look of a sales rep was peering surreptitiously down a typist's blouse, an expression of schoolboy lechery on his face.

'Oh goodie, a slimeball. I can't wait.'

She got up from the sofa and – to James's utter amazement – planted a kiss full on his lips. His unruly member twitched painfully inside his pants at the touch of her hands on his neck, the feel of her full breasts pressing hard against his shirt front. A thousand obscene fantasies coursed through his brain, making the tip of his glans weep tears of desperate longing. Oh God it was just too much; even the smell of her perfume gave him an erection. His fingers itched to reach out and grab great big handfuls of Soraya's gorgeous backside, but sheer panic kept his hands chastely resting on the waistband of her skirt.

'What was that for?' he managed to gasp as she released him.

'You know what I like best about you, James?'

'No, what?'

'You've never made a pass at me. Not once have you tried to put your hand up my skirt. You're not like the others – you're a real gentleman, James Delauney.'

Yes you are, James, you stupid bastard, thought Delauney as Soraya shut the office door behind her. More fool you.

It was late when Soraya got home from the office that day, tired and annoyed.

She'd been spot-on about Gavin, of course. A

14

malicious, lecherous tosspot with wandering hands, and a yellow streak as wide as Australia. He'd listened to her with that idiot smile on his face, and then told her quite frankly that if she wanted to get on in the Department she was going to have to be a whole lot nicer to him.

Well sod that, thought Soraya, stripping off her work clothes and turning on the shower. This was one relationship which was going to stay well and truly professional.

She stepped under the water – hot as she could stand – and let it warm her bones, taking away the horrible chill of a February night in London. Eyes closed, she let the water cascade over her face as she soaped her belly and breasts, savouring the luxury of the sensations. It was a pity Magnus couldn't be here, but he was at a conference in Reykjavik with that blonde girl from Fisheries and Foods. Not that Soraya was jealous – her relationship with Magnus had always been intimate, but not close. They didn't even see each other that often. No strings, no hassles; the payoff was mutual pleasure, and there was always plenty of that.

Imagination filled the void as she recalled how Magnus would soothe away the cares of a hard day at work. She ran her hands over her breasts, picturing him standing there in the shower with her, his strong hands kneading and stroking her body.

Soraya loved to touch herself. Orgasms were so wonderfully luxurious when you could allow yourself to be totally, unashamedly selfish. As tiredness and anger ebbed away, desire took their place; and she began gently pinching her left nipple between finger and thumb whilst her right hand slid down her belly towards the thicket of dark, lustrous curls between her thighs.

The intensity of the pleasure took her by surprise. Her love-lips seemed somehow larger and plumper than usual, more sensitive too, inviting her fingers into the dark warmth of her intimacy.

The wetness of her need mingled with the wetness of the hot soapy water coursing down her belly and forming little rivulets as it ran over the curly pubic hair. Fragrance filled her nostrils – the sweetness of the shower-gel, combined with the heady aroma of her own sex. Yes, Soraya was hot for pleasure tonight.

The lightest pressure of fingertip on pleasure-bud sent electric shocks tingling through her body, and she rubbed very gently, hardly touching the epicentre of her need. This pleasure was so close to pain, at the very edge of endurance.

Sliding her thumb over the slippery head of her rose-pink bud, Soraya let her middle finger dive into the luxuriant wetness of her vagina. Tight, hot, dripping with moisture, it welcomed the invader as it would welcome a lover's penis, pulsating with need as it tried to draw her finger ever deeper inside.

Such intensity could not last for ever. With a sigh almost of regret, Soraya surrendered to the onrush of orgasm. Warmth swelled in her belly, radiating out from her throbbing clitoris to fill her entire being as her womanhood clenched in the first of a dozen delicious spasms.

Oh yes, Soraya loved to pleasure herself.

Slipping on a robe and drying her hair, Soraya went out into the living room. It was dark but the curtains were open and a cold, clear light was spilling in from an almost full moon in a cloudless night sky. As she stood at the window, she could see the lighted windows in the exclusive apartment block opposite. She bent to turn on the table lamp but stopped, her attention suddenly attracted by something moving in one of the windows opposite.

Two figures were entwined on a bed, their naked bodies locked in silent ecstasy. Intrigued and slightly excited, Soraya stopped in her tracks. It wasn't that she was some sort of voyeur, oh no. This sort of thing didn't normally turn her on, but tonight . . .

Tonight, she seemed to have a more than usually avid appetite for sex. It really was a pity Magnus wasn't here. Magnus, or Peter, or Jonathan, or Lars: it didn't really matter. She just needed a cock inside her, needed a skilful tongue to lick out her honey-sweet juice. Her hand strayed instinctively to the front of her robe and slid inside, feeling for her pleasure-button as she watched the lovers' sensual play in silent slow-motion. If she didn't have a man to pleasure her, she must do the job herself. There was a risk that someone in the apartment block would see her standing there in the moonlit window, unfastening her robe, letting her hands stray over her own nakedness.

But tonight, in all honesty, she couldn't give a damn.

Chapter Two

Soraya parked the car and walked towards the office block, its tinted windows and blank façade offering no clue to the business conducted inside.

The message had been cryptic, but to the point: a few words typed on a postcard, depicting an old painting of Aphrodite. 'Bloomsbury Tower, 8 a.m. tomorrow. Absolute discretion essential.'

She'd thought about showing it to James, but James had been sent on a temporary transfer to Overseas Trade; and Gavin . . . well the less she saw of him the better. She'd been on the point of tearing the card up and throwing it in the bin, when she thought: why not? That was the thing about Soraya: she was an adventuress, a chancer. Which was how she'd acquired the Foreign Office job as 'cultural envoy' in the first place, and how she'd enjoyed such spectacular successes. Soraya Chilton just couldn't resist a challenge.

As insurance, she'd left the card on the telephone table in her flat. If anything untoward did happen, routine surveillance would be sure to track her down. The Department liked to keep tabs on all its employees, in case of mishap.

She gave the revolving door a shove, and stepped in; emerging on the other side into a sumptuous lobby, with modern sculptures tastefully arranged around a central fountain in the form of a statue of Aphrodite. Intrigued, she approached the reception desk, where a uniformed security guard greeted her with an appreciative nod.

'Good morning, miss.'

'Good morning. My name is Soraya Chilton. I've an eight o'clock appointment but I'm not sure who with.'

'Sign in here.'

The security guard slid a clipboard and pen across the desk, and rummaged in a box for a visitor's pass. Soraya couldn't help noticing the way his muscles rippled under his crisp white shirt, the way his dark hair curled enticingly at the nape of the neck, inviting kisses.

He handed over the pass, and she felt the warmth and strength in his grip.

'Don't lose it. Nobody goes in or out without one of these.'

With just a hint of nervousness, Soraya pinned the pass to her jacket. Bar-coded and anonymous, it gave no more clues than the blank windows or the nameless tight-lipped guard.

'Floor ten, room twenty-one,' announced the guard, consulting his list.

'Thank you.'

'And I shouldn't say this, miss, but . . .'

'But what?'

'Watch yourself. He eats pretty young ladies like you for breakfast.'

Does he indeed, thought Soraya as the lift ascended slowly with a muffled clanking of chains and gears. Well, we'll see about that. And all the time, her mind was racing on, wondering if it had been wise to come here, wondering who the hell this mystery man could be.

Floor ten loomed into view and the lift stopped with a thud and a jolt. The doors slid open to reveal a long, white-walled corridor lined with two rows of identical brown doors. This was a far cry from the luxurious

19

reception area, with its modern art and deep pile carpets. Yes, floor ten had a distinctly functional look about it.

She walked quickly down the corridor, counting the numbers on the doors – eleven, thirteen, fifteen, seventeen, nineteen . . .

Twenty-one. She raised her hand to press the button on the entryphone, then hesitated. Exactly what was she letting herself in for? What she was doing went against everything she'd been taught at training school: vet every contact in advance, make sure your section leader knows where you are at all times, don't leave yourself vulnerable to attack. This was crazy.

The sound of a man's voice almost made her jump out of her skin.

'So glad you could make it, Soraya. I'd almost begun to believe you weren't coming.'

The familiar voice was coming from the entryphone speaker, mounted at the side of the doorframe. Startled, she took a step back.

'Sir Adrian?'

'That's right, my dear. I've been watching you ever since you arrived. Nice car you have – red Mercedes, isn't it?'

Soraya scanned the door, the frame, the blank white ceiling for some sign of a hidden camera. Nothing.

'I shouldn't bother looking, my dear. The hidden cameras are extremely discreet and we do pride ourselves on the quality and range of our in-house security system. Wait for the buzzer then push the door open.'

'Yes, but – '

'I'm counting on you, Soraya. Don't let me down.'

A buzzer sounded and she turned the door-handle. The door opened into another white-walled corridor, shorter this time and opening out into an office at the far end. Framed in the doorway to the office was the broad-shouldered figure of Sir Adrian Graveney.

'Sir Adrian – but . . . the scandal! I was told you'd been transferred up north.'

Sir Adrian laughed. As handsome and well-dressed as

20

ever, he looked especially sexy when he was in a good mood, and he knew it. He treated Soraya to one of his most winning smiles, and she felt her suspicions melting away. She had resisted his amorous advances ever since joining the Department; but in that split second, she wondered why.

'The so-called scandal was just a smokescreen, my dear,' he explained, ushering her into a spacious office with deep-pile carpet and a massive antique desk with an embossed leather top. It certainly didn't look like the office of a man who'd fallen from grace. 'A simple diversion to ensure that no awkward questions were asked when sudden changes were made in the personnel structure of the Department. You see, my sweet siren, someone in the Department is not being entirely discreet, and I want to know who it is and why.'

He closed the door behind them.

'Do take a seat. I've given my PA the morning off, so we shan't be disturbed. Drink?' He indicated a well-stocked drinks cabinet.

'Er . . . no, thank you. It's a little early for me.'

'You won't mind if I do?' It was a statement rather than a question, and Sir Adrian proceeded to help himself to a giant brandy before sitting down opposite her. He'd chosen the seating arrangements carefully, to offer him the best possible view of Soraya's delectable thighs.

'Now, let me explain. It seems that someone within the Department – we're not yet sure who – has been selling classified information to the tabloid newspapers. Nothing damaging to national security as yet – just juicy scraps of tittle-tattle – but it's just a matter of time. I'm sure you can appreciate how damaging it could be should certain intimate details leak out regarding the Department's unorthodox methods.'

Soraya nodded, shocked by the news. She was ticking off a list of names in her head. James? Don't be ridiculous. Olivia or Stacey? Hardly. Gavin? But he'd hardly been there five minutes.

'At any rate, the bigwigs at Westminster have put me

21

in charge of the investigation, which is why I've been transferred to these offices. As of now, I'm working for CIU.'

'CIU?'

'The Central Intelligence Unit – a division of MI6. Officially it doesn't exist.'

'I see.' Soraya was having difficulty in digesting all this new information. Suddenly, she wondered if Sir Adrian was playing games with her, and she'd walked right into a specially-prepared trap. 'You don't suspect me, do you?' Nervously, she uncrossed her thighs, unaware of the stimulating effect this was having on Sir Adrian's already lively sexual appetite.

Sir Adrian chuckled and shook his head. A lock of wavy brown hair slipped down over his brow.

'Good Lord no. You're the last person I'd suspect. After all, you stand to suffer more embarrassment than most if we find ourselves splashed across the front page of the *News of the World*. No, not in a million years. In fact, that's why I asked you here this morning.' He paused for maximum effect and drained his glass in a single gulp. 'I want you to find out for me who it is.'

'Why me?'

'Because you're intelligent, sexy, discreet – and I trust you,' replied Sir Adrian, perching himself on the arm of Soraya's chair. 'And that's more than I can say for most of your colleagues. How long is it since we first worked together?'

'Three years.'

'Three years, Soraya, and you're the only woman in the Department I haven't had. Three years you've resisted me, Soraya, in the name of professional integrity.'

'I don't need to screw my boss to get to the top,' replied Soraya. 'You know that. Wherever I'm going, I want to get there on my own merits.'

'Yes, yes, exactly so. I know you're unimpeachable, my beauty, and that's why I want you to help me. But I know something else about you, Soraya – something you're not admitting.' He bent over her and ran his fingertips lightly over her cheek.

22

'What do you mean?'

'I know you want me, Soraya. You've wanted me for those three long years, just as much as I've wanted you. You refused to accept any favours from your boss – well fine; but I'm not your boss any more, am I, Soraya? I've gone, James has gone and that pathetic little wimp Gavin Pierce is running the show now. I'm . . . well, let's just call me your friend and adviser.'

Three years of resistance melted away like snow in the sunshine as Sir Adrian bent to kiss her, pushing his tongue between her lips into the hungry cavern of her mouth. Yes, she had wanted him, wanted to know how it felt to make love with him; yes, she wanted him now, this powerful man whose lips were crushing down on hers, daring her to push him away.

She could still reject him, even now, if she chose to do so. She could simply say no, and they would never speak of it again. Soraya Chilton was perfectly capable of looking after herself. But she had always fancied the man, and she was hungry for sensual adventure. Besides, all the reasons for resistance had been swept away from under her feet. So why not? Why the hell not?

Graveney's strong fingers slipped her skirt high up on her thighs, exposing the little black g-string that barely covered her pubis. She met his desire with her own, hooking her thumbs under the elastic and pulling the silly scrap of black cotton down over her haunches. Then her hands were pulling down his zipper, and she was sliding down in the chair until her backside was on the very edge, the scratchy moquette tormenting the delicate tissues around her anus as her buttocks parted in harmony with her outspread thighs.

He looked down at her quizzically.

'What – here? There's a perfectly good bed in the room next door. I'm sure we'd be far more comfortable.'

'No. Take me here.' Soraya wasn't going to let him call the shots. 'I don't want to make love with you in ten minutes' time, I want to do it right now.'

She reached out and gripped her lover's erect shaft,

23

sliding her fingers up and down the iron-hard flesh with a carefully-judged skill, so that the foreskin slid slowly back and forth over the sex-moistened glans. Graveney gave a groan of submission.

'You're the boss,' he grinned, slipping his finger between Soraya's sex-lips and teasing her bud of pleasure with a smearing of her own succulent love-juice. 'But then you always were, Soraya. You always were.'

Gavin Pierce was a total waste of space. That much was obvious from the way he'd handled – or rather mishandled – the arrangements for tonight's commemorative lecture.

Every five years, the Anglo-Arabian Society held a dinner at the Guildhall, at which eminent politicians and cultural figures delivered lectures on subjects of international importance. They spoke, and the world listened. Unfortunately, tonight's event had very nearly degenerated into a brawl. And whose fault was that? Gavin's, of course.

Gavin didn't seem to know the first thing about protocol, and consequently two Arab princes had found themselves sitting in the seats reserved for their servants. It was just as well he'd had Soraya on hand to pour oil on troubled waters . . .

It was also just as well – at least from Soraya's point of view – that the two injured parties were both so personable. Soraya certainly enjoyed her diplomatic duties far more when they involved having wild, uninhibited sex with attractive young men. And attractive these certainly were.

And so it was that after the dinner, in a private room at the Mansion House, Soraya was doing her best for Anglo-Arabian relations.

'Such a pleasing English filly,' observed Prince Al-Raschid, his fingers sparkling with gold and diamonds as he slipped down the shoulder straps of Soraya's evening gown. 'She would make a fine breeding mare for my harem, and an amusing concubine.'

'But has she the necessary skills?' demanded Prince

Kharim, a dark-eyed libertine with a notoriously insatiable appetite for all the pleasures of the flesh. 'A concubine must know a thousand ways to stimulate and satisfy desire. I have found that Englishwomen seldom have the gift of complete sensual abandonment.'

Soraya said nothing. She was remembering Gavin's panic-stricken words. 'For God's sake do something! Anything! Do whatever they want, just keep them sweet.' Well, she certainly had no intention of being dragged off to grace an Arabian harem; but she could perhaps teach these two young princes a few lessons in the English way of pleasure.

Slowly, she unbuckled Prince Kharim's belt, ran the supple leather over the palm of her hand, then handed it to the Prince with modestly lowered eyes.

'I am your slave, yours to command, masters,' she breathed. 'Yours to punish for the abominable insult done to your country by mine. Do with me as you will.'

Prince Kharim's eyes lit up at the very thought of such sport. Perhaps there were Englishwomen who understood the paths of pleasure, after all.

'You will submit to me, infidel slave? Submit to me utterly and accept your chastisement?'

'I will.'

'Then prepare for the kiss of the lash upon your sweet English flesh.'

Obediently, Soraya bent forwards, resting her arms and head on the carved wooden mantelpiece. There was a large gilt-framed mirror above, and as she watched with excited eyes, she saw Prince Kharim approaching, the end of the belt wrapped tightly round his hand. A thrill of anticipation ran through her as she felt Prince Al-Raschid's fingers wrenching down the zip of her evening-gown, baring her naked back.

With a swish of silk the gown slid to the floor, and in a second Al-Raschid had tugged down her panties, forcing her to step out of them. She was alone, vulnerable, naked save for the gold jewellery glittering at her throat and wrists.

'A pretty slave indeed,' murmured Kharim. 'But disobedient and in need of discipline.' He took Soraya's panties from his brother and breathed in their scent deeply. 'You are a little slut, Soraya! Your panties are full of the smell of your desire! How many men have you pleasured tonight? How many have you taken to your bed . . .?'

'I . . . dare not tell, master.'

'Then the truth must be beaten from you, my wicked slave!'

The game excited Soraya, and she gripped the mantelpiece tightly, anticipating the next move with a guilty pleasure. Why did it always turn her on so much to play the sweet little submissive? Perhaps because she knew that, when she chose, she could also play the cruel dominatrix to perfection. She wondered how it would feel if the situation were reversed, and Al-Raschid and his brother were at the mercy of her desire. One day, perhaps, she would find out.

In the mirror, she saw the reflection of Kharim, his arm lifted, ready to strike.

The makeshift whip whistled through the air and struck her back with a sensation like a thousand bee-stings. Again it fell, and now she was moaning and gasping for a mercy she prayed would not come. At least not yet, not before pain had brought a piquant pleasure to her martyred flesh. She bucked and writhed under a hail of blows that reddened her flesh from shoulders to backside; and little by little, her body submitted to the delicious discipline of the pain, opening itself up to its new masters. Soraya was enjoying herself; and all in the line of duty.

'Little slut, little slave,' spat Kharim, throwing down the belt and exploring Soraya's angry red flesh with greedy hands. 'Now it is time to teach you other lessons, lessons of pleasure.'

In the mirror above her, Soraya could see Al-Raschid, openly masturbating as he watched his brother preparing to enjoy his prey. And suddenly strong hands were

26

prising apart her bottom-cheeks, feeling for the soft wet haven between her thighs, moist with the urgency of need.

Her own desire was like a voice chanting inside her head, repeating the same phrase over and over again: give it to me, give it to me now.

His phallus entered her like a hot knife sliding into butter, and she let out a little sob of mingled pleasure and pain. The flesh of her back and buttocks was raw and tingling, but the intensity of sensation had spread between her thighs, and her clitoris was ablaze with burning, searing need. She heard Al-Raschid's voice behind her, laughing for the joy of his brother's conquest, and her womanhood began to clench in spasm after spasm of unbearable ecstasy.

'Take your pleasure quickly, my brother,' urged Al-Raschid. 'I hunger for this pretty slave to suck my cock.'

'I hear you did us proud at the dinner last night, Gavin. Damned fine show.'

Soraya glanced round from the exhibition stand, and saw Gavin beaming a slimy smile at Garforth Lythe, one of the junior ministers at the Foreign Office. It was a well-known fact that Lythe was close to the Foreign Secretary, so whatever Lythe chose to report, the Foreign Secretary would no doubt choose to believe. Her mind filled with murderous thoughts, all of them involving Gavin Pierce.

'Well, thank you, Minister. I did put in a great deal of work to ensure that the arrangements were exactly right.'

'I understand a couple of the Arabian princes were particularly impressed with our hospitality. They're talking about placing a large order with one of our steel manufacturers.'

Gavin's eyes met Soraya's, and his obsequious smile turned into a knowing leer.

'We at the Department always do our best to please. Isn't that so, Soraya?'

27

Soraya felt like killing Gavin. Slowly and painfully. Not only had the little toad managed to get all the arrangements hopelessly mixed up, and practically caused an international incident; now he was taking all the credit for what Soraya had done. She turned away in disgust, and felt a twinge of discomfort. Her back still bore the tell-tale traces of last night's diplomatic manoeuvrings. Not that she hadn't enjoyed them, of course, but the least Gavin could do was give credit where credit was due.

As Gavin bade the minister goodbye and returned to the exhibition stand, hands in pockets, Soraya stepped suddenly backwards, grinding her stiletto heel into his foot.

'Bloody hell, Soraya – what was that for?' he winced, rubbing his toes.

She smiled sweetly and picked up a pile of brochures from the stand.

'I believe everyone should get exactly what they deserve, don't you, Gavin?'

Taken aback, Gavin followed her rather sheepishly through the exhibition hall. Soraya could feel his eyes boring into the back of her head. Did he fancy her? Of course he did. Was he desperate to get into her pants? You bet. And did he stand a chance? Give me a break, thought Soraya; I'd rather screw a cockroach.

Still, in this line of work you couldn't allow personalities to get in the way of duty; and so here she was, doing her bit for the Department at a prestigious international IT exhibition – and keeping an unofficial eye open for any sign of what Sir Adrian would call 'suspect activities'. If she had not been especially watchful, she might not have taken any notice of the photographers grouped in front of a display of the latest Tuscan hardware, across the other side of the exhibition hall. A bikini-clad blonde was artistically draped across a micro-computer, her perfectly-manicured finger poised over the exit button and her candy-pink lips formed into a perfect 'O' of surprise.

The photographers – the usual raucous bunch – were calling out to her to pose for them as their shutters snapped away:

'Come on darlin' – push 'em out a bit further.'

'Give us a bit more leg, eh? You want these computers to sell, don't you?'

But one of the group didn't seem to be taking much interest in the publicity shoot. As Soraya paused and looked in his direction, she could have sworn she saw him lift his camera, point the lens at her and fire off five or six frames in rapid succession.

Intrigued, Soraya took a few steps towards him, but at that moment another pneumatic model arrived and the crowd surged forward. By the time Soraya reached the stand, there was no sign of him. The trail had gone cold.

Anton Kline was working late. The red 'safe' light gave the darkroom an eerie glow as he processed each print in turn, washed it and clipped it to a length of washing-line with a plastic clothes-peg.

The magazine shots were fine – two dozen shots of that big-breasted model, giving it all she'd got for the benefit of readers of *New Computer Monthly*. But it wasn't the magazine pictures he was interested in. It was these six shots of a woman in a green silk suit – luxuriant dark hair, coal-black eyes, long, long legs and full red lips that seemed made to whisper a single word. Sex.

He gazed at the pictures for a long time, little trails of water trickling off them as they dried. To him she seemed perfection – a flawless, utterly enchanting image of beauty and sex. Was it too much to hope that she might want him, too?

His penis ached, pressing uncomfortably against the waistband of his pants. He glanced at his watch. One a.m., and it was cold. Bloody cold. Spring? It felt more like the depths of winter.

'Anton! Come to bed, *chéri* – it's late.'

29

Mireille's voice floated across the corridor from the bedroom and he thought of sliding between crisp, white cotton sheets with a soft-breasted woman to warm him up.

The French girl greeted him sleepily as he threw off his clothes and slipped into bed beside her.

'How did the pictures work out?'

'Great. Just great.'

Better than you'll ever know, he thought to himself as he pulled Mireille towards him and ran his hands over her pert little Gallic backside. She responded with unexpected enthusiasm, returning his kiss with a thrust of her muscular tongue, and grinding her pubis against the swelling, sap-filled branch of his cock. Suddenly he felt a twinge of guilty conscience.

Spring fever, that was all that was wrong with him. The sap was rising in his veins and he was hungry for sex. But as he slid down Mireille's body and pressed his ardent tongue between her love-lips, it was not Mireille he was making love to – it was the dark-eyed woman in the photographs.

'Come in, Soraya, and sit down.'

Gavin was sitting behind James's old desk, his face a mask of smug self-importance. As she sat down on the soft leather sofa, she noticed an impressive pile of magazines and journals on the coffee table – *The Economist*, *International Affairs*, the *Frankfurter Allgemeinezeitung*: Gavin Pierce was still out to impress his bosses.

'What's all this about, then?' Soraya certainly wasn't setting out to drive Gavin into a paroxysm of lust, but with a short skirt on a low sofa, it was difficult not to. She watched his face go through different shades of pink and purple as his eyes fixed on the mysterious dark triangle he fancied he could just make out at the top of her thighs, beneath the hem of that much too provocative black skirt.

'What – ah, yes. The future, that's what this is about.'

'I'm afraid you'll have to be a little more specific,' Soraya commented acidly.

'I see the staff in this department as a team, Soraya,' continued Gavin, not taking his eyes for one second off her black-stockinged thighs. 'And that means working together, each member doing what he – or she – does best.'

'I see,' said Soraya, who didn't. 'This isn't a round-about way of telling me I'm sacked, is it?'

For the first time in weeks, Gavin laughed – and raised his eyes to the heavens.

'Hardly. I mean, you may have a bit of an attitude problem – and we're going to have to sort that out – but you're a valuable asset to this department. In fact, I'd go so far as to say that both you and I are an important part of its future.'

'Meaning?'

'Meaning that I intend to give you ample opportunity to do what you do best. I've seen enough of your work to know that you're a great persuader, Soraya. That's a valuable skill, and I'm sure you'll find it helpful to you in your forthcoming posting.'

A posting! At last. Soraya sat forward, eyes gleaming. 'Where? And when?'

'Ragzburg.' Gavin consulted his desk diary. 'Six weeks from today. So you'd better cancel the milk and get your bags packed.'

Ragzburg! Why did that place keep coming back to haunt her? She remembered the card in the travel agent's window, the inexplicable compulsion she'd felt just to get on a plane and discover the faraway city where her great-great-grandmother was born. She'd never been there, hadn't the faintest idea what the place was like, but it looked as if she was about to find out.

'Nothing wrong, is there?' enquired Gavin. 'Only you look a bit distracted.'

'Nothing at all,' replied Soraya. 'I can't wait.'

'That's good,' smiled Gavin, 'because neither can I. Seeing as you're one of our most experienced operatives, I feel it would be a valuable experience to observe your work in the field. Besides, I could use a break.'

31

'So you're . . .'

'So I'm coming with you to Ragzburg, Soraya – to hold your hand. Maybe we'll have a chance to get to know each other better. Won't that be fun?'

Chapter Three

'Taxi, pretty lady? Very good taxi, very fast, very clean.'

Soraya looked from the car to its owner, and back again. Very fast it might be – though from the sagging suspension she doubted it – but very clean? Hardly. Two chickens peered at her with beady eyes from a wooden cage on the back seat.

'Thank you, no,' she replied with a smile. 'Our own car will be arriving shortly.' It was lucky she'd specialised in central European languages at university – the local dialect was quite a challenge and the taxi-driver's English was rudimentary to say the least, with the thick, heavy accent of a gypsy.

'What the hell is he prattling on about?' demanded Gavin, panting from the exertion of dragging two enormous suitcases out of the baggage hall. Ragzburg International Airport was not big on modern conveniences like porters or conveyor belts. 'Get rid of him, will you? He's blocking our parking space.'

'Please,' smiled Soraya sweetly. 'You must go now – our car needs to park here.'

With a look of regret, the dark-eyed driver climbed back into the front seat of his car. As he opened his mouth in a parting smile, she noticed how white and perfect his teeth were, against the deep nut-brown of his skin.

'You like Janos, pretty lady?' He fumbled in the pocket of his grubby coat and pressed a card into her hand. 'You phone quick, and Janos will take you on night to remember, no?'

'Thank you,' replied Soraya, suppressing a smile. 'I'm honoured.'

'You must remember,' the driver insisted. 'Remember – Janos, he like you very much. He know how to give a pretty woman pleasure.'

This was becoming slightly embarrassing. There was a rough charm about the man; but the fanatical glint of his coal-black eyes made Soraya wary of this handsome Romany. She slipped the card into the inside pocket of her jacket.

'I'll remember. Now go – please.'

Gavin watched the ramshackle taxi clattering off into the distance with an expression of distaste.

'God, this is a hole,' he observed. 'They don't even have proper diplomatic clearance. And have you seen the state of the toilets?'

'Really?' Soraya was miles away. She was looking beyond the antiquated airport buildings towards the mountains, mysterious, dark and thickly forested, that surrounded the ancient city of Ragzburg.

Without even setting foot in the city streets she could sense a magic in this place, a timelessness that defied classification. With its skyline of crumbling spires and turrets, interspersed with occasional modern apartment blocks, Ragzburg was a city not wholly of the east or the west. It seemed caught in space and time, protected from the encroachments of the outside world by its dark, encircling hills. There was something very special here; something indefinable and unique.

'Are you listening to me?' demanded Gavin. 'Honestly, it's like talking to the bloody wall.'

'Sorry,' replied Soraya. 'I was distracted. Look – here's the Embassy car.'

'They've sent a Bentley – thank God for that. For a minute there I thought we were going to have to slum

34

it in one of the local rattle-traps. I knew I should have had the Porsche shipped over.'

Union Jack pennant fluttering on its bonnet, the Bentley drew to a stately halt outside the airport concourse, and a tall thin man got out, his hand raised in friendly greeting.

'Nick Drew, Cultural Attaché.' He extended a hand and Soraya felt the warm strength of his grip. She liked him instantly; fancied him, even – and the feeling seemed to be mutual. Certainly his eyes were twinkling with an appreciative glint of lust. 'And you must be Ms Chilton. I've heard a great deal about you from James Delauney.'

'That's a pity,' joked Soraya. 'And I thought we were going to get on so well!'

'Oh I'm sure we shall,' replied Nick, his hand brushing hers briefly as he lifted her suitcase and helped the chauffeur to load it into the boot of the Bentley. 'Quite sure.'

'I hate to break up this charming little tête-à-tête,' butted in Gavin irritably. 'But we're due for debriefing with the Ambassador at two o'clock.'

'Sorry Gavin. But you don't normally bring such charming female company with you. Ragzburg's a bit short on sophistication, as I expect you'll find out for yourselves. Here, let me take that.' Drew picked up the biggest suitcase. 'Bloody hell, Gavin – what have you brought with you – the entire departmental library?' He turned to Soraya with a smile. 'Gavin and I went through basic training together – and believe me, he doesn't know the meaning of travelling light. Always has his nose in some book.'

Or down the front of some poor typist's blouse, thought Soraya darkly. She hoped he'd keep his hands to himself whilst they were here in Ragzburg. After all, this was meant to be a business trip. Mind you ... She glanced at Nick Drew as he slid his long limbs into the front passenger seat. She had nothing against mixing business with a little pleasure.

Sitting on the back seat of the Bentley with Gavin, Soraya had ample opportunity to take in her new surroundings. The car slid almost noiselessly through the ancient gateway in the city's perfectly-preserved medieval walls, then almost immediately began bucking and bumping along a narrow, twisting road.

Drew turned round with an apologetic smile.

'Cobblestones, I'm afraid – the Ragzburgians are addicted to 'em. The twentieth century hasn't made much of an impact on this place, as you can see.'

The street curved upwards in a series of tortuous bends, and there was scarcely room for the Bentley, let alone for two cars to pass. A small boy on a rusty bicycle freewheeled past, almost scraping the wall, and Soraya wondered idly what would happen if they met another car coming down. But at this time of day Ragzburg was almost unnaturally quiet, its inhabitants taking their noonday siesta or working in the cool of the sheltered stone courtyards.

They drove on, dark buildings towering above them in a procession of picturesque, almost gothic shapes. Ever-changing images imprinted themselves on Soraya's mind. Stone-mullioned windows with tiny panes of painted glass, flashing in the rare shafts of sunlight that penetrated these dark streets; a massive door of weathered oak, set into a stone wall spotted with green and orange lichen; a black-clad peasant woman, eyes darting at them from beneath her white headscarf before she disappeared through a wrought-iron gate into the darkness of an enclosed courtyard beyond.

'In case you haven't guessed, this is the old town,' explained Nick. 'Nothing much has changed here for hundreds of years. People rave about the architecture, but personally speaking . . .'

'What?' enquired Soraya, her thoughts lost in every mysterious shadow, every twitching curtain behind a darkened window. She felt a curious excitement building inside her – an excitement, and perhaps just the faintest tinge of unease.

'It gives me the willies, it really does,' Nick continued.

'I'm not bloody surprised. It's a dreary dump,' said Gavin.

Further on, they left the old town and drove into broader streets, with massive, clean-lined stone buildings.

'This is the newer part of town,' Nick went on. 'The bit that was redeveloped by the Habsburgs in the eighteenth and nineteenth centuries. This is where most of the offices, shops and embassies are. In fact . . .' The car swung left and emerged into a busy square, complete with heroic statues and a fountain. '. . . this is it. We've arrived.'

'Hope you don't mind my disturbing you – only the door was open.'

Nick Drew was standing in the bedroom doorway, better-looking than any young man had a right to be on this warm, spring afternoon. Soraya greeted him with feigned indignation.

'Shame on you, spying on a lady when she's alone in her bedroom! Look, I'm still unpacking my underwear.'

Nick closed his eyes in mock ecstasy. 'Oh, don't torment me, it's more than a man can stand!'

Soraya burst out laughing. 'Give that man an Oscar!' She slid open a drawer of the polished walnut armoire and breathed in the scent of fresh lavender, sewn into a little heart-shaped satin sachet. One by one, she laid bras, panties and suspender belts in the drawer with deliberate slowness. Nick's eyes followed her every movement.

'I just wondered . . .'

'Mmm?'

'Well, I wondered if you might like to come out round the town with me this afternoon – I could show you the sights.'

And I could show you mine, thought Soraya wickedly, making sure that Nick got the full benefit of each new bit of lacy frippery.

37

'That would be great,' she replied, lifting up a flame-red suspender belt with black lace edging. She dangled it tantalisingly for a few seconds before packing it carefully in the drawer. 'I could do with a bit of fresh air after that briefing session.'

'Bad, huh?'

'Are you kidding? Listen, is the Ambassador always that boring, or did he make a special effort for me?'

Nick chuckled. 'Oh, old man Foley just likes the sound of his own voice. Look, when shall we go? Shall I call back in ten minutes?'

'Don't go – I'm almost ready. Just hold on a minute – I need to change out of this blouse into something a bit more casual.'

To Nick's astonishment, she unbuttoned her pink blouse and peeled it off, revealing the white strapless bra beneath, its lacy fabric pulled tight across her full breasts. With studied casualness, she turned and rummaged in her suitcase for a sleeveless shirt, making sure that Nick got the full benefit of her ample charms. Not for nothing was Soraya Chilton the Foreign Office's most valuable asset. And this afternoon, she was in the mood for fun.

Deciding that she had made him suffer enough, she selected a white silk vest and slipped it on over her head, tucking it deftly into the waistband of her short black skirt.

'Ready!' she announced brightly. 'I'm all yours.'

If only, thought Nick as she walked in front of him down the Embassy's grand central staircase, her backside wiggling invitingly in that smart but oh-so-tight skirt. Could there be any chance, however small, that she fancied him half as much as he fancied her? He fantasised about the creamy flesh he had glimpsed as she changed her blouse, there in her room. Was she just tormenting him, punishing him for daring to want her; or was she giving him the big come-on? In all honesty, he'd never been very good at judging the moment.

He wondered vaguely if Gavin had tried his luck, and

almost laughed out loud at the thought. He could imagine the result – a carefully-placed knee in the groin and an icy riposte from that razor-sharp tongue. Gavin was an idiot and ham-fisted with it, everyone at the basic-training school had worked out that much. Almost certainly, Soraya thought Nick Drew was an idiot, too ...

'Shall we take the car?' demanded Soraya as they showed their passes to the guard at the front door of the Embassy.

'Let's walk. It's a beautiful day – we might as well make the most of it. We get some really freaky weather-changes here, even in the spring and summer. I expect it's something to do with all these mountains.'

Ah yes, the mountains. Soraya gazed up at them. The heat-haze had cleared away now, and the tree-clad summits stood dark and forbidding above the town, looming over the huddled city. They seemed nearer now, as though they were moving in, trying to squeeze the life out of the ancient buildings. Or as if they were trying to get closer, so that the wind in the trees could whisper secrets; dark secrets that only Soraya would understand ...

She shook herself out of this curious train of thought. Strange, the magnetic pull that this place seemed to exert on her. She turned to Drew.

'Beautiful mountains, aren't they? So close, and yet so savage-looking.'

'There are quite a few strange stories about those mountains,' he replied, pressing as close to her as he dared as they walked down the Embassy steps and out into the square. 'Stories about weird creatures and people who've disappeared, never to be seen again.' He laughed. 'It's a load of old codswallop for the tourists, of course.'

'Yes, of course.'

Soraya was not laughing, though. She was thinking of the equally bizarre story that had been handed down through her own family: the story of her great-great-grandmother Alicia, the pretty girl from Ragzburg who had married a handsome English doctor. After her marriage they had gone to live in England, and all had been well for a year – until the day Alicia had returned to Ragzburg to see her relatives in a mountain village above the city.

She never returned.

Some said she had drowned in the swift-moving river that flowed along the margin of the city; others that she had been killed by wolves in the forests. But no sign was ever found of her, nothing at all. And Soraya's family had nothing to remember her by but a few faded photographs and a yellowed wedding dress. Nick's voice cut into her thoughts.

'Penny for 'em?'

'Oh, sorry, just thinking about my great-great grandmother. She was from Ragzburg, you know.'

'Really! I thought you had a look of the place – those dark eyes, that very pale skin and all that hair. Yes, I reckon you could pass for a native – though I don't know if you'd want to. This place gets under your skin somehow, makes you feel kind of jumpy. It's those hills, they're so claustrophobic. Sometimes I just have to get in the car and drive until I get to Prague or Vienna – anywhere, just to get away from here.'

They strolled together into the centre of the square, where a group of peasant-women were busily decorating the statue of one of Ragzburg's heroic founders with garlands of bright flowers.

'What's going on?' asked Soraya.

'Oh, you've come to our little city at rather an auspicious time. Tomorrow is the fertility festival – it happens every May, but this year it's a bit special. Every sixty years or so, there's a complete solar eclipse – and it just so happens that it's going to happen tomorrow. Astronomers will be coming from all over the place to watch it. So there'll be even more of a shindig than usual.'

'Sounds like fun!'

'Oh it is. But you want to watch the local wine, mind – it's dynamite. Last year, I had a bit too much and they

40

had to carry me back to the Embassy. Old man Foley was livid.'

'I bet. He looks like a guy with no sense of humour.'

'I bet you have though, Soraya. I bet you know how to let your hair down and have some fun.' Nick could hardly believe he was hearing himself talk like this. He was normally so unadventurous with women.

'Oh yes, Nick. I know lots of ways to have fun.'

Her body decided in that moment that it wanted him, and her heartbeat began to quicken with anticipation. Nick was standing very close to her, his hand on her bare arm; and the feeling was like glorious electricity, coursing through her veins. The chemistry was there; the time was right; he was bending down, his lips slightly parted as if to kiss her, and she was longing for him to take her in his arms.

A voice behind them made Soraya freeze.

'Pretty lady. Pretty English lady.'

Even before she swung round she knew that it was the taxi-driver who'd accosted her at the airport. This time he was standing beside the fountain, his arms overflowing with a riot of flowers.

'Pretty lady, Janos is waiting for you. His heart it ache for you.'

'Damn,' hissed Soraya under her breath. 'It's him again.'

'Do you know that guy?'

'Pretty lady . . . come to Janos. Come to him soon . . .'

'He's just a nutcase,' said Soraya. 'Walk a bit faster.'

Nick seized her arm and propelled her towards a narrow alleyway.

'Don't worry,' he smiled. 'I know somewhere quiet we can go. Somewhere where nobody will disturb us.'

Stetched out on the grassy river bank, Soraya looked up at Nick, his dark hair haloed with gold against the setting sun. She felt languid, lazy, sensual.

'Why don't people come here? It's so beautiful – so secluded. If I lived here, I'd want to come here every day.'

41

Nick squatted down beside her, pushing the thick, wavy hair back from his face. So what if he was practically a complete stranger – he looked pretty damn good right here and right now. Since the moment the plane had touched down in Ragzburg, Soraya had been aware of a growing warmth in her belly, a playful but insistent hunger that simply would not go away. Maybe it was just too long since she'd had a man.

'You know how it is – a few funny stories about a place, and people won't come near it. Werewolves, things that go munch in the night, that kind of stuff. It's all peasant mumbo-jumbo, but then that's what most of these people are – simple peasants. They won't come here without a pocketful of garlic and a pointed stick; but who cares? It's all the more secluded for sophisticated people like us.'

Soraya giggled and rolled over onto her back. She'd only had one glass of wine all afternoon, but she felt half-drunk. For all its weirdness, this place seemed in tune with her temperament, her desires. She felt at home among the swaying trees, listening to the river rushing by.

'You're saying I'm sophisticated?'

Nick was bending over her, his face very close to hers though she could hardly make out his features in the gathering dusk. The moon would be up soon, pale and almost full in the dark red sky.

'You're damn right I am. And believe me, I have excellent taste.'

He bent a little lower, and this time their lips touched. Reaching up, Soraya pulled him closer, crushing her mouth against his. He welcomed the initiative, pushing the tip of his tongue between her yearning lips.

Lying side by side on the river bank, they held each other very close, their kisses passionate and long. Nick pressed his belly hard against hers, and she felt his desire, hot and strong. So, he wanted her as much as she wanted him.

'You're one heck of a woman, Soraya Chilton. Look

what you've done to me! I don't normally get this intimately acquainted on a first date, you know.'

'Aren't I supposed to say that?'

'Shut up and let me make love to you.'

But Soraya wasn't accustomed to playing the passive little woman for any man. In retaliation she slid her hand between their bodies and unzipped his flies. His pants were moist with the urgency of his desire, his shaft hot and responsive to her touch. He murmured a half-hearted protest.

'You little . . .'

'I believe in taking what I want,' she retorted. 'And right now, what I want is you.'

Wriggling from Drew's grasp, she rolled him onto his back and straddled him with a proprietorial glee, her tight black skirt riding up high on her thighs. He was too surprised and too intrigued to resist as she pulled out his cock and smoothed it with her skilful hand.

'Mmm, that feels good,' he murmured. 'So, so good.'

Desires were coursing through Soraya's veins. So many things she wanted to do, so many needs whispering to her through the hot red mist of desire. No time to slow down, not now. No time for the pretty games that lovers play.

Sliding aside the gusset of her white panties, she pressed the tip of his penis between her swollen love-lips, and sank down onto it, impaling herself on the instrument of pleasure.

Drew gave a groan as his shaft was swallowed up by Soraya's eager womanhood. She felt so tight, so divine around his flesh, her smooth wet sheath sliding up and down, riding him ever-nearer to the summit of his own ecstasy.

Soraya threw back her head in silent laughter as she rode her steed, her hips rising and falling as she slid up and down on his ramrod-stiff shaft. Her index finger pressed to the throbbing bud of her clitoris, she controlled the rhythm of their love-making, the intensity of her pleasure. It hadn't felt so good – so natural – in ages. She couldn't remember a time when sex had lasted so long; when she had wanted it to go on and on and never end. It had never been this much fun with Magnus. Maybe that was why they'd split up.

Too soon, pleasure exploded within her with an almost painful intensity, and she pressed hard on her clitoris, prolonging the last spasms as Drew clutched her thighs and spurted the last of his seed deep into her belly.

'Soraya Chilton,' he murmured through half-closed lips. 'You're good enough to eat.'

'Then why don't you go right ahead?' laughed Soraya, slipping off her soaked panties and lowering herself onto his upturned face. Little trickles of mingled love-juice dripped from her, moistening his lips. 'Go on, Nick; eat me right up. And don't stop till you've licked out every last drop.'

The sea was deceptively calm today; a dull grey oily swell that lapped at the shingle beach with all the trepidation of a sixteen-year-old gigolo licking his sixty-year-old lover's nipple. Sir Adrian stood at the end of the Palace Pier and gazed down at the rusty pillars, disappearing into the murky depths. Brighton was a big bore, really. He couldn't understand how it had gained its racy reputation.

Chilly, too. It might be late spring, but Brighton seemed to have made up its mind to bypass the summer and sunshine altogether and go straight to autumn. Grey sky met grey sea, and Sir Adrian began to wish he'd worn a coat.

He glanced at his watch. Half-past four. She'd said she'd be here by quarter-past, but you couldn't trust them – any of them. And how had she made contact with him? He had to know. And so he had to wait.

The cacophony from the karaoke bar and the amusement arcade behind him was giving him earache. He moved a little further off, towards the very end of the pier, seeking solace in isolation.

Soraya would be in Ragzburg by now. Pity that. He'd hoped to retain her in the Department's London office to maintain continuous surveillance, but the posting had come up and he'd felt it would look odd if he opposed it. If she hadn't been chosen for the assignment, news was bound to leak out that Sir Adrian had been behind it, and since he was supposed to have had his arse kicked out of the Department for misconduct six months ago, it was rather vital that he maintain a discreet distance.

Soraya Chilton. The very thought of her warmed his belly and made him forget the screeching children on the waltzers, just yards behind him. Soraya, with her dark eyes and matchless breasts. He'd only enjoyed her the once, but it had been a memorable once – for her too, he was pretty sure of that. Now she was far away in Ragzburg, smoothing over another potential diplomatic incident. If only she was here in England, smoothing away his cares . . .

'I hope you haven't been waiting long. I got caught in traffic.'

He wheeled round. The woman was about thirty, by no means unattractive, with cropped blonde hair and green eyes that had a hard, acquisitive glint to them.

'Madeleine Berry?'

'The very same.' She produced a business card from her handbag. It read: 'Madeleine Berry, News Reporter, *London Daily Argus*.' 'And you must be Sir Adrian Graveney.'

Sir Adrian stared at his feet. 'You realise, of course, that I can make absolutely no comment on that whatsoever – or indeed on any other supposition you may care to make?'

'Of course.' She glanced round. 'Shall we go somewhere a little warmer and quieter? I could do with a drink.'

They walked together down the pier towards the exit, Sir Adrian cagey, Madeleine overly polite. He could sense that she was ready to pounce. Maybe he shouldn't

45

have come here. Maybe he should just have slapped a D-notice on her and prayed that no one else had got hold of the story.

At a bar just off the promenade, Madeleine bought them drinks and they sat in glum silence for a few minutes before she took the initiative – as he knew she would.

'Sir Adrian – as I mentioned on the telephone, my newspaper has been informed of certain . . . rumours.'

'You should never listen to rumours, Ms Berry.' The more he looked at the woman, the more he liked what he saw. She wasn't Soraya, but then who was?

'Indeed, Sir Adrian. But if we have no firm facts to go on, what can we do but listen to the rumours?'

'If you publish unfounded allegations, Ms Berry, you will be sued for libel. I should have thought that was obvious.'

'But are they unfounded, Sir Adrian? There's talk of a scandal hushed up, of pictures being taken of you with two call-girls. Why don't you just tell me the facts, Sir Adrian? Why don't you put the record straight? We could make it worth your while – money's no object, as I'm sure you can imagine. This would be quite a scoop for us.'

He wanted to laugh at her, but he was too busy lusting after her gorgeous body.

'Money is of no interest to me. I am already inordinately wealthy.'

'What then? What would tempt you to tell your story to the world?'

He paused. Then pounced.

'Sex, Ms Berry.'

'I beg your pardon?'

'Sex with you, to be more precise. Spend a night with me here in Brighton – no, make that two – and then I'll begin to start thinking about talking to you.'

He could see her mind working; see the journalistic cogs grinding round, weighing up the pros and cons; trying to decide if there might be extra mileage in the story if she came across. She wanted to, of course; he could tell. He could always smell a woman's desire, and Madeleine Berry reeked of lust.

'And if I did agree to sleep with you ... you'd agree to tell me your full and unexpurgated story, give us an exclusive?'

'No, Ms Berry. I said I would think about talking. You have to decide if that's good enough.'

Even before she replied, he knew she was going to accept his little proposition. Not because of the promise of a story – which he had been careful not to give – but simply because she was hot for him. He liked a woman who knew her mind.

As they walked off to check in at the hotel, Sir Adrian decided that Brighton was not, after all, quite as boring as he had thought. A little fun might perhaps be enjoyed behind the dull façade of its crumbling hotels. Madeleine Berry would not get her exclusive, of course. As soon as they'd spent a pleasant couple of nights together, he'd get Lord Grimsby to slap a D-notice on the story. And the two CIU agents he'd brought with him from London would ensure that she kept her mouth very firmly shut.

But that was all very firmly in the future. He didn't want to think about the little disappointments Madeleine was going to experience on Monday morning. Right now, all he wanted to think about were those two nights of pleasure between the sheets.

On that count, at least, he was pretty sure Madeleine Berry wasn't going to be at all disappointed.

Soraya woke early, refreshed and excited. Throwing open the wooden shutters, she breathed in the flower-scented air from the square below. Already, at six o'clock in the morning, the square was bustling with frantic activity as the inhabitants of Ragzburg and its surrounding villages prepared for the annual fertility festival.

She stepped out on to the balcony, revelling in the

47

early-morning coolness on her bare arms, the gentle breeze moulding the diaphanous silk of her flimsy night-dress to her body. She felt wonderful: strong, powerful, and intensely sexual in this place of primitive rhythms, mysterious shadows. It was as though she had come home.

A muffled protest came from the room behind her as bright sunlight flooded the darkness, and she turned round, smiling.

'It's a beautiful day, lazybones. The sun's shining, the birds are singing, and I can see five huge crates of red wine down there. Looks like we're in for some fun.'

Nick winced, hauling himself up on one elbow and shading his eyes. He squinted at the alarm clock.

'What time is it?'

'Just after six. Time to get up.'

'Six!' Nick fell back onto the pillows with a groan. 'Come back to bed.'

'Persuade me.'

Leaving the shutters wide open, Soraya sat down on the side of the bed. Nick lay naked across the mattress, the thin cotton sheet thrown carelessly across him, its gleaming whiteness contrasting with the golden tan of his chest. She smoothed a hand down his belly, stopping tantalisingly short of the sheet which lay in a tangle across his thighs and groin.

'There's a name for girls like you, Soraya Chilton.'

'Oh really – and what's that?'

'Prick-tease.'

'Is that so?' Playfully, Soraya slid back the sheet a few inches, to reveal the swelling shaft of Nick's manhood.

He sighed with satisfaction as her fingers slipped around the hardness, smoothing and stroking it. They felt so cool, so gentle and yet so knowing.

'Now take that back,' grinned Soraya. 'Or else I'll stop!'

'You win. Anything you say – only don't stop!'

He reached out for her and pulled her face down to his. His lips were hot and feverish, his kiss passionate and hungry. Laughing but excited, Soraya got into bed

48

and lay down beside him, still toying with the shaft of his penis. In the light from the open window, she took a good look at her latest conquest. He was nice-looking. Not really her type, of course, but somehow that didn't seem to matter. Not here in Ragzburg. This was a city of raw passions, transient but strong; a city where hunger could be satisfied and then awakened again . . .

Not for a very long time had Soraya felt this hot for sex; not since that night in London when she had watched the couple in the apartment block opposite making love, their naked bodies pale and dream-like in the silver-white moonlight. She had pleasured herself many times that night, in an attempt to satisfy the intense, gnawing hunger that overwhelmed her. And now she was hungry again.

'You gorgeous hussy,' growled Nick, suddenly taking the initiative and rolling her onto her back. 'You deserve to be taught a lesson, do you know that?'

'Oh, and you're the man to do it, I suppose?'

He straddled her, bending low so that his lips brushed her face, darting little kisses on her forehead, her chin, her cheeks.

'I can still taste your cum on my tongue', he whispered. 'I think it's time you tasted mine.'

His hands stroked her hair as he pressed his hardness against her lips, his balls soft and heavy against her face. She could have pushed him away, but she didn't want to. All she wanted was the touch and the taste and the smell of him, the animal strength of him thrusting into her, meeting and matching the strength of her own instinctive need.

She parted her lips for him, delighting in the powerful taste of their love-making, still fragrant on his cock-tip. Each thrust recalled the wildness of their sexual encounters last night beside the river. Not that she remembered many of the details – last night was a fuzzy memory, as though she had enjoyed a drunken romp. But she had not been drunk – or at least, not with alcohol. Her intoxication had come from an exhilaration of the senses, heady and sensual. Now all she recalled were the sensations, the feeling of flesh within flesh; and the cool moonlight, washing like springwater over their coupled bodies.

As the purple plum of his glans throbbed against the back of her throat, Soraya felt the power of pure sex rushing through her, strengthening and arousing her as it had never done before. Not until Ragzburg.

His thighs were strong and tight on either side of her, his flesh brushing hard across the juicy buds of her breasts, the sensation painfully pleasurable. The pleasure-garden between her thighs was dripping wet with need, and she squeezed her legs tightly together, desperate for the delicious friction of tongue upon clitoris.

Clutching his buttocks, she forced him harder, deeper into her throat. His engorged member was half-stifling her, but she didn't care. She just wanted more, more, more. And with a final thrust he came into her, his salty semen spurting in long, luxurious jets that filled and overflowed her mouth.

'Swallow it down, sweetheart; there's plenty more where that came from,' gasped Nick as the last waves of orgasm died away.

And Soraya spread her thighs and sighed with pleasure as he bent to coax ecstasy from her burning clitoris with his wicked, eager tongue.

'Hurry up now, everyone out onto the balcony, and please remember, you are representatives of Her Majesty's Government, not vulgar American tourists.'

Ambassador Foley was chivvying his Embassy staff onto the first-floor balcony like a tyrannical infant-school teacher. Soraya threw Nick a grimace that said 'what a prat'; but she could see that Gavin was lapping it up, hanging on the Ambassador's every word. Correction: what a pair of prats!

Down in the square below, the crowd was dancing to the primitive, pulsing rhythms of a gypsy band; the violinist swaying in a private trance as the melody swooped and sobbed. Soraya gave a little start as the crowd parted for a second and she glimpsed the nut-brown face beneath the colourful kerchief. It was the taxi-driver, Janos.

But almost instantly she forgot Janos and his strange pursuit of her. For the festival procession was entering the square: a long, colourful, straggling snake of Ragzburgians in national costume, bearing at their head brightly-painted wooden effigies of pagan gods and goddesses, naked and garlanded with flowers.

As Soraya sang along to the folk-tunes, she felt her gaze drawn to the first, and most magnificent of the effigies: the statue of a naked woman, her long dark hair like serpents coiling about her sleek golden body; her eyes the deep, glittering red of rubies and her teeth white and sharp as a beast's. About her feet lay the form of a sleeping wolf.

The dizziness of instinctive recognition silenced Soraya for a fleeting second, made her clutch at the balustrade, knuckles whitening with tension as she struggled to retrieve a memory, an image buried deep in her subconscious.

Nick glanced at his watch.

'Twenty to,' he whispered out of the corner of his mouth. 'It's almost time.'

'Time?' Soraya shook herself out of her reverie. She had almost forgotten why they were there.

'The eclipse – the total eclipse of the Sun.'

'Of course . . .'

Excitement coursed through Soraya's body as she watched the rippling mass of colour wending its way into the square, gyrating, swaying bodies moving together to the hypnotic rhythm of the music. Drink was flowing freely, glasses and bottles passed from hand to hand among the happy, chattering crowd.

'They'll be partying all day,' Nick went on, a hint of regret in his voice. 'And all night too – there's a full moon tonight.' He sniffed. 'Not much chance of us getting in on the act, mind you – not after my performance

51

last year. All Embassy staff are supposed to be confined to barracks.'

Up on the balcony, dressed in full ceremonial uniform, the Ambassador was surveying the scene with a mixture of amusement and contempt. He had long considered the Ragzburgians to be a particularly unsophisticated peasant breed; and regarded their festivals as more of an annoyance than anything else. Her Majesty's Diplomatic Corps must maintain its dignity at all costs; and he hadn't forgotten Nick Drew's shameful display during last year's festival. He wasn't taking any chances this year. If the occasion had to be celebrated at all, it was to be done in the most British of ways.

'A small dry sherry for everyone,' he instructed Pascal, the Embassy servant. 'This is a special occasion, after all.'

Was that a tinge of darkness in the clear blue sky; a shadow beginning to nibble at the edge of the Sun's perfect, golden disc? Soraya shivered, a dizzy excitement overwhelming her, making her suppress a giggle of girlish wickedness. Desire was in her, too; her senses sharpened, her appetites intensified.

'What's the matter, Soraya? Are you all right?' demanded Nick as she stepped back from the balustrade and pushed her way through the little gaggle of watchers, into the first-floor drawing room of the Embassy.

'I'm fine.' Soraya walked quickly across the soft Afghan carpet towards the door that led to the landing and the central staircase.

'Where are you going?' Nick pursued her across the floor, conscious of the way this must look to the Ambassador. He hoped he hadn't noticed their desertion.

'To get a drink.' She opened the door and stepped out onto the landing.

'But . . .'

'You heard. I'm going to join in the parade.' She turned round and Nick saw that there was a wicked smile on her face, a glint of defiance in her dark eyes. 'Want to come?'

52

'I . . . I can't, Soraya, you know I can't. Foley will blow his top. And you can't either!'

'More fool you,' Soraya retorted, very clearly and very calmly. 'You can do what you like, but I'm going to get myself some fun.'

She turned and hurried down the staircase to the open front door of the Embassy. Nick stood and watched her for a moment, unsure whether he ought to follow her and drag her back. What the hell had got into the girl? But no; last year had been bad enough. He couldn't afford to blot his copybook yet again with old man Foley. He turned back and rejoined the sedate gathering on the balcony.

Stepping out of the Embassy into the furnace-like heat of noon, Soraya felt wild, excited, hungry for new sensations. Her body was vibrating to the rhythm of the music, every nerve-ending stimulated to an almost unbearable degree of sensitivity. Laughing and singing with the crowd, she slipped off her blouse and danced in her black lace bra, uninhibited and exhilarated.

A bottle was thrust into her hand, and she drank deeply, the rough red wine rich and coppery on her tongue. But she didn't need the wine to feel drunk – already she was intoxicated with the moment, the noise and the scent and the taste of the excitement all around her.

'It's happening. It's happening . . .'

The voices around her took up the litany, a mad chorus that stilled suddenly to a hushed whisper, rippling again and again through the assembled throng.

Soraya shaded her eyes, squinting at the disappearing sun through a proffered square of smoked glass as the Moon's round disc slid across, and the sky darkened to a premature night.

'What the . . . isn't that that girl – what's her name? – Chilton?' demanded the Ambassador, his attention suddenly drawn to a semi-naked girl dancing drunkenly among a crowd of peasants in the gathering twilight. His features set in a mask of cold outrage as he gripped the balustrade. 'What is the meaning of this?'

Gavin butted in, eager to exonerate himself and throw all the blame onto Soraya.

'I gave her strict instructions to behave herself, Ambassador,' he insisted. 'But the girl is headstrong.'

'Oh shut up, Pierce,' snapped the Ambassador, pushing him aside. 'If you cannot control your own staff, you should not be travelling abroad on Departmental business. I shall be submitting a report to your superiors on your return to London.' He turned to Nick, now little more than a silhouette in the rapidly-closing darkness. 'Drew, get down there and remove the girl. Now.'

'Yes sir. Right away.'

Nick pushed his way off the balcony and made his way down the central staircase, grateful for the electric light cutting through the gloom. If he didn't get a move on, it would be too late. He'd never find her in the pitch blackness of the eclipse.

Still dancing in the crowd, Soraya saw pictures in her head. Vivid pictures that made her want to laugh, and cry, and fuck. There was hunger and thirst within her, but not for food, not for wine. The bottle slipped from her fingers and fell with a crash onto the ground, but she did not notice the glittering shards of glass around her dancing feet. She was looking at the pictures, the pictures that grew ever more vivid as darkness fell.

Suddenly, there was no more light. The Moon's disc snapped across the last remnant of the Sun, obliterating all but the faintest halo of golden light.

But the pictures kept on dancing in Soraya's head; the faces smiling and the voices whispering to her of the sweet, savage pleasures of the flesh. She stretched out her hands to them, but as soon as she tried to touch them, they were gone.

Lost in the crowd, Nick's last image of Soraya was of a whirling, swaying figure disappearing into a sea of engulfing flesh, her arms stretching out to something he could not see.

And then everything went black.

Chapter Four

Need, need, need . . .

The woman's breath was coming in harsh, staccato gasps now as she ran over the rough bracken, dry twigs snapping and rustling beneath her bare feet. The sounds of pursuit were very close behind, but she was not afraid. She was exultant. Some deep, dark part of her yearned to be captured. Only then would she be able to turn the tables on her pursuer, release the fierce power within her.

Panting, she paused for a moment on the hillside, a half-smile on her lips as she listened to the pounding footsteps, coming ever-closer. The moon was very full, very high in the velvet-black sky, its cool silver light coursing over her naked flesh like a shimmering water-fall. Excitement crackled and fizzed through her body, the electricity of pure, savage desire, and she lifted her face to the moonlight, letting it kiss and caress her with a lover's tender, seductive skill.

The dark-haired woman threw back her head and her moist scarlet lips parted, revealing the glint of teeth as sharp and perfect as diamonds. Her cry of lust filled the darkness, stilling the sounds of the creatures of the night; vibrating to the rhythm of her dark and sensual need.

And that need was growing stronger with every second that passed. She had already feasted, already gorged her desires on one unwary young man who had been all too ready to couple with her beneath the night skies. But he had been a long time ago – minutes, hours? She tried to focus the images, but could not quite recall what had happened. Everything had grown so vague, so muddled in her mind, lacking the painfully sharp definition of her overwhelming desire.

She could not even recall his face. All she remembered now was his young, strong body, sweating and straining beneath her as her bare white thighs straddled him and the hungry muscles of her womanhood engulfed him in their hot, wet folds. In her mind she was riding him again, bucking and thrusting as his cock impaled her and she fed on the strength of his young, impetuous desire.

With each thrust she felt her strength grow, felt the power of desire within her like a mighty ocean-swell, rising and tumbling in her belly. Her whole body was hypersensitive, charged with a ferocious energy that made her want to devour her prey, drink in the sexual energy that pulsed out of him in great waves. Her nipples were hard as iron, her labia swollen and throbbing to the rhythm of her swollen clitoris.

Desire became a desperate hunger and at last pleasure came, white waves crashing on a distant rocky shore in the glistening moonlight. Pleasure: but not the sating of lust. With each orgasm, the lust within her doubled in intensity, the need becoming both pleasure and pain, agony and ecstasy.

The pretty boy had afforded some small pleasure, met the need for a few fleeting moments. His blood was still caking her fingernails, a reminder of her savage joy as he thrust into her with long, luxurious strokes.

But that was long ago, too long ago. A memory lost in the dark need that enfolded her; images dissolved by the moonlight that whispered to her of desires as yet unsatisfied. She must have sex. Must have it soon. Must ease this terrible, aching hunger gnawing at her belly with an ever-greater intensity.

A cloud drifted across the sky, veiling the moon's face for a few moments; and she knew that it was time. The sound of footsteps pounded ever nearer, echoing the thunderous beat of her own heart.

Laughing, she took to her heels and raced down the hillside, lithe limbs rippling with hidden strength as she ran through the bracken, deeper into the secret shadows of the ancient forest. She would enjoy the pursuit.

And later, when she had allowed herself to be captured, her pursuer would understand what it meant to feed this gnawing hunger in her belly.

'My God . . . how much did I have to drink?'

Hand shading her eyes, Soraya squinted painfully in the sudden light from the drawn curtains, her head thumping, senses reeling.

'Time to get up, Sleeping Beauty.'

She rolled over, shook her head and forced herself to open her eyes.

'Oh God, I was having the weirdest dream. There was this naked woman, running through a wood . . .'

Gavin Pierce was standing by the bed, a cup and saucer in his hand and a contemptuous sneer on his face.

'Get a move on and drink this. You obviously need it.'

She accepted the cup.

'What's this – room service?'

'Black coffee. It'll help clear your head. Nick Drew told you that local plonk was strong stuff, but would you listen? The Ambassador is absolutely furious. I hope you're quite satisfied.'

'What the hell happened to me?' She scrabbled around on the top of the bedside table for her watch. 'What time is it?' With a groan, she took a gulp of coffee. It scalded her throat, but at least its bitter strength took away the taste of the cheap red wine. 'My mind's a complete blank.'

'It's getting on for seven o'clock at night. You've been asleep since lunchtime – you keeled over during the eclipse.' He sighed in exasperation. 'God you can be annoying, Soraya. Don't you remember anything?'

'I remember being in the town square – at the summer festival. All those fertility statuettes and flowers everywhere. We were waiting for the lunar eclipse of the Sun. I was dancing, and I suppose I had a bit to drink . . . And then, nothing. Not a damn thing.'

'Typical! Well, drink your coffee and then hurry up and get dressed. If you recall, you have a very important civil servant to corrupt tonight. Anyhow, the state you were in, maybe it's just as well you don't remember.'

Gavin sat down on the edge of the bed. He didn't look so bad in the half-light, mused Soraya. In spite of the muzzy ache in her head, she realised that she was feeling distinctly randy. Why, she could almost fancy him. Fancy Gavin Pierce! Funny, that. She'd always thought of the little toad with utter contempt. The perfect po-faced Whitehall Under-Secretary: the perfect prat.

She sighed.

'Go on – tell me the worst. Was I completely embarrassing?'

'Embarrassing!' snorted Gavin. 'Humiliating, more like. Honestly, I always thought you could take your drink. And you didn't have time to have more than half a bottle of red wine, thank God. But when the eclipse started, you started behaving extremely oddly. Nick went down to try and fetch you back, but he lost you in the crowd. The next thing I knew, it was getting dark and you were hallucinating – and then you passed out.'

'Oh God, did I really do that? Look, I'm sorry, truly I am.' Soraya sat up in bed, and the bedclothes slid down, uncovering the tops of her bare breasts. Realisation dawned and she giggled, feeling playful in her nakedness. 'Gavin – you undressed me! You wicked boy . . . you haven't been taking advantage of me, have you?'

Gavin flushed scarlet and edged a little further away.

'Uh-huh; not guilty, sweetheart. Some woman doctor

58

from the Belgian Consulate sorted you out and put you to bed. Said you'd probably had too much wine and too much sun, and you needed to sleep it off.'

Soraya pouted in mock disappointment. She was in the mood for fun.

'So you don't fancy me after all? Not even a little bit?'

'Well . . .'

Soraya grinned. She really was feeling very odd indeed. She'd never even remotely fancied Gavin in the past – heavens, back in London she wouldn't have given him a second look. He was dead boring, everybody knew that. Devious too, and malicious – a right little creep. You couldn't trust him further than you could throw him. And yet, here he was sitting on the side of her bed at the British Embassy in Ragzburg, and suddenly, for some unaccountable reason, he didn't look too bad. Not too bad at all. Soft, wavy brown hair framing a tanned face; broad shoulders and slim hips; surprisingly sensitive fingers that might yet be taught to give a woman pleasure.

She let the bedclothes slip further down, exposing the full swell of her breasts. Her nipples were already puckered with excitement, her womanhood hot and moist with the anticipation of pleasures to come. Slowly, her right hand strayed towards Gavin's thigh. His eyes widened in surprise, but he made no attempt to move away.

'What . . .?'

Soraya kissed her fingertip and placed it on Gavin's lips.

'Hush. Just let me.'

He gasped, giving a little outrush of breath as Soraya's skilful fingertips traced the swelling outline of his burgeoning cock. It was much bigger than she had expected, and hardening by the second. Her pulse was racing, her mouth dry with a delicious apprehension.

And suddenly Gavin Pierce – staid, unpleasant, humourless Gavin with the grey suits and the greyer personality – seemed the most exciting man in the world.

59

But at this moment, any man would have seemed exciting: Soraya justed wanted sex; sex with any man who would have her. It just so happened that Gavin Pierce was here – hot and ready for the taking.

Deftly, she tugged down the zipper on his pants and slipped her fingers inside, feeling for the front vent in his cotton boxer shorts. Gavin might like to play the cold-blooded Englishman in public, but his shaft was so eager that it practically leapt into her hand. Her tongue passed fleetingly over her lips as she anticipated the taste of the glistening cock-tip, the feeling of it entering the depths of her hungry mouth.

She gave the engorged member a playful little massage, and was gratified by Gavin's shuddering gasp of helpless pleasure. So he wasn't as emotionless as he pretended to be. Desire was hot and strong in her belly now, urging her on to ever-greater audacities. Well, she'd come this far – she might just as well take the game to its natural conclusion. If she was going to tease and torment her boss so shamelessly, why not go the whole way and screw him too?

'Lie down on the bed, Gavin,' she pleaded, slipping out from between the cool white sheets. Already her dark pubic curls were glistening with droplets of clear love-juice. Her heart was pounding with the delicious anticipation of sex. 'What shall we do first? I know – why don't I suck you off?'

Soraya sat on the terrace of the Hotel Radetsky, sipping a glass of chilled white wine and watching the world go by. Her contact would be here soon: a Mr Mankiewicz from the Ministry of Mines and Public Works. She patted the bag on her lap, feeling for the reassuring bulk of the envelope inside – whatever happened, she must not lose it. Her instructions were quite clear – deliver the package safely, turn on the charm, be the perfect companion. Don't lose the cash, don't come back without clinching a deal – and above all, don't do anything which might embarrass Her Majesty's Government.

Soraya smiled to herself. She'd done enough of that already. Obviously she'd better keep off the local red wine.

After three years at the Department, Soraya was used to these under-the-counter deals. Some might call it corruption, but the Prime Minister preferred to refer to it as 'oiling the wheels of commerce'. The Germans, the Americans, the French – everybody did it. And in places like the Republic, the only way to take a short cut through the miles of government red tape was to make a few friends in high places – and pay them well. That was what Soraya was here to do. She'd been told to get Mankiewicz's support for the British plan to build a hydro-electric dam in the mountains above Ragzburg – and she had no intention of failing.

Soraya wriggled uneasily on her seat, suddenly uncomfortable in her smart evening suit and high heels. This was just an ordinary evening, an ordinary deal; and yet tonight, she felt different, somehow. Tonight felt like an adventure – and the excitement was like fire deep in her belly, a boiling, white-hot river soaking the wispy lace gusset between her thighs. Despite the amusing little episode with Gavin, Soraya was feeling randier than she could remember having felt in a long, long time. Sex with Gavin had left her with a thirst that chilled white wine just couldn't satisfy. A sixth sense told her that it could only be slaked by more – and better – sex. This wasn't like her. Tonight, she felt wild, abandoned ... predatory?

Dismissing the thought with a chuckle, Soraya took another sip of wine and gazed up at the evening sky. It was beginning to darken to a light royal blue, the first pin-pricks of starlight just appearing above the turrets and pinnacles of the ancient city.

Rising above the dark, looming shape of the distant mountains was the pale disc of the full moon, still rather indistinct against the mid-blue sky, yet already achieving a strange, effortless domination over the city below.

Soraya shivered, her eyes drawn to the moon and yet

repelled by it. She felt odd: a little dizzy, feverish perhaps. That's what comes of mixing bad wine and sunshine, she thought. She drained the wine glass and topped it up. The wine was ice-cold, yet it seemed to have no effect on her burning, shivering body. Her nipples felt hypersensitive, aching as they rubbed against the black lace of her bra; and she longed to release them from their prison, feel the night breeze cooling her overheated flesh.

Strange place, Ragzburg. A city of the brightest lights and the darkest shadows, where the ancient rubbed shoulders with brash modernity. But the ancient seemed more real, somehow. How had the city changed in the hundred years since her great-great grandmother left to marry young Englishman Josiah Chilton? And what had happened to make the young woman leave her home in England, disappearing back into the shadows and secrets of ancient Ragzburg?

A voice interrupted her reverie; an annoyingly familiar voice; and she looked up, dreading the inevitable.

'Pretty lady . . .'

Her heart sank. Janos. Just her luck.

The dark-eyed gypsy was standing beside her table, still clad in the gaudy folk-costume he'd worn that afternoon at the festival; and his violin tucked under his arm. He swayed a little and stank of drink as he bent to speak to her.

'Pretty English lady want . . .?'

'No.' Soraya cut him dead. 'I don't want you to play for me, and I don't want a ride in your disgusting taxi. I just want you to leave me alone, don't you understand? Look, here's a couple of zloty.' She rummaged in her handbag and threw the coins onto the table. 'Go away, for goodness' sake. I'm waiting for somebody.'

But Janos responded with a laugh, and to her surprise sat down opposite her.

'You not understand, I think.' His eyes glittered with an intensity which Soraya recognised with alarm. There was no mistaking that look of manic lust.

'But I understand you, pretty lady. My little princess with the heart of a wildcat.'

Suddenly his hand was on hers – his great hairy paw stroking and caressing the white flesh, as though he longed to possess her. Speechless, Soraya stared back at him as he continued.

'I know who you are – what you are. And so do they. Those others who pass by on the other side of the road. They look at you and they desire; and yet, they are afraid to look.'

'What? I'm afraid I don't quite . . .'

He grinned, and his teeth glistened sharp as a wolf's in the lamplight. 'They know what you are, also. Can you not feel their eyes on you? They fear you, but they are just poor, superstitious peasants.' He spat contemptuously on the tiled floor of the terrace. 'But I have no fear. Your faithful Janos is not afraid, even of you.'

Soraya felt herself trembling again, now with an intoxicating mixture of fear and excitement. Outrageous though they were, this man's words seemed to strike a chord within her. She didn't understand, and yet it was as though he understood her – better than she could ever have believed possible.

He tightened his grip on her hand.

'You want it too, don't you, my little she-cat? Tonight you have a need deep within you . . .'

'No . . . I . . . don't understand.'

'Come with me. Come with your friend Janos. Let him show you the truth of what is within you. He will play your sweet young body more skilfully even than he play this violin. And he will make her sing so, so sweetly . . .'

'No, no, get off me.' She tried, without success, to draw her hand away. 'Leave me alone. I'm waiting for somebody. He'll be here soon. If you don't leave me alone, I'll –.'

Janos leant close and kissed her on the forehead, running his fingers over her cheeks, her lips, the erect crests of her nipples.

'But Janos has been waiting for you for a long, long

time, my little one. He will not let you go now, not now that he has found you. Come with me now.'

Soraya tried desperately to pull her hand free, but Janos had it fast in his. There was a wildness in his eyes that terrified and yet excited her. He was a good-looking man, strong and beautiful, and he wanted her so very much. The scent of his need seemed to surround her, making her head spin. But she fought the tide of desire bubbling up within her, urging her to give in, to abandon her body to desire.

She glanced round – people were pretending not to be looking, but she knew they were staring at this curious little scene. In a convulsive attempt to get away, she grabbed at Janos's embroidered shirt, ripping it open to the waist. She gasped.

'The scars of love, sweet lady.'

Soraya stared in horror at his tanned skin, criss-crossed with deep scars and gouges that looked like the legacy of an attack by some wild animal.

'Now you understand what it is that I crave, little wildcat. Give it to me, my sweet vixen. Ride me between your hot, strong thighs, possess me, tear me with your claws. Hurt me, harm me, rend me, tear me apart, I beg of you . . .'

Janos was beside her now, dragging her to her feet and pressing his hardness against her belly. She could smell his desire. Why didn't anyone come and help her? Why were they shrinking away from her, trying to avoid her eyes?

'No, no . . . you're crazy!'

'Hurt me, hurt me! You know you want to, little vixen! You can feel the hunger in you, feel the need to tear my flesh. Pain, there must be pain . . .' He seized her hand and pressed it to his chest, trying to force her to scratch him with her fingernails.

All thoughts of illicit pleasure forgotten, Soraya tried to pull free of him, but he held her fast.

'Let me go – you're frightening me.'

'It is almost time; see how sky darkens as the full

moon rises. Do you not feel your desires darken, also? Your claws, she-cat! My cock inside you. Your claws in my flesh . . .'

'No, no, no!'

With a supreme effort, Soraya succeeded in pulling free from him, prising his fingers from her flesh.

'I told you – leave me alone!'

Suddenly Janos was no longer the menacing demon-lover he had seemed. He sank back onto his chair, cringing and trembling, a pathetic figure as he stretched out beseeching arms to her, and whispered:

'Pain. There must be exquisite pain. I know you want it too. I have seen the darkness in your soul. Why will you not give me what I crave . . .?'

No, no. He was talking nonsense – it couldn't be true. Couldn't be true that she wanted to do these terrible things to him.

Revulsion overwhelming her, Soraya broke away and stumbled off across the terrace, pushing her way between the tables and bumping into the staring diners as she fought to rid herself of the black thoughts that overwhelmed her, the treacherous desire that made her whole vulva throb with suppressed power.

As she rushed out into the cool night air, a man loomed up out of the darkness. She almost cried out and tried to turn away, but he stopped her, laying his hand gently on her arm.

'Miss Chilton? And in such a hurry to leave? Allow me to introduce myself. My name is Lukas Mankiewicz.'

In the misty drizzle of an English spring afternoon, Anton Kline was wishing himself somewhere – anywhere – else but here.

The photo shoot had got off to a bad start right from the word go. To begin with, the weather had turned bad almost as soon as he'd set up his equipment in the grounds of Caversham Manor, and he'd only managed one roll of film before they'd had to retire inside to drink black coffee and dry out the frocks.

In the drawing room of the old stately home, Anton improvised. The House of Luxor was shelling out two million on this advertising campaign, and they weren't paying to have a photographer, two lighting technicians and six models sitting around eating Hob-Nobs all day. Since they were inside, he might as well make the best of it and set up a few atmospheric indoor shots.

At exactly the right moment, the owner's velvet-coated Weimaraner wandered into the room and Anton snapped his fingers. Nice dog; classy. Just the prop he'd been looking for.

'Get that dog and make it lie down in front of the fireplace,' he ordered his assistant, who prodded the dog rather ineffectually in the direction of the hearthrug. 'And you, Antonia – drape yourself all over it, that riding-outfit looks good, but undo a couple of the top buttons. Nice little flash of tit – remember, these are for *Esquire*. For God's sake get that bloody dog to stick its tongue back in, it looks obscene. Now, sultry looks everyone . . . great.'

He snapped off another couple of rolls of film in rapid succession, but the light was getting so bad that they had to bring in all the auxiliary tungsten lamps. Only six o'clock, but already it was getting dark. Maybe there was going to be a storm? The hairs on the back of his neck were standing uncomfortably erect, as they always did when there was a hint of electricity in the air. Now the whole room was starting to take on an eerie look, all chiaroscuro like *Nosferatu* or a French *film noir*. OK, OK, he was a professional; he could handle that.

'Black cape, Sophie. And the gloves, the ones that go up to your elbows. Full riding-kit, Jeremy – and the boots.'

At that moment, Caz the technician put her head round the door.

'Amanda's arrived, Anton. Her plane was grounded in Athens, and she's only just made it off the M25.'

'About time too. Well, now she's here we'd better use her. Tell her lots of scarlet chiffon, and to get a move on.'

He fiddled irritably with the lens cap on the Leica. Models. Prima donnas the lot of 'em. The worst thing about them was, none of them was a patch on that gorgeous dark-haired beauty he'd caught sight of at the IT exhibition, all those months ago.

Smitten? He'd been having wet dreams about her ever since. It wasn't like him not to be able to get a woman's face out of his mind, but this one had got him so bad he'd even gone to the trouble of finding out her name: Soraya Chilton. Even now, just the thought of her made his penis throb. He wondered vaguely who she was screwing on this damp, dark evening; and the thought of that made him burn with a ridiculous but inescapable jealousy.

Five minutes later, Amanda del Rio entered the room; and Anton knew she'd been worth the wait. Tall and aristocratic, with dark hair and flashing blue-black eyes, she curled her crimson lips into a smile and he went instantly weak at the knees.

'Mr Kline – so lovely to meet you at last. I've heard so much about you.' Her voice was husky and deep, with that vague Continental accent he had always found impossibly sexy. She extended her ringed hand and he felt a silly romantic urge to kiss it. He pressed his lips to her hand and her soft, white flesh had a faint scent of violets.

'All bad I hope,' joked Anton, feeling somewhat uneasy. This sultry beauty had got him hot under the collar, and it was tough trying to maintain his habitual veneer of arrogant charm.

'So you're a bad boy, are you?' teased Amanda, kissing an immaculately-manicured fingertip and placing it playfully on his lips. 'This I must see.' She nodded towards the fireplace and the dog, now sleeping with its head on its paws. 'Now, where do you want me?'

He was painfully aware of the double meaning in the question. Anton Kline was no young innocent. He'd never lacked for female companionship, and he could spot a feminine chat-up line a mile off. But his heart was pounding and his mouth was surprisingly dry, and it was a couple of seconds before he could reply.

'Anywhere you like, darling,' he replied, taking off the lens cap. 'Just do whatever feels right.'

Amanda purred her satisfaction as she draped herself, belly-down, across the hearthrug. He realised with a thrill of schoolboy delight that he could see right down her dress, to the juicy swell of two small but perfect breasts.

'That's just the way I like it,' she smiled as the motor-drive whirred away. And as he knelt a few feet in front of her to take a close-up, she whispered words that made him shiver with excitement. 'Maybe later on you could show me what feels good for you?'

Later, they would get together in Amanda's hotel room, and it would be great. Maybe a spot of dinner at San Lorenzo's first, no point in rushing things; but she was his for the taking. Or was he hers? He didn't really care. He wanted her, and she wanted him. Their bodies would come together in perfect synchronicity, and at last he would be able to free himself from this burning, all-consuming need to make love to her.

The only thing that bothered him, as he packed up the camera, was a feeling of dishonesty. It wasn't as if he was cheating on the woman, no, not really. Only, he knew exactly why he wanted Amanda so much, and he didn't feel particularly heroic about it.

He wanted her because she reminded him of Soraya Chilton.

'You have the package?'

Soraya nodded.

'It is as we agreed. Five thousand, plus the extra – administrative charge.'

'Good, good. But not here, Soraya. I fear there are too many prying eyes. Nearby is a small hotel I know – very safe, very discreet. We shall attend to our business transaction there.'

They walked on down the main street, turning into a

shadowy alleyway which led into the very heart of Ragzburg's old town. It was getting very dark now. The sky had deepened to a rich indigo, and the moon hung, huge and white, above the city. Its light felt cool and sensual on her bare shoulders and arms – yet somehow alive, like quicksilver running over her flesh. They were walking very close together, their bodies almost touching. Soraya could feel the heat radiating out of Lukas's body, and longed to feel his naked flesh against hers. How would it feel to be taken by him here, now, with her back up against the crumbling stone wall and her skirts up round her waist?

What was happening to her? Why couldn't she get sex out of her mind? And why did she feel so odd? She glanced down at her fingertips. They felt all tingly, as if she had pins and needles; and her mouth was dry and hot. She moistened her lips with the tip of her tongue. Was she ill? She didn't feel ill – just very strange; and very, very hot for sex.

Lukas Mankiewicz was certainly a very desirable man. Who could blame a red-blooded young Englishwoman for lusting after his Slavic good looks? Tall, dark and brooding, with piercing blue eyes, he pressed himself close to her and she knew instinctively that he wanted her too. As her hand brushed against his, she felt a spark of energy pass between them, uniting their lust.

Need, need, need. Such a thirst. Such a hunger, deep within.

The moon stretched thin, pallid fingers of light even into these ancient, unlit alleyways where rats scurried and cats' eyes gleamed for a second before being swallowed up in the darkness. This was a place of guilty secrets, half-heard whisperings. Elusive sounds played games with her mind – half-heard for a few seconds, then lost. Could she really hear voices whispering in her head? What were they saying? Was she losing her mind?

Got to keep it cool, calm. Got to keep it professional – her instructions had been quite clear on that score.

Soraya tried hard to get a grip on herself. If she blew this deal, Gavin could quite easily have her demoted, or sent off to manage some God-forsaken outstation at the back end of Belgium.

'Here we are, my dear.' They were standing in front of a peeling white door, illuminated with ghostly clarity by a hanging blue lamp. Mankiewicz turned and flashed her a smile which revealed perfect teeth. He rang the doorbell and a few moments later, the door swung open. An unseen figure invited them inside, then disappeared.

Mankiewicz ushered her into a sparsely-furnished room on the first floor. It was a typical room in a cheap Eastern European hotel, with little to commend it – two chairs, a bed, tatty dressing table and French windows leading out onto a small balcony. The windows were open, and as Soraya sank onto a chair her eyes were once again drawn by the pale, placid disc of the moon, so huge now that it seemed to fill the entire space bounded by the window-frame, dominating the night sky.

'Drink, Miss Chilton? I have only a rather cheap brandy, I'm afraid. Good brands are so hard to come by.'

'Brandy will be fine.' Soraya shook herself, making an effort to be efficient and charming. She slipped the package from her bag and laid it on the small coffee table. 'I think you will find it is all there.'

'In used notes?'

'Of course. Swiss Francs, as you stipulated.'

Lukas smiled, flicked briefly through the bundle of notes, then slid the package into a drawer of the dressing table.

'I am glad to be doing business with such a charming young lady.' His hand touched hers fleetingly as he handed her the brandy, and Soraya felt a shiver of pleasure run through her body.

'You will expedite the British company's application to build the hydro-electric dam?'

'Certainly I shall do all I can, but . . .'

Irritation mingled with desire. Surely he was not going to renege on the deal now. 'There is a problem?'

'In this country there are always problems with bureaucracy, my dear.' He sat down on the edge of the bed, facing Soraya, and slipped off his jacket. 'Difficult people to convince, officials to influence. Sometimes the process can take many months.'

'Please get to the point, Mr Mankiewicz.'

'Very well, my dear. I think we can approach the problem in a civilised way, no? This is what I propose. Sleep with me tonight, and the British application will proceed unhindered. Refuse, and ... I can give no guarantees. Things can of course go wrong. It is often the way in Ragzburg.'

Soraya was listening, but it was as though Lukas's words were reaching her from the far end of a very long tunnel. Her eyes had strayed once more to the window, and to the moonlight which was flooding the unlit room, bathing her skin with a silvery glow. Her fingers were tingling more than ever now. She looked down at them, and the varnished nails seemed to glisten with a deeper, richer crimson than she remembered. Were they longer and sharper, too? No, that was pure nonsense.

'Soraya ...?'

She didn't answer, but picked up the brandy and lifted it to her lips. What was happening to her? She could hear the blood pounding in her veins, feel her clitoris pulsating with a painful intensity between her thighs. Every sense seemed sharpened – sight, sound, smell, taste, touch. She could hear the whispering voices in her head again; only this time, she could make out some of what they were saying.

Take him, Soraya. Take, feed. He is prey, Soraya. Your prey. He is there for you. Can't you feel yourself getting wet, just at the thought of it? He is helpless, Soraya. Sweet, succulent, helpless prey. You know you want to fuck ... You know you have to take him ...

She looked down at her hand again. It was trembling. Her whole body was shaking convulsively.

71

'What is the matter, Soraya? Are you ill?'

Shaking; shaking like a rag doll, helpless to resist a power far greater than itself. Desire and need were the only forces that existed within her now. An inhuman strength flooded through her, like mountain streams swelling the spring tides. She stared at the hand holding the glass, and suddenly she knew that she was gripping it too tightly. She tried to loosen her grip but she couldn't – the strength within her had taken over, and she kept on gripping it tighter, tighter . . .

Suddenly the glass shattered in her hand. Glittering fragments scattered in all directions. A single drop of blood formed a lustrous crimson bead in the palm of her hand. Entranced, Soraya put out her tongue and lapped at it as a she-cat laps cream.

'My God, Soraya! What on earth . . .'

But Soraya was not listening to Lukas Mankiewicz any more. She was listening to the voices in her head, to the throbbing, insistent pulse of her need and her desire. She lifted her head to the night air and breathed in deeply. Sex. The air was filled with the scent of sex. She could smell Mankiewicz's fear and desire, mingling to form the most intoxicating, exquisite aphrodisiac.

She had forgotten why she came here. All thoughts of the deal banished from her mind, she thought of nothing but the sexual pleasure that she must have; the hunger that must be fed. Lukas Mankiewicz was no longer her contact, her enemy or her potential lover. Now he had become her prey.

Maddened with hunger for his sex, Soraya tore off her clothes, desperate to feel the cool, silver moonlight caressing her bare flesh. The silk blouse and skirt, the bra, the little white lace panties and pale stockings joined her jacket in a crazy jumbled heap on the floor.

As she stood naked before Mankiewicz, she caught sight of her reflection for a second in the mirror which hung behind the old iron bedstead.

She was beautiful with an unearthly, ethereal beauty, her lips and nails a glossy crimson against the silver-white pallor of her naked skin. Her eyes were no longer a deep blue-black. They burned deepest red like the smouldering embers of a volcano, awakening to rage and destruction. Lust consumed her, overwhelming reason and leaving in its place only passion's blind instinct. Still the voices whispered on in her head.

Got to have him. Got to have him, now.

Soraya turned, the terrible sexual hunger overwhelming her. Little whimpering cries of lust escaped from her glossy red lips, and Mankiewicz was backing away from her slowly, a look of alarm on his face.

She sprang, pawing at her prey. Panting and gasping with need, she tore at his clothes, ran her scarlet-taloned fingers down the curve of waist and hip and plump, swelling cock.

'Want you, want you now . . .' she breathed. Her voice seemed as distant as Lukas's, as distant and unreal as the room in which they were struggling, their bodies locked together in a convulsive embrace.

Mankiewicz cried out, tried to push her away; but the stength was in her and she was invincible, irresistible, insatiable. Her hands were on him and he was falling back onto the mattress, his mouth opening and closing in silent anguish as she fell upon him with savage lust.

Desire was the only truth now. He was naked beneath her and nothing stood in the way of her pleasure. Instinctively she sought out his shaft with her lips, her tongue, teasing him with the points of her little sharp teeth. He tasted so good on her tongue, the saltiness of his precum filling her mouth and making her thirst for more and still more.

Mankiewicz groaned and writhed, but she held him fast, pressing him down onto the soft bedcovers as she sucked him to the point of surrender. His balls were so big, so full of love-juice. She let go of his shaft and started licking the velvety purse between his thighs, delighting in the way it tensed at her touch, growing heavier and more expectant by the second. His hands reached out, trying to touch the fullness of her breasts, teasing the hypersensitive flesh of her iron-hard nipples.

He came into her mouth, and the taste of his semen turned Soraya's desire into a wild, untamed frenzy. In a second she was on top of him, furiously pumping his shaft back to painful stiffness with her hands.

'No more . . . no more . . . I can't . . .'

She was not listening to him. All she could hear were the sounds of her own laboured breathing, the voices whispering their chorus of delight in her head as she straddled Lukas's rampant cock, taking him inside her with a brutal urgency.

He was hers now; and pleasure was very near. Pleasure that would begin to slake the terrible thirst that made her throat burn and her sex-bud throb with unsatisfied need. Her thighs tightened about Lukas's hips, drawing him deeper inside her, using his body to give her the pleasure she so desperately craved. His hard, sleek penis was filling her, stretching her, swelling to ever-greater hardness as their passion climbed towards the peak of frenzy.

As she came, she clutched convulsively at Lukas's flesh, her sharp scarlet talons raking across his chest and belly in a paroxysm of ecstasy, raising angry red welts that would bear witness to her hunger for many days to come. The pain made Lukas gasp with pleasure, and his back arched as his balls tensed and delivered up their opalescent tribute.

Soraya's womanhood tensed in the first spasms of orgasm. Wave upon wave of exquisite pleasure followed, shaking her body and tearing apart her soul. There had never been pleasure like this before, pleasure that was strong enough to be pain. As she sank down upon the body of her unconscious victim, her head reeled. Where was she? Who was she? What was she?

A creature of the moon. A creature living only for the sex that fed its hunger – and already that hunger was stirring in her belly once again. Tonight, there would be no rest until pleasure had been taken to the furthermost extreme, ecstasy drained to the very last drop.

Invigorated by the strength of her need, Soraya

pushed Mankiewicz away and got off the bed. He was of no consequence now. She had already forgotten his name, almost forgotten he had ever existed. She needed sex, more and wilder sex.

Drawn by the moonlight, she walked across to the French windows and stepped out onto the balcony. The cool moonlight danced patterns on her naked white skin, soothing and yet intensifying the fever.

Come to us, Soraya. Join us. Run with us tonight.

The voices were whispering to her from the shadows in the garden. Soraya looked down into the darkness, but the garden was a shadowy mass of bushes and trees.

Come to us. It is time. Come and share our need, our pleasure.

Eyes. There were eyes in the darkness, glowing like tiny red coals. Clouds drifted over the face of the moon, changing the pattern of shadows, picking out moonlight on an arm, a hip, the swell of a naked breast.

We are waiting Soraya. Waiting for you . . .

Exhilaration washed over her like wild sea spray, and Soraya climbed over the balcony rail. It was not far down into the garden. With a cry of joy, she jumped, landing on hands and knees on the soft grass. Hands touched her, soothed her, welcomed her; and a moment later she was running across the grass and into the night.

Running with the pack.

Chapter Five

The morning sunlight filtered through the dense canopy of foliage, spreading a warm odour of pine and leaf mould.

Something scuttled away through the undergrowth, and Soraya paused for a moment, her naked flesh very white against the greenish-black tree bark.

She still felt confused, memories of last night's adventure coming back only fitfully. Images fluttered in and out of her mind: a big, silver moon in a dark blue sky; laughter and excitement and sweet, savage sex. The best sex she had ever had in her entire life.

Had it all been a dream? None of it seemed to make sense in the bright, uncompromising light of day. But if it had been a dream, how had she come to this place, awakening alone in the forest at dawn, her flesh scratched and bruised and her body thrilled by the fading memory of a strange excitement?

The feeling of exhilaration was still with her: a profound, peaceful exultation that made her want to laze like a lizard in the summer sun, soaking up the warmth and living only for languid, effortless pleasure.

Something smelt good. The scent of meat cooking brought Soraya back to her senses. She was hungry, she was naked and – although she had lost all track of time

– she knew that if she didn't get back to the Embassy pretty damn quick, Gavin would be sending out a search party to look for her. It wasn't that he cared about something bad happening to her: he'd be more worried she'd gone walkabout with his fifty thousand Swiss Francs.

Soraya pushed her way cautiously through the trees and found herself on the edge of a small clearing. In the centre stood a small ramshackle wooden hut, with a plume of dirty grey smoke emerging from a hole in the roof. Food! Could she steal herself some breakfast without anyone seeing her? Better still, she spotted a row of clothes drying on a line stretched between two trees. There didn't seem to be anyone around. Surely she could sneak up and appropriate something to cover her embarrassment. After all, she could hardly make her way back into Ragzburg stark naked – though the thought was a diverting one . . .

Darting out from her cover, Soraya made for the washing line. That old shirt and pair of tatty corduroy pants would do. The smell of food cooking was driving her mad, but there wasn't time to think about breakfast. Hastily she pulled the shirt off the line and reached out for the pants. Suddenly she felt a hand on her shoulder. She froze.

'Such a pretty little thief . . .'

She wheeled round, eyes wide with horror; thanking her lucky stars that she'd bothered to learn the local dialect.

'I . .. I'm sorry. I needed clothes . . .'

'I can see that.' It was hard to tell if the blond woodsman was angry or amused by her predicament. His grey eyes were feasting on her nakedness, drinking in every curve of breast and hip and thigh. He was a powerful man, strong arms rippling with well-honed muscle. Strong, and perhaps a little dangerous too.

She tried to push him away, and managed to prise his hand from her shoulder; but that only made matters worse. Now he held her fast again, his strong hands

77

round her waist and her back pressed up against a thick tree trunk.

'You are a stranger . . . a foreigner.'

'English,' stammered Soraya. The woodsman's face was very close to hers, his breath hot and spicy on her cheek. To her surprise she realised she was not afraid. If anything, she welcomed the way his body heat soaked into her naked flesh, welcomed the rough denim of his overalls grinding into the fragile softness of her pubis, demanding her to surrender to pleasure.

He took one hand from Soraya's waist, and let it explore the territory he had conquered, skimming thigh and hip, cupping her breast and smoothing surprisingly gentle fingers across her cheek.

'English,' he repeated. 'So my beautiful little thief is an Englishwoman. And yet there is the look of the Slav in those deep, dark eyes.'

'My . . . great-great grandmother was from Ragzburg.'

'Ah . . .' He smiled, a self-satisfied grin. 'Vaclav is never wrong about a woman.' He slipped his hand back down to Soraya's breast, and pinched one of her nipples. She gasped. 'And Vaclav knows something else about you.'

'W-what?'

He laughed.

'Vaclav knows that you love to fuck.'

Soraya felt herself blush; but she didn't see why she should let a peasant get the better of her.

'You want to have sex?'

'Vaclav wants to make love with every beautiful woman in the whole world.'

'Why the hell should I do it with you?'

Vaclav nodded towards the old shirt and pants, now lying on the dusty, trampled grass where two goats were grazing peacefully.

'Everything has its price. I have what you want, and you have what I want. Only I think you want it, too.' He slipped his hand down Soraya's belly and let his fingers toy with the dark curls on her pubis.

78

Soraya gave a little moan of reluctant pleasure. She knew she could resist him, push him away, persuade him that he was wrong – even scream and shout. But he was right. A familiar, lazy warmth was spreading over her, reminding her of the summer night when – as a tipsy schoolgirl – she had surrendered her troublesome virginity to a young sports master behind the school pavilion. Then, as now, she had wanted to deliver herself up to a man, abandon all responsibility and reason, and just let him make passionate, indulgent love to her.

Encouraged, Vaclav pushed his fingers down between Soraya's thighs and into the hot, moist sanctum of her womanhood. Soraya welcomed his entry with a sigh of sensual pleasure. If this was the price ... it was well worth paying.

One finger, two, three slipped into her eager haven, parting the fleshy folds and skating over the slippery love-juice to discover the secrets within. The rough bark of the old tree chafed her naked skin, but Soraya didn't even notice. Vaclav's fingers were inside her, pressing again and again on the spongy g-spot that made her juices run in crazy, abandoned rivulets down the inside of her thighs.

'I know a woman's body,' panted Vaclav, his fingers working in and out of Soraya's slippery womanhood. 'And I understand your body, my pretty little thief.'

Soraya closed her eyes, not daring to move or speak in case the pleasure stopped. She was close, so very close to her climax; and now Vaclav's lips were closing on her nipple, sucking and biting and teasing it to new peaks of excitement.

Suddenly, Vaclav was kissing her – his lips crushed against hers, his tongue jousting with hers, forcing its way into the hot wet cavern of her mouth as his fingers explored the garden of delights between her thighs. And then he was sliding down her body, kissing neck and shoulders, breasts and belly and soft, springy pubic curls.

When the tip of his tongue probed between her thighs,

parting her love-lips, Soraya could not suppress a sob of pleasure. He had not lied. He did indeed understand a woman's body – or at least, he understood hers, knowing instinctively all the little tricks and caresses which would take her to the brink of dazzling, breathtaking ecstasy.

'Oh give it to me, give it to me now ...' she gasped. One hand was on Vaclav's shoulder, gripping him tight, whilst the other was on the nape of his neck, twisting and winding the corn-blond curls about her fingers as she strived for the elusive summit of pleasure.

Elusive, because Vaclav was in no hurry to take her to her destination. She knew he wanted to torment her first, show her the power that he had over her helplessly sensual body. And today she did not care about power games – yearning only for the pleasure to go on forever; the exquisite, effortless pleasure of his fingers and tongue between her sex-lips.

Kneeling between her parted thighs, Vaclav ran his questing tongue along and between the folds of her inner labia; making circles that narrowed, gradually coming ever closer to the throbbing heart of her desire.

It was like a glorious, golden dream, being sucked and licked by this handsome young woodsman in a forest clearing. Through her closed eyelids, Soraya sensed the changing patterns of light as the sun moved towards its zenith, and the branches swayed lazily in the gentlest of breezes. Today was not a day for wild, abandoned sex; for savage lust and joy so intense that it was almost indistinguishable from pain. She had given up trying to understand what had happened to her. Today was for sweet, slow pleasure and warm sunlight on naked flesh.

Ecstasy was coming: rising and swelling within her as the warmth spread out from the pink bud of her clitoris and seemed to fill her abdomen, her thighs, her breasts, her entire body.

Vaclav pressed his face closer to her swollen lower lips as her vulva tensed in the first, blissful spasms of orgasm, releasing a flood of the sweetest love-juice he had ever tasted. He growled with delight as the heady mixture trickled out of her and onto his tongue.

Gasping and moaning with pleasure, Soraya opened her eyes. The whole world seemed to be spinning, trees and sky and sun-dappled leaves all whirling around her head.

A shadow appeared in front of her eyes: the sun-haloed head of Vaclav. With the sun behind him, she could hardly make out his features at all. He was her faceless lover, and it did not matter, because at this moment she was faceless too: just a pleasure-seeking body, longing for release.

Pants quickly unbuttoned, his hands held her thighs apart and he entered her in a swift rapier thrust that left her breathless. She had still not even stroked his cock – had not made its acquaintance with kisses and caresses. As it entered her, she closed her eyes, savouring its size, its power, its delicious hardness, and surrendering to it willingly. All that mattered here and now was the pleasure.

Vaclav rode her expertly, a magnificent animal for whom instinct was the only guide. If he recognised something dark and powerful within her, he chose to disregard it. He was the stallion and she was his sprightly filly, a willing partner in his games of lust. His finger slipped between his body and Soraya's, bringing her to a second orgasm with a few careless strokes across the head of her clitoris.

With a grunt of satisfaction he gave a final thrust, holding her very tightly as the last drops of love-juice oozed from him.

At last he withdrew from her and buttoned up his pants. Soraya opened her eyes and realised that she had not even seen the instrument of her pleasure. Still, it mattered little. Freed from Vaclav's vice-like embrace, she stretched, smiled, stepped forward and planted a kiss on his cheek.

'I take it the price is paid?'

He chuckled.

'Paid in full.' He picked up the shirt and pants and handed them to her. 'Hungry?'

'Ravenous. But I have to get back to Ragzburg as quickly as I can. My boss . . .'

'Come into my cottage and we shall eat together. Afterwards, I will take you back to Ragzburg in the truck – it is not many miles, and I am sure you will find ways of entertaining me on our journey.' He paused on the threshold of the shack. 'These woods are dangerous – there are some who say they have seen wolves. Tell me, Englishwoman – how did you come to be here?'

Soraya shook her head.

'That's the trouble,' she replied. 'I just don't remember.'

Showering in her room at the British Embassy, Soraya took the time to reflect on what had happened. But what exactly had happened? As she smoothed the citrus shower-gel over her skin, she tried to sort the images out in her mind.

One minute she was sitting in that cheap hotel with Lukas Mankiewicz, drinking brandy and looking out at the moon. Mankiewicz was smiling at her, proposing a little deal, and she was feeling stranger and stranger – overwhelmed by a sexual hunger that she had never experienced in her life. Then they were having sex, only it wasn't like any sex she'd ever had before. It was the slaking of her hunger upon Mankiewicz's body, using him for the pleasure her own body demanded again and again, with ever-greater ferocity.

The next minute, Mankiewicz wasn't there any longer and Soraya was standing in the moonlight, naked and hungry and laughing for the sheer joy of lust.

What had happened next? Everything after that moment was just a jumble of crazy images – faces, bodies, sensations . . . and always moonlight. Always the huge, silver moon dominating the vast blackness of the night sky.

The next thing she remembered distinctly was waking

up in the woods. It was early morning and she was curled up in the bracken on a wooded hillside, miles from Ragzburg. There were bites and scratches on her skin and her body ached all over, yet she was filled with the most incredible sense of well-being: a deeply sensual awareness that made her yearn for the luxury of passive, unquestioning pleasure. The ferocious sexual hunger of the previous night seemed to have evaporated along with the last shadows of night.

She tried to piece together the fragmentary images in her brain, but it was no use. Nothing made sense. Besides, she was wary of exploring the possibilities; uneasy about getting too near the truth. Today she felt wonderful; she was safe and well; she'd had innocent fun with Vaclav – well, that was enough to be going on with.

She couldn't help giggling when she thought of the guards' faces as she rolled up at the doors of the British Embassy in a broken-down timber truck. Or Gavin's when he saw she was dressed in nothing but a threadbare old shirt and a pair of well-patched corduroy trousers. He'd taken one look at her and snapped:

'Debriefing – my office, half an hour. Sharp!'

As she dried her hair, Soraya looked at herself in the mirror, remembering how she had looked last night. Had her eyes really glowed red? It must have been an optical illusion, a trick of the light – or the after-effects of her fainting fit at the fertility festival. Suddenly, as she gazed at her reflection, she noticed something very odd. A few hours ago, her breasts and flanks had been crisscrossed with a tracery of fine scratches: now, there was nothing – not a mark, not a bruise. In those few short hours, her skin had returned to its former flawless beauty. Her body was positively glowing with health.

This wasn't something she wanted to think about; it short-circuited her brain, opening up the dark maelstrom of questions she would really prefer not to answer. Throwing on a smart navy dress and matching high-heeled shoes, Soraya gave her long black hair a final brush and turned away. She was due in Gavin's office in five minutes – and she couldn't afford to keep him waiting. Besides, she owed him an explanation – if she could think of one to give him.

Gavin was standing beside the ornate carved fireplace, drumming his fingers on the mantelpiece. He turned sharply as Soraya walked in, and glanced at his watch.

'Two minutes late. Still, you're here now, so you can start explaining to me exactly where you've been since last night.'

Soraya stared at her shoes, trying desperately to come up with something that would placate Gavin. Obviously Mankiewicz had complained about what she'd done to him last night. He'd expected a pleasant night's casual sex, and what had he got? Some crazy woman screwing the life out of him. She swallowed hard.

'Well, I delivered the money as you instructed: fifty thousand Swiss Francs. Mankiewicz made the rendezvous at the Hotel Radetsky, as arranged. Then we went to a hotel to ... talk business.'

Gavin raised a quizzical eyebrow.

'Business? Perhaps you'd care to be more specific.'

Irritated, Soraya looked him straight in the eye.

'OK, Gavin, if that's the way you want it. Here's what happened. The creep took the money, then he decided to change the rules a little. Said if I slept with him, he'd make sure the British bid went through, no problems. But if I didn't, things were liable to go wrong. What did you want me to do, Gavin? You made it pretty damn clear I mustn't come back without getting a deal. In the circumstances, I did the only thing I could.'

'You had it off with him, right?'

'Right.' Her heart was beating too fast. It looked like she'd really screwed it up this time. 'Sorry. Only you've never complained about my methods before.'

To her amazement, Gavin's face broke into a broad grin.

'Thank God you did, Soraya, that's all I can say.

Because whatever you did to him, it worked.' Gavin picked up a sheet of paper from his desk, and pushed it across for her to look at. 'I received this by fax from Mankiewicz this morning.'

Soraya glanced down at it.

'The contract! You mean . . .?'

'Signed, sealed, delivered – well, good as, anyway. But that doesn't explain why you've been wandering the countryside half-naked all night, does it?'

Soraya sighed.

'No, Gavin.'

'But . . . well, your private fetishes are your own affair, just so long as they don't jeopardise your work for the British Government. Luckily, the Ambassador is so pleased with the contract that he seems to have forgotten all about your little escapade yesterday at the festival. Let's just say that I'm prepared to forget your little indiscretions too, let bygones be bygones, if . . .'

'If what?'

Gavin came round from behind the desk. Soraya saw at once that his cock was already swelling beneath his dark grey flannels. She groaned inwardly. It really had been a big mistake, getting friendly with him last night. She should have known it could only lead to trouble. How could she have been so stupid as to let lust get the better of her good judgement? And what had possessed her to lust after the odious little creep in the first place?

'If you're nice to me, Soraya. Really nice.'

He advanced. She stood her ground, though what she really wanted to do was turn tail and get the hell out of Gavin's office. She shouldn't show him how much she despised him. He was her boss, after all.

'Nice, Gavin? Whatever do you mean?'

Gavin smiled – a nasty, thin-lipped sneer that reminded Soraya of a crocodile. He took hold of Soraya's right hand, and guided it to the front of his Savile Row pants.

'Feel that, sweetheart?'

She nodded. She could hardly miss it.

'Why don't you stroke me, tease me – squeeze me like you did last night? Go on – you know you want to. You play it so cool but you're just a slut at heart, aren't you, Soraya?'

Soraya slid her hand down his flies until her fingers were cupping his testicles, very lightly, very seductively.

'You want me to do it like this?'

Gavin half-closed his eyes and gave an appreciative murmur.

'Mm, yes. Like that. Just like that.'

In a single savage movement, Soraya clenched her fingers, squeezing his balls in a vice-like grip that made him howl with sudden pain.

'Forget it,' she snapped, turning on her heel and slamming the door of the office behind her.

Gavin was annoyed. It was hardly surprising really. First of all he'd got the brush-off of his life from Soraya, and then the Foreign Secretary had rung through from London to tell him there was a crisis in Iceland that needed sorting out. The upshot was that they were both being pulled back to London, ASAP.

As Soraya waited with her bags on the front steps of the Embassy, she gazed out at the bustling streets of the ancient city. She'd only been here a few weeks. She'd hardly begun to get to know the place, let alone understand the city where her great-great grandparents had met and married.

The mountains encircling the city in a protective bowl; the villages and scented pine-forests where nothing disturbed a routine which had continued for centuries; the city streets where horse-drawn carts still outnumbered trucks and limousines. Ragzburg was a secret city hardly touched by progress or the march of time. It was a crazy place, but Soraya would miss it. Maybe one day she would get a chance to return.

'Defiler! Devil woman!'

Soraya turned in astonishment to see an elderly,

black-clad peasant woman on the other side of the narrow street, staring at her with an expression of mingled fear and hatred. Could it be the same crazy old woman she had noticed staring at her in the town square, just after she'd arrived?

Heads turned at the sudden commotion. Rooted to the spot, Soraya stared in amazement as the old woman fought her way across the crowded thoroughfare, still babbling her crazy nonsense.

'The power – the power of darkness. I have seen it, devil woman!' she screeched. 'You deny it, but it is within you, a tenfold curse upon your desire.'

She was only feet away from Soraya now, and seemed afraid to approach closer. She backed away as Soraya took a step towards her.

'What are you talking about? I don't understand. What curse?'

The old woman cackled with mirthless laughter.

'You think you are so clever, Englishwoman. You think you can use the power for your own pleasure, but in time the power will use you.'

'Power? I . . .'

'On a night when the full moon is crowned with blood; then you will understand.'

At that moment, two burly Ragzburg policemen appeared from the shadows and seized hold of the struggling woman. The captain turned to Soraya.

'I apologise, madame. She is just a trouble-maker, a little sick in the head, no?'

As they dragged her away, the old woman turned back, the thin screech of her voice carrying above the noise of the midday traffic.

'You can never leave Ragzburg! Never! Ragzburg is in the darkness of your soul for ever!'

The old woman sat on a wooden bench in the main square. It was market day and the square was filled with noise and bustle, but she paid no attention to anything around her. She was too busy staring at something in her hand.

It was a very old and very tattered sepia photograph of a woman in Victorian dress. A beautiful young woman with jet-black hair and dark, lustrous eyes.

A woman who bore an uncanny resemblance to Soraya Chilton.

Chapter Six

Amanda del Rio slid her silken thighs between the sheets, and pressed her perfect body up against Anton's back.

Drowsy and relaxed, he gave a soft murmur of pleasure and rolled around to face her.

'You're insatiable, Amanda!'

'It's not like you to complain, darling.'

Anton laughed. Amanda was good for him, he knew that. She gave him good sex and fun times, and she kept bringing him back down to earth whenever he got too big for his boots. Was it so terrible to want that extra something more?

'I want you, Anton, and you'd better give me exactly what I want because I'm a tiger when I'm roused.'

'Is that so?'

Amanda ran her spiky fingernails lightly down his bare back, making him shiver with the sudden sensation as reddish-pink tracks appeared on his golden flesh.

'See? Tiger-stripes. Now you're a tiger, too. Come here and screw me, tiger.'

Side by side in Anton's king-size bed, they kissed. Slowly, Amanda lifted her right leg and slid it over Anton's thigh, parting her swollen sex-lips. It was the simplest of manoeuvres to take hold of Anton's smooth, hard shaft and press its tip against the entrance to her womanhood. She was wet and excited, more than ready for him; the fragrance of her designer perfume easily engulfed by the fragrance of her sex.

Anton needed no second bidding. With a swift thrust he was inside her, his cock in up to the hilt. As they moved together slowly, luxuriously, the fingers of his left hand crept down over her backside, feeling for the succulence of her secret furrow.

As the tip of his index finger toyed with the puckered rosebud of her anus, Amanda sighed and moaned, clutching him tight, riding him harder and faster. His fingertip penetrated her and she cried out in sudden ecstasy. There was no controlling the onrush of pleasure now, she was on the brink of orgasm and there was no going back.

'I'm coming, I'm coming!'

Her vagina tensed in spasm after spasm of ecstatic delight, and she felt herself tumbling, falling in a glittering cascade of perfect pleasure.

'Wonderful,' groaned Anton, spurting deep into his lover's belly. 'Just wonderful.'

He fell back, exhausted, onto the pillows, and they lay together, still coupled, for many minutes; not speaking, but listening to the halting rhythm of their heartbeats, gradually slowing as passion died away.

In the darkness of the night Amanda listened to Anton's breathing; slow, regular, deep. He was sleeping.

Slowly and carefully, she slid out of bed, dressing quickly in the darkness. Slipping on her shoes and evening jacket, she felt in the pocket for the letter and laid it on the bedside table, where he would find it when he awoke.

She hadn't wanted it to end like this. When she'd first seduced him into her bed, she'd been in search of nothing more than a few nights of innocent, libidinous fun. A couple of weeks on, she realised that she had broken her one unwritten, inviolable rule: she had got in too damn deep.

He did not wake as her lips brushed his cheek in a farewell kiss. A pang of jealousy stung her as she wondered if he would miss her at all. She still wanted him; wanted him like crazy – but Amanda del Rio would never share her man with another woman.

She crossed the room and opened the door softly, the 'do not disturb' notice swinging gently on the outer handle. She didn't look back; as far as she was concerned, Anton Kline was just one torn-out page in a book with many chapters.

Yes, she wanted him; but she knew she wasn't what he really wanted. She'd seen the photographs he kept in his desk drawer, even caught him looking at them once; and as soon as she saw the dark-haired woman in the pictures, she'd understood. Incomprehensible though it was, that was what he truly wanted.

Time to let go. Time to forget all about Anton Kline and his inexplicable infatuation with a woman called Soraya Chilton.

'Hurry up, Soraya. We're late enough already.'

Gavin stalked through the green channel, leaving Soraya to push the luggage trolley in his wake, silently cursing the arrogant little sod. Ever since she'd turned down his advances, that night in Ragzburg, Gavin had been more unpleasant towards her than ever; and she wished to goodness she'd never seduced him. In fact, the more she thought about it, the more she wondered how she could ever have fancied the man, even in her wildest, most bizarre dreams.

Two uniformed customs officers were standing beside the entrance to the green channel, one with an Alsatian dog on a thick chain leash. As soon as Soraya got within ten yards of the anmal, it began barking and cringing, seemingly desperate to get away from her. That was odd. She'd always got on well with animals – but this one couldn't get away fast enough.

One guard flashed the other a knowing look.

'Steady, Sabre. Calm down, old boy.'

'Excuse me, miss.' The second guard walked swiftly over, and Soraya's heart sank. 'I'd like a word, if I may.'

'What about?' Soraya's voice faltered as nerves overtook her. Why did she always feel guilty whenever she went through the green channel, even though she had nothing to hide?

'Do you have anything to declare?'

'Nothing at all. Is something wrong?'

'Perhaps. Perhaps not. Would you come with me please, miss?'

'But – I'm travelling on a diplomatic passport.' Soraya rummaged in her pocket and extracted it, handing it over with a triumphant flourish.

'Indeed, miss.' The guard accepted the passport, and rather than look at it, shoved it deep into the pocket of his uniform trousers. 'Well, I'm sure we can sort all this out in due course, in the interview room. Now, if you'll just come with me . . .'

'Yes, of course, but –'

Soraya searched round desperately for Gavin, but by now he was conveniently out of sight. No doubt he had made a swift exit as soon as the dog started barking. Gavin had a natural gift for distancing himself from trouble. Soraya felt her cheeks turning crimson, aware that all eyes in the airport concourse were on her.

'OK, OK, I'm coming. Just let go of my arm, will you?'

The guard's grip on her arm was strong, almost painful, and Soraya felt utterly helpless as he led her through the concourse towards a door marked 'H M Customs. No Admittance.'

'Look,' she reasoned, hoping that a display of feminine vulnerability would get her out of this tight corner. 'There's been some mistake. If you think there's something in my luggage –'

'Something, Miss Chilton?'

'You know . . . something that shouldn't be there.'

'Those were your words, Miss Chilton, not mine. I would advise you not to say anything which might incriminate you. In fact it might be better if you didn't say anything at all until you have a solicitor present. Now, if we could just sort this out . . .'

'Yes, OK. I suppose we must,' sighed Soraya as the guard pushed open the door of the interview room, ushered her inside, then turned to lock the door.

'Dr Anderson will conduct the examination.'

'Examination!' Soraya looked from the guard to the stern-faced doctor, and back again. She had heard tales about the sorts of examinations people had to undergo at airports.

'If you would please strip,' instructed the doctor dispassionately. He was a tall, slender man with fine features and sensual lips, but today there seemed no ounce of interest in him, let alone sensuality.

'What – here?'

'Here. The guard will ensure that we are not disturbed.'

Soraya swallowed hard. This couldn't be right, stripping naked in front of these two men. But something inside her, something mischievous and dark, found the whole idea quite diverting. Well, if strip she must, she might as well make it an entertaining experience for them all . . .

'There is a screen,' commented the guard, indicating a government-issue monstrosity of green printed cotton, stretched over a tubular steel frame. 'If you wish to undress behind it.'

'No need for that,' replied Soraya. 'I have quite a good body, and I'm not ashamed to show it.' She reached behind her and slid down the zipper of her dress. 'At least, most men seem to like it. See what you think.'

The men's eyes widened in disbelief as she casually peeled the dress down over her shoulders, her breasts, her hips; wriggling her lissom hips as she let it slid with a swish around her stockinged ankles. She was the focus of attention now, and she loved that. Their eyes were travelling downwards, down to the thicket of dark curls between her thighs. No panties today, and it was an added bonus to see their faces redden as they took in the seductive vision of their captive, naked but for her bra and stockings.

She wanted to giggle, the seriousness of the situation completely lost on her now. Yes, she wanted to giggle and be shameless. With playful fingers she unhooked her bra and lifted it, with agonising slowness, away from the ripe swell of her breasts. What demon was inside her, making her play these dangerous games?

'I think I'm ready for you now, gentlemen,' announced Soraya, resplendent in stockings, suspenders and high heels. 'As you can see, I have absolutely nothing to hide.'

'Bend over the table,' instructed the guard, his voice dry and almost cracking with emotion. She knew the torments he must be going through as his eyes roamed over her nakedness.

'I'd be delighted to,' replied Soraya, smug now in the certainty that she was now in control. 'How would you like me – like this?' She bent over modestly, legs together and breasts modestly concealed by the falling curtain of her hair.

'Or like this?'

She raised herself on her arms, exposing her breasts; thrusting out her backside and parting her thighs so that the purplish-pink of her love-lips was just visible beneath the dark tangle of her maiden-hair. Ah yes, that was better. She could tell from the quickening pace of their shallow breathing that they very much appreciated the artistry of the pose.

No one spoke or moved for a few seconds; somehow unwilling to disturb the pretty little tableau. It was Soraya who broke the silence, craning her head back to look at the doctor. There were little beads of perspiration on his brow; and she wondered how he would like it if she offered to lick them off, one by one . . .

'You can begin now,' she smiled. 'Of course, you won't find what you're looking for; but I'm sure we'll have fun trying . . .'

It was late evening when Soraya reached home, and

darkness was falling over the little cluster of exclusive apartments where she lived.

Turning the key in the lock, she felt inexplicably nervous. Funny. She didn't generally have any qualms about returning home after an overseas posting, but this time . . . this time, something was different. Something had changed – but was it her, or just the neighbourhood?

Certainly she seemed to be behaving differently these last few weeks. Goodness knows, she'd always been an adventurous girl who liked to have fun; but what she'd done back at the airport – well, it surprised even her. She smiled as she remembered the look on Gavin's face as she'd walked free from the interview room, thrusting the screwed-up ball of her suspender belt into the top pocket of his jacket.

Adventurous? That was just plain malicious! Still, Gavin had asked for it by running off and leaving her, the cowardly little slimeball.

She pushed open the door and dragged her suitcase into the hall, stepping with difficulty over five weeks' worth of post and free newspapers. Almost immediately, she was aware of the smell of the place – not just the obvious smell of the pot pourri that her cleaning lady insisted on leaving in little bowls all over the flat, but a whole jumble of subtler smells, harder to define.

Beeswax and camomile. Ground coffee – yet surely the only coffee in the flat was in an unopened foil pack in the top kitchen cupboard. How could she possibly smell that? Then there was sweat and sex and the sweetness of the herbs she grew – outside in a window box, behind a double thickness of glass. It was crazy, but ever since that weird night in Ragzburg, her senses had seemed sharper, sometimes unbearably so. She had even found, to her amazement, that she could sometimes identify a person by his or her smell, seconds before that person even entered a room.

She stepped into the living room and clicked on the light. Colours assailed her. Colours everywhere. Had that picture really been so brightly-coloured before? She

95

stepped forward and examined it more closely. The lines in it seemed more sharply defined, the colours almost startling in their intensity. In fact, the whole flat felt, smelt, looked . . . different.

Strong coffee, that's what she needed. It wasn't surprising that she was feeling peculiar after the long flight from Ragzburg with Gavin, not to mention that weird scene at the airport. As she set up the cappuccino machine, she felt a vague pang of regret that Nick Drew wasn't here. He'd been fun, a welcome antidote from Gavin and from the bizarre events that had pursued her in Ragzburg.

But that was all behind her now, wasn't it? She'd always said the same thing, after every trip abroad: close the door, turn around and walk away. Nick Drew had been fun, yes; but that was all. No strings, no entanglements, no complications. Like Magnus, like Jonathan, like all the rest, Nick Drew was history.

She turned on the television in the kitchen, and a game-show host with a ginger wig and spangly suit was working up an audience of housewives into a frenzy over tonight's star prize – oddly enough, a weekend for two in Ragzburg. Soraya shivered momentarily at the coincidence, and turned to get the milk out of the fridge.

The sound of the doorbell made her jump. She glanced at her watch. Ten o'clock – late for a casual visitor. She opened the door a few inches.

'Yes?'

She didn't recognise the man on the landing outside – an unappealing-looking man, about forty, balding and with an appalling taste in clothes.

'Good evening.' The man's face lit up with possibly the most disconcerting smile Soraya had ever seen. 'My name's Christopher Dane. I'm your new neighbour.'

'Neighbour, oh – I see.' Soraya hesitated in the doorway, unsure of what to do next. There was something a bit creepy about the man, and she wasn't at all convinced that she wanted to invite him in. On the other hand, she couldn't just slam the door in his face.

96

'Yes, you know,' continued Dane, shuffling from one foot to the other as though expecting something, 'from number ten, just across the hall.' He paused. 'Bit chilly tonight, isn't it?'

'I suppose it is. A little,' replied Soraya. 'Look – is there anything I can help you with, only I'm just about to have a shower and go to bed. I'm very tired.'

'I was just wondering if you'd got any milk you could lend me,' replied Dane. 'I've completely run out, and it's miles to the all-night shop.'

'Milk?' It was a good thing Mrs Travers was so thorough. As soon as she'd heard Soraya was coming back to England, she'd gone out and bought bread, milk, butter – the lot. 'Yes, I think I can let you have some.'

She turned to go back into the flat, meaning to leave Dane outside; but he was right on her heels, eager as a puppy, and before she realised it he was following her down the hallway towards the kitchen.

'Nice flat you've got here, Miss ...'

'Chilton. Soraya Chilton.' Soraya fumbled in the fridge for the spare pint of milk, hoping heartily that she wouldn't have to offer this creep a coffee as well.

'Soraya. That's a lovely name. So ... sensual. Don't you agree?'

Alarm bells rang in Soraya's head as Dane took several steps closer, forcing her to retreat until her back was up against the open fridge door.

'I really don't know, Mr Dane.'

'Call me Christopher. All my close friends do.'

Oh yes, thought Soraya. Well you needn't think I'm going to be one of them. She stood up, pushing him away from her with the proffered carton of milk. Her hyperactive senses picked up his smell – sour, hungry, threatening.

'Do they really – Mr Dane? Here's your milk.'

He looked crestfallen; and hesitated for a moment.

'An espresso machine – how lovely! I've been meaning to get one for ages. I bet the coffee tastes really great, just like the stuff you get in Italian restaurants.'

'Yes, it does.' Soraya slipped away from Dane and closed the fridge door. She glanced at the kitchen clock. 'Goodness me, ten o'clock already. Well, I mustn't keep you.'

'I could stay a little while. Maybe we could get acquainted? That would be nice, wouldn't it?'

He put out his hand to stroke her bare arm, but she recoiled from his touch. His fingers were as cold and clammy as a dead man's. The smell of sex emanating from him was almost overpowering now, and all she wanted to do was get him out of her flat.

'I'm so sorry, Mr Dane. But I'm afraid I'll have to ask you to go now. I've just returned from a long journey, and I'm very tired.'

With a smooth strength which evidently surprised Dane, she guided him firmly down the hallway towards the front door, reaching past him and opening it.

Dane turned to leave. She could see frustrated hunger in his eyes – a hunger which might not easily be denied next time; if there was to be a next time. She would have to be very careful indeed how she dealt with Mr Christopher Dane.

'I'll return the milk – maybe tomorrow?' Dane was not giving up that easily.

'I'll probably be out tomorrow,' replied Soraya, making a mental note to ensure that she was. 'Don't worry about it.'

To her surprise, Dane smiled. But it was not a friendly, open smile; his lips were curved upwards, but his eyes were as cold as two lumps of glass. When he spoke again, his voice was a guttural whisper, hoarse with excitement.

'You have to understand, Miss Chilton; some of us are sensitives, we can see what you are, feel what you are.'

'I don't know what you're talking about. If you'd just please go now, Mr Dane . . .'

'There's no need to be afraid – your secret is safe with me, Soraya. I won't tell them what you are. You'll see, you can trust me.'

Before Soraya had a chance to reply, he was gone;

scuttling across the darkened landing like a stick insect, and disappearing into his flat with a triumphant click as the front door snapped shut.

Nutcases. She seemed to be surrounded by them these days. Maybe it was time she found a new place to live. Something subtle and intangible had changed; and she had the strangest feeling that things would never be the same again.

Over the next few months, Soraya thought of several dozen different ways to murder Gavin Pierce. She'd overstepped the mark in Ragzburg, it was true; but ever since they'd got back, Gavin had made it very plain that she was going to pay for her mistake – in full.

One dismal October afternoon, when the sky was already a misty royal-blue at five-thirty, Soraya was fighting hard to concentrate on the latest boring job Gavin had dumped on her: writing a report on the forthcoming visit to London of an Albanian trade mission, intent on buying several million tons of steel bolts for a bridge in Tirana.

'Mussolini wants to see you in his office, like yesterday,' announced Stacey Reed, one of the section officers, as she passed Soraya's desk. 'And he's in one of his malicious moods.'

'When isn't he?' sighed Soraya, throwing down her pen. These last few months had been sheer bloody murder – nothing but paperwork and escort duty at boring political lunches. 'One of these days, my girl . . .'

'Well, if you're going to stab him through the heart with the letter-opener or something, give him one from me. He's just had my Harry posted to Trondheim.'

'Bastard,' chipped in Maria Naismith, once James's personal assistant and now – to her chagrin – Gavin's. 'Do you know, he had me counting every paperclip in the stationery cupboard yesterday, 'cause I threatened to report him for trying to stick his hand up my jumper. You've got to have eyes in the back of your head – not like with James; he was a real gentleman.'

Soraya suppressed a smile. It was common knowledge in the Department that Maria had been hopelessly, helplessly in love with James Delauney – but he, alas, had been too much the gentleman to notice, despite numerous heavy hints from various members of staff. She sighed. She was missing James, too. They all were.

'You want to watch yourself with him,' commented Stacey. 'I reckon he's got it in for you – can't think why. Must be because you aren't desperate to get inside his pants.'

'Not like Beth,' observed Maria.

No, not like Beth, thought Soraya, jabbing the final words of a memo into her antiquated electric typewriter. Beth was the new girl in the Department – bold, brassy, and bright enough to know that if she wanted to get to the top, she needed to keep Gavin happy. This she seemed more than willing to do, and on one occasion Soraya had actually walked in on the pair of them when Gavin was undoing her blouse.

Not surprisingly, Beth's enthusiasm had been rewarded with a series of prime assignments, and she was going off to the States on a job next week. Soraya, on the other hand . . .

'Right. I'll go in and see him now.'

She got up from her desk, smoothing her skirt. She was looking and feeling good today; whatever axe he wanted to grind, Gavin wasn't going to get the better of her this time.

Beth gave her a sly smile as she walked through the open-plan office, passing the screened-off section where Beth did her 'private and confidential' paperwork. There were others, less charitably-minded than Soraya, who had suggested the screening was there for other, more recreational purposes.

'Off to see Gavin, darling?'

Soraya paused, suppressing her irritation. Beth Fielding was *not* going to get to her, with her low-cut blouses and her glossy-red, bee-stung lips.

'Uh-huh.'

'Lucky you. He's such a hunk.'

Soraya raised an eyebrow but did not respond. She wondered if it was just, vaguely possible that Beth really did find Gavin irresistibly attractive. It was an intriguing concept.

'Give him a message from me, will you, darling?'

'Sure. What is it?'

'Tell him I'll see him tonight, at my place. And not to forget the pink champagne!'

Soraya pushed her way into Gavin's office.

'You wanted to see me?'

Gavin raised his eyes from a file with a little scowl of annoyance.

'I've told you before to knock before you come in.'

'Stacey said it was urgent.'

She sat down on the sofa without waiting for an invitation. Gavin got up, walked round and perched himself on the front of his desk.

'I've got a job for you, Soraya. This one's just up your street.'

'That's what you said about the last one.'

'Didn't you enjoy taking Lord Grimsby's children to the zoo? He tells me they had a wonderful time.' Gavin's smile was smarmy, his tone sarcastic.

'I'm employed to work on sensitive diplomatic assignments, not as a nursemaid. You know damn well where my skills lie.'

'Ah well, you're not the only one with those skills, are you Soraya? Beth Fielding is a very promising trainee. Very promising indeed.'

Soraya's frayed temper snapped. On her feet now, she confronted Gavin eyeball to eyeball.

'She's a scheming bimbo, and you're screwing her senseless. Oh and by the way, it's her place tonight, and don't forget the pink champagne.'

'Not jealous, are we?' Gavin's voice was mocking now. But Soraya could see the glint of lust in his eyes, and knew that no matter what he did or said, she was still the one in control. He simply couldn't resist her.

He was punishing her for not giving him the one thing he desperately desired: her body.

'No Gavin. But I think you are.'

He didn't reply. Suddenly his eyes seemed glazed, his gaze distant. They were standing very close, and in an almost robotic movement he slipped his hand round her waist, smoothing the open palm over the curve of her backside, sleek in its skin-tight skirt. Startled, she wondered if he was feeling for the tell-tale line of her panties; well, he would have a long and fruitless search . . .

Her senses were working overtime. She could smell the desire in him, sweet like the sickliness of decay. And she could feel a power within herself, too. A power that recalled the way she had felt on that dark dreamlike night in Ragzburg when she had stepped into a world of erotic fantasy.

Realisation exploded like a hand grenade. If she chose, this man could be hers. Not a man; her prey. She could eat him up, spit him out, captivate him. Destroy him. As he gazed deep into her eyes and stroked her backside with a hypnotic slowness, she knew that she had him in her grasp; had him fixed as a stoat fixes a rabbit, in that ecstatic moment of glorious expectation before it plunges needle-sharp teeth into the sweet, soft throat.

The traffic in the street outside and the chatter of voices in the office seemed to rise into a deafening crescendo around her, a confusing drone that filled her head. And above the roar of background noise sounded the manic thumping of her own heart, the treacherous whisperings of her desire.

Yours, Soraya. Yours if you want it. Its flesh is not sweet, but you would relish the strength it gave you. He is yours; why not feed on the prize that is offered to you . . .?

His body was pressed up tight against hers, and she felt his helpless desire pulsing on her belly, tasted the hunger on his breath as his mouth drew closer to hers, his lips pleading, beseeching . . .

What was happening to her? What unseen demon was

within her, driving her to this hunger, this madness? Did she want his sex – or his submission? With a gigantic effort of will, she snapped her gaze away; and saw a look of astonishment pass over Gavin's face as she freed herself from his grasp. His face was sickly-white, his lips bloodless and pale as though some tremendous force had drained the very life from them. He was clutching at the desk, as though too weak to stand.

Soraya went in for the kill.

'I couldn't care less who shares your bed, Gavin, as long as it's not me; and I don't give a damn how much you spend on pink champagne. But what I do care about is being exploited.' She dragged Gavin across the room and slammed him up against the wall, her body suddenly a storehouse of powerful and exultant energy.

'Soraya . . . I . . .' he gasped, half-choking.

'Find me another assignment, Gavin. A proper assignment. Or you can get someone else to do your dirty work for you.'

Turning on her heel, she pushed him away and wrenched open the office door. Eyes swivelled in her direction, taking in the intriguing image of Soraya striding back into the main office; whilst behind her, slumped on his own sofa, sat Gavin, his face fixed in the horror-stricken expression of a hunted animal.

What have you done, what have you done now? demanded a little voice at the back of her mind; but Soraya felt good. She'd said what needed to be said. If Gavin gave her the push – well, it was just too bad. And anyway; he wouldn't dare.

'There's a message for you,' chattered Maria breathlessly as Soraya stalked back to her seat. 'On your desk.'

'Oh great. Who's this one from – Mothercare?'

She stopped dead in her tracks as she saw the envelope lying on her desk. A white envelope edged with gold, and lying across it, a single velvety red rose. Intrigued, she picked it up and looked quizzically at Maria.

'Who . . .?'

'No idea. They came by motorcycle messenger, but he didn't have a sender's name and address. Go on, open the envelope! How can you bear to wait? It's so romantic.'

It was indeed. Half a dozen conflicting thoughts were chasing each other through her mind. Maybe it was from Nick, in Ragzburg? Or could it be from that creep Dane? But how could he have found out where she worked?

She ripped open the envelope. Inside was a piece of plain white paper, wrapped around a photograph.

'I have to see you. I just can't get you out of my mind. Can we meet soon? I'll be in touch. Anton.'

Anton? Did she know anyone called Anton? Puzzled, Soraya turned over the photograph and looked at the image. It was a picture of herself, wearing that emerald green suit; and Gavin following behind, his usual prattish self. Recognition clicked in. The exhibition. But who . . .?

There *was* one man who could have taken that picture – the magazine photographer she'd spotted at the international IT exhibition, months ago. But who the hell was this 'Anton'? There was no address, no way of contacting him. More to the point, did she really want to meet him?

But on the other hand – why not? Her fingers curled around the thornless stem of the rose and she felt her heart pounding faster at the thought of a much-needed adventure. Why not . . .

It was a misty October day, threatening rain; and the park was deserted save for a few dejected-looking nannies, pushing their charges through the crisp, golden and brown autumn leaves which had begun to collect on the ground. Not a good day, perhaps, but certainly an excellent place for a discreet meeting. Ideal, even.

Sir Adrian watched the long-legged girl striding towards him across the grass, her long dark hair flowing out behind her like a banner, and felt his spirits soar. She wasn't his, and she probably never would be; but Soraya Chilton was one hell of a woman.

He got up from the park bench and walked quickly to meet her, intercepting her beside the lake.

'Glad you could make it, my dear.'

'Did I have much choice?'

'You seem rather annoyed, if you don't mind my saying so. Is there a problem?'

'In a word, Gavin.'

Sir Adrian snorted.

'Pierce? That little tosspot? You don't want to worry about him. He's nothing – less than nothing.'

'It's easy for you to say that. He threatened to sack me last week.' Soraya still smarted from the humiliating apology Gavin had forced out of her, the day after her outburst of temper.

Sir Adrian chuckled.

'Ah. That little contretemps over Beth Fielding.'

'You knew?'

'Of course I knew. It's my job to know. And in my opinion you handled the little toe-rag rather well. Next time, he'll think twice before he messes you about like that. In any case, he may not even be around to cause you problems in future. People in high places have been talking about sending him to Murmansk. Now, why don't you tell me what you've got for me?'

Soraya reached into her bag and took out the brief report she'd typed up the night before. It was embarrassingly scanty.

'If you know so much, what do you need me for?' she demanded, handing it over.

'I don't know everything, my dear,' replied Sir Adrian. 'You're there to keep an eye on things, fill in the gaps.' He caught the haze of autumn sunshine on her glossy hair and felt curiously romantic. More typically, he glanced appreciatively at the figure-moulding suit she was wearing, remembering the succulent flesh beneath. Intelligent, sexy, insatiable. One hell of a woman.

They walked on past the deserted bandstand, still dripping wet from the previous night's fog.

'Information is still leaking out of the system,'

explained Sir Adrian. 'And I need names. The PM won't be patient for ever, and whilst things continue the way they are doing, we are each and every one of us under suspicion.'

Soraya stiffened.

'All of us? Even me? But you said . . .'

He felt genuinely sorry. He'd always had a thing for Soraya, but she was more than capable of standing on her own two feet and he couldn't keep the truth from her any longer.

'I'm sorry, Soraya, but I'm afraid it's true. From now on we're all going to have to watch our backs. Even you.'

Soraya was seething. Fair enough, the job shepherding an Albanian trade delegation round a South Wales steel mill had been allocated to a junior member of the Department; but what about that business over the Canadian petrochemical deal? That needed an experienced operative, someone who knew what she was doing. Someone with the subtle skills to cajole, persuade, seduce.

And who had got the job? That bimbo Beth Fielding.

And so here she was, making small-talk with a crowd of insignificant MEPs at the opening of 'Artists of the EC' – definitely one of the Tate Gallery's less inspired exhibitions. Still, the champagne was good and plentiful, and it was an opportunity for her to do a little covert surveillance. Sir Adrian's words had worried her, perhaps more than she realised.

'OK, ladies and gentlemen. The press have arrived. If we could just get you all together for a photocall.'

A woman from the Department was shepherding everyone into a close-packed group, and Soraya slipped in at the back; but the exhibition's artistic director grabbed her by the arm and led her round to the front of the group.

'Can't have you hiding your light under a bushel now, can we?' The man bustled around, pushing everyone into exactly the correct photogenic formation. To her embarrassment, Soraya found herself right at the front, dazzled by the lights from two dozen flashbulbs.

'Smile everybody,' called out one of the photographers.

Click, whirr. Click, whirr.

'Girl in the front row – the one in the red dress. Give us a great big smile . . . lovely.'

Click.

'OK, all done. Just a couple more shots of the MEPs with Mr Cavendish and Mrs James . . .'

Relieved, Soraya split from the group and went through into the empty ante-room, to get herself another glass of champagne. As she picked up the glass she heard a voice behind her.

'Soraya – Soraya Chilton?'

She wheeled round. He was youngish and powerfully built, with honey-coloured hair and soft grey eyes, and the twist of a slightly embarrassed smile at the corner of his mouth.

'Who . . .?'

'My name's Anton Kline. I was beginning to think I'd never get a chance to be alone with you.'

'Anton! The photographer who . . .'

'That's right. I . . . Look, I'm really sorry about all this. It took me ages to track you down.'

Soraya put down the glass and folded her arms.

'I ought to be furious with you, you do realise that?'

'Yes. Of course.'

'Give me three good reasons why I shouldn't send you away with a flea in your ear.'

'I can't even think of one.'

'What exactly did you think you were playing at?'

'Playing? Oh, it wasn't a game, you mustn't think that. I'm completely serious about this. Have been since the moment I first set eyes on you.'

He took another step forward, reached out and brushed his fingertips lightly across Soraya's cheek, almost wonderingly, as though he wanted to make sure

107

that she was real. His fingers were reassuringly warm, surprisingly sensitive for such a strong man, but they trembled just a little as flesh met flesh.

'Look, I know this must seem like a crazy thing to do, and you probably think I'm barmy. I don't even understand it myself. But the first time I saw you there, at the IT exhibition, well – you just knocked me out. It was like being struck by lightning – I've never felt anything like it.'

Soraya said nothing. She hardly knew what to think, but she did not shy away from his touch. Oddly enough, she felt not the slightest inclination to reject him. There were no alarm bells ringing in her head. Already she was breathing in his scent, instinctively relaxing in the aura of warm sensuality that surrounded him. It seemed that her body, at least, had already made up its mind about Anton Kline.

But he took her silence as a rejection and stepped back, his hand falling to his side.

'I've really made a fool of myself, haven't I? I knew I shouldn't have come here. You must think I'm unhinged.'

Instantly Soraya experienced a wave of regret, a curious sensation of loss.

'Did I say that?' She moved closer to him again, her body seeking him out even though her rational mind urged caution. After all, there was always a chance he might turn out to be another Janos, another Christopher Dane. 'Maybe I'm crazy, too.'

Caught between laughter and confusion, Anton ran his fingers through his tousled mop of blond hair. The gesture made him look vulnerable and almost child-like. On a ridiculous, dangerous impulse, Soraya planted a kiss on his cheek.

Immediately, as though a binding spell had been broken, his arms closed around her and he crushed his mouth against hers, his passion hot and honest and strong.

It felt like coming home.

Chapter Seven

'What do you think of me in this? Or this, maybe?'

Soraya ran her hand along the rail of clothes, occasionally plucking out something that took her fancy, and holding it up against herself for an opinion. She loved the feel of the silks and satins between her fingertips, adored the sensual luxury of wispy chiffon or heavy brocade, sliding gently over her naked flesh.

'How do you like me in this one?'

'Wonderful, brilliant,' laughed Anton, clicking away on the Leica as Soraya draped a long wine-coloured velvet cape around her bare shoulders. The rich burgundy of the cape showed off her creamy-white skin to perfection. 'You're a natural. But do you know something, Soraya?'

She giggled, letting go of the cape so that it fell open, sliding slowly down over her bare shoulders and arms.

'What?'

'I like you best in nothing at all.' Laughing, Anton grabbed hold of her and she wriggled free of the velvet cape, savouring the long, slow caress as it slid smoothly down over her back and thighs, forming a crimson pool around her bare feet. He kissed her, his probing tongue graphically conveying the message of what his cock would like to do; and she responded hungrily, grinding the hardening points of her breasts against his shirt front. The rough cotton abraded her soft flesh, awakening new sensitivities, new thoughts of pleasure and play.

'I thought we came back to your studio for a photo session,' she gasped through her laughter and her desire.

Anton responded by holding her tighter, his muscular thigh pushing its way between hers, pressing hard against the secret places she no longer had the slightest desire to veil from him.

'Darling,' he murmured, kissing her neck and breasts tenderly. 'Darling, I can think of a hundred more interesting things to do with you than take photos. No, make that a thousand. Why don't we do a few of them right now?'

He held her tight and lifted her up into the cradle of his arms, as effortlessly as if she were a tiny child; and Soraya was more than content to lie there, her arms wrapped loosely round his neck as she kissed him again and again. He carried her purposefully out of the studio and across the landing into his bedroom. She made no protest. Why should she? She wanted this just as much as he did.

In the week since she'd first met Anton Kline, Soraya had been awakened to a whole new world of tender sensuality, quite different from anything she had ever known with her many other lovers. The moment they had shared their first kiss, Soraya knew that she wanted Anton for more than just the physical beauty of his young and eager body. From that first moment of passion, she was addicted.

They had spent the whole of that first afternoon and night in bed together at Anton's flat, scarcely aware of the time passing, or the clouds drifting across the sky, obscuring the distant eye of the waxing moon. On that night, they were not interested in the world outside, only in each other.

The following morning, when Soraya had arrived

extremely late for work at the Department, Gavin had glared at her, but said nothing. It might have been that Sir Adrian's 'friends' had had words with him, but Soraya suspected a rather different reason. Since that day when she had confronted him in his office, Gavin had been noticeably less unpleasant towards her. Why? Because he was scared of her, that was why.

This secret knowledge gave Soraya a pleasing thrill of triumph. It felt good to have won a first, small victory over Gavin. Despite continued worries about the internal investigation at the Department, things seemed to be going better for her. In ways she could not begin to comprehend, that brief trip to Ragzburg seemed to have unlocked an inner potential, put her back in touch with some lost wholeness she had not even realised she possessed – if, of course, you believed in that sort of New-Age philosophy. Whatever the cause, Soraya had reason to be profoundly grateful, because these days she was feeling good and sex was great – *really* great.

They entered the bedroom and Anton laid her down gently on the rumpled sheets they had left only an hour ago. Work seemed like a distant irrelevance, and as for the photo session, that was long forgotten. It seemed there could be no end to their appetite for love-making. They embraced, and Soraya challenged her lover between kisses:

'Want me?'

'Want you. Now.'

She kissed him on the end of his nose.

'What, again?' Her voice was full of feigned incredulity.

'Again. And again. I just can't get enough of you, Soraya.'

And the truth of the matter was that she wanted Anton just as much as he wanted her – she could smell and taste and touch the powerful need in him, and the knowing only made her own yearning more intense. Soraya tugged and fumbled at the buttons of his shirt, her fingers clumsy in the urgency of her need. Anton took hold of her hands and kissed each individual finger with a playful tenderness.

'Hush. Lie back, and let me . . .'

She sank back, glad now to feel his strength and certainty. With Anton there was no need to prove a point. With Anton, it was all so natural.

He threw his clothes into a jumbled heap on the floor, and returned to lie beside her. Greedy but languid, she reached out and stroked his tanned nakedness, wonderingly.

'You're beautiful, Anton.'

He put his arms round her and they kissed.

'And you're a miracle, Soraya Chilton.'

'I still don't understand why you wanted me so much – why you did what you did.'

'Nor do I.' His fingers toyed with her dark pubic curls, tantalising without satisfying, spicing the anticipation with the sweetest drop of frustration, making the need linger and grow. 'But I'm incredibly glad I did.'

Soraya rolled onto her side, pressing the curves of her back and buttocks into the hollow of his belly. They fitted together perfectly, like the missing pieces of a jigsaw puzzle.

'So,' breathed Anton, wriggling up closer to put his arms around her. 'You want it like that, do you?'

Soraya did not reply. She was too busy enjoying the warm sensation of flesh on flesh, the intensely pleasurable friction as, very slowly, she began rubbing her bottom up and down Anton's rapidly-stiffening manhood.

'Yes. Oh, yes,' murmured Anton, his hands sliding up Soraya's smooth belly to the ripe curves of her breasts. They nestled in the palms of his hands so beautifully, their juicy firmness contrasting with the iron-hard tips of her nipples. Gently he rolled them between finger and thumb, and Soraya started to moan very softly, very distantly, as though lost in a trance of pleasure from which only he could awaken her. 'That feels so, so good, Anton. Don't stop.'

Still she rubbed herself up against him, rejoicing in the

112

silken sensation of his hardness, slipping easily down the crease between her rounded buttocks. She wanted him so much, had to have him inside her; and yet this simple pleasure was almost too much. How could she bear the intense delight of having his cock deep, deep within her belly? As though answering her, she heard Anton's voice, soft and low in her ear:

'I've got to have you, Soraya. My cock's burning for you. If I don't have you now, I'll explode . . .'

'Take me slowly,' she sighed. 'I want this to last forever.'

Anton took his hands from her breasts, and felt for the glorious roundness of the globes of her bottom. His touch on her flesh made her shiver with delight.

'Mmm. Yes, yes . . .'

Gently he parted her buttocks and introduced the glistening purple head of his glans. It slid easily down the furrow between her bottom-cheeks, teasing the amber rose of her anus for a fleeting moment before it disappeared into the white-hot heart of her sex.

'Anton, Anton, yes!'

She thrust back gently, engulfing him with her hot, wet womanhood. Anton gasped. It felt like fire swallowing him up, a delicious inferno from which he might not emerge unscathed. But he did not care. All he cared about was the ecstasy of being with his perfect, once-in-a-lifetime lover.

'Slowly, Anton, keep it slow,' pleaded Soraya.

They moved together in slow, silent harmony, locked together in an embrace so close it seemed they could never be separated. The pleasure was intense, overwhelming, and yet there was no urgency in it. It flowed over them like the tidal swell of a warm, blue ocean, lapping at the shores of a tropical isle.

Soraya felt her whole body relaxing into the gentle rhythm of sweet, slow pleasure. The wildness of Ragzburg, the strange happenings and the savage desires of her dreams, all seemed very far away in this warm, soft bed where the only sounds were the gentle sound of breathing and the distant tick tock of an old grandfather clock. Nothing could disturb the tranquil perfection of her love for Anton.

Outside, a dog howled in the distance as dark, rain-bloated clouds scudded across a cold black sky, obscuring the swollen white disc of an almost full moon.

'Ah, Ms Chilton. What a delight it is to see you again.'

Sir Reginald Manners, Assistant Governor of the Bank of England, made it a point never to lie, except on matters of national security. When he said it was a delight to see Soraya again, he meant it. The girl had both class and common sense in abundance, not like that idiot Pierce. Gavin Pierce was living proof that even the finest public school education money could buy could not make a silk purse out of a sow's ear.

Manners welcomed Soraya with a bone-crushingly firm handshake.

'You have come to supervise the disposal of the obsolete non-EC currencies?'

Soraya nodded, and consulted the briefing document Gavin had given her. 'As I understand it, twenty million each of old Czechoslovak, Yugoslavian and Soviet banknotes?'

'Yes, plus a smaller quantity of mixed silver-based coinage. If you would like to follow me, I will take you down to the furnaces. I do apologise for all the locking and unlocking of doors, but as I'm sure you can appreciate, we have to maintain absolute security. Can't have Joe Public wandering off with the nation's bullion reserves!'

Soraya followed Sir Reginald down a bare flight of concrete steps and through a thick steel door into a series of long, maze-like corridors illuminated by harsh white striplights. Security cameras tracked their progress – red, winking eyes following them down the corridor with an electronic hum.

Passing through a second steel door, they found themselves in a huge underground chamber. Soraya stepped back, overwhelmed by the sudden stifling heat.

Sir Reginald smiled apologetically.

'I'm sorry, I should have warned you. It does get a bit overpowering down here, but one gets used to it. Makes a good blaze though, don't you think? Now, if you could just come this way and sign the necessary authorisation, we can begin.'

Soraya walked over to a small desk where Sir Reginald had laid out the usual sheaf of papers relating to the destruction of obsolete currency. She sighed. The Foreign Secretary was a stickler for form-filling. She wondered idly if he did *everything* in triplicate . . .

'If I could just have your signature as authorising officer. There. And there.' Manners indicated the relevant sections of the form and Soraya signed, after scanning the small print for any incongruities. She had to be careful – this was the first remotely responsible job Gavin had entrusted her with since the Beth Fielding incident. Speaking of which . . . she wondered how Beth was enjoying it at the Croydon sub-office. It must be a bit of a come-down after New York.

She signed the forms, placed Gavin's copy in her briefcase and shielded her eyes from the fierce orange glare as the furnace doors opened and she watched huge shovelfuls of banknotes disappearing into its hungry maw. She couldn't help noticing how good-looking the foreman was, stripped to the waist; his impressive musculature glistening with runnels of sweat as he pushed lank blond hair back from his forehead.

Hungry.

She shook herself, trying to rid herself of the whispering, coaxing thought. It was just plain silly. She was perfectly happy with Anton, she adored the gentle intensity of his love-making and wasn't looking for anyone else. Positively not.

Hungry, Soraya. For sex.

She forced herself to turn away, trying to banish the incongruous images filtering into her too-receptive mind. Images of sudden, intense, ferocious sex. What would the foreman look like if she was to strip him of those grimy, sweat-soaked overalls? How would his skin feel and taste to her thirsting tongue?

Embarrassed by the force of her own imagination, she looked up and caught the foreman's eye. He was grinning at her, as though . . . almost as though he could read her thoughts, and was even now approving her desire.

Quickly she turned back to Sir Reginald.

'The coinage. I believe you mentioned there was also some coinage to be disposed of?'

'Ah yes, over here, Ms Chilton. Not very much, as you can see. A few hundred thousand at most. But the small percentage of silver can be extracted and recycled.'

With a child-like wonder, Soraya plunged her hand into the immense vat of coins, scooped up a huge handful and let it fall in a glittering, tinkling cascade.

'I've always wanted to do that!' she laughed. So much money. It was like being in Aladdin's cave.

One coin, slightly larger than the rest, caught her eye: a thick circle of blackened silver, worn almost smooth with age. She felt a sudden urge to touch it and picked it up to examine it more closely.

The obverse of the coin depicted some long-forgotten General with a big nose, his balding head topped with a luxuriant laurel leaf. She flipped the coin over, and her heart missed a beat. A bas-relief of clustered buildings, huddled together in the shadow of a dark mountain, seemed to leap out at her from the worn surface, demanding recognition. And above, in the blackened sky, hung the tiny shape of a perfect crescent moon.

The oddest sensations began rushing through her. Pictures began forming in her mind – a wild whirl of coloured images that left her dizzy and clutching the side of the steel hopper. Laughing faces in narrow, twisting streets; other faces, twisted in horror and fear as something inexplicably terrifying bore down upon them in the darkness; children playing in the shadow of a wooded mountain; a man and woman screwing in a dark alleyway; a handful of silver coins lying on a cobbled roadway, pale and unreal in the moonlight . . .

116

Hungry. So hungry. Feel the hunger burn your belly, sharpen your claws. Feel the moonlight on your flesh, and hunger . . .

She snapped back to reality with a start, fervently hoping Sir Reginald had not noticed her confusion. He saw the coin lying in her palm, and took it from her, turning it over in his hand.

'Ah yes, a five-zloty piece. Quite old, but of no intrinsic value to a collector. They were much too heavy and unwieldy to be practical – the new government in Ragzburg phased them out when they came to power last year.'

Ragzburg.

'If you like it, perhaps you'd like to keep it as a souvenir?'

'Keep it . . .?'

'I'm sure the Bank won't miss one five-zloty piece. They're very common, you know. Do take it.'

'I don't know, I . . .'

He placed the coin in her palm. It felt cold and clammy on her feverish skin. As her fingers closed over it, she fought the treacherous desire to know more.

Common? No, this coin was anything but. This was something very strange; something that Soraya Chilton was afraid to understand.

The moon, Soraya, the moon.

Soraya got out of her car and locked it, trying not to gaze up at the crystal-clear sky above, spangled with bright pin-points of starlight. High above them, at the very zenith, hung the moon's pallid disc, silent and unmoving in the velvet black canopy.

Her eyes strayed to the sky once again as she slipped the car keys into her pocket. It was only the moon, for goodness' sake. Nothing sinister, nothing unusual – and certainly nothing to be afraid of.

She wished she was seeing Anton tonight, but he was away in Devon, working on some major-league beer commercial; and so she walked alone towards the apartment block, nodding a mute good evening to the concierge as she pressed the lift button and waited.

Anton. Why couldn't he be here when she wanted him? No, not wanted; needed. Her body was silently screaming for the touch of his knowing fingers, the caress of his wicked tongue, flicking back and forth across the hot, juicy bud of her clitoris. She was always ready for good sex; readier than ever these past few weeks; but tonight, she needed it like an addict needs a fix.

The moon. Its image wouldn't leave her. Here she was, stepping into the lift cage, and if she closed her eyes it was still there; the insolent, insistent moon, teasing and coaxing her, daring her to deny its magnetic attraction. What *was* it about the moon? Why were her dreams full of it these past few days? She shrugged. Maybe watching that eclipse in Ragzburg had affected her more than she'd realised. Maybe that crazed old peasant-woman's words had had more of an impact on her than she dared admit.

At the second floor the lift jolted to a halt, and Soraya groaned with impatience. Why was there always someone else wanting to share the lift when she was in a hurry to get home and get silently drunk in front of the TV?

As the doors slid open, her heart sank.

'My dear Soraya! I've been trying to get in touch with you for weeks, but you were never in. You haven't been avoiding me, have you?'

'No, of course I haven't,' she lied. 'I've just been rather busy, that's all. You know how it is, Mr Dane.'

Dane. Christopher bloody Dane. That was all she needed – a trip up to the fifteenth floor in a sealed box with a total nutter. She eyed the control panel, half-inclined to get out at the next floor up and walk; but of course he would volunteer to walk up with her, and besides, he was standing right in front of the control panel. To get at it, she would have to get dangerously close to touching the man. The very thought made her stomach churn.

'Oh yes, my dear. I know exactly how it is,' replied Dane cryptically. To Soraya's consternation, he reached out and jabbed the stop button. The lights flickered momentarily, then the lift jerked to a stop between floors. Now he was inching nearer, and Soraya could smell his excitement, hear it pulsing out of him.

'I don't know what you're talking about, Mr Dane.' She tried to get to the control panel, but he was blocking her way.

'Oh but you do, Soraya.' In the dingy yellow lighting of the lift cage his smile was a ghoul's, fixed and chilling; and those small dark eyes, beady and glittering like a bat's, unnerved her despite her determination to shrug him off. To her alarm, his fingers closed about her wrist. She tried to snatch it back, but he was surprisingly strong.

'What . . .?' she gasped, momentarily lost for words.

'Don't lie to me, Soraya,' said Dane, squeezing her wrist so tightly that she gasped with the pain. 'I promised I would keep your secret, but in return you must do something for me.'

His lecherous leer gave a graphic explanation of what that something might be.

'I know what you are, my little wild one,' he continued. 'But I am not afraid. I have a taste for women like you, and I have waited a long, long time . . .' He laughed. 'What luck that we should meet again on the night of the full moon.'

The moon. The image of its pale disc seemed to fill her brain now, a swelling, engulfing, monstrous presence that annihilated every other thought. Her eyes were open and she was looking at Dane's face, but all she could see was the moon.

Hunger. Can't you feel it?

No! Soraya fought off the whispering need inside her head; the need that made her fingers tingle, her clitoris burn with the forbidden excitement of the thought.

You are hungry. He is nothing but a fool. He will not be missed.

No, she would not succumb to this madness! With a sudden anger that gave her renewed strength, Soraya flung Dane away from her, wrenching his fingers from her wrist. She turned a face full of hatred on him, and her voice was cold as ice.

'How dare you touch me. How dare you come near me. Get your filthy hands off me.'

Startled and suddenly afraid, Dane shrank away, his tall thin frame quivering – with fear, or with desire? Soraya stared at him with a calm hatred and saw the swelling cock beneath his pants, pulsating with a pathetic need. The memory of that afternoon in Gavin's office came back to her, and she wanted to laugh out loud at the crazy sense of victory filling her up, making her stronger than she could ever have believed possible.

More startled than alarmed by her own power, she watched in satisfaction as Dane seemed to shrivel up, sliding down the wall of the lift and subsiding into a crumpled heap on the floor. Calmly she reached out and restarted the lift.

A few moments later, the cage jolted to a halt at the fifteenth floor.

The doors slid smoothly open and Soraya got out, stepping disdainfully over Dane's shaking figure. He was sobbing now; sobbing with disappointment and fear – and the terrible joy of submission; his mind filled with the image of a beautiful, cruel woman with eyes that glowed red as coals. He wanted her. Longed for the bliss of her displeasure; but now she was gone. As her high heels tapped away down the corridor, his parched lips opened in a single, ecstatic gasp:

'Mistress.'

Soraya did not look back, but hurried across the landing to the front door of her apartment. She fumbled for her key, then jabbed it into the lock.

Home. At last.

Gratefully, she pushed the door shut and stood for a few moments with her back pressed against it, as though afraid that Dane might come looking for her, tap-tapping at the door for her to let him in. She hadn't even the strength to switch on the light. Her heart was thumping, her head reeling, and she wiped the back of her hand across her forehead, only to discover that it was covered with beads of cold sweat. She felt very odd – could she be sickening for something? So cold, and yet so hot. It felt as though a fever was raging inside her, and yet her fingers and toes were icy, tingling in almost the way they did when she was about to get chilblains.

Tap. Tap, tap.

Soraya nearly jumped out of her skin. For a moment she really believed he was there behind the curtains, his features twisted into a Norman Bates smile as he mouthed the words: 'I'm just a regular guy . . .'

Don't be silly. Dane was a harmless wimp and she'd shown him exactly where to get off. It was odd, though; the way he'd shrunk away at her command, like a kicked spaniel. Come to think of it, an awful lot of odd things had been happening lately. And now, standing here in the gloom of her darkened flat, the air felt claustrophobic and stifling.

Tap. Tap, tap.

She snapped on the light but the room seemed even tinier, even more constricting. It wasn't as if she was normally prone to panic attacks or anything like that, but tonight she felt like a mouse in a trap. She needed fresh air; cool, cold air that would calm her down and take away the feverish heat within her. More than that, she needed it to rid her of the stale, sickening stench of Dane's lust.

Her mouth was dry, her pulse racing as she walked across the room towards the window, the heavy, floor-length drapes still closed from the last night she'd spent here, three days ago. Something beyond those dark, unmoving curtains was calling to her, enticing her, drawing her on. With each step she took, the carpet felt thicker and deeper under her feet, the air about her heavy and almost unbreathable.

Hot. So hot. Yet cold as ice.

She reached out for the curtain-cord, a heavy twisted rope of yellow silk, and gave it a tug. The curtains swished open, revealing the apartment block opposite and behind it, the immense dark canopy of the night sky. Slowly, almost mechanically, the trapped end of the sun-blind was being blown against the outside of the glass.

Tap. Tap, tap.

Framed in a window on the seventh floor of the block opposite, a couple were making love, eyes closed as their naked bodies entwined. But Soraya did not even notice them. Her eyes were drawn high above the buildings, towards the zenith where a huge full moon shimmered and floated in a sea of deepest black, its pale disc ringed with a deep crimson haze, like a bloodshot eye.

The moon. The distant moon, swollen and expectant; lustrous and sensual. It seemed to be calling to her, caressing her with silvery fingers of light.

And then Soraya remembered the old woman's words: *On a night when the full moon is crowned with blood, then you will understand.*

A sudden *frisson* of excitement made her shiver, and she clutched at herself, tingling fingers clutching at her arms as wave upon wave of moonlight washed over her upturned face.

Hungry. So hungry. It is long since you last feasted.

Quickly, she unfastened the window catch and the pane swung outward, admitting a rush of cold air. The night-breeze outside was crisp and chill, and already the first powdery grains of an early, light frost were diamond-dusting pavements and rooftops.

It is time, Soraya. You cannot resist the hunger.

She closed her eyes, overwhelmed by the raging tempest of sensations rushing in on her. Her body seemed racked by some strange fever that sent hot and cold shivers running all over her flesh. Delicious shivers, that filled her with a new and intense longing. The longing for wild, untamed sex.

122

Her whole body felt as though it were on the point of orgasm, an unbearable intensity turning every sensation into a torment, every desire into a throbbing, pulsating need. Her clitoris was hot and hard, her love-lips moist and swollen with the urgency of passion. There was no tenderness in this feeling, only an animal hunger that must be sated.

A sudden, unexpected joy filled her being and she threw back her head in laughter, her lips glossy as ripe red berries in the moon's silvery glow. Rational thought evaporated, disappearing into the night like a wisp of fine mist as raw instinct took over, turning her cool sophistication into a driving engine of sexual hunger.

Time.

She turned away from the window, the red coals of her eyes glowing hot with the turbulent power within her. The moist pink tip of her tongue flicked greedily across her lips, quick as a lizard's. The city at night was a big place, a place of shadows and secrets; of mysterious darkened streets and doorways where the unwary might be lured into the sweetest, the most succulent of honey-traps.

One vast new hunting-ground.

A thousand nameless faces peopled her dreams; but when she awoke, she was alone. And very, very cold.

A sullen grey dawn was just coming up over the park as Soraya opened her eyes; and the first thing they focused on was a group of unconcerned fallow deer, huddled together in the shade of the spreading oak tree that was sheltering them all from a biting east wind.

Where the hell . . .?

The grass was damp and cold beneath her, and she struggled to her feet, trying to remember what had happened to her. Where were her shoes? She stared down in disbelief at her bare feet, bruised and blue with cold. The memories were all jumbled up in her head, and she couldn't make any sense of them. She could remember an unpleasant encounter in the lift with that creep Dane and later, standing in her flat looking out of the window at the moon, huge and white with a bloody red haze around it. Then – nothing.

Well, not absolutely nothing. A few vague, disturbing images danced tantalisingly before her eyes, the fragments ... of what? Of dreams or of a reality too bizarre and frightening to contemplate? The faces of strangers, hunger, nakedness, savage pleasure – but fleeting impressions were all that she could recall. Nightmare and reality seemed inextricably blurred together.

It must have been quite a night. Apart from her shoes, her watch and jewellery had mysteriously disappeared, and as she looked down at herself she saw that her dress was torn across the breast, exposing the bare flesh beneath. Had she been attacked? She seemed to be covered in bruises and scratches ... and was that a trace of dried blood under her fingernails? The thought made her heart skip a beat. No, not attacked. Some other truth, far wickeder, hid beneath the level of her conscious thoughts. If only she could remember ...

Cold, hungry and struggling with unanswered questions, she leaned against the tree trunk, trying to clear her head, trying to face the unpalatable, unfeasible truth. The same, strange thing had happened to her again. Not in scary, creepy Ragzburg this time, but in sensible, rain-sodden London where the inexplicable simply didn't happen. It was late, and there would need to be explanations when she finally made it to work – but what explanation could she give if she couldn't even explain this to herself?

Just what had happened between the moment when she left her flat, and the moment when she awoke, scratched and dishevelled, in the deer park on Richmond Hill? Quite frankly, she wasn't sure she even wanted to know. But it had been something sexual, of that she was instinctively sure. She could still recall the warmth of sex deep in her belly, still feel the embers of a desire hot enough to coax passion from a stone. Something powerful too – so powerful that she seemed to have no control over it. There were dark corners of her mind that had closed themselves off, as though to protect her from something she must not know – and that was more scary still.

The whole mystery seemed utterly crazy in the cold, grey light of an October dawn. Crazier still that, despite the cold and the hunger and the apprehension, she felt alive, excited, exhilarated.

And that really was frightening.

'Soraya . . .'

'Will it wait, Stacey? If I don't get this finished by half-past and get over to MAFF, Gavin's going to blow a fuse.'

'Sorry, but I thought you'd want to see this.'

'What?'

'The morning paper. Look, page two: "Foreign Affairs – FO plays it dirty". What do you reckon to that?'

Soraya scanned the page. So it was still happening; someone within the Department was still feeding juicy snippets to the tabloids. The stories were getting uncomfortably close to home.

'See what I mean?' Stacey pulled up a chair and sat down. No names thank goodness, but it's getting a bit close for comfort, don't you think? I thought all this stuff was over when they sacked Sir Adrian, but honestly, it just seems to be getting worse.'

Soraya nodded.

'It's worrying.' Just one more thing to worry about, she mused as she re-read the story. No clues. Another mystery she wasn't even sure she wanted to solve. 'First that piece about backhanders in the *Mirror*, and now someone's been blabbing about our . . . special ways of doing things.'

'Gavin's secretary says he's furious,' remarked Stacey.

'When isn't he?' replied Soraya. 'Mind you, I see he's got Beth to comfort him.' Beth had returned from the Croydon sub-office only two days ago, but already she and Gavin seemed to have got reacquainted remarkably quickly. As she glanced towards Gavin's office she could see them through the glass screen, heads together as they laughed and drank coffee. 'And he doesn't look very upset to me.'

'Well, I'd keep clear of the little rat if I were you.'

'Don't worry, I intend to.'

Stacey got up to leave.

'Are you OK?'

'Yes, sure I am – why?'

'It's just that you look a bit ... well, you look as if you've got something on your mind.'

As Soraya finished typing and began putting papers in her briefcase, she wondered how Stacey would have reacted if she'd told her exactly what was on her mind. How did you tell someone about something you didn't even understand yourself – something that scared and tormented and excited you?

Needless, to say, a cryptic call from Sir Adrian's PA about this morning's little exposé had only made matters worse. It seemed his masters were getting impatient, demanding results. She picked up her briefcase and wished Anton was here right now. It seemed a long, long time until tomorrow night.

As she walked through the office towards the lift, she glanced towards Gavin's office and something clicked. She wished it hadn't, because it made things more complicated than ever. But the more she thought about these leaks to the press, the more she became convinced that there was only one person who could have known it all – and had the malicious streak to tell it.

And that person was Gavin Pierce.

Chapter Eight

The sound of a key turning in the lock startled Soraya out of her daydream, and she leapt to her feet, dropping the newspaper onto the coffee table. Did she look all right? Should she have worn the black dress instead of the fuchsia silk suit?

Anton appeared in the doorway to the living room, and the breadth of his grin banished all her fears. He flung his overnight bag and camera case onto the sofa, and tore off his overcoat. His eyes were twinkling with delighted lust.

'Soraya darling, you look good enough to eat. How could I be stupid enough to spend even one night away from you?'

Anton opened his arms and Soraya melted into the huge, soft warmth of his embrace, lifting her face so that he could kiss it again and again, brushing his lips over her forehead, her cheeks, her lips, the nape of her neck.

'I've really missed you,' she sighed, as his hands smoothed her long dark hair and wandered down the curve of her back to knead the firm flesh of her bottom.

'Well, I hope you've been horribly bored without me,' replied Anton jokingly. 'Can't have you enjoying yourself whilst I'm away, can we? You might decide you don't need me any more.'

'Oh I shouldn't worry, nothing interesting happened; nothing at all,' murmured Soraya. How could she find the words to tell him about that cold dawn in Richmond; the savage encounter with Gavin; that newspaper article . . .?

She gave a little gasp of sheer delight as strong fingers ruched up her skirt, exposing the black stockings and g-string that Anton adored. He murmured his appreci-ation, smoothing his hands over Soraya's firm flesh.

'You're a shameless temptress,' observed Anton with a chuckle.

'But only for you.' Soraya offered herself to his ca-resses with a joyful abandonment. Sex with Anton was so powerful and yet so gentle. All she had to do was be guided by her desires, and sensual instinct would do the rest. There was no darkness in the sun-bright pleasure that they shared.

Anton peeled off Soraya's little fuchsia silk jacket and fumbled with the tiny pearl buttons on her sleeveless blouse.

'Oh God, why do they make these things so difficult to get into?' he moaned in mock frustration. 'It's enough to drive a man mad.'

Soraya giggled.

'Think of it as gift-wrapping,' she suggested, guiding Anton's fingers; showing him how to unfasten the but-tons quickly and easily. 'You know how it is, darling – the best part of any present is unwrapping it.'

'Rubbish!' laughed Anton, victorious at last in his quest to get rid of the offending blouse. He held the crumpled handful of white silk to his nose for a few seconds, breathing in her unique fragrance, then let it go and it floated to the ground. 'The best part of you . . . is having you naked!'

He tugged down the zipper of her skirt, and she wrig-gled her hips obligingly, helping him to undress her. Her desire was every bit as strong as his, perhaps even stronger. Over these last few days, she'd grown to crave the delicious normality of sex with Anton, the only antidote to the increasingly bizarre events and sensations that seemed to be crowding in on her. Here, in broad daylight in Anton's apartment, she could close her mind to the image that seemed to fill her thoughts day and night: the insolent, unforgiving face of the full moon. What did it all mean? Here at last, in Anton's arms, she could stop tormenting herself with questions that had no answers.

As his fingers unhooked her bra, she swiftly unbuttoned his shirt, delighting in the animal warmth of the flesh beneath, lightly scented with talc and sweat. She savoured the spicy tang of his desire, and it hungered her still more – but she wanted to take their love-making slowly, make the feelings long and luxurious and lasting. She unbuttoned his 501s with desperate, tantalising slowness, and slid the skin-tight denim down over his slim hips, over the hard bulge of his penis and the tanned pillars of his thighs.

He stepped away and slipped off his shoes, socks and jeans. The white cotton boxer shorts only served to accentuate the light golden tan of his skin, the insane hardness of his cock, so aroused that its tip was oozing clear, salty juice that dampened a little patch on the front of his underwear.

With a teasing smile, he hooked his thumbs under the waistband. The message to his lover was clear: if you want me, come and get me.

Soraya needed no persuading. Bare-breasted, her dark hair falling in glossy tendrils almost to her waist, she covered him with kisses; beginning at his lips and moving slowly downwards, over throat and nipples and chest and belly to the heartland of his sex.

As she slid down she prised away his hands, and with playful fingers she smoothed over the moving swell of his shaft. It was curved like a bow stretched to breaking-point in the second before it let fly its arrows. Its arrows of burning desire . . .

On her knees before him, she opened her mouth and fastened it around the tip of his dancing phallus, darkly pink and wet through the thin cotton fabric. Anton's eyes were on her, feasting on the sight of his lover, tasting him through the material, breathing warm, moist breath that teased and excited his already-swollen glans as she flicked her tongue lightly across the tip. Her fingers slipped up under the hem of his shorts, feeling for the ripe plums which hung beneath, heavy with juice and aching with the need to be touched, caressed. They tensed within their loose purse of flesh as her fingertips brushed the thick golden curls, and Soraya shivered with the pleasure of knowing herself to be desired.

Slowly, she took her lips from Anton's cock and slid down his boxers, unveiling the secret treasure beneath. He was more beautiful and more exciting even than she remembered. She longed to taste his nakedness.

Her lips slid smoothly over the tip of Anton's member, and he let out a sigh of extreme delight.

'Oh Soraya, Soraya; you're a witch, that's what you are. It feels so good!'

He tasted salty and strong on her tongue, as delicious as some rare and exotic delicacy; and she ran her tongue-tip down his shaft with a greedy delight. Then, to Anton's surprise, she began licking his balls, moistening them with little flicks of her tongue before engulfing one in the warm, soft depths of her mouth.

It was wicked, luxurious pleasure and Soraya felt her whole body tingling with excitement. As she sucked and licked she looked up, and Anton's eyes were fixed on her, full of wonderment and exultation. This was good – no, it was better than good. It was magical.

'If you . . . if you don't stop that, you'll make me come all over your face.'

Soraya rather liked the idea of that – of thick, creamy-white spunk spurting and spitting all over her upturned face. She went on sucking and caressing and stroking.

'Soraya . . . for pity's sake. I'm going to . . .'

He came, the juicy globe in Soraya's mouth tensing a micro-second before his cock twitched and the first of a dozen creamy gobbets of semen fell onto her face. It was like warm, wet snow, cooling quickly to a thick gel. Releasing Anton from her unforgiving kiss, Soraya smiled up at him. Still panting, he bent down and ran his fingers through the cold, white droplets of his seed; and Soraya licked the salty cream from his fingertip.

'Look what you've done now, you wicked girl,' he observed, kneeling on the ground with her and kissing the white foam from her lips. 'And I was trying to save myself for you.'

Soraya smiled slyly.

'You've got plenty more for me.'

'Oh yes?'

'Oh yes.' Soraya retaliated by seizing the still-hard shaft of Anton's cock. 'See – you're hard for me again already.'

Anton ran his fingers down her belly with a playful defiance, and unfastened the two little bows which held Soraya's entirely inadequate g-string in place. The two black ribbons yielded easily, and with a little tug he removed the tiny scrap of lace, sliding it out from between her thighs.

'You know, Soraya, you really should wear something more substantial, don't you think? I mean, look at you – naked and completely helpless. What's to prevent me having my wicked, wicked way with you?'

What indeed? thought Soraya, revelling in the lewd yet gentle touch of Anton's fingers on her glossy pubic curls. She prayed that he would take her quickly, release her from the prison of desire which the sight and taste of his orgasm had only intensified.

A moment later, he slipped his hand between her thighs and she felt herself instinctively opening to him. Soraya shuddered with the wonderful suddenness of the pleasure as the side of his hand parted her love-lips, and encountered the hot, slick wetness of her womanly haven.

'Oh yes, yes. Do it to me, Anton.'

Anton rubbed her harder, and she felt wave after wave of need wash over her. Little trickles of juice were escaping from between her sex-lips, moistening Anton's hand and her inner thighs with the fragrant betrayal of her desire.

'Take me, Anton. I need you inside me now,' gasped Soraya. 'If I don't have you, I'm going to go insane.'

'How about something a little different?' suggested Anton, giving Soraya's nipple a lascivious tweak.

'Anything,' sighed Soraya, sinking to the ground as he teased her to the very brink of ecstasy.

As she lay there belly-down on the living-room carpet, Anton planted little trails of kisses over the inviting swell of her generous backside, moving gradually upwards towards her shoulders and the hypersensitive nape of her neck, with its child-soft covering of dark curls.

'Let me take you from behind,' breathed Anton, his kisses hot and urgent on her neck. 'You know how I like it. And I know how you love it too.'

Shivers of anticipation sent another flood of love-juice gushing from between Soraya's love-lips. Hungry for the pleasure it would bring her, she pulled herself up onto her hands and knees on the silky Chinese carpet, where a dragon's face gazed up at her with deep green eyes as she thrust out her bottom to receive Anton's eager tribute.

His cock-tip slid down the furrow between her buttocks, seeking out the heart of her desire; nuzzling against the secret gate of her anus that had so seldom been breached. A buzz of excitement brought the intriguing thought to her mind: maybe if he was to bugger her, take her roughly in that other tight passage . . .? But no, this was Anton and already the tip of his shaft was sliding tantalisingly down, down, down towards the wet heart of her sex: her vagina pulsing gently with the sorrow of its emptiness. Anton was big and hard. He would fill it up; he would give her what she needed.

'Yes!'

With a sudden, smooth thrust, Anton was inside her; his shaft feeling huge and hard within the soft wetness of her intimacy. She could feel it distending her vagina, stretching the delicate tissues to an almost unbearable pitch of sensation. Sex had never been this good before – in the forgotten days before Ragzburg. Sensations had never been so intense, now so sharp that she fancied she could see them; many-coloured lights that flickered in her head as her bud of pleasure throbbed and she glimpsed the delicious onrush of her orgasm. The questions were still there, at the back of her mind. So many questions, demanding answers. But this was not the place for questions; not here, not now. This was the place for pleasure.

Her imagination carried her into a world of erotic fantasy, where she was a lustful vixen, offering herself to the dog-fox who desired her, courted her with his strong hard phallus that searched out the soft, vulnerable feminine tissues and plunged, dagger-sharp, into their depths.

The pleasure was so intense that Soraya's head was swimming, and she began crying out softly with each new stroke. Her buttocks thrusting out, she sought to take her lover ever-deeper inside, to feel his cock-thrusts pressing against the neck of her womb.

Anton's voice was soft and breathy in her ear:

'Come for me, darling. Come for me. I want to feel you swallowing up my cock . . .'

His fingers slipped underneath her, and one hand toyed with her nipple whilst the other sought out the heart of her secret garden, the little pink rosebud of her desire.

She hardly knew what she was saying, but her mouth was open and she was babbling her joy as Anton masturbated her, his skilful fingers seeming to know every path to her pleasure, every little trick to awaken the tumult of sensation lying dormant within her.

'Come for me, Soraya. I'm coming soon. I want you to come with me.'

'Pinch my nipple, Anton. Pinch it hard.'

'But Soraya . . . I'll hurt you!'

'Pinch it. Please.'

133

How could she explain the sudden, crazy fancy that had entered her head – pleasure demanding the piquant spice of pain?

Anton gave the hardened flesh a tentative nip.

'Harder. Much harder. I want you to hurt me.'

Puzzled, he pinched Soraya's nipple hard between finger and thumb.

'I don't understand. You don't usually like this sort of thing.'

A sob of ecstasy tore itself from Soraya's lips as she abandoned herself to the tyranny of pleasure, her womanhood tensing and untensing in the long, expansive spasms of orgasm. Seconds later, she felt Anton give a final thrust.

'I'm coming, Soraya . . .'

His testicles were hot and heavy against her backside and he clasped her to him as his orgasm wracked through his body in wave after wave of desire.

'What was all that about?' he gasped as they lay side by side on the carpet. 'I didn't know you were into pain.'

'I'm not,' replied Soraya, surprised at the vagaries of her own desires. 'Believe me, Anton, I'm not.'

Anton kissed her, then got up to go to the bathroom.

'How about a long, sinful afternoon in bed?'

Soraya stretched luxuriously, like a cat that has just lapped a saucer of stolen cream.

'Wonderful. Tell you what, I'll pour us some drinks and bring them to bed, shall I?'

'You're a wicked temptress and I love you.'

'Does that mean yes?'

'Darling.' Anton bent low and nibbled Soraya's earlobe. 'I could never say no to you.'

As Anton disappeared into the *en-suite* bathroom which led off the master bedroom, Soraya poured a couple of whiskies, adding a few very small dashes of ginger ale as an afterthought.

'I'm getting into bed,' called Anton from the other room. 'What's keeping you?'

134

'I'll just be a moment. Keep it warm for me.'

As she screwed the top back on the ginger ale bottle, Soraya caught sight of the newspaper again, lying where she'd dropped it, on the coffee table. It was only a small item, way down at the bottom on page seven, but her eyes were drawn to it as though to a magnet:

'MISSING MAN FOUND IN RICHMOND DEER PARK'

She'd read it over and over again, and she knew it by heart – all about the London businessman found wandering naked in the park, babbling incoherently about 'devil women' and 'the moon'.

The moon. She really didn't understand any of this. Didn't want to understand, maybe. All she wanted were Anton's strong arms about her and the delicious grind of flesh on flesh. All she wanted in the whole, wide world.

'Come to bed, Soraya. It's getting cold in here without you.'

She picked up the newspaper and dropped it into the wastepaper bin with all the rest of the rubbish. Then she turned back and called to Anton: 'Better get ready for me, darling. I'm coming.'

Dr Hal Pendersley-Griffin slid across the panel and peered in through the small grating into the room beyond.

'No change?'

Nurse Janice Walker shook her head sadly.

'It's the worst case I've seen in a long time. All he's done since they brought him in is lie curled up in the corner like that. It's as if he's scared of something.'

'Hmm. If this continues, we may have to try ECT. Have the relatives been informed?'

'The girlfriend, yes. Mind you, she didn't seem overly bothered about his health – more interested in why her live-in lover had been found wandering around naked in Richmond Deer Park, covered in scratches. Apparently they haven't been seeing eye to eye recently – seems he has a habit of sneaking off up west to pick up girls.'

Pendersley-Griffin slid back the panel with a sigh. Another day, another head case.

'Well, it looks like he picked up more than he could handle this time. Have you seen those scratches on his back? It's almost as if a wild animal had attacked him.'

Nurse Walker nodded.

And he still keeps on babbling about the moon. I thought he'd maybe taken something, but the blood tests came back negative.'

Pendersley-Griffin consulted the patient's TPR chart.

'Well, continue with the Diazepam for the time being, and we'll see if he comes out of it. The police are quite keen to talk to him. Mind you, I'm beginning to wonder if it wasn't a mercy, his mind blanking everything out like that. Because whatever happened to him that night, it's scared the living daylights out of him.'

'Don't you want to know what happened to him, Doctor?'

'I don't know, Nurse Walker,' replied Pendersley-Griffin, scratching his ear reflectively with his red pen. 'I really don't know if I do.'

The studio at Bush House was surprisingly dark and dingy, the walls lined with chocolate-brown soundproofing tiles and the centrepiece a shabby Formica-covered table, in the middle of which lay a microphone and two sets of earphones.

'It is here – here that I must make my speech?'

'Yes, it is here. Take a seat and I'll phone down to the engineer to set up the line.'

Soraya could hardly blame Captain Maracek for the note of doubt in his voice. After all, it was hardly what the world might expect of the illustrious BBC. But the World Service was feeling the pinch right now; Maracek was lucky to be able to make his broadcast at all. The 'self-operating studio' would just have to do, and Soraya had been sent to Bush House to make sure that nothing went wrong.

The assignments had been getting marginally more interesting recently. It wasn't that Gavin had had a change of heart; he was just playing things safe since Sir Adrian's 'friends' had had a quiet word in his ear – and since the day when Soraya had put the frighteners on him. She still couldn't help smiling at the remembrance of Gavin's white-faced expression of horror. If she really had to work for Gavin Pierce, that was exactly how she wanted him: well and truly under her thumb.

A red light flashed on the telephone; the engineer was calling through to confirm that the airways were open.

'You're on. Just put on the headphones and speak into this microphone when you're ready. Don't worry – you'll be fine.'

She gave Maracek's hand a squeeze, and his eyes filled with mute gratitude. She hadn't missed the looks of lust he'd been giving her in the taxi, all the way from Heathrow, and he was a pretty tasty-looking man: tall, aristocratic, with a sweep of dark hair that from time to time fell over his eyes. Nice-looking, yes; but Soraya intended to keep this relationship strictly professional. Keep an eye on the guy, make sure he made the broadcast, then get him back to the Foreign Office: that was her brief, and she was sticking to it. The exiled captain was a very sensitive international commodity: this was neither the time nor the place to indulge in freelance sex.

As Maracek prepared to begin his broadcast, the door of the studio opened a few inches and Soraya glimpsed a familiar face in the ante-room beyond. Charles? Charles Christensen? It couldn't be . . .

She got up quietly, crossed to the door and slipped outside, into the corridor.

'Long time no see, Soraya! How's it hanging?'

Soraya giggled.

'Charles Christensen – well I never! I thought Sir Adrian had sent you to Nepal.'

'And so he did. But the posting's just come to an end. I'm back on the loose in London for a couple of weeks to brush up on my French, before they send me off to Ouagadougou. I tell you, Soraya, it's nothing but the bright lights in Her Majesty's Diplomatic Corps!'

137

'So what are you doing here?'

'Oh, I'm meeting the head of French language broadcasting, for a bit of the old private tuition.' He winked outrageously. Soraya got the message. She couldn't vouch for the quality of the language tuition, but Davinia Ducasse was universally agreed to be drop-dead gorgeous. 'I heard you were here nurse-maiding old Maracek, and thought I'd pop over for a bit of a gossip.'

'You old reprobate. Well, there's nothing much to report. The Department's much the same as ever – except that we've now got a creep for a boss.'

'Gavin Pierce? I heard. I knew someone who was at Oxford with him. Right little tosser, by all accounts. Used to cheat in his exams.'

'I shouldn't say this, but he's a nasty little piece of slime. He nearly got me the sack, you know.'

'I hear you've had a bit of trouble with . . . er . . . confidentiality problems, too. One or two indiscretions in the tabloid press. Could be unfortunate, that.'

Soraya shrugged awkwardly.

'Maybe, maybe not, but I can't talk about it, you know that. It's all strictly under wraps.' She didn't even like thinking about it, not since her suspicions about Gavin had surfaced. She'd be obliged to tell Sir Adrian at their next meeting, of course; but what if her suspicions turned out to be completely ill-founded? And then again, what if they were true and she didn't do anything about them . . . ?

'No, no. Of course not, I quite understand.' Charles leant up against the wall of the shabby, half-lit corridor and surveyed the peeling paintwork around him. 'Smelly hole this, isn't it?'

'Pretty ghastly. You can see how we lost the Empire.'

Charles's expression brightened.

'I say, fancy a drink? Just you and me? We used to be quite close.'

Soraya patted his hand.

'Sorry, sweetie. Nice thought and all that, but I'm

138

fixed up. Great guy by the name of Anton. And the best thing of all is, he's got absolutely nothing to do with the Department.'

Charles scowled in mock outrage.

'I'll kill him.'

'Tell you what,' grinned Soraya. 'Why don't you have a torrid night out with Gavin? Perhaps you could get him drunk and push him in a canal, somewhere nice and quiet. Somewhere with rats.'

'Oh, I wouldn't worry too much about Gavin,' scoffed Charles. 'I hear he's going to have competition.'

Soraya's ears pricked up.

'How do you mean?'

'Well, you know James Delauney has been seconded to Overseas Trade for God knows how long?'

'Yes, of course, but . . .'

'He's coming back as Departmental Controller, Soraya, or at least that's what I've heard on the grapevine. Looks like Gavin's getting himself a new boss.'

Greenwich Market bustled with tourists, packed together so close inbetween the stalls that it was almost impossible to move backwards or forwards.

'Are you sure this was a good idea?' panted Anton, forcing his way between two enormous Texan matrons haggling over the price of a battered plaster dog. 'I mean, I can get crushed any Friday night in Tesco's, and it's cheaper.'

'You know I've been delegated to get a leaving present for Stacey,' scolded Soraya. 'I promised – and besides, she loves these antique Bakelite telephones.'

'Yes, well, now we've got one can we go home?' pleaded Anton, pushing his way into a relatively empty space. 'Only I can think of much more interesting ways of spending a Saturday afternoon with you.'

'That wouldn't be in bed, by any chance?'

'You read my mind every time.' Anton's smile was rakish. 'So how about it then? Just you and me and a great big bottle of Dom Perignon, snuggled between the sheets.' He pulled her towards him, juggling awkwardly with the parcel under his arm as he pushed the hair back from her face and kissed her softly on the forehead.

'You're insatiable.'

'And you're not? I could have sworn you were enjoying it this morning, when you seduced me in the park.' The memory of their unexpected outdoor romp, spiced with the fear of discovery, was making him unbearably hot for her again.

Soraya was remembering it, too. Al fresco sex was taking on a whole new dimension for her these days. That morning in the park, she'd loved the feeling of the cold wind on flesh, the fresh scent of the frosty earth beneath them as she rode her lover, helpless with the tight grasp of her strong, bare thighs. Oh yes, she'd enjoyed it very much indeed.

'Come on Soraya – let me take you home. Let me take you back to bed.'

'Sounds wonderful. Only . . .'

'Only what?'

'I have to go to the craft market first. Maria asked me to get her some of those coloured glass tumblestones you put in flower vases.'

'It isn't like you to put duty before pleasure,' observed Anton. 'You're not going off me, are you?' he teased.

Soraya laughed and slid her fingers down his belly, giving him a surreptitious grope as the crowds milled past.

'Darling, the day I go off you is the day I go off sex – and you know how likely that is!'

'True.' Anton slipped his hand between their bodies and through the unbuttoned front of Soraya's jacket. Her breasts weighed heavy in his hand, her nipples hard and thrusting against the brushed cotton fabric of her checked shirt. 'Sure I can't tempt you?'

She gave a little animal growl.

'Cheat.'

'All's fair in love and war.' He squeezed a breast gently and she felt herself melting at his touch.

'Out of the way, for gawd's sake! Bleedin' love-birds . . .'

The fat, middle-aged stallholder shoved past, forcing Soraya even closer against Anton so that she felt his desire, burning and hard, thrusting against her belly. But the spell was broken, and with a little kiss she broke away.

'The craft market,' she said. 'And then . . . just wait and see!'

Greenwich's craft market was crammed into an old covered market hall called the Bosun's Yard, the stalls squeezed into an inadequate space made even more cramped by the hordes of shoppers, all intent on that essential pre-Christmas bargain.

Soraya and Anton pushed and shoved their way towards the back of the hall, where Soraya made her purchase and pocketed the change.

'Home?'

'Home.'

A voice behind her, muffled and distant amid the lunchtime cacophony, made Soraya turn round.

'Read your aura, lady?'

The young Irishman sat in a battered Lloyd-loom basket chair amid the paraphernalia of his craft. A crude hand-painted sign proclaimed: 'Theophilus Reilly – psychic and healer.'

'Read your aura?' he wheedled. 'Only five quid.'

Soraya opened her mouth to decline, but Anton was already reaching into his pocket: 'You'll have a go, won't you Soraya?' He pushed her forwards and thrust a five pound note into the Irishman's slightly grimy hand. 'This I have to see,' he muttered into Soraya's ear. 'I just love this mumbo-jumbo.'

'Well OK, but you first.' Soraya paid for Anton's reading. If she was going to be made to look silly, so was he.

To Soraya's surprise, Reilly picked up a battered old Polaroid camera and took a snap of Anton.

'Is that it?' she demanded. It didn't seem much for five pounds.

141

'No, no, 'tis just to capture the aura, y' see,' he explained, waiting for the picture to develop. 'Of course, we use a special type of film, to bring out the colours, like.'

Of course, thought Soraya. Anything to pull the wool over the punter's eyes. Experience had made her just as cynical as Anton. She had once been sent to investigate a bogus Polish medium on behalf of the Department, and the experience had certainly opened her eyes. Plastic ectoplasm, trick mirrors, she'd seen it all.

'Ah, now, here we are,' announced Reilly, holding up the snapshot. It showed a bemused-looking Anton standing in the middle of a rainbow of multicoloured light.

'Good God, how did you manage that?' exclaimed Anton, genuinely surprised.

'Ah, now, that would be tellin'. But 'tis a fine healthy aura you're havin', if I may make so bold, sir.'

'Thank you,' replied Anton, unsure of what to say.

'Now, this bit of green here – that shows you have the stress, sir. But all this red and yellow ... well, sir, 'tis a fine passionate sex-life you must be havin', an' no mistake.' His voice lowered to a conspiratorial whisper as he looked Soraya up and down. 'You lucky devil.'

'How about my friend here?' demanded Anton, by now thoroughly embarrassed. 'I'm sure Soraya has a much more impressive aura.'

Soraya giggled as she posed for the obligatory snapshot, then waited. Twenty seconds passed in what seemed an eternity, passers-by sneaking furtive glances of amusement at the gullible punters Reilly had managed to con.

Reilly pulled the photo out of the camera with a flourish.

'Well, what does it say about me, then?' demanded Soraya. 'Have I got a passionate aura, too?'

Reilly did not answer. He was staring fixedly at the photograph, the colour draining out of his face by the second.

'Is there something wrong? Let me see.' Soraya prised the photograph from his fingers. 'What? I don't understand . . .'

'Devil woman.' Reilly's voice was a faint, trembling whisper.

'What? What do you mean? What's the matter?'

'Devil woman. Just you keep away from me.' He was cringing away, trying to get out of his chair without getting any nearer to Soraya. She held out the photograph to him, but he shrank away. 'Don't touch me.'

'But this photograph, I want you to explain. I don't understand.'

He was on his feet now, trying frantically to push his way through the crowd towards the exit.

'Leave me alone, devil-creature. 'Tis inside you, the power. Can you not feel it?'

'I . . . She reached out to steady him, to hold him back, but he bared his teeth in a hiss of fear.

'Get away from me!'

And he was gone, pushing and scrambling through the jostling masses, disappearing into the crowd as eyes followed him, incredulous and apprehensive.

'What on earth was wrong with him?'

Anton and Soraya looked at each other, then at the photograph. Soraya felt a rush of unease, but that was just silly. Words echoed in her mind: not just Reilly's, but those of an old gypsy-woman in a Ragzburg street.

Devil-woman. You can never escape . . .

Anton put his hand on her shoulder. His voice was warm and concerned, but it sounded a million miles away.

'Is something the matter, Soraya? Look, you don't want to take any notice of idiots like that.'

She fought to free herself from her foolish fantasies. Something had obviously gone wrong with the developing process, that was all. Where Soraya's face should have been, at the centre of the photograph, the picture seemed grossly over-exposed, leaving nothing but a jet-black silhouette, surrounded by a curious halo of light.

143

A silver-white circlet of moonlight. Like a total eclipse of the sun.

'Two o'clock, Soraya. I was beginning to think you weren't coming.'

Sir Adrian carried on throwing bread to the ducks as Soraya sat down on the bench beside him.

'It's been a busy morning at work. You know how it is.'

He glanced across at her.

'You're looking tired. I hope the strain is not affecting you too much. I am relying upon you, Soraya.'

'I'm not particularly worried about the Department, no. It's just ... well, a few peculiar things have been happening to me lately. And it's amazing how I seem to attract nutcases these days. There's this guy who's moved into the flat opposite mine. A real grade "A" weirdo ...'

'Ah yes, that would be our Mr Dane.' Sir Adrian's voice held an unmistakable note of irritation. 'I fear I invested somewhat unwisely in that man's services.'

Soraya stiffened.

'What do you mean, "invested in his services"?'

'I had to be certain, Soraya. You will understand that, I am sure. I had to be certain that your loyalties did indeed lie with the Department – and with me.'

'You mean ... you've been paying that nutcase to spy on me?'

Sir Adrian shrugged.

'In the event, the experiment was not a particularly successful one. Dane's mental condition appears to have deteriorated quite dramatically over the last couple of weeks, for some unaccountable reason, and it seems he is no longer able to provide me with coherent information.'

'Pity,' muttered Soraya sarcastically. 'I really enjoy having my privacy violated by a head case with a penchant for S & M sex.'

Sir Adrian sighed, crumpling up the paper bag that had held stale bread crumbs.

'You are a senior agent working for the Special Operations Department of the Foreign Office, Soraya, not an assistant manager at Woolworths. You have no automatic right to confidentiality – none of us has. And your inability to locate the source of these leaks of information does raise a few questions if not about your loyalty, then certainly about your competence.'

'I see.' Soraya's eyes flashed with sudden anger. 'Well, if you have so little faith in my ability, why don't you get someone else to do your dirty work?'

'That will not be necessary. My superiors are satisfied, for the moment, that you are not the major security risk. And if you can prove yourself by identifying who is . . .'

'Prove myself! Four years with the Department and I'm still having to prove myself?'

'National Security cannot take account of personalities. Not even yours – or mine. In this job, we are all trying to prove ourselves twenty-four hours a day.'

Soraya took a deep breath.

'OK, I'm sorry.' She reached into her pocket and took out an envelope, containing her latest report. 'In any case, I think I've found your culprit.'

'I'm glad to hear it.' Sir Adrian took the envelope and placed it, unread, in the inside pocket of his coat.

'It's Gavin Pierce,' continued Soraya. 'It has to be. No one else had access to all the information at the right times. And no one else is malicious enough to have done it.'

'Gavin, eh? Well, I must say you don't greatly surprise me. And you have collected together all the evidence we need to confront him with this allegation?'

'No, not yet. But I will.'

Sir Adrian took off his gloves, laid his briefcase across his knees and flicked open the catch.

'I think I know just the way to trap him,' he announced with a smile. 'And you, Soraya, are going to be the bait . . .'

145

Chapter Nine

'Call for you on line two, Gavin – it's the Junior Defence Minister.'

'Tell her I'm out.'

Beth Fielding raised a pert eyebrow in surprise. Could it possibly be that Gavin was losing his cool?

'You told her that this morning.'

'Well tell her again. Tell her I'm in a meeting and I'll call her back. You know I can't speak to her until I've got those figures from Geoff. I'll probably be up all night working as it is.'

'But sweetie – what about our date tonight? You said you'd take me to *Mon Plaisir*.'

Gavin gave an exasperated sigh.

'Yes, well you'll just have to get someone else to take you, won't you? Now go away, I'm busy.'

A head popped round the door of Gavin's office.

'You know that report for the Foreign Secretary – the one on the Albanian trade mission?'

'What about it, Peter? You know I'm busy. James is on my back and it seems I'm surrounded by complete cretins who can't even organise their own workload.'

'Ooh, who got out of the wrong side of the bed this morning?' bitched Peter, exchanging knowing glances with Beth.

'Get on with it,' snapped Gavin.

'Well, before she left for Moscow, Stacey said she'd put together all the information I'd need and she left it in the top drawer of my desk. Only it isn't there any more. The thing is, the Foreign Secretary's seeing the PM tomorrow morning, and he's pushing me for the report. What do I do?'

Gavin chucked an untidy bundle of papers across the desk at him.

'Stacey's rough notes. Get on with it. And if you have any problems . . .'

'See you?'

'Wrong. See James. It's his baby now. Frankly, I couldn't give a flying toss about the Albanians.'

From her desk outside Gavin's office, Soraya watched the silent pantomine of Gavin waving his arms about and scowling at a procession of people with problems. What they possibly didn't realise was that their problems were as nothing compared to Gavin's. James was back in the Department, and Gavin was in major-league shit.

She felt almost sorry for him, pale-faced and harassed behind a steadily-mounting pile of paper as he struggled to catch up on the backlog of work before James realised quite how ineptly he'd been managing the Department. Almost, but not quite. Because – harassed or not – Gavin was still an unpleasant prat, and of course there was the pressing question of his loyalty. Sir Adrian had made it perfectly clear that there had to be answers – and soon; otherwise the powers that be might start looking for a scapegoat. Soraya, for instance.

'Coming for coffee?' Maria passed by on her way back from the deli on the corner of Gricewell Street. The bagels and blinis looked particularly appetising today.

'You'll get fat,' observed Soraya with amusement.

'Not me! I never put on weight. Must be all that healthy exercise I'm getting . . .'

Maria's steamy romance with a hunky BBC camera-man was all round the Department, and she made no

147

secret of their all-night romps. The mere thought of it sent Soraya's pulse racing with thoughts of Anton, of great sex and fine champagne between silk sheets. Over these last few days, she had felt her need for sex growing, a delicious irritation like a burning itch that demanded to be scratched. She had been greedy, insatiable, aggressive even in her demands for ever more intense pleasure; and she sensed that tomorrow night, when she saw Anton again, the hunger would be still more savage and unremitting.

She tried to put the thought from her mind, but it was still there, niggling and insistent. Last night, when she stepped out onto the balcony of her flat, she had watched the moon appear from behind a cloud, its cold, blanched face seeming to leer at her, taunting her with a secret she did not want to know.

The moon is almost full. The moon is almost full.

She fought the hunger with all the force of her willpower. Yes, she needed sex. Of course she did. She was a red-blooded woman, with a natural appetite for sensual pleasure. But she was in control – this bizarre, frightening need was not going to overwhelm her, not again, not ever. Whatever was going on inside her, it had nothing to do with the moon.

'You OK, Soraya? You're looking a bit pale.'

A deep breath calmed her down. So she wanted sex. Fine. But that was for later. For now, she had important things to do.

'Yes, fine – sorry, I was miles away,' she replied. 'But I've no time for coffee today. I'm up to my eyes in work, what with these weekly progress meetings James is initiating. Our daily gossip will have to wait.' She got up from her chair and picked up her Filofax, her eyes lighting longingly on a squidgy cream cake. 'See you later, Maria – and have a blini on me.'

As she crossed the carpeted floor to the swing doors, she noticed a sycophantic group of junior managers fawning round a tall, brown-haired figure at the far end of the open-plan office. There was no question about it

148

– James Delauney was the man of the moment; Gavin Pierce decidedly was not.

There were a couple of payphones out on the stairwell. It was a bit risky, but Sir Adrian had been very precise about what she was to do; and besides, if the plan worked and Gavin fell into the trap, there would be no need for further secrecy. Soraya was just doing her duty.

She flipped through her Filofax to the little wallet of business cards. There, hidden among them, was the scrap of paper she needed, with the scribbled name and number. She hesitated for just a moment; then dialled.

There was hardly time to get her breath, to think out what she was going to say. Two rings and a clipped female voice answered: '*Daily Comet*, can I help you?'

'Damien Greenway, please.'

A distant purring and then the phone was picked up. 'Greenway, News Desk. What can I do for you?'

'Mr Greenway. You don't know me, but I think I have some information which may interest you. There have been some interesting goings-on at the Foreign Office . . .'

The Canadian Ambassador was good-looking. Too good-looking, perhaps, mused Soraya as she ushered him down the front steps of the Canadian Embassy and into the sleek black limousine.

Reaching forward, she rapped on the glass screen which separated the passengers from the chauffeur. Charlie inclined his head, listening for instructions.

'Drive on. Afternoon tea at the Palace, then drinks with the PM and his wife.'

They drove off, the black Mercedes sliding almost silently into the heart of the rush-hour traffic.

'It's real good of you to show me round like this,' drawled the Ambassador, sneaking an appreciative peek at Soraya's long, black-stockinged legs. 'I really like you, Soraya. Maybe we could get . . . better acquainted?' He half-turned towards her on the roomy back seat, so that their knees touched. Heat pulsed into her from the sudden contact. 'I'd be honoured to take you out for dinner.'

It was a ham-fisted pass, and Soraya's rational mind dismissed it out of hand; but her body was pleading yes, yes, feel the warmth of his touch. His scent was strong and musky, she could almost taste it on her tongue, like a starburst of perfumed oil. Whatever she said, she mustn't risk upsetting or annoying him – even if he was half-drunk on James's single malt. She flashed the Ambassador one of her most winning smiles.

'You're too kind, sir. But . . .'

He placed his hand on hers. The touch felt like raw electricity, sending shock-waves rushing and sparking through her body.

'Call me Ed.'

'Well, it's really kind of you, Ed, but I'm sort of fixed up.'

The excuse sounded lame even to her; and it did nothing to dent the ardour of her transatlantic suitor.

'You're a fine woman, Soraya Chilton. I don't want you to think I come on this strong with every pretty girl I meet. Hell, I hardly know you, but – well, there's just something kinda special about you, know what I mean? And I thought, well, maybe you might think I'm kinda special too. Whaddya say, huh? A discreet dinner for two at the Embassy, no strings attached . . .'

She turned away, pretending to look out at the traffic in the gathering gloom, but she could taste him on her lips. How could she possibly confess to him how tempted she was by his clumsy proposition? Beneath the level of her conscious control, her mind was already picturing how it would be to have him, right here and now, on the soft white leather back seat. And yet, good-looking though he undoubtedly was, she wouldn't normally look twice at the guy. So why did she want him so suddenly, so powerfully?

'I'm sorry about the traffic,' she said, swiftly changing the subject. 'It's always bad this time of day. We could be stuck here for ages.'

'Suits me,' replied the Ambassador, with a broad smile. 'I reckon it would be a long, long time before I got bored.' His hand squeezed hers, a prisoner of his will. The Ambassador was not accustomed to dealing with refusals. 'Now, whaddya say about that dinner date, huh?'

Her right hand was clenched so tightly that the manicured nails were starting to cut into the flesh of her palm. It was the only weapon she had against the overwhelming need threatening to engulf her, its fiery tide drowning her reason in wave after wave of desire.

'Aw, you're not angry with me, are you, hon?' He pushed a little closer to her, and Soraya heard the blood thundering round her veins, her heart pounding in her chest. 'Just dinner and a show. Where's the harm in that?'

His hand crept up her arm to her shoulder, the sheepish gesture of a man intent on conquest but hampered by his own innate politeness.

'Honey – I'm sorry. Just look at me, will ya?'

Hunger. Hunger. Taste the exultation of his sex. Feed on the joy of his lust . . .

'No!' Soraya wheeled round and suddenly she was spitting fire. Desire burned in her like a furnace, consuming, devouring; the flames like claws raking her flesh as a treacherous voice whispered in her head: *prey, prey, prey . . .* But she would not give in to it, would not let it destroy her as it was willing her to destroy this man who so desired her. 'No.' Her voice was a hoarse, dry gasp of agony.

The Ambassador shrank away, his expression suddenly changing from debonair seduction to alarm. He put up his hands, as though to defend himself.

'OK, OK, little lady, I get the message. There's no need to go over the top, right?'

Calm came over Soraya with the same fierce suddenness that had heralded the onset of desire. What was she doing – what was she saying? She forced herself to smile, reached out and touched the Ambassador's hand. He flinched.

'I'm sorry. Don't know what happened there. Just didn't feel too well, all of a sudden.'

'That's quite all right. I understand.' The Ambassador was coldly civil now, his face an impassive mask of diplomatic politeness.

Soraya turned away from him and wound down the window a little, needing the cold rush of late autumn air to cool down her burning face. At least they were moving again – at this rate they'd not be too horribly late.

As she looked out, she caught a glimpse of her reflection in the rear-view mirror. The image of a pale-faced woman with dark eyes; and behind her, the round white disc of a full moon.

Her heart thumped against her ribcage and she looked away, her mouth suddenly dry with fear. The moon? But it wasn't even dark yet – even at four o'clock on a miserable November afternoon, it was only just dusk.

When she looked into the mirror a second time, her reflection gazed back at her with huge, frightened eyes; but there was no sign of the moon.

It had quite simply disappeared.

'Where are you, Soraya?'

Soraya slid a little further down into the sea of fragrant bubbles, revelling in the luxury of the shell-shaped sunken bath. She needed desperately to relax, she'd been so uptight these last few days. All this stuff about the moon was fast becoming an unhealthy obsession. She listened to Anton's footsteps coming up the corridor from the front room of the apartment. He was early – but why shouldn't he see her in the bath? They might even have some fun.

'In here. Why don't you come and get me?'

Anton's blond head popped round the door, his face wearing a broad and lascivious grin.

'Heck but you're gorgeous, Soraya Chilton.'

'We aim to please.'

Anton threw off his jacket and tie, and came to sit on the edge of the bath. Soraya greeted him with a kiss and a blob of creamy lather on the end of his nose.

152

'It's sad but we don't have much time tonight. Remember, I told you that my boss wanted me to work late from home.' She hadn't been able to tell Anton much. How could she explain that tonight, she was waiting for a trap to be sprung: waiting for Gavin Pierce to walk straight into the spider's web of intrigue she had prepared?

If Sir Adrian's suppositions were right, Damien Greenway's journalistic curiosity – and suspicion – would get the better of him. Offered a juicy exclusive by an unfamiliar Foreign Office contact, he would be bound to get in touch with his regular informant – Gavin. And it would not take Gavin long to work out which of his Departmental colleagues was stealing his thunder.

Tonight, unless she was very much mistaken, she would be receiving a little visit from Gavin Pierce.

Anton nodded ruefully.

'It beats me what they're up to at that Department, getting you to meet contacts at your flat. Are you sure you wouldn't like me to stay and keep an eye on things? You can't be too careful, you know . . .'

Soraya chuckled.

'You're sweet, Anton Kline. A great big soft-hearted, sexist pig!' She sat up and reached for the soap, and the clinging blanket of iridescent bubbles slid slowly and languorously down the soft swell of her breasts, tickling and teasing as they dripped from the hard points of her nipples into the warm scented water beneath. 'I can look after myself, you know that. In fact . . .' she pulled his face down to hers and held him in a vice-like grip as she dotted kisses all over it, '. . . I could have my wicked way with you here and now, if I wanted to.'

'Oh yeah?'

'Oh yeah.' She released him from her grasp, and slid down into the foamy water. It felt so good, like a warm caress on her bare skin. Maybe they didn't have a lot of time, but surely there was enough for a little innocent fun.

'I think I should teach you a lesson,' grinned Anton,

unfastening the top button of his shirt and pulling it off over his head. 'Tormenting a red-blooded Englishman like that. It's just not right!' He stepped out of his trousers and eased his underpants off, revealing the strength and urgency of his desire. Soraya watched approvingly: she liked a man who knew exactly what he wanted.

'Come here and say that,' she teased, stroking his flank as he bent over her, one knee balancing on the side of the bath. She knew what she wanted, too . . .

Seizing him by the arm, she gave it a playful tug and he overbalanced, landing on top of her in the bath with a splash that sent water and foam flying all over the bathroom floor.

'What the . . .'

Laughing and spluttering, they rolled around in the water, play-fighting in the foamy depths as levity turned to desire. For a moment Anton had the upper hand, straddling her with his strong thighs as his cock danced like a tempting sweetmeat on her belly.

'You're an absolute menace,' he laughed as he fought to hold her down beneath him. 'I've still got my shoes and socks on, you know – that's two hundred quid down the drain for a start off!'

'Typical!' retorted Soraya. 'Here you are with a gorgeous naked woman between your thighs, and what's the first thing you think of? Your precious hand-made shoes!'

'I really do think I ought to teach you that lesson, you know,' continued Anton, his voice soft and sly. 'Maybe I should give you a good spanking. Or should I just make that a damn good screwing?'

'Beast!' Soraya was shrieking with laughter as she pushed him off her, rolling round with a sudden strength that caught Anton completely off his guard. Defeated, he slipped underneath her, his head just clear of the water as she trapped him between her thighs. He looked so tempting lying there; so luscious and full of life.

And then she wasn't laughing any more.

'What's ... what's the matter, Soraya?'

She did not reply immediately. She was breathing deeply, inhaling her lover's scent, savouring the spiciness of it as she slid her hand down his belly and grasped the sap-filled stem of his cock. Desire ...

'I've got to have you, Anton. Got to have you *now*.'

Before Anton could reply, she was straddling him, the scented water swirling madly as she positioned herself to take the knife-thrust of his penis. The need was upon her, the wildness within her and she had to satisfy it. Now.

'Soraya. Soraya. What's happening to you?'

Anton felt her hot flesh engulf him, and then she was riding him like some mad creature, half-famished for the need of sex. It felt so good, so exciting; he'd never had anything like this before, not with Amanda, not with Mireille, not with anyone. This was something crazy, something dark, something that tapped passions too deep to be spoken of. This was wild, primeval sex – and he was loving every second of it, caught in the no-man's-land between ecstasy and fear.

Soraya's strength was overwhelming tonight, her slight frame controlling and imprisoning him within the framework of her own needs and desires. Anton gazed up at her, implored her to look at him, but she seemed to be staring straight ahead of her – at what?

Her heart was thumping, her womanhood white-hot with pleasure as she pumped up and down on Anton's belly, her swollen love-lips parting as she ground her clitoris against the root of his cock. The need for pleasure was frantic, the hunger gnawing at her belly as she rode her lover towards the dazzling high peak of pleasure. And her fingers, normally so gentle and sensitive, began raking sharp nails over the surface of his skin.

The mirror on the wall opposite the bath was partly steamed over, but as the steam swirled and danced on the warm air, it cleared momentarily, providing tantalising glimpses of a fuzzy, clouded reflection. No.

It couldn't be. The silvery-white glimmer was a trick of the light, a lie from the depths of a disordered brain.

How could it be? The bathroom was windowless. Whatever she had glimpsed in the mirror, it could not be the reflection of a full moon. No, not that . . .

Trapped beneath her, Anton felt his spunk rush out in a series of wonderfully hot jets as her vice-like thighs pressed in on him, pushing him inexorably down as orgasm shook her body. The water was lapping at his chin, his mouth, threatening to engulf him. And still she refused to look down at him, her eyes fixed on some faraway object that he could only guess at. Something fascinating and terrifying, that only she could see.

Panic overtook him. He struggled in his fear, but her grip on him only tightened. A dizzy sickness lapped at his consciousness as he saw a single drop of blood dissolving into the warm bathwater from the scratch she had gouged on his chest. The water was rising, lapping over his mouth, his nose, his eyes. With a supreme effort he managed to lift his head out of the water, for just a second.

'Soraya!'

And, as though awakened from a trance, she looked down at him. It took a second, maybe two, for her eyes to focus and register the horror of what she saw.

'Oh my God. Anton!'

She held him, embraced him, lifted him up out of the water as she kissed the fear from him.

'What on earth were you doing there?' spluttered Anton, coughing up water. 'Trying to drown me?'

Soraya held him close, smoothing the wet hair from his forehead as she kissed his throat and tried to chase the bad dreams away; the bad spirits that kept whispering in her ear.

Prey. This is prey. Feed, destroy, rejoice.

'I think you'd better go now,' she whispered, holding him very tightly. 'Because I don't think we've got much time left.'

Maybe none at all.

* * *

It was dark in the flat. She hadn't bothered to put on the lights after Anton left. It was all she could do to keep it together until he'd gone, to hide from him the all-consuming lust which was tearing through her like a forest fire. But the living room curtains were still wide open, and the room was awash with silvery, silky moonlight that deepened and softened the slowly-moving shadows.

Naked, except for a towel, Soraya sat curled up on the sofa, gazing out at the moon. Its light seemed to wash over her, engulfing and caressing her as it awakened her to a new world of pleasure and need.

Her fingers tingled almost painfully, her nails glossy and red in the shimmering white light as she pushed the dark hair back from her forehead. She was listening intently to the voices, whispering to her on the night air – or were they in her head? Voices that soothed and teased, urged and cajoled, calling her to join with them in the hunt.

Hunger. Prey. It has been too long. Feel the moonlight, Soraya; feel it on your flesh and know that again it is time . . .

She no longer fought the need within her; the strength to resist had gone, and now all she cared about was the raging hunger. Outside, in the darkness of the moonlit night, there was prey. She could smell its scent, wafted on the night-wind, carried in the first tiny flakes of snow that swirled against the window-pane. Still she waited. She was waiting for someone she knew would come – someone who must be punished.

Prey.

The sound of a key turning surreptitiously in a lock made her stiffen and turn to face the door. As she turned, her face caught the moonlight, her eyes glowing red as slow-burning coals against the pallor of her cheeks. The tip of her tongue flicked over her lips, her fingers raking over her own bare flesh in anticipation of other, sweeter prey.

He had come.

Her love-lips swelled with need, her clitoris

blossoming into a small, sweet fruit that yearned for the savage pleasures of the night. Her nipples were like betel-nuts, hard with the juice of an unholy desire. Appetite coursed through her, and she crouched in the shadows, waiting.

His footsteps came slowly along the corridor. He was trying to be unobtrusive – typical Gavin. No doubt he thought she was out, and he could ransack the apartment without having to confront her. Typical cowardly Gavin.

She crouched, ready to spring.

The door to the corridor opened, and she saw him standing there. At first, her fragmented consciousness could not understand. This . . . this was not the one she had been waiting for. His scent was sweeter, his flesh more succulent. This was not the one, and yet. And yet, this was prey.

She sprang at him out of the shadows, a glistening-white chimera with eyes and lips and claws of purest scarlet.

'Soraya – my God, Soraya. What –'

He was no match for her, her strength at its height and her savage sexuality irresistible in its dark power. She gasped her need as she clawed at him, tearing at his clothes, exposing the delicious flesh on whose sexual energies she would feed.

Got to have sexual pleasure. Got to have it now. Take the prey, it is ours. Tonight, the whole world is our prey.

Kneeling over him on the floor, she gave a cry of triumph as she felt the hardness between her fingers, the juicy heaviness of his testicles. He struggled feebly, but he was no match for her. His own desire would be his downfall. He was hers, to pleasure or destroy. And perhaps both . . .

Clawing at him with red-tipped fingers, she ran her tongue and teeth over the length of his body, savouring the firmness of his flesh, the salty seasoning of his sweat, the delicious slipperiness of his cock-juice, weeping from the very tip of his swollen-headed glans.

And then she was upon him like a wild beast, her vagina closing about his stiff rod like the mouth of a sea-anemone about its prey; sucking the pleasure from him as she would suck a juicy fruit dry. The pleasure was wild, insane, brutal; her fingers gripping and raking her lover's flesh with a crazy intensity.

Time no longer existed. As the moon moved slowly across the sky, marking the progress of the night, the two figures moved together on the floor of the apartment, twisting and writhing in a shadow-play of untamed passion.

Until at last, one of them lay still.

Soraya got to her feet, her transient lover sprawled helpless and unmoving on the floor. Her pulse was racing, the hot blood pounding in her veins with a new and exhilarating life. And the voices were calling much more loudly and clearly now, exhorting her to join them in their pretty night-games.

Come. Run with us. Answer the need within you.

Her face, turned towards the moonlit panorama of the night sky, was a mask of hunger – and fear. Not this. No more, no more. Please. No more. She looked down at the still, white figure on the ground and realisation stirred within her, the dagger-thrust of a memory that would not go away.

She did not understand. Why had she done this to James Delauney? And why was he here, in her apartment? She put her hand to her forehead, trying to make sense of the dizzy, broken images that raced through her mind.

One thread of sense did burn its way through the fog of her altered consciousness. Anton. It had so nearly been Anton. And what if it happened to him next time – what if she could not stop it and she did something terrible to him, something irrevocable?

Confusion, dizziness and desire overwhelmed her; but above it all rose a single certainty, clear and unswerving.

She had to run. Now, somewhere, anywhere. She had

to run away from this place and keep on running; perhaps for ever.

Sir Adrian scratched his head in baffled amusement.

'And you say that Soraya Chilton ...?'

'Yes. I told you.'

'No, I can't believe it. She's a hot-blooded young woman, I'll grant you, but this?'

He looked at the sorry spectacle of James Delauney, being helped away to the ambulance by a couple of burly police officers. If Soraya really had done this, she'd made one hell of a mess of him. Scratches and bites everywhere; and pale – the man looked as though he'd seen a ghost.

Well, more fool him, he reflected. Though admittedly it had come as a bit of a surprise to discover that it was Delauney, and not that waste of space Pierce, who'd been leaking scandalous stories to the press. In retrospect, of course, it all made perfect sense. James was an ambitious young fellow, keen to get on in the Department – but loyal too. By providing the tabloids with a steady stream of juicy but relatively harmless stories, he'd succeeded in destabilising the Department without actually doing anything seriously to compromise Her Majesty's Government. Very clever. Just what Sir Adrian would have expected of him.

And of course, when called upon to ride to the rescue of the ailing Department, James had been only too happy to play the knight in shining armour. Naturally, within weeks of his arrival as Under Secretary, the leaks would have ceased and James would have taken the credit. A nice little plan; indeed, it was the exact same one that Sir Adrian had used to get his first important promotion as a young diplomat. The difference was, he hadn't got himself caught.

Ah well, it was all over now. There was just one question remaining.

What on earth had happened to Soraya Chilton?

Chapter Ten

'Mid-European Airways regrets the cancellation of its delayed flight No. ME 78965 to Budapest.'

The cold grey mist of dawn lay over the airport like a stifling blanket, muffling all sound. Wetness dripped from the roofs and wing-tips onto the tarmac. The sky was an impenetrable dome of thick, sickly-grey smog.

Fog-bound. That was all she needed. Soraya stood at the observation window, staring out at the inhospitable morning, shivering in her thin woollen dress. There hadn't been time to pack properly, not even to think properly, for that matter. And now, two days later, in the cold light of day, she was almost beginning to wonder why she had ever come this far.

Almost, but not quite. Because memory had stirred within her, and now there was no escape from the horror of what she was, of what she had done. Before, there had been no clear recollection, no understanding to concentrate her thoughts and make her take action. But the nightmare world was opening to her now, and every time she closed her eyes she could see the moon shining coldly through the falling snowflakes, casting eerie shadows over the still whiteness of James Delauney's body.

Had she ... had she killed him? She had no way of

knowing. She was afraid to know. All she understood was that something powerful and dark had entered her soul on the night of the last full moon, filling her with a blind, unforgiving lust, taking away her will to resist. The rest of that night's events were still hazy in her mind. Perhaps her subconscious was still battling with the truth, trying to force it below the level of her conscious memory. But she recalled disturbing images and impressions: dark alleyways where she had run barefoot in the settling snow, impervious to the cold; the feeling of the blood boiling in her veins as she hunted for prey to assuage the burning fever of desire that consumed her; the face of a man, his mouth opened in ecstasy or fear as she took her pleasure from his helpless body.

So many unholy, unforgivable desires. And she had satisfied every last one, without conscience, without consciousness. She hugged herself in misery as she stared out at the fog, the chill of fear settling on her as she realised how close, how desperately close, Anton had come to being one of her victims.

That was why she was here, standing in the departures hall of a grotty German airport, waiting for a flight, which, it seemed, would never get off the ground. Even the weather seemed to be conspiring against her, trying to prevent her from getting back to Ragzburg, finding out what it was about that infernal city which had got underneath her skin, triggered off this dark moon-madness in her helpless soul.

Ragzburg. She had to get back to Ragzburg. Somehow, in the depths of her being, she knew that the key to this dark secret must lie there. And the more distance she put between herself and Anton, the safer he would be. Sadness filled her heart as she thought of him, alone and uncomprehending, without so much as a note to explain where his lover had gone. Would he understand? How could he? And she could never explain to him how nearly he had fallen victim to the cruel, capricious savagery of her helpless love.

'Das Wetter ist ganz schrecklich, nicht wahr?'

Soraya looked up, to see a tall, bespectacled man in a dark grey suit.

'I beg your pardon?'

His face creased into a smile, and he extended his hand in a gesture of greeting.

'Ah, English! I should have known – so elegant, so . . . *soignée*. They say that it is the Frenchwomen who are chic, but for me, I find Englishwomen quite, quite irresistible.'

Soraya accepted his handshake, but returned his gaze blankly. She was still wary, still instinctively afraid of everyone and everything after the events of two nights ago.

'The weather – it is quite atrocious, ja?' The stranger's eyes peered into hers, full of warmth and concern. Disconcerted, she turned away and went back to staring out of the window. He seemed undeterred.

'But please forgive me, I have not introduced myself. Heinrich Zoll, Sales Director of Essen Steel Fabricators. My friends call me Heini.' He glanced at his watch. 'I have a meeting at two o'clock this afternoon, but evidently I am not going to make it. It is just so frustrating!'

Soraya sighed. Time seemed to be against everyone; against all of these silent, grim-faced people lining the hard wooden benches ranged along the walls of this shabby little airport. She turned away from the window to look at Herr Zoll.

'Soraya,' she said. 'Soraya Chilton. Pleased to meet you.'

'Might I offer you a coffee, Fräulein Chilton? You look as if you need it, if you don't mind my saying so. These December days can be appallingly cold, up here in the mountains.'

She answered with a weak smile. How could he know the half of it?

'Coffee would be wonderful. It's very cold in here, isn't it? You'd think they'd put the heating on.'

'Here – let me put my coat round your shoulders.' Zoll slipped off his soft cashmere overcoat and put it round her. The warmth was blissful, a cocoon of security in this cold, grey world; but the stranger's kindness baffled her, made her feel uneasy.

'You're very kind.'

Zoll put his head on one side, studied her with a twinkle in his pale blue eyes.

'And you're very beautiful, Fräulein Chilton.'

Sophisticated young career woman that she was, Soraya was deeply embarrassed to feel herself blushing scarlet. She felt suddenly more like a naïve teenager, flirting with a man of the world for the very first time. But that dark, moon-filled night had left her not only with a lingering sense of guilt and shame, but with a deep and rapturous hunger, a simmering, ravenous appetite for sweet, comfortable sex. And the man beside her was good-looking, intelligent, witty. He would know things; know how to bring pleasure to her lonely, yearning senses.

'Let me carry your case.'

'No, it's OK, I'm fine,' protested Soraya, picking up her flight bag.

'Is that all you have with you?'

'I . . . left in a bit of a hurry. I didn't really have time to pack properly.'

They walked together across the dingy airport concourse, past the Mid-European Airways check-in desk, where a harassed girl was doing her best to pacify a dozen disgruntled Russians, marooned in the middle of Germany on their way to a soccer tournament in Southern Italy. It seemed as if the whole world had ground suddenly to a halt, stopping normal life dead in its tracks.

'This is one hell of a place to get stuck in,' sighed Soraya as they walked towards the coffee bar. 'Like the end of the world.'

Zoll laughed.

'You English, you think we Germans are so technologically advanced, so wonderfully organised. But you have not seen the terribleness of our provincial airports, I think!'

At the coffee bar Zoll ordered two large espressos, and persuaded Soraya to stir three large sugar-cubes into her cup before presenting her with a warm croissant and jam.

'You need it. I can tell. You are too pale, Fräulein.'

'Thank you. Please call me Soraya.' Soraya sipped at the coffee. It was thick and treacly, like a bitter-sweet black syrup on her tongue. The warmth spread quickly down her throat to the pit of her stomach, bringing colour back to her cheeks. 'Do you mind if I ask why you're being so kind to me?'

Zoll shrugged and took a sip of his coffee.

'I am no Good Samaritan, I confess it, Soraya. Perhaps it is just that I like to be near beautiful women.'

Soraya could not help smiling to herself. An appealing air of vulnerability could help sometimes – she knew that only too well from her own experiences. How many times had she used her femininity to soften the resolve of some hard-hearted foreign dignitary and get her own way? And none of them had ever even glimpsed the steely strength beneath the velvet glove. And now here she was, in the middle of nowhere with a complete stranger; and for the first time in her life her vulnerability was unfeigned.

A muffled German voice cut through the low babble of chatter. Hardly anyone even bothered to listen. It was obvious, from the thickening blanket of fog, that nothing was moving in or out of the airport for quite some time.

'Mid-European Airways regrets . . .'

'It is really too bad,' observed Zoll, glancing again at his watch. 'Perhaps I must make alternative arrangements.'

'Alternative?'

'Take the train,' explained Zoll, finishing his coffee. 'If I take a taxi to Leipzig station, there should be plenty of trains out east. I may perhaps make it to Ragzburg by tomorrow, at least.'

'Ragzburg!'

'Yes, of course. There is an engineering symposium at the university. You know the city?'

'Know it? Not very well.' Soraya toyed with her cup, making the most of the last waves of warmth as they soaked into her hands. 'But that's where I'm heading, too.'

Zoll thumped the counter with such enthusiasm that his cup jingled in its saucer.

'Then of course you must come with me, my dear Soraya.'

Soraya looked at him with interest, considering the proposition, savouring the soft-eyed gaze of the handsome German. Did she want to travel across Europe with him? Could she trust him? More to the point, could she trust herself? The full moon had left the sky for now, but its whispering, shimmering rays were lodged deep in her soul, and she could still feel the tingling-hot embers of a passion that had brought her close to destruction. She couldn't be sure what her desires might make her do.

But this was not Anton. No one, not even this handsome hunk with his blue eyes and his taut, athletic body, could come close to what she had had with Anton. She put down her coffee cup and confronted Zoll with a searching gaze.

'No strings?'

'No strings.'

'Just friends?'

'Of course.'

Sliding off her barstool, she picked up her flight bag.

'OK. Let's go.'

As they were walking towards the front doors of the airport, Soraya felt Zoll's hand brush hers briefly. And she wondered if, besides the simple pleasure of friendship, there might not be other simple pleasures to lighten the dull hours of a long train journey.

'Mr Kline? Mr Anton Kline?'

Anton smoothed a hand over his stubbly chin and cursed the half-bottle of brandy he'd swallowed the night before. It had been a bad, bad night – lonely and cold and hellishly dark. So lonely, he'd almost picked up the phone and called Amanda del Rio. But what was the point of doing that? She'd given him the brush-off and quite right too. Both of them knew she could never be more than a poor second best to Soraya Chilton.

He tried to shake the sluggish desire for sleep out of his head and avoided catching sight of his reflection in the mirror. He was only too aware what he must look like – unshaven, red-eyed, sloppy and unkempt in his dressing-gown and slippers. He beckoned to the two men in suits in an apologetic gesture.

'You'd better come in. I'm sorry about the mess.'

IDs were flashed, but Anton barely glanced at them. He'd been expecting a visit from the Foreign Office ever since Soraya disappeared. Soraya. Every time he thought about her his heart seemed to plummet like a lead weight with the unbearable heaviness of his sorrow. Where had she gone? More to the point, why had she gone? These were the questions these men would want to ask, and they were the same questions that Anton wanted answering himself.

He ushered them into the living room and brushed a sheaf of two-day-old newspapers off the settee.

'Sit down. Shall I put the kettle on?'

The older of the two men shook his head and sat down gingerly on the settee.

'Mr Kline, I am Gerald Sutton and this is my colleague, Alistair McKenzie. As you may have gathered, we are from the Central Intelligence Unit of the Foreign Office, and we would like to ask you a few questions about Ms Soraya Chilton.'

'If you want to know where she's gone,' sighed Anton, sinking into the depths of his favourite armchair, 'I think I'd better tell you that you're not the only one. I haven't the faintest idea what's happened to her. One minute she was here – the next, she'd vanished into thin air. And if you think I've got something to do with it—'

McKenzie, flicking back through the pages of his notebook, put his hand up to silence Anton.

'At this stage no one is accusing anyone of anything, Mr Kline. We simply want to establish a few of the facts surrounding Ms Chilton's sudden disappearance. But I am sure you must be aware of the ... sensitive nature of Ms Chilton's job.'

'I knew she worked for some hush-hush department at the Foreign Office, yes – but she never told me much about her work.'

'I am glad to hear it.' McKenzie reached the page he was looking for. 'The less you know, Mr Kline, the better. Now, on the night of Ms Chilton's disappearance, you spent some time with her, am I right?'

'Yes.'

'Could you please tell me exactly what happened?'

Anton felt embarrassment rising in him like an incoming tide. He wasn't normally easily embarrassed, but when it came to talking about Soraya, well – that was something private. They'd done things together that he didn't want to talk about with anyone, let alone two sour-faced goons from the FO.

'What – everything?'

'Everything you can remember.'

'Well. I got to Soraya's flat around six, I suppose – or maybe five-thirty. I wasn't expecting her to be there, but she'd left work early and she was in the bath. I wanted to surprise her, I mean, I'd been away on a photo-shoot for two days, and I was kind of keen to get reacquainted with her if you know what I mean.'

'And did you ... get reacquainted with her?'

In spite of himself, Anton felt his face crack into the beginnings of a smile. Had they? They most assuredly had.

'Yes,' he replied, staring Sutton straight in the eye. 'We had sex. In the bath.'

'I see.' Sutton's gaze did not flinch, but Anton noticed him fiddling with his collar. 'It's a little warm in here, don't you think?'

'Did you notice anything strange about Ms Chilton?' butted in McKenzie. 'Anything unusual in her behaviour?'

'No. Not exactly,' replied Anton slowly.

'Meaning?'

'Meaning she seemed a bit edgy, that's all. And she was a little over-enthusiastic about sex. She half-drowned me in the bath, she got so carried away. But we hadn't been together for days. It's hardly surprising we were a bit overheated, is it?'

'That's not really for me to say, Mr Kline,' replied McKenzie, scribbling in his notebook. 'And what time did you leave?'

'Around seven-thirty, as I recall. Soraya said she had to work late at the apartment, that her boss had arranged for her to meet someone there. A man. I wasn't too happy about her being alone, but she insisted.'

'And that was the last you saw of her?'

'The very last. Yeah.'

Even as he spoke the words, he felt all the hope draining out of his body. He felt like crying, but he was damned if he was going to cry in front of these two.

'Is that all?'

'Almost. Just one more question.' Sutton cracked his knuckles absent-mindedly, setting Anton's teeth on edge. 'Can you think of any reason why Ms Chilton would want to flee the country?'

'Flee the country! You think she's gone abroad? You don't think she's been spying or something like that?'

'I didn't say that. Answer the question, please.'

'No. No, of course not. In fact, she told me she was enjoying her job much more, now that her old boss was back.'

'James Delauney?'

'Yeah, Delauney, that sounds like the guy. But to be honest, I don't really remember. Like I said, she didn't tell me any more than the bare minimum.'

Sutton got to his feet.

'Well, I think that's all for now, Mr Kline. But we at the Department would appreciate if you didn't take any long journeys in the near future. We may need to question you again.'

Anton thought of the lucrative three-week assignment he'd been offered in Tasmania, and mentally cursed the Department. Not content with robbing him of his lover, it seemed they were also working on taking his livelihood away.

McKenzie held out his hand, but Anton pretended not to have noticed.

'Goodbye, Mr Kline. We'll be in touch.'

No doubt you will, thought Anton bitterly as he closed the front door. But will Soraya? Will I ever see her again?

Dejected, he went back through the living room. He really ought to get dressed, go down to the studio and do some work. But what was the use? He just couldn't get it together since Soraya had gone. Maybe he'd just go back to bed with the rest of that bottle of brandy.

Throwing his dressing-gown over the bedside chair, he noticed for the first time the little overnight case Soraya had left at the flat, the one she kept her toothbrush and make-up in. He pulled it out from underneath the chair and sat for a few moments on the edge of the bed, just looking at it. Silly really, but a little thing like that brought her right back. He clicked open the catch and her favourite perfume wafted out at him, making him catch his breath.

He reached into the case, feeling the softness of her lacy bra, the silkiness of her black satin panties. It was like touching her skin, caressing her, holding her close, surrounded by the aura of her perfume. And then, under the softness of her clothes and the jumble of her make-up and toiletries, he felt something hard and oblong; something unmistakable.

A book?

Curiosity getting the better of him, he lifted the book out of the case. It was a plain, green leather-bound volume, about seven inches by five. As soon as he opened it he realised what it was. It was Soraya's diary.

Guilt twisted a knife in his heart. He really shouldn't be looking at Soraya's personal diary – she wouldn't like it, he was sure she wouldn't. Besides, there might be things in there he'd rather not know. And yet ... he needed to have hope, a chance of finding out something that might give him a clue about what had happened to her, where she'd gone.

Closing the book momentarily, he opened it again at random, and began to read.

'Tuesday, 7 June. Ragzburg is the most beautiful city I have ever seen. It fascinates me, as though it holds me under some sort of spell. When I look up at the dark, mysterious mountains, I begin to understand why my great-great-grandmother found it impossible to stay away. And yet, there is something that frightens me about the place, too. Something dark that has got under my skin and won't let me go.

'Nick Drew came to my room tonight. He means nothing to me, and yet I wanted his body more than I could say. Since I have been in this place, I have had a thirst for sex that nothing can satisfy.

'I try to look at Nick objectively, tell myself that he is an unremarkable young man and not even my type. But whenever I am with him my blood seems to race faster in my veins, and I feel dizzy and light-headed with the excitement within me. Tonight, when it was dark, I heard him turn the handle of my bedroom door. I lay very still, pretending to be asleep, but my heart was pounding in my chest so hard that I swear I thought he would hear it. There was just a glimmer of silvery moonlight to see him by – there was a perfect crescent moon last night – and he looked like a beautiful bronze statue as he slipped off his robe and slid under the covers of my bed.

'As he lay pressed up against my back, his hands roamed all over me, teasing me into wakefulness, and I felt as though he were playing a symphony of sensations on my body. I cannot begin to recall on paper how wonderful it felt.

' "Are you awake?" he whispered.

'I did not reply, but when his fingers slid down to the

171

base of my belly, and started playing with my pubic curls, I betrayed myself with a little gasp of pleasure.

' "So you want to play games, do you?" he breathed in my ear. "Well I can play games too."

'I couldn't help myself. I wriggled my bottom into the hollow of his belly as he twisted and pulled my curls, making my swollen sex-lips tingle and ache with sensual need. The stiff baton of his penis seemed to slip naturally into the deep crease of my backside, and I seemed to feel it pulsing against my intimate flesh, with its own urgent life.

'It's mad, I know – or at least, it looks very strange written down on paper like this – but I didn't need to be able to see Nick's face or hear his voice, or even feel his touch on my skin. I could smell his desire – not just the tang of his sweat, or the sweet spiciness of his cologne. Nothing so ordinary. This was something quite different – an indefinable scent of pure, hungry sex. And I could taste the need on his lips, his tongue, his cock – long before our mouths met and we kissed.

'Quite honestly I don't know what this place is doing to me, and sometimes it frightens me, just a little. People look at me strangely in the street – and there's that lunatic gypsy, Janos, who seems obsessed with wanting me to hurt him. There's the way I feel, too – the way things seem to have changed inside me since the day of the total eclipse of the Sun. I can't define the change, but somehow I feel brighter, hungrier, more alive. I don't see how any of this could even remotely be bound up with being in Ragzburg, and yet . . . I feel strangely at home in this place, once my great-great-grandmother's home, now mine for a little while. I find questions filling my head, but always desire wins me over, stops me questioning the things that have happened to me and which are still happening.

'The moon. Why, when I close my eyes in the darkness, do I see its pale, round face staring back at me from a midnight-black sky; as though the moon itself were the question. And the answer?

'Utterly mad, isn't it? Sometimes I start thinking I'm going mad. I'm sure Gavin would like to think I was – he's furious about what happened that afternoon in his office, and no doubt there'll be big trouble once we get back to London. There's so much I don't understand, fleeting shadows I seem to glimpse out of the corner of my eye, but when I turn to look at them, they're gone. Scary. But exciting, too. I want the feelings inside me to stop now, but I want them to go on forever, too.

'I pushed all thoughts of shadows and fear out of my mind. Nick's fingers seemed inspired. He seemed to know exactly what to do to pleasure me, and all I had to do was just lie there and take all this amazing, unbearable pleasure. After a little while, when I was half-mad with lust for him, he let go of my pubic curls and I felt his fingers slide slowly, coquettishly, between my love-lips.

'I heard myself whisper "Yes, yes", but I hardly knew what I was saying. My pussy was on fire and all I wanted was to be made love to, screwed until the savage need was gone and I could take no more. Nick, however, seemed to share none of my urgency. He wanted to play with me, tease me, make me beg for release from my torment. His fingers slipped inside my vulva and it was slippery-wet and hot around his fingers.

' "All ready for me, aren't you?" he whispered. "All ready for a nice fat cock inside you ..."

' "Yes!" I gasped as his fingers skimmed my white-hot love button, sending electric shocks of desire running through me. "Please ..."

' "Nick said nothing, but began rubbing me, very lightly, with his fingertip – the pressure so light that it was barely more than a butterfly's breath, a tiny flutter of wings rippling across the hypersensitive bud of my womanhood. My body was on fire for sex, yearning for the release of orgasm, but Nick held me there, on the brink of ecstasy, and sweet clear fluid began trickling from between my thighs.

'The mountains around the city turn Ragzburg into a boiling cauldron at noon, and even in the middle of the night the air is often stifling and unbreathable. Lying pressed up against Nick, heat and desire moistened my flesh with little rivulets of sweat that coursed over me, glistening on my breasts, trickling down between my shoulder-blades to the hollow of my back.

'Suddenly and silently, he slid his hardness down the furrow between my buttocks, slipping into the moist slipperiness of my haven with a single thrust. I tried not to cry out – it wouldn't do for the Ambassador to over-hear, and Gavin's mad enough with me already! – but I could not prevent a little shuddering cry as Nick entered me, impaling me on his stiff manhood.

'It felt wonderful. In that moment, I had everything I could possibly want: pleasure, deep-down irresistible pleasure, that washed over me in wave after languorous wave. I thrust out my buttocks to take him in deeper, wanting to swallow him up inside me, drink in his de-sire and the creamy whiteness of his ecstasy. I could taste his need, and it was pungent and spicy on my tongue, reawakening an insatiable appetite that has pur-sued me since the first day I set foot in Ragzburg.

'And then there was the pleasure. Pleasure, coming in long, wild waves; a turbulent ocean crashing down on a lonely sea-shore, fingers of spume-flecked water raking the shingle as they clawed their way back into the bosom of the sea.

'We lay together in the darkness for a long time, our sweat-soaked bodies still intertwined as we listened to the quiet sounds of the night: the low clicking of insects in the trees in the square outside; the distant shriek of an owl swooping down on its prey in the overgrown Embassy gardens.

'And then I rolled around to face Nick, my lover's face sculpted into an eerie mask by the faint glimmerings of moonlight that filtered through the shutters. We kissed, and at once I felt the tide of desire rising in me again.

' "Shall we . . .?" I hazarded.

' "I thought you'd never ask," replied Nick, and he slid down the bed to suck the musky juices from me.

174

'Last night was wonderful, but I still don't quite understand why it happened. What I have enjoyed with Nick Drew is nothing – the stuff of brief pleasures, fleeting liaisons. Yet I felt a raging, burning desire that even a long night of lust could not satisfy. For a wild, stupid moment I even found myself wanting Gavin, for goodness' sake! I look around me, and see ordinary men, uninteresting men with uninteresting bodies. At times, it seems to me that I desire them all.

'What is happening to me? Only in the secrecy of these pages dare I ask myself the questions that keep creeping into my mind. What is it about Ragzburg that has awakened these passions within me; and what terrible thing happened to me on the night of the full moon, causing me to wake up naked and bruised, yet filled with a deliciously sensual glow?

'And answer me this: what scratches and cuts and bruises can heal within hours, leaving no trace? I have to know the answers – but where can I find them?

'The shutters of my bedroom window are open, and I am looking out into the square, over the jumbled rooftops towards the darkening mass of the mountains. The city seems huddled, mysterious, as though it is hiding a secret from me. But that's insane. Cities don't have secrets, and the full moon is nothing more than an inert lump of rock, hanging in an empty sky.

'If only I could be sure . . .'

Anton stared blankly at the diary. He felt no compulsion to read on, though he knew that he must. Emotions battled for the upper hand – jealousy, lust, pain . . . and perhaps just a glimmer of hope. As he flicked through the pages, the truth he had glimpsed began to take on a more solid form. These pages were packed with Soraya's fears and mysteries and questions, and there was only one place she would go to find answers to those questions.

The ancient city of Ragzburg.

As the train slid along the valley floor towards the

far-distant mountains, Soraya began to feel her panic subside. Tomorrow morning they would be in Ragzburg, and – strange as it was – she was already beginning to feel as though she was going home.

Drifts of dazzling white covered the hilltops and blanketed the branches of the close-packed conifers, individual grains seeming to sparkle with a bluish fire as the sun moved slowly across the smoky-white sky. One or two fat white flakes drifted down, sticking to the carriage window for a few seconds before the slipstream dragged them away.

'It is cold out there, ja?' observed Zoll, taking a sip of his lunchtime liqueur. 'But not in here – in here, we are so very warm and cosy.'

His eyes twinkled with a mirthful lust as he flashed a smile at Soraya. Sitting across the table in the restaurant car, she responded with a smile and a nod. She didn't feel apprehensive of him any more. Perhaps she should – hell, she was supposed to be a career diplomat, a fixer, continually suspicious of everything and everyone. But with each mile of track the train ate up, it was carrying her nearer to Ragzburg and the answers she had to have. That made her feel relieved of an enormous burden, very nearly playful. And since Anton was not here, who was she going to play with?

A waiter glided over to the table, broad-shouldered and slim in his tight-fitting uniform. Soraya put her hand over her mouth, suppressing a giggle. In her present state, she felt an uncontrollable desire to be silly and girlish and flirtatious. She'd only had one tiny glass of red wine, but it felt as though she were on that dangerous margin of drunkenness, intoxicated as much by her own nervous excitement as by the alcohol. And in her present state, the waiter looked good. Too damned good for his own safety.

'Will sir or madam be requiring anything further?' he asked, his voice cool and syrupy with a hint of East European charm. 'Only, you are the last diners, and it is necessary to close the restaurant car very shortly.'

176

Soraya almost opened her mouth to make an outrageous comment, but fortunately for international relations Heinrich got there first.

'That will be all thank you, Yuri.' He slipped a couple of crisp notes into the waiter's pocket. 'But we are quite comfortable in here for the time being. I take it there is no great urgency in sending us back to our seats?'

Yuri looked doubtful.

'Well, sir, there is a strict schedule which we are supposed to keep to, and of course we must prepare the dining car for the evening meal.'

Soraya watched, intrigued, as Zoll peeled another three crisp notes from the roll in his inside pocket, folded them neatly and slid them into Yuri's top pocket.

'I take it we shall not be disturbed for – say – an hour?'

Yuri's face unclouded into a winning smile.

'No sir. Most assuredly not. I shall ensure that you and the lady are quite alone.'

'Excellent.'

As Yuri retreated into the galley, Soraya looked Zoll up and down with amusement.

'You're a crook, Heini, do you know that?'

Heini shrugged modestly.

'You say the sweetest things, my dear Fräulein Chilton. Let us say that I know ways of getting what I want. Quickly.'

'Is that so?'

Soraya toyed with the bottle of Tia Maria, eyes lowered coquettishly. Did she want to play Zoll's game? Maybe . . .

'And what was all that about, anyway?' she challenged him.

'All what?'

'Bribery and corruption, Heini.'

'Is it a crime to want a little privacy? Especially when one is in the company of a delectable young English lady . . .'

'You could have all the privacy you wanted back in the sleeping compartment,' she teased.

177

'Why spoil the mood by going all the way back there? I believe in spontaneity in all things, don't you?'

Soraya started as she felt something touching her leg, very gently, very surreptitiously at first. What . . .? Then she realised. The shameless letch. He'd taken off his shoe, and his foot was caressing her stockinged calf, climbing its way slowly up her leg to her knees. Then it paused, his toes gently insistent as they tried in vain to persuade her to part her knees. As though nothing had happened, he topped up his glass and raised it with a suave smile.

'Are you sure, you won't have some, my dear? I'm sure you'd enjoy it.'

So that was how he wanted to play it. Well, she wasn't going to let a man like Heinrich Zoll see that he'd got the better of her. Looking him straight in the eye with an unwavering gaze, Soraya slipped off her thin jacket to reveal the black body-hugging dress beneath, a bright red zip fastener drawing a dramatic line between neck and navel, throwing the twin mounds of her breasts into relief.

Still looking him in the eye, she tugged down the zipper in a single swift movement. Naturally, she was not wearing a bra underneath. That would have spoilt the clinging line of the dress; the rather chic effect of her bare, stiffened nipples pressing against the thin woollen jersey.

A sound, almost inaudible, reached her ears, but Soraya did not bother to glance round. She knew who was watching, knew that somewhere to her left Yuri would be standing in the doorway to the galley, his eyes as round as saucers as he watched the sophisticated English lady stripping for her pleasure.

Calmly, she peeled away the two sides of the dress, pulling the stretchy black and red fabric down over her shoulders to reveal inch after inch of perfect, creamy-white flesh. She knew exactly what she was doing to Zoll, for all his feigned impassivity; she had calculated precisely what he was now seeing. Her breasts were

178

pink-white globes, luscious and warm against the cold black of the dress, her neck and shoulders eminently kissable roundnesses in the angularity of her spare, lithe frame. So he wanted to play. Well, Soraya Chilton knew how to play too.

With an unfaltering grasp, she seized his hand and guided it and the liqueur glass to her mouth. She drank slowly, allowing the golden-brown fluid to moisten her lips before pushing Zoll's hand gently away.

She licked the last of the liqueur from her lips.

'I'm not sure if I like it or not,' she announced. 'Maybe you can persuade me.' She rubbed her hands over her bare breasts, not sure which excited her more: Zoll's pretended coolness or Yuri's desperate attempts to muffle his heavy breathing.

Her own touch felt good on her skin, her fingers well-practised in all the arts of self-love. No one could pleasure her like she could – except perhaps Anton Kline.

Zoll's gaze shifted away, towards the window where the snow was falling faster now, the thick wet flakes plastering the outside of the glass. Soraya felt a momentary pang of disappointment, then realised that Zoll was watching her every movement, reflected in the glass. With deliberate slowness, she let her right hand slide down her belly, following the track that the zipper had taken, towards the triangle of flimsy white cotton that covered her pubic bone. Her clitoris was warm and swollen already; it would welcome the touch of its mistress's skilful fingers.

Her actions were pre-empted by Zoll's foot, climbing back up her leg – more insistently this time. She wanted to laugh. Men were so funny, they got so outraged if they felt they weren't in control. Maybe it was better if he did not realise that she could brush him off like a fly if she chose. Soraya Chilton didn't do anything she didn't want to do, anything she wasn't in control of.

A little warning voice sounded inside her head. Really, Soraya? Not even on nights of the full moon?

The sudden thought flashed through her mind like a

lightning bolt, but she was too fast for it. She banished it with a supreme effort of will, reaching down and catching hold of Zoll's foot. It was a nice foot, granted, but of course, a foot wasn't what she was looking for. She pushed it away.

She smiled.

'If you want to persuade me, you're going to have to do better than that,' she teased, her lips still moist from the flick of her thirsty tongue-tip.

'Really, my dear Soraya, you underestimate me.'

Soraya's sharpened senses picked up a maelstrom of colours and scents and tastes. She could smell the snow as it tumbled out of the leaden sky, carrying with it the faraway pine-sharpness of a mountain forest, a forest near Ragzburg. She could smell Zoll's need, taste his excitement as he stood up, his cock bulging stiffly under the soft woollen fabric of his suit trousers. She had almost forgotten how tall he was, and now he was standing beside her, towering over her as he unzipped his flies. Her own desire was a dazzling spectrum of flickering coloured lights, swirling inside her head. She felt dizzy, dizzy and exhilarated as she turned to face Zoll, swinging her long stocking-clad legs off the chair so that they were touching his. Her dress was a ruff of black and scarlet fabric about her bare hips, veiling the thin cotton panties she longed to discard. She looked up at him.

'You were saying?'

'I think we have said enough, Soraya. Don't you? There are other ways of talking, we have no need of words.'

The bulge of his erection was a tempting fruit, inches from her face. From where she was sitting now she could quite clearly see Yuri, a shadowy figure inadequately concealed behind the door to the galley. Was that his hand she could see, manipulating the stiff, naked shaft of his engorged penis? She wanted to giggle with the realisation of this devastating power she had suddenly acquired – this power to be the centre of so many men's attentions. Yuri's scent was strong and sharp, with the muskiness of the wild stag in rut. She could no longer resist the delicious torment of her desire.

The train sped on silently through the snow, swallowing up the miles between eastern Germany and the enigmatic city of Ragzburg. And, suddenly warm and playful, Soraya opened her lips to welcome Heinrich Zoll's member into the warm cavern of her mouth.

The smooth pink baton of flesh sprang eagerly into her hand, its upward-curving arc straining for release. And she rewarded its eagerness with the soft moistness of her lips and tongue. Zoll clutched at the back of her chair as the train rounded a bend, throwing him onto her, so that his cock thrust deeper into her throat, half-choking her.

She could hear his breathing, knew how much she was exciting him. He was hers utterly, his pleasure caught in the palm of her hand, which was cupped lightly around the soft, heavy bulbs of his testicles. She ran her tongue over Zoll's cock-tip, teasing the flesh gently with the points of her teeth, and felt him tremble at her touch. It would take little to bring him to climax. But Soraya wanted to make it last . . .

'Soraya . . .'

Zoll's voice was a faraway whisper, a convulsive gasp as he shuddered in the grip of a runaway passion he could no longer control. His head was thrown back and he was shaking slightly, his body racked with the first spasms of extreme pleasure. The train seemed to be going faster now, plunging between dark hills as the snow fizzed and sizzled on the hot metal casing of the engine. Soraya could sense Zoll letting go, his spirit falling through empty space as she sucked harder on his shaft, delighting in the salty-smooth ooze of love-juice collecting in huge droplets on her tongue.

She squeezed his balls with a wicked gentleness that teased as much as it stimulated, holding him back, making him wait for the pleasure to come. She was wet between her thighs with a glorious, triumphal lust, and her stiff-nippled breasts were thrilling to the feeling of the rough fabric of his clothes rubbing against them as she brought him slowly to the very peak of his pleasure.

Now. She clasped his hips and took him deep into her mouth, so that the swollen purple tip thrust hard against the back of her throat. With a shudder and a groan he emptied his desire into her, flooding her mouth, her throat; and little threads of white, silky spunk escaped from her lips, leaving a wet trail that led beneath her chin to her throat and right down between her breasts.

Somewhere nearby, Yuri was milking himself to a climax, the little sobbing gasps reaching Soraya's ears as she swallowed down the last few drops of Heinrich's semen. Zoll seemed almost paralysed with pleasure, unable to speak or move; and she pushed him away gently, withdrawing him from the tight red sheath of her lips.

As though awakening from a dream, he gave a little start and looked down at her, his eyes at first unseeing as though he were looking at a stranger. Remembrance lit up his gaze and he smiled.

'You're good, Soraya Chilton.' He bent and ran his finger over her lips. She put out her tongue and licked him like a she-cat, full of a playful malice.

'Yes,' she replied simply.

'But my cock's still stiff for you. I want you again. I want to take you, Soraya.'

She took his finger between her lips as though it were a pencil-slim shaft, sucking and licking it with a wicked concentration. When she released it, he was panting slightly, his eyes full of lust. 'Well, if you want it to be *really* good, you're going to have to do a little something for me,' she responded.

'There's nothing I'd like better.'

In a second Zoll was on his knees on the carpeted carriage floor, holding her, pressing her to him, kissing her with a raw hunger that took Soraya by surprise. Then he kissed her on the cheek, the throat, and left a trail of kisses that followed the trail of his own semen, leading down through the deep valley between her breasts.

His fingers drew patterns in the thick, pearly-white fluid, smoothing it over the flesh of her breasts and onto the crests of her nipples. She shivered with anticipation as he pinched the super-sensitive flesh between finger and thumb, then carried on his progress down her belly until his tongue reached the tiny spunk-filled well of her navel.

His thirst temporarily satisfied, he seized the scrunched-up fabric of her dress and pulled it up, revealing black stocking-tops and suspenders framing creamy-beige thighs and the chaste triangle of her white cotton panties, now moist at the crotch from the intensity of her sensual excitement.

This time, she made no attempt to resist him. As his fingers took hold of the waistband of her panties and tugged them down, she assisted him with a wriggle of her hips. In a few seconds they were gone, the wisp of damp white cotton a crumpled memory on the carriage floor. Now his hands were on her thighs, his strong hands, unused to resistance. He would most certainly not take no for an answer.

Both seduced and the seducer, Soraya anticipated his insistent demand and spread her thighs wide, shamelessly displaying the treasures of a fur-lined casket at the heart of which glistened a single moist pearl, rose-pink and succulent.

No words were spoken. They had long since left behind the need for language. The only sounds in the carriage were the gentle chink of empty wine-glasses rattling on the table-top as the train sped through a remote country station, and the soft harmony of the lovers' breathing, rising to a delicious crescendo of need.

Strong, insistent fingers stroked the softly-wooded mound of her pubis; brushed over the crinkly curls with such wicked restraint that Soraya could hardly bear the agony of suspense. When would he touch her – when would he touch her *there*?

He ran his fingertip lightly down the length of her crevice, and her sex-lips opened instinctively to welcome him. He bent his head, pressing his face between her outspread thighs, and she gave a great juddering sob of ecstasy as she felt the first touch of his warm, smooth tongue on the pink pearl of her clitoris.

As he began to lick her out, Soraya felt an overwhelming sense of well-being washing over her; a warmth and a coolness that enlivened and relaxed her, making her tingle all over with a wonderful excitement. A dazzling lightness of being, like being bathed in moonlight . . .

Sir Adrian took a sip from his coffee cup, then replaced it carefully in its saucer, wiping away a small drip from the side. He was a man who believed in the old maxim: there's a place for everything, and everything in its place.

The place for Gavin Pierce and Beth Fielding was, apparently, the Borneo Consulate. Well, so be it: it was no more than the little worm and his malevolent floosie deserved. He agreed with the PM and the Foreign Secretary: the sooner those two losers packed their bags and got the hell out of London, the better. Gavin Pierce had cocked up his last Departmental initiative.

The Foreign Secretary stood looking out of the window, hands clasped behind his back.

'It's a pity about Delauney,' he observed, without bothering to turn round.

'Indeed,' nodded Sir Adrian. 'He showed exceptional promise.' Even now, he was kicking himself for not realising the identity of the 'mole' sooner. The trouble was, he tended to take people at face value, and on the face of it James Delauney was a nice, loyal, well-bred young gentleman who wouldn't know what a tabloid was, let alone sell sensational stories to it. Which just goes to show what a gullible old fool I am, thought Sir Adrian grimly.

'Of course, we had to get him out of the way,' the Foreign Secretary went on, still gazing out at the lawns behind his country house, where a pretty boy in tight

184

jeans and a T-shirt was raking up dead leaves, apparently oblivious to the biting December chill. The Foreign Secretary liked pretty boys. That was one reason why men like Delauney had to be got rid of – and sharpish. Couldn't have *that* sort of story hitting page one of the *Comet*. 'We simply can't condone that sort of behaviour from our diplomatic staff,' he explained.

'Of course not,' agreed Sir Adrian. 'What have you done with him, incidentally?'

The boy disappeared from sight, and the Foreign Secretary turned back from the window.

'He's counting penguins in the South Sandwich Islands.'

'Important work,' observed Sir Adrian, working hard to conceal his amusement.

'Certainly it is. Apparently their numbers are in decline. But most important of all, this assignment will keep him out of the way for as long as we deem necessary. He'll have neither the time nor the energy to make trouble, and that's how I like it.' The Foreign Secretary walked quickly back to the desk and sat down. 'Now, have you thought any more about a replacement for Delauney? The Department can't function without an Under Secretary forever, you know.'

For once, Sir Adrian was at a loss for words. Whilst investigations continued, he had been careful to keep Soraya's disappearance from the ears of the PM and Foreign Secretary – but it had been almost three weeks now. How much longer could he do it? It was a risky business, and what if he was wrong, as he had been wrong about James Delauney?

'I . . . have someone in mind,' he replied, somewhat evasively, draining his coffee cup. 'But she's on leave at the moment.'

'She – so you're thinking in terms of a woman? Splendid. It's about time,' observed the Foreign Secretary, whose lack of sexual interest in women was matched only by his enthusiasm for them as Departmental workhorses. 'So, what's this filly's name then?'

'Chilton,' replied Sir Adrian, uneasily. 'Soraya Chilton.'

'Ah yes, the Chilton woman. I've heard good things of her – tireless in the pursuit of Britain's interests and all that. I'm sure she's up to the job. Well, I trust you'll bring her in to see me when she gets back from leave.'

'Yes sir. Of course I will.'

Yes, of course he would: if only he could find her.

The illuminated sign above the window of the hotel opposite was impossible to shut out. Even with the lights on and the curtains drawn, Soraya could clearly make it out: red, white, red, white, pulsing into her brain like the sound of a dripping tap.

Leaving the door ajar, she threw her room key onto the bedside table and lay down on the bed. On the table lay a pathetic jumble of papers – the sum total of almost three weeks' research since she had arrived back here in Ragzburg. Mentally she ran through them: her great-great-grandmother's marriage certificate, dated 1880; a couple of old newspaper articles mentioning the arrival of her great-great-grandfather in the city, in search of his missing wife; and now the battered sepia photograph she had found pushed under the door of her hotel room the previous afternoon.

Soraya reached out and picked up the photograph. The likeness was quite astonishing. If she were not dressed in a Victorian satin gown, with her dark hair scraped back into a bun, the woman in the picture might very well be Soraya Chilton.

She knew that it was a photograph of her great-great-grandmother, Alicia; she had seen a few old photographs of her at her grandmother's house. It was no great secret in the family that Soraya was very like her. The question was: who had put this photograph under her door – and why? The thought nagged at her, made her feel more ill at ease than ever.

The city had drawn her here, and it felt right to be here; and yet, there were certainly people in this city who feared her, some she had even seen crossing the road to avoid walking with her. She had heard an old man whispering under his breath, recalling the words of Janos and the old gypsy-woman:

'Devil-woman . . . cursed child of the moon.'

What did it all mean? She had tried asking questions, but no one would talk to her. Sometimes, it felt like a huge conspiracy to drive her mad, to convince her that there really was something supernatural about her, something powerful and dark and perhaps a little evil. As the words whispered menacingly in the back of her mind, she thought of poor mad Christopher Dane, dragged sobbing from the apartment block by men in white coats who refused to listen to his talk of moon-cursed devil-women. The trouble was that, here in Ragzburg, it all seemed so much more plausible.

She avoided looking out at the night sky. The moon was not yet at its height, but its rays, reflected by the blanket of snow that covered the city, made the evening seem unnaturally bright, even through the drawn curtains. Flicking off the bedside light, Soraya closed her eyes to try to rid herself of the brightness. The city was calling to her, begging her to immerse herself in its snow-bound streets, to accept the part of her that belonged to Ragzburg. But Soraya was tired. She wanted darkness; warm, secure darkness in which to find some tranquillity and think. What was she doing here? What had she achieved? Whatever was she going to do next?

Time passed, and she must have dozed off, because the next thing she remembered was the door creaking slowly open, and the tell-tale crack of the broken floorboard just inside the doorway.

Training took over, and she leapt off the bed, making a grab for the heaviest thing she could find – a half-full bottle of local cider. Scrabbling around for the light switch, she flicked it on.

'Who the hell . . .?'

Blinking in the sudden light, they stood staring at each other for seconds that seemed an hour long.

'Soraya, I'm sorry, I thought . . .'

'Anton!'

Soraya's arm fell to her side, cider trickling from the upturned bottle onto the carpet.

'I'm really sorry, honestly I am. I saw the open door and I thought maybe something bad had happened to you . . .'

Soraya feigned indignation.

'Haven't I told you before, I can look after myself.'

'Yes . . .'

'I nearly hit you over the head with this bottle of cider!' She set it down carefully on the bedside table.

They looked at each other. Soraya's nerve was first to crack.

'How on earth did you track me down? This wasn't supposed to happen, you know.'

Anton took a faltering step forward.

'You were one hell of a problem to find the first time, Soraya. Did you really think I'd let you get away from me that easily? And if you think I'm letting you out of my sight again . . .'

A sudden wave of relief overcame Soraya and she flung herself into Anton's outstretched arms, longing for the warm security of his strong embrace. All her fears for him forgotten, she craved the incredible pleasure of feeling his nakedness against hers, or just simply being with him.

'Missed me, Soraya?' he whispered into her ear as he planted kiss after kiss upon her bare throat, running his hands all over her scantily-clad body.

'Not one bit,' she sighed, and lifted her face to be kissed, over and over again. 'So don't go flattering yourself.'

'So I'm to go away again then, am I?' demanded Anton, running his hands over her buttocks, round and appealing in the flimsiest of silky French knickers. 'Shall I make my excuses and leave?'

'Well, maybe not just yet,' replied Soraya, responding passionately to his kisses. 'Seeing as you're here we might as well have some fun . . .' Stripping off his jacket, she began unbuttoning his jeans, feeling for the hidden warmth of his prick.

She found it. It was hot, hard, and willing.

'Come to bed,' she urged Anton, massaging him with long, smooth strokes.

'I hope you realise you've got a lot of explaining to do, young lady,' retorted Anton.

'I'll explain everything later,' promised Soraya, leading him towards the bed. 'Now, for pity's sake Anton, take me to bed and fuck me.'

Chapter Eleven

'You mean ... I didn't kill James Delauney?'

Soraya propped herself up on her right elbow, and gazed intently into Anton's eyes.

'Well he looked perfectly all right to me.'

'You've seen him!'

Anton kissed her gently.

'Don't worry. I was careful. But I wanted to find out what the hell was going on – and more important, I needed to know what had happened to you. I didn't speak to him. But I did ask around, just a few discreet questions. It seems your friend James has been packed off to some far-flung corner of the South Atlantic, and as for Beth and Gavin—'

'Yes?'

'Borneo.' Anton put his arms round Soraya and pulled her on top of him, easing the quilt over their naked bodies like a warm, dark tent. The bed creaked arthritically, but what did he care? So what if this was a cheap hotel in the seedy end of Ragzburg. He was alone again with Soraya, flesh to flesh, their bodies melting into one. Whatever bad things had happened, everything was going to be all right now. He could feel it in his bones.

Soraya snuggled close, stroking Anton's hair as she punctuated her words with kisses.

'So – I suppose it was all over the papers?'

Anton shook his head.

'Not at all. They've kept it very quiet. The *News of the World* had something about "sudden changes of personnel at the Foreign Office", but that was about it.' He held her tight, the stiff rod of his cock pressing insistently against her flat belly. 'The thing is, Soraya . . . they're looking for you. You must have known that they would. Somebody somewhere is very worried about what's happened to you, and you're going to have to go back and face the music sometime.'

'I know.' Soraya gave a sigh and buried her face in the crook of Anton's shoulder.

'Whatever it is, Soraya – however bad it is – I can help.'

She raised her face and gave a dry, humourless laugh.

'Anton. You read my diary. You *know* how bad it is.'

'You don't know for sure that anything terrible is happening to you,' protested Anton. 'Maybe you're imagining all this moon stuff.'

'Listen to me.' She placed her fingertip on his lips, silencing him. 'Strange things have been happening to me, there's no doubt about that. Things that seemed like fun at first, but now – now I'm beginning to understand what's been happening to me, and it scares me half to death.

'I had to come back to Ragzburg. I don't understand how it ties in with this moon business, or with any of the other things that have been happening to me, but this is where my great-great-grandmother disappeared, and I'm convinced that's got something to do with all of this.

'And now I know that someone here, in Ragzburg, also knows that I have come here, and knows what I am looking for. Yesterday, when I came back here, I found a photograph of my great-great-grandmother Alicia, pushed under the door. There was no message. No clue. Nothing. Somebody out there is playing games with my mind, and I don't like it one little bit.

191

'The thing is, Anton, I'm terribly afraid of this ... darkness inside me because it's something beyond my understanding and my control. Each full moon it's been getting stronger, wilder; and when I left James lying there in my apartment, I swear I thought I'd killed him.'

Anton kissed her, stroking tender fingers down from the nape of her neck to the small of her back.

'He's fine, Soraya – I told you. There's nothing to be afraid of.'

'There's everything to be afraid of! Haven't you been listening to a word I've said?' Soraya's eyes glistened with unshed tears. 'If I don't find out what's going on before the next full moon, I've a feeling it could be too late. And you, Anton, are in the most terrible danger. That's why you have to leave me. Now. Go back to England and forget you ever heard of Soraya Chilton.'

She made as though to pull away, but Anton held her fast, fixing her with his blue-grey eyes.

'You know I'll never do that, Soraya. I didn't come half-way across Europe just to turn round and go straight back again. I don't care what happens to me: I'm never leaving you again.'

'You're mad to stay.'

'I'd be madder still to go.'

In a turmoil of mixed emotions, Soraya submitted to the warm, comforting security of his embrace. He was strong, tender, full of certainty: maybe Anton was right and she was wrong. Maybe, when the full moon rose in three days' time, nothing bad would happen.

His penis was appetisingly firm under her belly. If she slid down just a few more inches, its tip would be at the entrance to her pleasure-garden, already slippery-wet with the memory of their last coupling. Slowly and sinuously, she worked her way down Anton's belly, her love-lips parting slightly as they rubbed over his tanned flesh, her clitoris lightly grazed by the wiry blond hairs that beckoned her down towards his pubis.

Instinct guided her, not rational thought. In Ragzburg, she now knew, there was no place for reason. This was a city of dark desires, of sensual mysteries centuries-old and hidden behind the mask of phoney tranquillity. If she was to find what she was seeking, she must first open herself up to the secret life of this ancient place.

As Anton's fingers slid over her buttocks, parting her cheeks and toying with the secret garden within, Soraya let go, throwing herself into the flood-tide of passion which threatened to engulf her, washing away the stagnant black waters of fear.

Anton and Soraya walked slowly through the winding streets of the old town, their feet sliding around in the grey slush that covered the ancient cobbles. A light dusting of fresh snow was falling out of a featureless white sky, frosting their eyelashes and hair as they walked through it. Far away, on a distant hillside, a lone church bell tolled a long, slow lament.

'This place is off another planet,' observed Anton, kicking sticky clumps of snow from his shoes. 'And the people! Did you see those guys in the bar when we went in to ask for directions?'

'They were afraid of me,' replied Soraya simply. 'You can't really blame them.'

Anton snorted.

'You're taking this thing too far. It's not like you to be scared off by a bunch of superstitious peasants.'

Soraya did not reply, but went on walking, head bowed. Anton caught up with her and gave her a hug.

'Look, I'm sorry, really I am. I'm just finding all this a bit much to cope with.'

'And you think I'm not?' Soraya and Anton walked on together, arm in arm, grateful for each other's warmth in this cold city of dark shadows and prying eyes. Soraya pressed close to Anton, wondering what she ought to say. How could she tell him about the danger she could feel building up inside herself, about the sexual hunger growing ever-stronger in her belly as each new day brought them closer to the next night of the full moon?

'Just look at that!' remarked Anton, directing her attention to a carved wooden figure hanging, gargoyle-like, under the eaves of a half-timbered medieval house.

Soraya looked up at the carved figure with curiosity. Like a man with the head of a wolf, it seemed to grin down with a malevolent glee, its mouth open to display two rows of white-painted fangs. She shivered. They walked on.

'Ragzburg's full of curiosities,' observed Anton as they crossed a small enclosed courtyard lined with tiny leaded windows. He paused in the middle and pulled up the collar of his coat. 'I've been reading the guide-book. I mean, take this place, for instance. This is the old medieval square, where they used to burn heretics and witches. Look – you can see how the stone flagstones are all singed and cracked. And see all those windows?'

Soraya nodded.

'That's where the really important townspeople used to gather so they could get a good view of the show. Nice people!'

At the far side of the courtyard they emerged into the long, narrow alleyway which led to the cathedral, a massive medieval building of blackish stone which dominated the old town. A sudden chill ran over Soraya. For, at the far end of the alleyway, as though at the very end of a long tunnel, she had glimpsed a familiar figure.

An old peasant woman. Surely the very same one who had screamed abuse at her in the street outside the Embassy, taunting her with talk of curses and devilry.

'What's the matter, Soraya?' Anton called after her as she wrenched herself free of him and ran down the alleyway towards the place where she had glimpsed the fleeting figure. 'Wait!'

But Soraya was already half-way down the alleyway, her feet slipping and sliding on the cobblestones, slippery with wet snow and ice. It seemed suddenly very dark, as though the slimy, moss-covered walls were crowding in on her, the spire of the cathedral looming over her head like an accusing finger, or a sword-blade threatening to fall.

Sounds filled her head – the eerie noise of wild animals howling above the thin screech of the icy wind. The chorus filled her head, urging her to run faster, stumbling blindly to the end of the alleyway and emerging into the cathedral close, crowded with a party of Japanese tourists.

All eyes were on her, startled, fearful. Behind the crowd, in the distance, Soraya glimpsed the old woman for a moment longer, then she disappeared and the crowd closed in. She was gone.

But the howling was still there in her head, and the tourists were looking at her, exchanging incredulous glances and whispers, backing away from her as though she were some dangerous wild creature, or just a crazy woman.

A crazy woman, standing in the cathedral close in broad daylight, howling at an invisible moon.

'Bloody hell, Soraya,' panted Anton, catching up with her and seizing her by the shoulders. He turned his most venomous stare on the surrounding tourists. 'Have you quite finished gawping? Why don't you just piss off and find something interesting to do?'

Whether or not they understood his words, the Japanese seemed to get the gist of his tone and duly shuffled off in the direction of the next photo opportunity.

Anton put his arms round Soraya's shoulders. She was trembling violently.

'I'm sorry, darling. I'm sorry and I'll never doubt you again. There really is something weird happening to you, isn't there?'

'I saw her,' said Soraya faintly, clutching at Anton. 'The old woman. You've got to believe me, I saw her.'

'I believe you.' And he did. He believed her with every fibre of his being, and it scared the hell out of him.

Soraya straightened up, forcing herself into an uneasy composure.

'We have to find her, Anton. She knows what's

happening to me. She thinks she can play games with me, but she's wrong.'

'We'll find her,' promised Anton. 'I promise you we will.' He took off her glove and rubbed her hand. It was icy cold. 'Come on, you're chilled to the bone and there's a refectory in the cathedral. You can buy me some of that hot chocolate Ragzburg's supposed to be so famous for.'

The interior of the cathedral shimmered with hundreds of tiny candles, their orange glow radiating from the steps in front of the altar where old women in black were kneeling in prayer. All around was bathed in deep shadow, relieved only by the multicoloured pools of light cast by the rather fine medieval stained glass windows.

Anton and Soraya walked self-consciously across the nave, talking in uneasy whispers.

'This is where Alicia married my great-great-grandfather, Josiah Chilton,' explained Soraya.

'It doesn't seem to have changed much since 1880,' remarked Anton. 'I mean, haven't they heard of electric light?'

Soraya stopped beneath one of the massive stained-glass windows, her eyes drawn by something in the design that she had not noticed before.

'Look.' She pointed to the bottom left-hand corner.

Anton followed her gaze and saw.

'Wolves, threatening a flock of sheep. This place is certainly big on wild animals,' commented Anton.

'Look more closely. Right in the very corner.'

Anton took a step back, craning his neck to make out the small, intricate detail.

'That's no ordinary wolf, Anton. Not that one there. Can you see it?'

He nodded, hardly believing the evidence of his own eyes.

'It's . . . a wolf with a woman's face.'

'That's right, Mr Kline. A wolf with the face of a beautiful woman.'

196

Anton and Soraya spun round at the sound of the man's voice. Soraya's heart missed a beat. Even in the semi-darkness of the cathedral, the voice and the face were familiar.

'Lukas – Lukas Mankiewicz?'

He clicked his heels together, acknowledging Soraya's greeting with a respectful nod.

'We meet again, madame.'

Anton looked from Soraya to the dark stranger and back again.

'You know this man?'

Soraya nodded. She only had to look at Lukas Mankiewicz, and the sexual itch came back – the insistent, nagging itch that demanded to be satisfied. Here, in the gloom of the cathedral where thick, black shadows seemed to eat away at the edges of the light, the sensations were especially strong. She fought the urge to close her eyes, knowing what she would see behind her closed lids. The swelling disc of the waxing moon . . .

'We did a little business together once, the last time I was in Ragzburg,' she explained. 'Foreign Office business – isn't that so, Mr Mankiewicz?'

'It is indeed. I have not forgotten the pleasures of our last encounter, nor shall I, Soraya. I only wish that this meeting could be in less formal circumstances.' He beckoned, and two more men appeared from the shadows, clad in identical dark coats and black leather gloves. 'We are interested to know why you are here in Ragzburg, Soraya.'

Irritation bubbled up in Anton. 'Why the hell should she—'

'Please be quiet, Mr Kline, or Henryck will have to persuade you.'

Henryck took a step forward; mean and gorilla-like in his black overcoat. Anton fell silent.

'Now, Soraya,' continued Mankiewicz. 'I believe you have something to tell us. As I understand it, Her Majesty's Government are rather anxious to speak with you. It would be a great pity if they were to stumble upon your whereabouts before you were ready to speak with them.'

'I see.' Soraya's pulse quickened. 'But I should have realised that you were capable of blackmail, bearing in mind what happened last time we met.'

For a moment, Mankiewicz's face cracked into a smile, and his laughter rang out around the huge empty spaces of the cathedral.

'My dear Soraya, I seem to recall that you were more than happy to use pleasure as a weapon for persuasion. Perhaps your friend Mr Kline would like to hear how you sucked my cock and raked me with your sharp little fingernails?'

'I came back to Ragzburg to find out what happened to my great-great-grandmother,' replied Soraya quickly.

'And also . . .?'

'And also to find out what is happening to me. There have been strange things I cannot explain. Questions I need to have answered . . .'

'Regrettably, it is precisely as I had surmised.' Mankiewicz reached into the inside pocket of his overcoat and took out a slim Manila envelope, which he handed to Soraya. 'In this envelope you will find directions to a remote village in the mountains. Follow them closely – you will not find the village of Vokolitz on any map.'

'Vokolitz?' butted in Anton. 'Why should we want to go to some mountain village?'

'Mr Kline.' Mankiewicz's voice was cool and clinically precise. 'If you and Ms Chilton know what is good for you, you will follow my instructions precisely, and without question.' He turned to Soraya. 'If you stay in this city, Soraya, you and your companion are in grave danger. Those cursed by the moon are not welcome in Ragzburg. You must leave. No later than tomorrow.'

As he and his companions turned to leave, Mankiewicz paused and looked back.

'By noon tomorrow, Soraya. Or your British Foreign Secretary may hear news of a certain missing diplomat . . .'

When they had gone, Soraya and Anton stood together in silence, gazing after them into the darkness. In the distance, voices soared to the vaulted ceiling, chanting the words of an ancient anthem, weaving a dizzying net of brittle sound.

'Vokolitz,' murmured Soraya, clutching the envelope very tightly.

'You have heard of it?'

Soraya shook her head, but there was a question mark at the back of her mind. Vokolitz. There was something familiar about it, something mysterious that made the hairs on the back of her neck stand on end.

Perhaps Vokolitz would provide the answers to her questions, an end to the tormenting need that made her clitoris throb with painful, irresistible desire.

Snow was falling heavily over Ragzburg as the jeep rattled over the cobblestones towards the western gate of the city.

'It's a bad day to be travelling anywhere,' observed Anton, wiping condensation off the windscreen.

Soraya steered the hired jeep through the gate, trying to ignore the dark figure of a man standing by the roadside, his hand raised in a gesture of farewell. Lukas Mankiewicz was taking no chances.

'There's no time, Anton. No time to lose. And if we make good time, we should be there before nightfall – it says so in the notes Mankiewicz gave us.'

Anton looked out of the window at the swirling snowflakes, drifting in an unending curtain across the city. The ancient towers and turrets of the old town thrust like black spikes through the whiteness, now visible, now veiled by the drifts of snow. Irritated though he was to be run out of town by some two-bit civil servant, he was relieved to be leaving Ragzburg. There was something stifling and unhealthy about the place, something that made his flesh creep. How many times had he caught sight of something out of the corner of his eye, only to turn and find that there was nothing there? In Ragzburg, it seemed, even the shadows played games.

The jeep's heavy-duty tyres crunched satisfyingly on the fresh snow as they began to climb up out of the basin that held the city captive. Anton felt himself begin to relax. Maybe this Vokolitz place would give Soraya what she needed. And if not, maybe he could persuade her to abandon the chase, go back to London with him and take up the reins of a normal existence. He touched her thigh lightly, and she flashed him a smile.

'Don't tempt me,' she grinned.

'Fancy me then?'

'Like crazy, you know that. But you'd better not distract me, or we'll end up in the hedge!' How could she tell him just how much she wanted him? Her whole body was vibrating to the secret rhythm of a sensual energy, deep within her. She could shut her mind to the whispering voices, but not to the sly tide of desire washing over her, filling her mind with images of glorious sex. It was getting much, much too close to the night of the full moon . . .

At the crest of the first hill they hit the crossroads, and most of the vehicles in front peeled off right, heading west towards Prague and Leipzig. Soraya swung the jeep left onto the mountain road, overtaking an old farmer in his broken-down Trabant. Even with a clear road ahead of them, they couldn't go much faster. Compared to the main route west, this road was little better than a track; and the lack of traffic had left it treacherous, a narrow, winding band surfaced with several layers of hard-packed ice, frosted with a couple of inches of powdery snow.

Trying to keep her mind and her eyes on her driving, Soraya resisted the flood of images invading her brain. It was so tempting to give in to the thought of Anton lying naked beside her, his fingers and tongue exploring her body. Already she could taste him on her lips, smell the sweet muskiness of warm sex filling the air. The wheels slipped on the frozen surface, and she changed down into first gear to take the steeper gradient.

'The weather's closing in,' she observed, peering

through the small arc of glass cleared by the windscreen wipers. The world before them was a whirling mass of white, the road almost invisible as she steered the jeep between towering banks of piled-up snow. Headlamps loomed up out of the distance and she swerved, the off-side of the jeep grazing the bank as she wrestled with the wheel. The grey shape of a van slid past, its wheels spraying up a cloud of dirty snow.

They carried on, climbing higher and higher into the mountains above Ragzburg. Looking down out of the window, Anton realised that he could no longer make out the black, needle-sharp spike of the cathedral spire, spearing the white sky. Ragzburg had disappeared into the fast-falling snow, a ghost in a world of blinding white.

Want him. Want him like crazy. The wanting came in wave after wave, refusing to go away. Anton's hand was still resting on her thigh, his desire surrounding her like a sweet perfume.

A few miles further on, they reached a fork in the road and Soraya brought the jeep to a halt.

'Left or right?' demanded Soraya.

Anton consulted Mankiewicz's notes.

'It doesn't say.' Forcing open the door of the jeep, he stepped out into the snow and surveyed the scene through a whirl of white flakes. 'No signpost,' he shouted to Soraya through the high-pitched shriek of the wind. 'But it must be left – the other road probably leads back down to Ragzburg.'

He got back into the jeep, snow melting to tiny trickles of water on his face. Soraya looked at him yearningly, longing to kiss the snowflakes away, one by one. Wishing she could slake her thirst for love on his beautiful body.

She put the jeep into gear and eased it into the left-hand fork. The road worsened. It was now barely wide enough for one car let alone two; and framed on either side by an impenetrable forest of larch and spruce. The windows were tight shut and the heater was on full blast, but Soraya could smell the cold, spicy tang of the mountain air. They were getting close. They must be getting close.

An hour later, when the track petered out into nothing, they had still not found Vokolitz.

'Face it, we're lost,' sighed Anton. 'And in an hour's time it'll be dark.'

Soraya wound down her window a couple of inches, and a wild swirl of snowflakes gusted in on an icy blast.

'We have to do something,' she announced. 'Get the jeep somewhere safe, and find ourselves a place to sit out this blizzard.'

As though right on cue, the snow seemed to part for a second, revealing a dark shape a hundred yards or so further on, nestling under a canopy of trees. Soraya pushed open the jeep door and jumped down, sinking almost to her knees in soft snow. She shaded her eyes against the glare.

'It looks like some kind of wooden hut,' she announced. 'Probably a hunting lodge or something. Maybe there's someone there who can help us.'

They left the jeep in the lee of the trees, and trudged towards the low wooden hut through the blizzard, almost losing it from sight as the wind blew stinging gusts of snowflakes into their eyes. Soraya reached the hut first and rattled the handle.

'Locked, dammit.'

'No problem.' Anton applied the sole of his boot to the rusty lock on the wooden door and at the second attempt it burst inwards, with a cloud of powdery snowflakes.

They dived inside, slamming the door behind them gratefully. The interior of the hut was sparsely furnished but surprisingly warm, with a low wooden bed covered with a couple of rough brown blankets; a small pot-bellied stove with a kettle and a pile of firewood; a couple of chairs and a table, with a small oil lamp and a box of matches. A shotgun lay across the table, with a couple of spent cartridges beside it.

'Looks like someone's intending to come back,' commented Anton, lighting the oil lamp and laying his hand on the side of the stove. 'It's still warm. I don't suppose he'll be any too pleased when he finds out we've kicked his door in.'

'Whoever it is, they won't be back just yet,' replied Soraya, slipping off her jacket and jumper. 'Nothing could make it through this weather. And it's getting darker outside. Looks like we're going to be all alone tonight . . .'

Pulling off her boots and corduroy pants, she stretched out on the bed, pulling the blankets over her. They were rough and scratchy, but that only added to the fun, caressing her with every move she made, teasing and tormenting her willing flesh.

'Why not join me? Come and keep me warm.'

It had been too long since she had enjoyed Anton's body, and a languorous warmth was spreading through her, exciting her to new heights of passion. A sweet, sensual hunger made her whole body tingle, swelling her love-lips with the promise of pleasure to come.

'Come to me. I want you so.'

Anton was not slow to respond, throwing off jumper and pants and sliding underneath the covers. His flesh throbbed hot and dry against the coolness of Soraya's flesh as he unfastened her bra and slipped it from her breasts.

'You *are* cold,' he whispered. 'Let me warm you up.'

Dropping Soraya's bra on the floor, he began kissing and gently rubbing her breasts, warming her with the heat from his breath and the warm trails of his saliva, winding round and round the little hillocks of flesh that felt so wonderfully firm and heavy in his hands. Her nipples responded swiftly, erecting into the hard, conical spikes he loved so well. They fitted so beautifully between tongue and teeth, forefinger and thumb.

Soraya's lips and hands were working too, kissing and caressing her lover with tender urgency as he answered the call of her desires. She hardly noticed night falling, darkening the windows of the little log cabin as the fat white moon rose in the sky, its near-circular disc casting kaleidoscopic patterns through the swirling snowflakes.

All she noticed was the mounting strength of the desire within her, warming her belly and making her crazy for Anton's sex. Seizing hold of his manhood, she guided it between her thighs. Anton looked down at her, surprised by this sudden hunger. Perhaps he was remembering that night, a number of weeks ago, when they had made love in the bath at Soraya's apartment. That fateful night when she had been so deliciously, dangerously predatory: the night she had half-killed James Delauney.

'Now? You want me now?'

'Now. Please take me now. I can't bear the waiting any longer.'

He entered her, and she met him with a powerful thrust of her hips, her womanhood swallowing him up like the maw of some carnivorous creature. They lay together, facing each other, Soraya's thighs parted and their limbs entwined; and slowly began to move, their instincts setting their own rhythm as the pleasure grew.

Hunger. Hunger.

The whispering grew louder in Soraya's head, and she fought to banish it. This was not her prey. This was her lover, the only man who could give her more pleasure than she could give herself. This was Anton, and he was loving her with a glorious, tender intensity.

Hunger. So strong.

'You're so beautiful, Soraya,' groaned Anton. 'My cock feels like it's on fire.'

Faster now, they moved in instinctive synchronicity, their breathing harsh and laboured as they climbed towards the glittering summit of their pleasure.

'Take me, Anton. Oh, take me . . .'

Her nipples were rubbing hard against his chest, her love-lips opening to the delicious grind of his pubis against hers, stimulating the white-hot nerve-centre of her delight. Anton's seed spurted into her belly, and in a lightning-flash of release she came, tumbling into an infinity of coloured lights and exquisite sensations, lulled by the sweet music of ecstasy.

As she lay in Anton's arms, listening to his breathing grow slower and easier, another sound filled the air, making her stiffen with an instinctive, primeval recognition. It was a howling, the thin high chant of beasts; and it was closing in.

'Wolves?' Anton listened, puzzled. 'It can't be, surely. There aren't any wolves in these mountains – they died out years ago.'

But Soraya was not listening to Anton's voice. Her ears were attuned to the ghostly sound, the doleful cries of a dozen voices, maybe more; calling to her from out of the darkness. Drawn to the window, she slipped out of Anton's embrace, scooping up one of the blankets and wrapping it round her against the cold.

With her face pressed up against the window, she searched the night for the source of the sound. At first she saw nothing, but as the moon emerged from behind a cloud, illuminating the snow in a blaze of white fire, she saw their eyes, glinting a baleful orange as they waited among the trees.

Waited for their mistress.

Suddenly they raised their muzzles to the cold dark air and chorused to the moon. Anton called to her sleepily from the bed.

'What's the matter, Soraya? If it is wolves don't worry – they can't hurt us, not in here.'

She said nothing. The blanket slid from her shoulders and she stood naked in the moonlight for a few seconds before walking towards the door. As she wrenched it open, eddies of snowflakes gusted into the interior of the hut on an icy, bone-chilling wind. But Soraya was oblivious to the cold.

'Soraya – shut the door, it's bloody freezing in here.'

She took a step outside, and her bare feet sank almost knee-deep into the snow. In the shadow of the trees, the wolves were waiting patiently for her.

'For God's sake, Soraya, come back!'

Anton leapt out of bed and rushed after her, seizing her by the shoulders and forcing her to turn and look at him. There was a wild gleam in her deep, dark eyes.

'We have to follow them, Anton,' she whispered excitedly. 'They've come to lead us to Vokolitz!'

Chapter Twelve

'Two English gentlemen to see you, sir.'

Heinrich Zoll looked up irritably from his computer screen. European sales figures were down on the previous month, and the last thing he needed now was an unexpected disturbance.

'What do they want?'

His personal assistant, Gaby, shook her head.

'I'm afraid they wouldn't say.'

'Tell them I don't see anyone without an appointment.'

He turned back to his terminal and punched in another string of figures. A multicoloured bar chart appeared on the screen and he groaned. The long-term projections were not looking at all good. It was becoming increasingly likely that someone's head was going to roll, and Heinrich Zoll was determined to make sure that it wasn't his.

A man's voice ate into his concentration.

'Mr Zoll? Mr Heinrich Zoll?'

Annoyed by yet another interruption, he looked up to see two strangers standing in his office. He could tell at a glance, from the unfashionable cut of their Savile Row suits, that they must be Englishmen. Gaby was standing behind them, hopping about and trying to attract his attention. His temper snapped.

'I thought I made it quite clear . . .'

'I couldn't stop them, sir. They were most insistent.'

'I see.' Heinrich pressed a button and the computer terminal slid silently down into a neat little niche at the side of his workstation. He folded his arms and confronted the two visitors with a hard stare. 'Well, gentlemen, this had better be exceptionally important. You have precisely five minutes in which to convince me that it is.'

The taller of the two men pulled up a chair and sat down. Apparently undisturbed by Zoll's show of strength, he leaned across the desk, until they were almost nose to nose.

'Mr Zoll, I would advise you not to do or say anything which might compromise your already rather delicate position. Kidnapping and espionage are very serious offences.'

Zoll stared back, for once in his life completely baffled.

'Kidnapping! Espionage! Is this some kind of bad joke?'

'Let me explain.' Sutton pulled a warrant card from his pocket and tossed it onto the desk. 'I am Gerald Sutton, from the Central Intelligence Unit of the Foreign Office, and my colleague here is Alistair McKenzie. We have come here to ask you a few questions about a certain young lady who seems to have disappeared off the face of the earth. A Miss Soraya Chilton. Our sources tell us that she was last seen in your company, at an airport in southern Germany.'

'Soraya!' The memory came flooding back in all its delicious detail. Their encounter in the restaurant car, the wonderful inventiveness of her love-making as they lay together in the darkened sleeping car, on a trans-European express train speeding through the night.

'So you admit seeing her?'

Zoll chuckled.

'Admit it! Any man would boast about it.' He rummaged in his desk drawer and took out a handful of

208

credit card receipts. Sorting through them and selecting one, he pushed it across the desk and Sutton picked it up. 'There you have it – that is the receipt for our train tickets. You see, I have absolutely nothing to hide.'

'Train? But according to our information, you and she were waiting for a plane.'

'That is indeed true, but the airport was fog-bound that day. The weather was so bad that we decided to make for the railway station and take the overnight sleeper.'

'I see.' Sutton crinkled the receipt thoughtfully between finger and thumb. This was an entirely new development which he hadn't reckoned with. 'Tell me about your train journey. And tell me about what happened to Miss Chilton. Where were you going together? What were you doing? I want to know everything.'

'There is remarkably little to tell,' replied Zoll. An ingrained sense of Teutonic honour prevented him from going into all the details of the intimate hours they had spent together, their bodies intertwined as passion's flame burned within them again and again. In any case, he judged, such details would be of little interest to these faceless, bloodless bureaucrats. 'But I can tell you this much, gentlemen. The last time I saw Soraya Chilton was on a night train heading into eastern Europe. The next morning, we parted at the central station in Ragzburg; and I haven't seen her since.'

Morning dawned crisp and clear over the mountains, the snow lying thick and undisturbed, and the sky a fragile eggshell blue.

Soraya scrambled through the close-packed trees, towards the summit of the mountain, Anton panting in her wake. She had to know if what they had glimpsed last night through the fast-falling snow was real, or just some wild hallucination of their brains crazed by the icy cold. Surely it had all been a dream, and they would reach the summit to discover nothing on the other side but more snow, more ice, more impenetrable forest.

Pushing through the last of the spindly larch saplings, she found herself at the top of the ridge, gazing down on a sight that made her gasp. Catching up with her, Anton halted dead in his tracks, his eyes round with disbelief.

'No! That's just not possible.'

Immediately below them lay a perfect valley, cradled in the gentle hollow between two high mountain peaks, and completely isolated from the world below. Along the valley bottom, a tranquil stream wound its way through a little village of perhaps twenty or thirty simple timber cottages, thin white ribbons of smoke drifting upwards from their chimneys into the flawless blue sky.

Incredibly, there was not a trace of snow or ice anywhere. On the gently sloping valley sides, flooded with yellow-gold sunlight, cattle and goats grazed peacefully on grass so lushly green it seemed hardly real. A thick carpet of wild flowers spread over the meadows, and the air was summer-warm and fragrant. Soraya suddenly felt very out of place in her thick jacket and heavy boots, still fringed with the last traces of melting snow.

'This place, Soraya . . .' began Anton, hardly knowing what to say, his mind struggling to come to terms with the unfeasible truth of what he could see. 'Are we dreaming this place? How can it look and feel like spring here when it's the depths of winter everywhere else?'

Soraya put her arms round him and kissed him, trying to hide her own fear.

'I don't understand it either. But it's very beautiful, isn't it?'

Anton gripped her arm.

'It's creepy, Soraya, that's what it is. I don't think we should go anywhere near it.'

'We have to, Anton. Don't you see? You can turn back if you want, but for me there can't be any going back, not any more. I have to know, Anton. I have to know before it's too late.'

'Then we go together.'

Hand in hand, they began the slow walk down the hillside towards Vokolitz.

Nurse Janice Walker peered down at her patient over the top of her horn-rimmed spectacles. Even the thick leather straps could scarcely hold him to the bed, he was straining so hard against the steel buckles.

'His condition is definitely deteriorating again, Doctor. The ECT doesn't seem to have done any good at all.'

Dr Hal Pendersley-Griffin scratched his head with the end of his pencil.

'And you're absolutely sure that these bouts of disturbed behaviour occur in regular cycles?'

Nurse Walker opened the patient's file and handed it to the doctor.

'Roughly every twenty-eight days, Doctor, as you can see, and they last for a few days at a time. He's quite docile most of the time, but round about the time of the full moon, he starts to become extremely violent.'

'And you're quite sure this has got something to do with the moon? It couldn't be something else we haven't thought of?'

'Positive, Doctor. Even pictures of the moon drive him to distraction. Sister Phillips has to be very careful what she lets him watch on the television.'

'And he's just entering one of these ... phases now, I take it?'

Nurse Walker consulted the calendar.

'Twenty-seven days since the last episode of delirium, so he's right on cue. As you can see, if we didn't restrain him he'd be a danger to himself as well as the staff and all the other patients. He keeps trying to scratch and bite himself, you see. And he has this peculiar obsession with the full moon. If we don't keep all the windows firmly shuttered, he tries to climb out in the middle of the night.'

Pendersley-Griffin stared down at the man, baffled and frustrated. Here they were with a genuine lunatic on their hands, and he hadn't the faintest idea what to do with him. Still, if nothing else it might make an interesting scientific paper.

'Pump him full of Largactyl, and we'll see what we can do with him when he calms down. Maybe more psychotherapy will throw something up.' He wrote up the prescription. 'Administer it twice daily, by intravenous injection.' He glanced out of the window at the darkening sky and the full, fat disc of the moon. 'On second thoughts, make that three times a day. You can't be too careful.'

'I greet you in peace and in the sisterhood of the moon, my child.'

The dark-haired woman stood with arms outstretched beneath the dark wooden archway which spanned the road leading into the village. She was raven-haired and dark-eyed, and Anton was immediately struck by how much she reminded him of Soraya. The thought disturbed him. But she was certainly beautiful. Her long, white robe floated about her tall, slender form in the light breeze, the filmy fabric moulding itself to the curves of her delicious body. Her voice was husky and musical as she addressed them in heavily-accented English.

'My name is Emilia, and I have been sent to guide you. You and your companion are most welcome in this sacred place.' Her dark eyes flashed an appreciative glance at Anton, who felt suddenly very uncomfortable. But the woman's embrace seemed warm and genuinely welcoming; perhaps he was imagining the hint of menace he had glimpsed in her deep, dark eyes. 'It has been many long years that we have awaited your coming. It was written that one day you must come to avenge the past, but we had almost begun to disbelieve the legend.'

'This place,' blurted out Anton. 'I don't understand how . . .'

Emilia raised her hand to silence him, and Soraya noticed how unearthly white and flawless her skin was, so translucent that the light seemed to shine right through it, showing up the fine spider's web of veins beneath.

'Your questions shall be answered,' she said. 'But first you must rest after your journey, and prepare for what lies ahead. Follow me. A place has been prepared for you.'

They followed in obedient silence, still scarcely able to believe that they were here, bathed in the warmth and fragrance of an unseasonal spring. Anton glanced at Soraya. If she was afraid, she did not show it. Instantly he felt ashamed of his own weakness.

The main road through the centre of the village was no more than a broad track of beaten earth, winding among the cottages: each a simple structure of weather-beaten wood with a small garden. As Soraya and Anton followed Emilia, other women appeared at the doors of their cottages and came out to greet them. Like Emilia, they were all dressed in thin white dresses that showed the womanly curves of their bodies. And like Emilia . . .

Soraya shivered, a *frisson* of unease rippling through her. Like Emilia, all the women were dark-haired, dark-eyed, young and beautiful. There was no denying the striking resemblance between these women and their guest, Soraya Chilton. Again, apprehension gripped her. Had she been mistaken in coming here, throwing herself willingly into this strange, unearthly place which could so easily turn out to be a trap for an unwary fool?

As they walked past the cottages, each woman in turn came out of her house and joined them, forming a long, slow procession through the village. Anton was alarmed to feel them closing ranks around him, their nubile bodies pressing against his, separating him from Soraya, now walking several yards in front with Emilia. He wanted to turn round and face the women, but they were pressing so close around him that he could hardly breathe; all he could do was keep on walking.

Their voices wove a net around him as they whispered among themselves. He could not understand the language they spoke, but the meaning of their words was not difficult to guess at. Their fingers brushed his body, their slender hands testing and pinching the firmness of his flesh, the palms of their hands smoothing over his back, appreciating the lithe curves of his body. Anton Kline was no stranger to women, and he had never in his life been afraid of the strength of their desire. Now, suddenly, he felt an urgent need to turn tail and run, and keep on running until Vokolitz was a long, long way behind him.

And then the real strangeness of this alien place struck him. Where were the men of this mountain village? Where were the old women, the children? What kind of village was it where all the inhabitants were beautiful, raven-haired young women, so alike that they might all be sisters?

He wanted to talk to Soraya, wanted to take her by the hand and lead her out of this sinister paradise, but now he was separated from her by the jostling women, whispering and giggling as they surged around him, pawing at him; caressing and arousing him in spite of his unease. One girl reached up and pulled his face down to hers, forcing her lips against his. Her breath tasted unnaturally sweet, like a mixture of violets and rosewater. He tried to push her away, but her strength amazed him. Seemingly without the slightest effort she held him fast, her companions laughing and sighing and chattering around him as her muscular tongue-tip probed the interior of his mouth, possessing him as a man possesses a woman.

At last she tired of her game and he was free of her, the nauseating sweetness of her lingering in his mouth as she licked her lips provocatively with the tip of her moist pink tongue. Struggling to extricate himself from the encircling crowd, he searched for Soraya. She was a long way ahead of him now, listening intently to something Emilia was saying. Could she sense nothing amiss behind the flawless façade of this too-perfect place?

'Soraya!'

She turned and held out her hands to him. To his surprise the group of women immediately parted to let him pass, and he put his arm about her waist, afraid to let her go.

214

'They are taking us to their guest house,' explained Soraya as Emilia led them towards a low wooden building. Atop the shingled roof, a weather-vane in the form of a silver crescent flashed white in the sunshine as the breeze caught it and spun it gently around.

Emilia pushed open the door.

'Wait. I must prepare the way.'

With that, she scooped up a handful of flower-petals from an earthenware pot outside the door and disappeared inside, strewing the petals on the beaten earth floor.

'Doesn't this place give you the creeps?' hissed Anton.

'Of course it does.'

'Then why not leave now, before things get any weirder . . .?'

She squeezed his hand tightly.

'I've told you why. Because I have to know. I'm just sorry I brought you here, it was selfish. You should leave now, Anton. If anything was to happen to you . . .'

'If you're staying, so am I. You can't kick me out of my own nightmare.' Anton looked the building up and down. 'I suppose you've noticed the weather-vane.'

'Another moon. This place is full of them. All the cottages have little silver crescents painted over the door, did you see?'

Emilia reappeared with a welcoming smile.

'All is as it should be. You may now enter.'

The flower-petals beneath their feet released a sweet, fresh odour as they followed Emilia down a short passageway into the warm twilight of the guest house, leaving the whispering crowd outside, their voices fading to a distant murmur.

'This is the room we have prepared for you.' She flung open the shutters, letting in the golden sunlight and a bouquet of fragrant flower scents. The room was simply furnished with a carved wooden bedstead and dressing-table, but as Anton glanced up at the ceiling he saw that it was decorated in the dark blue of a night sky, dominated by the silver globe of the moon.

215

Emilia laid a single white lily on the embroidered bed-spread.

'And now I shall leave you to rest.'

'But . . . I need to talk to you,' pleaded Soraya. 'There are questions I have to ask.'

'When dusk falls and the moon rises over the mountains, I shall return,' promised Emilia. 'There is much to tell you, and much for you to learn before the night of the full moon.'

Beth Fielding walked out of the bathroom with all the panache of a girl who knew her way around – which of course, she did. Gavin Pierce had not been the first of her conquests, and no doubt Sir Adrian Graveney would not be the last.

'Let me in, honeybunch,' she simpered. 'It's cold out here.'

Sir Adrian slid obligingly sideways and she slipped under the covers, making sure her companion got a really good look at the new bra and panties she'd bought especially for his benefit. She'd chosen a pretty black lace half-cup bra, that pushed up her small, round breasts and gave a wicked glimpse of her nipples, hard as hat-pegs from the icy-cold water she'd run over them with the shower-hose. The new panties were sexy too, black satin-edged with scarlet ribbon that led tantalisingly into the dreamworld between her well-toned thighs. She wondered how long it would take Sir Adrian to realise that her sexy black panties were open at the crotch . . .

'Come here, Beth. My, but you're a fine handful of a woman.' Sir Adrian made a grab for her breasts, squeezing them hard through the underwired lace. She smiled seductively. Actually, she didn't mind him playing a bit rough. She liked a bit of that sometimes. That had been one of the most irritating things about Gavin: he was such a wimp, he couldn't countenance the thought of a little pain, not even when she wanted him to do it to her. Mind you, he hadn't been as bad as that before he went to Ragzburg. Beth blamed it all on that Soraya woman, playing games with his head. Cow.

She snuggled up to Sir Adrian, and let him run his hands all over her backside, exploring the divine roundness she'd worked so hard to perfect in the gym. It felt nice. Sir Adrian was a real blue-blooded aristocrat, not like the other men she'd seduced. It had been a genuine pleasure offering herself to him in return for his promise to get her posted somewhere better than Borneo. It was her secret hope that, whenever Soraya Chilton came back from her extended leave, she'd walk in to the Department to find Beth Fielding sitting at Gavin's old desk. Wouldn't *that* be fun . . .

'Lovely firm breasts you've got,' observed Sir Adrian, wrestling with the clasp of Beth's bra. 'Pity they're so damned hard to get at.' Giving up the struggle, he reached into Beth's bra-cup and pulled out first one breast, then the other, so that they looked like twin sweatmeats on a confectioner's shelf. Two glacé cherries on little pyramids of whipped cream. He shuddered with anticipatory pleasure. So much to choose from. He hardly knew where to start.

As he took her nipple into his mouth, he enjoyed the sensation of Beth's practised fingers curling about his shaft. He felt good and randy today, and Beth was just the girl to give him what he wanted.

He slid his hand down Beth's belly and thrust a couple of fingers between her thighs, forcing her legs apart. He knew a pair of split-crotch panties when he saw them, and the mere thought of getting his fingers wet in Beth's honeypot made him almost come on the spot.

Beth gasped and wriggled as her lover's fingers penetrated her, thrusting through the scarlet gash in her panties and parting her fat, shaven love-lips. Oh yes, she liked it a bit rough sometimes.

'Do it to me, do it to me,' she panted as the strong fingers slid in and out of her with merciless precision, rubbing and pumping her towards a powerful climax.

Tonight at least, her enthusiasm was entirely genuine. She hadn't realised Sir Adrian was such a skilful and experienced lover. If she had, maybe she'd never have given Gavin bloody Pierce the benefit of her considerable talents.

Suddenly, he stopped. She opened her eyes and looked at him reproachfully. 'Honeybunch!'

He soothed her with a kiss, wriggling his fingers deep inside her and then sliding them out. He licked the clear, sweet honeydew from his fingers with relish.

'Tell you what, Beth, why don't *you* do it to *me*?'

She needed no second bidding. Sir Adrian had got her hotter than an August noon, and she was quickly astride him, stroking his prick and testicles as she prepared to take him inside her, then positioning him at the entrance to her womanhood. With a long, luxurious sigh, she sank down on the upraised spike of his cock, impaling herself in a delicious martyrdom.

It felt pretty good for him, too. He felt a touch guilty really, stringing her along like this. But she really was an appallingly ruthless little floosie, and her own worst enemy at that: the silly girl had fallen for his well-worn chat-up hook, line and sinker. Still, how was she to know that the Borneo posting had fallen through anyway, and that in a week's time the Foreign Secretary was having her packed off to Colombia?

In any case, he had more to think about than Beth Fielding's next career move. He had troubles of his own to occupy his mind. Even as Beth was sitting astride his member, her strong slim thighs pressed hard up against his hips, he was visualising his career ambitions spiralling down the drain.

Fat chance he had of making it to the House of Lords if Soraya didn't show up pretty damn soon. If Sutton and McKenzie's wild goose chase didn't produce results in the next week or two, the Foreign Secretary was going to start asking questions which even Sir Adrian Graveney, master of quick-witted deception, would find hard to answer.

No matter how he tried, he couldn't get the woman out of his thoughts. If she wasn't worrying him half to death, visions of her body were tormenting him into stubborn rigidity at all sorts of inconvenient moments. Yes, it was amazing how a woman like Soraya Chilton could screw up your life.

Soraya woke from sleep and rolled over to kiss Anton. He was curled up into a ball, still fast asleep. For a moment, she panicked, forgetting where she was and why she was here. What was this strange place, this place where it was as warm as springtime in the black heart of winter?

The shutters were still wide open, and the sky had now darkened to a patch of royal blue, dotted with the first stars. Sitting up in bed with her arms clasped round her knees, Soraya looked out at the coming night, and remembered. A shiver of fearful expectancy ran through her. It would soon be time.

Even as she sat there, gazing out at the gathering darkness, she could feel it. There was a power in this place, an intensity like the low hum of an electrical generator. This village was the centre of it all, the guardian of secrets which she must, at any cost, unlock. She could feel the sensual power vibrating through her, awakening her body to the familiar ache of unstoppable desire. How much greater would the power be tomorrow night, the night of the full moon?

Anton stirred beside her, and she slid down under the covers to join him.

'Where . . .?'

'Vokolitz. Don't you remember?'

'Vokolitz? I thought it was just a crazy dream.'

She caressed him and he held her tight, his warm strength radiating into her, his embrace reassuring and secure. He kissed her hard, pressing her against the swelling hardness at the base of his belly.

'So what do we do now?'

She snuggled close, and whispered in his ear: 'We have sex.'

In spite of himself Anton laughed, grabbing hold of Soraya and flinging her onto her back on the soft, down-filled mattress. He pinned her down by her arms, kneeling astride her slender nakedness.

'Do you know what you are?'

'Tell me.'

'You're the most beautiful woman I've ever set eyes on, Soraya Chilton. And I want you even more than I wanted you that first time, at the studio.'

'Let's fuck,' whispered Soraya.

He slid into her and she gave a little sigh of pleasure, her yearning senses at last satisfied by this longed-for coupling. She raised her hips to meet his thrust and they moved together, smoothly and silently, the only sound the quiet harmony of their breathing.

They had no need of words tonight. They had long since passed the point where spoken language could express their fears and their desires. They communicated now with the language of sensations, their kisses and caresses expressing the warm, sweet pleasure of their joining.

Anton bent to kiss her breasts, running his tongue over the smooth, flattened globes of firm, juicy flesh. She shivered with delight, her nipples growing stiffer still as the soft night-breeze played across the moistened flesh, thrilling it to new heights of sensation. Anton's scent was strong and spicy tonight, the taste of his need filling her being, making her dizzy with excitement.

Suddenly, Anton rolled sideways, taking her with him, and they were coupling like hungry animals, gasping and panting with lust as the thrusting grew faster, more urgent. Soraya felt hunger taking her over, urging her on to a frantic climax as she clasped her lover to her, so convulsively that her fingernails dug into the flesh of his naked back.

She shuddered as she came, receiving jet after jet of pearl-white seed as Anton pumped into her, his eyes closed at the very height of ecstasy. The world was spinning behind Soraya's closed eyelids, a mist of unreality veiling her consciousness; and she clung on to Anton for a long, long time, the steady thump-thump of his heart her only point of reference in a turmoil of uncertainty.

A whispered summons broke the spell.

'It is time, Soraya.'

Soraya opened her eyes to see Emilia standing alone in the open doorway. She was naked, her flesh ghostly-pale in the moonlight. Framed in the window, the night sky loomed black and cloudless, each star a clearly-defined pin-prick of light and the globe of the waxing moon a mere hair's-breadth from its zenith.

'You must come with me now. Alone. None but you shall see what I must show you.'

Emilia stretched out her hand, and Soraya freed herself from Anton's embrace, sliding quickly out of bed. Anton tried to follow, but Soraya kissed him and pushed him gently back onto the soft pillows.

'You can't come with me, but I'll soon be back, I promise.'

'You're joking, Soraya. I can't let you go alone. What if . . .?'

Soraya fixed him with a steely gaze that made his heart lurch suddenly.

'Do this one thing for me, Anton. There could be danger for us both if you defy her. Promise me you won't follow.'

'I . . . OK, yes, I promise.'

Anton watched in silent torment as Soraya took Emilia's hand and the two women walked out into the night, their bare flesh gleaming unearthly white under the star-filled night sky.

The women of the village sat naked in a circle on the ground, their faces upturned to the rising moon. They paid no heed to Soraya or Emilia as they entered the village square. They seemed far away, entranced.

'They seek the blessing of the moon,' explained Emilia. 'See how its light washes over them, soaking into

221

their flesh, bringing them a new strength and a new hunger.' She turned to Soraya, and her eyes were like glittering lumps of jet in a deathly-white face. 'You too have felt the hunger, haven't you Soraya? You too have been gifted with its terrible, wonderful strength.'

Soraya's hand trembled in Emilia's.

'Strange things have happened to me, things I cannot explain,' she replied. 'And now this village . . . There is so much I cannot begin to understand.'

'Be seated in the circle,' Emilia instructed her. 'Sit at its very centre, for Vokolitz is the centre of the power, and tomorrow night, when the full moon rises, you shall be its most powerful embodiment.'

Puzzled, Soraya sat at the centre of the circle. Emilia remained standing, her tall, pale figure like a living statue in the moonlight.

'You speak of a power . . .'

'The power, yes, Soraya. The power that has pursued you ever since the day of the eclipse in Ragzburg.' Noticing the look of surprise on Soraya's face, she smiled. 'Yes, we know about that day, Soraya. We know everything there is to know about you. As soon as your face was revealed to us in the waters of the crystal lake, we knew that you must be the one.

'Many years ago, Soraya, a woman from a village near Ragzburg was called to us. Few are chosen, but she had the power deep within her and nothing could quench it. Each full moon she was called to the hunt, to slake her thirst for pleasure. But this poor, misguided girl sought to fight the power. She met a man – an Englishman – and foolishly believed that by marrying him and going to England she could escape. She was very like you, Soraya Chilton.'

'That woman was Alicia Chilton,' said Soraya, softly. 'She was my great-great-grandmother.'

Emilia nodded. Her eyes were lowered, and she was tracing patterns with her bare foot in the dust.

'She was indeed. Alicia left us, but we knew she would return, for she was our sister. One year later, on the night of the full moon, she returned. The hunger was greater than ever within her, a raging, burning forest-fire that would no longer be denied. We begged her to listen to us, to forget her foolishness and return to us, but she paid us no heed. Her mind was made up: she was determined to rid herself of the power.'

Soraya leaned forward, fascinated.

'There is a way – a way to get rid of the power?'

Emilia gave a dry laugh.

'I see that you are indeed the true guardian of Alicia's spirit,' she observed. 'But beware the arrogance that leads to folly. Yes, there is a way; but it is a dangerous and terrible way. All who have taken that path have failed. And the penalty, sweet Soraya . . .' She looked up, and her eyes flashed a warning. 'The penalty for failure is destruction.'

Soraya's heart was thumping so hard that she was sure Emilia must be able to hear it. She glanced around, and saw that the other women were still gazing up at the moon, utterly enraptured.

'The sisters are preparing themselves,' said Emilia. 'Tomorrow night is the winter solstice and the night of the full moon. There will be great sport for those who hunger.' Her voice grew more animated. 'Listen to me, Soraya. The women of Vokolitz want for nothing. This is our paradise on earth. Our village is blessed with eternal youth, eternal springtime; we suffer no death, no pain, no fading of our beauty. Here, we have no need of men to protect us. And to answer our craving for pleasure, we have the nights of the full moon, when our strength and our desire mingle and there seems no end to our sweet, savage joy.

'It is indeed a tragedy that Alicia could not accept the blessing of her power. She might have been the greatest, the most accomplished of all our priestesses. If she could only have learned to accept her power as a blessing . . .'

'It is not a blessing. It is a curse,' countered Soraya. She was remembering that night at the apartment, when she had looked down at James's body and believed that she had killed him. 'And that is why I have come here, to you – to rid myself of the torment.'

Emilia fixed her with glittering eyes that seemed to search the very depths of her soul.

'Destiny has drawn you here, Soraya, not the force of your own will. I have already warned you, and I pray you heed my words. The danger is immense, the penalty for failure – death. Will you not stay here with us, in this place of eternal youth and springtime? Will you not accept the power – and the pleasure it offers?'

'I cannot. The last time it happened, I almost killed a man. What if, the next time, it is my lover Anton?'

Emilia shook her head in disbelief.

'One man is not sufficient for you, my dear Soraya. With us you will have many lovers, men who will serve you for one night before you cast them away and seek new prey. Your pretty boy Anton is an appetising morsel, I grant you, but he is nothing. Forget him. Join us and we will turn him free in the mountains. He will come to little harm. Join with us, Soraya. Forget this madness and accept what you are, what you have become. A daughter of the moon, a beautiful she-wolf of the sensual darkness.'

Soraya sat in silence for a long time. When she looked up, Emilia was again staring at her intently, as though willing her to give in.

'You know that I cannot.'

'Then I am bound to show you what fate has in store for you, Soraya Chilton. Come.'

Emilia took Soraya by the hand and led her out of the circle of women. They paid her no heed, their bodies white and still as polished marble.

Soraya and her guide crossed the village in silence, their bare feet sinking slightly into the cool, moist grass as they approached a tall, dark, octagonal building which stood apart from all the others. High on the roof glittered a silver moon and stars.

'This is our temple,' said Emilia as she turned the handle and pushed open the door. 'You may enter.'

Soraya stepped inside, momentarily dazzled by the bright white light which filled the vaulted chamber, pouring in through a circular opening in the high roof.

'Kneel and feel the power of the moon,' whispered Emilia. 'It is at its strongest here. On nights of the full moon, the brilliance of the light is almost blinding.'

But Soraya was scarcely listening to her guide. Her eyes growing accustomed to the light, she was staring straight ahead, at a grotesque tableau in the centre of the chamber. On a raised dais stood the life-size figure of a tall, muscular man, carved from a black stone with the metallic sheen of haematite. His upward-arching penis was massively erect, its tip sheathed with polished silver, and at his feet lay four carved wolves, their bellies bared in submission to their master.

Their wolf-headed, razor-clawed master, whose maw gaped open in a ferocious snarl, his teeth glittering fangs of yellowed ivory and his eyes two wine-coloured rubies.

'This is the shrine of our master, the moon-beast, source of all power, who heaps his matchless blessings upon us,' whispered Emilia in reverential tones. 'If you serve him well and accept his laws, he will bless you by strengthening the power within you tenfold.'

'And if I resist?'

'If you resist, Soraya, the beast will assuredly destroy you, as effortlessly as the winter wind bends and breaks a sapling on the mountain top.'

Soraya fell silent for a few long moments, listening to the pounding of her heart in her chest. But what task must she perform to break free that could be so terrible, so impossible to contemplate? She was a sensible Englishwoman, not a superstitious peasant. How could a stone statue possibly do her any harm?

'Tell me what I must do to be free of the power.'

'Forget this foolishness, Soraya.'

'Tell me.'

'Once in sixty years, the winter solstice falls on a night of the full moon. On that night, it is said that the statue will come to life, and none may approach in safety. She who would free herself of the power must couple with the beast. His sensual hunger is insatiable, Soraya; it destroys as it consumes – as long ago it destroyed Alicia.'

'But if I succeed, I shall be free?'

'If you fail, you will be destroyed.' Emilia's lips curved into a smile, but her eyes were cold and unforgiving. 'And your pretty boy Anton will become our prey. The women of Vokolitz will take the greatest pleasure in feasting on his soul.'

Chapter Thirteen

The telephone rang, and Sir Adrian surfaced unwillingly from sleep. Beth hadn't left until almost midnight, and after a marathon session like that he needed his beauty sleep. He glanced at the alarm clock with a grunt of annoyance: just after ten in the morning. Who the hell could be ringing him at this hour? Everyone who was anyone knew that Sir Adrian Graveney never rose before noon. It was just like being back full-time at the Department.

He picked up the receiver. 'Graveney.'

'Sir Adrian? It's Alistair McKenzie here. I thought I'd better give you a progress report.'

'Good God, man, what time do you call this? Couldn't it have waited till a more civilised hour?'

'Well yes, Sir Adrian – only Sutton and I thought you'd want to know.'

'Know what – you don't mean you've actually found Soraya Chilton?' He sat up in bed, suddenly very interested indeed. His life peerage was hanging in the balance. This could be its salvation.

'Er . . . sort of. We know she took the overnight sleeper to Ragzburg a few weeks back. She was travelling with a German by the name of Heinrich Zoll. Anyway, they parted once the train arrived and he hasn't seen her since. But . . .'

'Get on with it, man!'

'We've found the hotel where she was staying – nasty little rat-hole it is, too – and it seems she was visited by a man closely answering the description of Mr Anton Kline.'

'Kline! Excellent.' Sir Adrian mentally tried on the ermine-trimmed robes. They suited him very well indeed. 'So where are they now?'

'That's the trouble,' replied McKenzie uneasily. 'We're not sure.'

'What do you mean, not sure? They were there, in the hotel, what more do you need to go on?'

'Seems they hired a jeep a couple of days ago, and headed up into the mountains.'

'Then follow them.'

'It's ten below out there, there's a blizzard and the snow's nearly a foot deep,' he pleaded. 'All the roads into the mountains are closed.'

'I don't care how you do it,' snapped Sir Adrian. 'But if you haven't found them by . . .' he consulted his diary for the time of his next meeting with the Foreign Secretary, '. . . this time on Wednesday, you're both fired.'

He slammed down the receiver and mopped his brow with the sleeve of his pyjamas. Damn, damn and triple damn. That Soraya Chilton was getting dangerously close to being more trouble than she was worth.

In the guest house at Vokolitz, Soraya sat up in bed, watching the shadows lengthen as afternoon turned into evening. She could feel it happening already, the need rising inside her like a black tide as the sun sunk towards the far horizon.

Hunger. Listen to the hunger, let it pleasure you.

Already the tremors of sensual need were shaking her body, and their intensity frightened her. This place, this night, the strange statue of a man with the head of a wolf . . . How much more powerful would the hunger be tonight, as the full moon rose over Vokolitz?

'Try to explain, Soraya.' Anton put his hand on her shoulder, and for an instant she recoiled, fearing the touch of human warmth lest it arouse the fierce need for flesh with which she was battling. Not here. Not now. She took his hand and kissed the palm, folding over his fingers to keep the kiss safe, then curling her own hand over his. They sat like that for a little while before Soraya spoke. How much could she tell him? And how much could he take?

'I don't know where to begin. Tonight, my power is to be tested. You have to leave, right now. It may even be too late.'

'You keep telling me I have to leave, Soraya, but you won't tell me why. For God's sake, I thought we'd promised to share all the secrets.'

'OK, I'll try.' Soraya lay down beside Anton, putting her arm across his chest. 'But it sounds crazy. There's a statue in their temple. Tonight, when the moon rises, legend says it will come to life, and I must give my body to it, pleasure it. It's the only chance I have to rid myself of this cursed power. But if I fail . . .'

'Tell me, Soraya. I have to know.'

'They say they will harm you. Why stay here and face the danger, Anton? Why not leave now, while there's still a chance?'

Anton hushed her with caresses.

'I've told you before, if I'm going, you're coming with me. And frankly, I don't see what's to stop us just packing our bags and walking right out of here, this minute. This madness has gone far enough.'

'I can't. You know I can't. You've seen what happens to me.'

'Then we stay.'

He held her close, and the warm strength of him surged into her as the blood pumped round his body. She tried not to drink in the scent of him, the animal piquancy of sweat and sex. Tried so hard not to be aroused by her lover's skilful touch . . .

'Besides,' Anton added. 'I know how peculiar this place is, but honestly it still sounds like mumbo-jumbo to me. Living statues? Give me a break.'

Yeah, mumbo-jumbo. Of course it was, Soraya tried to

tell herself as her desire took over and she submitted to Anton's caresses. She couldn't dwell on the fear or the reality for long, because if she did, it would take over and then there would be nothing left but fear.

'No, no, we mustn't,' she murmured, but her protests were scarcely audible. She didn't want to have sex with Anton, mustn't give in to this desperate desire for him. The danger was too great. The voices were all around her, and their whispering seemed to drown out every other sound.

Sweet prey. Sweet prey.

She forced herself to blot out the sound, and returned Anton's kiss with tender passion. She so needed to feel him close, to understand that in this nightmare world where nothing was as it seemed, there was still something real, something true.

'Hold me,' she gasped as Anton's strong arms enfolded her. She wanted him to go on holding her all through this crazy night, to hold her until the first glimmerings of dawn hovered rosy over the mountains and once again, the danger was past.

He sank back onto the soft mattress, pulling her on top of him. Something inside Soraya's head was laughing madly, and she wanted to tell him: no, not this way. Tonight, I want you to be in control, I want you on top of me, denying this tide of power that's rising within me, drowning me in dark lust.

But she could not voice her fear. Lying there on top of her lover, she felt the seductive savagery of the moon-lust twisting and turning in her mind, confusing dream and reality. She had to fight to remember that this was not her prey; this was her lover Anton.

The moon. Without turning to gaze out of the window, she could feel its magnetic pull as it rose slowly, only just behind the crest of the mountains now. The sunset was a bloody stain on the blue-black sky, another innocent victim of the moon's hunger for flesh.

Instinctively she touched and stroked him, the tingling tips of her fingers hypersensitive almost to the point of pain as her nails raked the length of his belly with an automatic skill, leaving little white tracks that in seconds had turned a livid red.

Anton did not protest. He was mesmerised by her. Tonight, Soraya was more beautiful and more irresistible than he had ever known her. Silhouetted against the darkening sky, her body seemed more silky-smooth and sinuous than he could ever remember it, her limbs strong as iron as they held him pressed to the bed. He could not see her face, but her eyes seemed to glitter with a deep-red inner light, drawing him into her desire, awakening passions he could not question; only submit to with a joyful abandon.

Helpless as some forest creature, caught in the ecstatic, entrancing moment before the sharp teeth strike, Anton found himself swept along in Soraya's dangerous game. Dangerous? He had forgotten the meaning of the word danger, half-forgotten even who and where he was. All he knew was that the most beautiful woman in the world was sucking his cock, her needle-sharp teeth teasing and tormenting his shaft with a skill that made him want to cry out his joy.

And then she was straddling him again, pinning him to the bed with a vice-like grip as her womanhood imprisoned him, the soft wet flesh fitting snugly round his rigid member like an iron hand in the silkiest velvet glove.

Borne away on the tide of her lust, Soraya too was helpless, completely unable to fight the turmoil within her, the soul-deep urge to revel in the hot, white sexual energies that flooded into her from her lover's body.

Pleasure, Soraya. Feel the pleasure. Satisfy the hunger within you.

The strength in her was growing truly inhuman now, the urge to satisfy her hunger far wilder and far stronger than it had ever been. She was a rag-doll, shaken by the force of her own need. Hungrily she rode Anton's cock, forcing the pleasure from him as she ground her clitoris against the hard base of his shaft.

Her fingers raked his flesh again and again as the frenzy overtook her; but he did not struggle. He wanted it, wanted it all – even the sharp pain that knifed through him as Soraya's fingernails dug into the soft flesh of his belly. His eyes grew wide with a fascinated lust as she threw back her head and screamed the ferocity of her pleasure, the spasms of orgasm racking her body with wave upon wave of unbearable joy. It excited him so much that his balls tensed, sending powerful jets of semen spurting up his shaft.

As the pain and pleasure died away, the first glimerings of awareness began to seep back into Soraya's consciousness. She looked down at the figure on the bed, scratched and bloody. He seemed barely conscious, his eyes half-closed. She hardly recognised him.

Prey, Soraya. Again. Don't fight it. Destroy him for your pleasure . . .

Horrified, she sprang away. A thin white trickle of semen escaped from her love-lips. Anton – she had almost done the very thing that she had so feared.

Even as she backed away, the voices within her were whispering softly to her, urging her on. The desire for pleasure was a smouldering furnace in her belly, threatening at any moment to burst forth again into a raging inferno. And this time, Anton might not be so lucky.

Already understanding was ebbing away again, as lust fought to take control of her body. The wildness was in her and she must get away. A low whimpering filled her head, the sound of a suffering animal; and she realised with a shock that the sound was coming from her own lips. She backed away, towards the window where the first rays of moonlight were creeping into the room. She placed a hand on the sill, and as she looked down at it she saw that her nails were sharper, glossier, curving into talons of menacing crimson. Her fingers were tingling with an agonising insistence, itching for the work they longed to do again. The rending, the tearing, the unbearable savagery of pleasure.

She looked out into the night, trying desperately to ignore the delicious scent of her lover, lying in the bed behind her. Above the throbbing pulse of her heartbeat, the surging roar of the desire boiling and bubbling in her veins, she fought to remember the work she must do before sunrise.

She was a hair's-breadth from oblivion. She must do it, and do it now, before it was too late.

The voices called to her seductively from the still warmth of the night. *Sweet Soraya, our beloved sister. Come to us. The night is warm and welcoming with the scent of prey. Come to us, run with us . . .*

Something moved in the darkness, and Soraya followed it with her eyes as moonlight illuminated pale shapes moving in the darkness, hands reaching out to her and eyes glittering furnace-red. She felt something touch her arm and looked down to see a claw-like hand stretching in through the open window, gripping her wrist with sharp red talons.

It is not too late, Soraya. Come to us now, and paradise shall yet be yours . . .

An inhuman strength surged into her, and she wrenched her hand away. Turning to the dressing table, she picked up the lighted oil lamp and flung it out of the window into the gloom.

'Get away from me!'

The lamp hit the ground with an explosion of burning oil, and whitish shapes recoiled from the glare, retreating into the safety of the shadows. With a last backward glance at Anton, Soraya whispered her farewell.

'Forgive me.'

And then she was gone, leaping through the open window to land soundlessly on the ground outside. Seconds later she was running through the village, her bare feet padding silently on the soft turf as instinct led her towards the temple.

In the darkened, snow-filled side streets of Ragzburg, a man stood gazing up at the rising moon.

He started momentarily as a thin black cat darted from the shadows, in search of prey. Janos smiled. Cats would not be the only creatures out hunting tonight. On nights of the full moon, the mountains were full of the cries of the wolf-children.

The Englishwoman had thought she could ignore the power, believed in her arrogant naïveté that she could escape it. But no one could escape it. Tonight, she would be running with them in the mountains, her delectable naked body streaked with the sweat and blood of the night's conquests.

The Romany licked his lips, remembering the first time; the mountain-woman who had given him the deep scars he still bore today. Perhaps one day he would meet the Englishwoman again, and this time she too would bestow on him the mark of her savage love.

Taking the violin from its case, he lifted it and placed it carefully under his chin. He drew the bow lightly across the strings, and a plaintive music trembled from beneath his fingers: the ethereal cry of his yearning heart.

And from the mountains above Ragzburg came an answering music: the cry of a lone wolf, baying at the moon.

Eyes seemed to follow her, gleaming ruby-red and yellow from the shadows. All about her, the cries of the night-creatures rose to a baleful chorus, and she was howling with them as the whispers filled her mind, malevolent and frightening now.

Turn back, Soraya. He will destroy you. His power will tear you apart . . .

She had lost touch with the reality that was Soraya Chilton. Now she too was a creature of the night, a dark-spirited phantom racing through the darkness in search of prey.

The temple rose above her, dark and loathsome. She halted for a moment outside, and the moonlight washed teasingly over her like a cool waterfall, kissing the sweat from her skin as she drew in long, shuddering breaths of night air. Above her, the moon was riding high in the dark canopy of space, tormenting yet arousing her with its full, white, leering face.

She placed her hand lightly on the door handle and the door swung open without a sound, almost as though someone or something was expecting her, welcoming her in. She stepped through the door into the interior, and a ferocious energy seemed to gust out, buffeting and swirling around her.

Suddenly, all was darkness and silence. Soraya struggled to accustom her eyes to the gloom. There was a scent here – a scent of evil.

'And so I have you at last.'

The rasping voice seemed to fill the darkness. Heart pounding Soraya swung round to hear the heavy wooden door slammed shut behind her, obliterating the last vestiges of light. She looked up, but this time there was no circle of bright stars to comfort her. There was nothing but darkness, and the heavy thump of her heart.

'You are afraid?'

'I am afraid of nothing.'

Soraya fought to make out shapes in the shadows, trying to imagine the statue as she had seen it, tall and black and menacing.

'Would you like to see my face?' The tone of the voice was mocking. 'The face of your demon lover Azrael?'

A grating sound made her look up, to see the round panel in the roof sliding away, revealing a circular patch of night sky, now almost filled by the swollen disc of the full moon. The temple chamber was suddenly flooded with white light, and for a moment Soraya was blinded.

'Am I not beautiful, Soraya? Is my phallus not the most handsome you have ever seen?'

Her eyes growing accustomed to the light, Soraya looked again towards the statue, and saw it sculpted in light and shade by the dazzling moonlight, the powerful body of a young man transformed into a moving tableau of glistening black curves and hollows, obscenely crowned by the massive head of a wolf. His prick seemed impossibly huge and swollen, an instrument not of pleasure but of torment, its silver tip catching the light as the creature turned fiery red eyes on her, its most succulent prey.

'And so you dare to challenge the violence of my desire.' The wolf-creature's mouth was open in a snarl of contempt. 'But I can smell your fear, Soraya Chilton. It reminds me of the scent of another young woman who once challenged me, long ago. She failed, as you will fail.' He laughed, and Soraya trembled at the sight of the forked tongue between the yellowing teeth.

Trembled not only with fear, but with a perverse desire, burning and unquenchable. This creature was terrifyingly beautiful, his young man's body the glistening embodiment of sex, powerful and strong. She wanted him; and she wanted his submission.

He spoke again, and Soraya caught the rancid sweetness of his breath.

'Her flesh afforded me some small sport. I trust yours will not disappoint me too severely.'

'I do not fear you,' said Soraya, very firmly and distinctly, as though she were trying to convince herself that it was true.

'Then come to me, sweet little Soraya,' he taunted. 'Come and couple with me, and let me possess that ripe and fragrant flesh.'

The deep-red eyes of the man-wolf Azrael seemed to bore deep into her soul, reading all her secrets, mocking all her hidden terrors. His manhood jutted vast and threatening before her, a curving sabre daring her to match his lust with her own.

A cry filled the air: the high-pitched baying of a she-wolf, crying to her mate. And as Soraya screamed out the power of her desire, other voices answered: the wolf-children calling to their sister from the distant mountain-sides.

Moments later, she sprang; and he captured her in his powerful embrace, his claw-like fingers burying themselves in her flesh as he hoisted her aloft, to impale her on the merciless upraised spike of his glistening black penis.

As they coupled, fire flashed blue-white across the night sky; and suddenly, all was darkness.

Chapter Fourteen

Sir Adrian Graveney re-read the letter with satisfaction. In all honesty, he hadn't expected the life peerage quite so soon, but all things considered, this was a most pleasing outcome to a stressful episode.

It had been a close-run thing, but he'd managed to prevent the Foreign Secretary finding out any of the embarrassing details of the Soraya Chilton affair. In fact, Soraya and that Kline fellow had turned up just in the nick of time. It was six months now since Sutton and McKenzie had found them, lying naked and unconscious on a fire-scorched hillside near Ragzburg.

During intensive debriefing, they had come up with some confused nonsense about wolf-women and full moons, but under the circumstances that was only to be expected. Bizarre hallucinations and temporary memory loss were typical features of the type of subtle brainwashing at which Lukas Mankiewicz excelled.

Sir Adrian had no way of knowing exactly how long Mankiewicz had been playing games with Soraya's mind: possibly ever since their brief liaison in Ragzburg. Well, it was all over now and Mankiewicz wouldn't be troubling any more British agents, not since he'd been consigned to that nice cosy psychiatric hospital in the mountains.

There was really no need for Soraya ever to know that she'd been used in this way. The effects had clearly worn off and she seemed perfectly normal now, happily settled behind James's old desk and making a damned fine fist of it.

Sir Adrian's mind flew back to the fleeting dalliance he'd enjoyed with Soraya, over a year ago. That had been indecently good fun. Of course, now that she was in a position of high responsibility he felt duty bound to keep an eye on her, to check for any signs of recurring problems. He'd probably have to spend a lot of time getting close to her, maybe wine her and dine her a little – all in the line of duty, naturally. How remarkably tiresome it would all be.

Life can be such a bitch, thought Sir Adrian, smugly rubbing the swelling bulge in his pants. But it's OK, I can take it.

Soraya flung her briefcase into the far corner of Anton's new studio. It was almost six months now since she'd moved in with him, only a little while after that strange night at Vokolitz.

But they didn't talk about any of that, not now. Here in staid, respectable south-west London it seemed inappropriate and more baffling than ever. Vokolitz? It could all have been a bad dream. And perhaps that's all it ever was.

She stripped off and joined Anton in the shower, and they caressed as hungrily as if it was their first time. That was the great thing about sex with Anton: it just kept getting better and better.

'How about a little afternoon delight?' murmured Anton, his strong fingers rubbing lather between her parted thighs.

'I'm all yours.'

Without bothering even to rinse off the soap, he gathered her up in his arms and carried her, giggling, into the bedroom where he deposited her unceremoniously on the bed.

She lay there, naked and glistening in the afternoon sunlight, her skin lightly tanned against the whiteness of the bedspread, her desire for him hot and strong.

'I want you now,' she breathed.

And they sprang together like creatures possessed, the wildness of their lust surprising even them. The sun cast long, golden shadows across their moist flesh as they coupled with a joyful abandon.

When Anton gazed deep into Soraya's eyes, for a second he could have sworn he caught sight of twin reflections in their dark depths; the faraway, pearly discs of the full moon.

But that was impossible. And when he looked a second time, sure enough they had gone; melted away into the dark, deep pools of Soraya's lustrous eyes.

BLACK
lace

NO LADY
Saskia Hope

30 year-old Kate dumps her boyfriend, walks out of her job and sets off in search of sexual adventure. Set against the rugged terrain of the Pyrenees, the love-making is as rough as the landscape. Only a sense of danger can satisfy her longing for erotic encounters beyond the boundaries of ordinary experience.

ISBN 0 352 32857 6

WEB OF DESIRE
Sophie Danson

High-flying executive Marcie is gradually drawn away from the normality of her married life. Strange messages begin to appear on her computer, summoning her to sinister and fetishistic sexual liaisons with strangers whose identity remains secret. She's given glimpses of the world of The Omega Network, where her every desire is known and fulfilled.

ISBN 0 352 32856 8

BLUE HOTEL
Cherri Pickford

Hotelier Ramon can't understand why best-selling author Floy Pennington has come to stay at his quiet hotel in the rural idyll of the English countryside. Her exhibitionist tendencies are driving him crazy, as are her increasingly wanton encounters with the hotel's other guests.

ISBN 0 352 32858 4

CASSANDRA'S CONFLICT
Fredrica Alleyn

Behind the respectable facade of a house in present-day Hampstead lies a world of decadent indulgence and darkly bizarre eroticism. The sternly attractive Baron and his beautiful but cruel wife are playing games with the young Cassandra, employed as a nanny in their sumptuous household. Games where only the Baron knows the rules, and where there can only be one winner.

ISBN 0 352 32859 2

THE CAPTIVE FLESH
Cleo Cordell

Marietta and Claudine, French aristocrats saved from pirates, learn their invitation to stay at the opulent Algerian mansion of their rescuer, Kasim, requires something in return; their complete surrender to the ecstasy of pleasure in pain. Kasim's decadent orgies also require the services of the handsome blonde slave, Gabriel – perfect in his male beauty. Together in their slavery, they savour delights at the depths of shame.

ISBN 0 352 32872 X

PLEASURE HUNT
Sophie Danson

Sexual adventurer Olympia Deschamps is determined to become a member of the Legion D'Amour – the most exclusive society of French libertines who pride themselves on their capacity for limitless erotic pleasure. Set in Paris – Europe's most romantic city – Olympia's sense of unbridled hedonism finds release in an extraordinary variety of libidinous challenges.

ISBN 0 352 32880 0

ODALISQUE
Fleur Reynolds

A tale of family intrigue and depravity set against the glittering backdrop of the designer set. Auralie and Jeanine are cousins, both young, glamorous and wealthy. Catering to the business classes with their design consultancy and exclusive hotel, this facade of respectability conceals a reality of bitter rivalry and unnatural love.

ISBN 0 352 32887 8

OUTLAW LOVER
Saskia Hope

Fee Cambridge lives in an upper level deluxe pleasuredome of technologically advanced comfort. The pirates live in the harsh outer reaches of the decaying 21st century city where lawlessness abounds in a sexual underworld. Bored with her predictable husband and pampered lifestyle, Fee ventures into the wild side of town, finding an urban outlaw who becomes her lover. Leading a double life of piracy and privilege, will her taste for adventure get her too deep into danger?

ISBN 0 352 32909 2

AVALON NIGHTS
Sophie Danson

On a stormy night in Camelot, a shape-shifting sorceress weaves a potent spell. Enthralled by her magical powers, each knight of the Round Table – King Arthur included – must tell the tale of his most lustful conquest. Virtuous knights, brave and true, recount before the gathering ribald deeds more befitting licentious knaves. Before the evening is done, the sorceress must complete a mystic quest for the grail of ultimate pleasure.

ISBN 0 352 32910 6

THE SENSES BEJEWELLED
Cleo Cordell

Willing captives Marietta and Claudine are settling into an opulent life at Kasim's harem. But 18th century Alergia can be a hostile place. When the women are kidnapped by Kasim's sworn enemy, they face indignities that will test the boundaries of erotic experience. Marietta is reunited with her slave lover Gabriel, whose heart she previously broke. Will Kasim win back his cherished concubines? This is the sequel to *The Captive Flesh*.

ISBN 0 352 32904 1

GEMINI HEAT
Portia Da Costa

As the metropolis sizzles in freak early summer temperatures, twin sisters Deana and Delia find themselves cooking up a heatwave of their own. Jackson de Guile, master of power dynamics and wealthy connoisseur of fine things, draws them both into a web of luxuriously decadent debauchery. Sooner or later, one of them has to make a life-changing decision.

ISBN 0 352 32912 2

VIRTUOSO
Katrina Vincenzi

Mika and Serena, darlings of classical music's jet-set, inhabit a world of secluded passion. The reason? Since Mika's tragic accident which put a stop to his meteoric rise to fame as a solo violinist, he cannot face the world, and together they lead a decadent, reclusive existence. But Serena is determined to change things. The potent force of her ravenous sensuality cannot be ignored, as she rekindles Mika's zest for love and life through unexpected means. But together they share a dark secret.

ISBN 0 352 32912 2

MOON OF DESIRE
Sophie Danson

When Soraya Chilton is posted to the ancient and mysterious city of Ragzburg on a mission for the Foreign Office, strange things begin to happen to her. Wild, sexual urges overwhelm her at the coming of each full moon. Will her boyfriend, Anton, be her saviour – or her victim? What price will she have to pay to lift the curse of unquenchable lust that courses through her veins?

ISBN 0 352 32911 4

April '94

FIONA'S FATE
Fredrica Alleyn

When Fiona Sheldon is kidnapped by the infamous Trimarchi brothers, along with her friend Bethany, she finds herself acting in ways her husband Duncan would be shocked by. For it is he who owes the brothers money and is more concerned to free his voluptuous mistress than his shy and quiet wife. Alesandro Trimarchi makes full use of this opportunity to discover the true extent of Fiona's suppressed, but powerful, sexuality.

ISBN 0 352 32913 0

April '94

HANDMAIDEN OF PALMYRA
Fleur Reynolds

3rd century Palmyra: a lush oasis in the Syrian desert. The beautiful and fiercely independent Samoya takes her place in the temple of Antioch as an apprentice priestess. Decadent bachelor Prince Alif has other plans for her and sends his scheming sister to bring her to his Bacchanalian wedding feast. Embarking on a journey across the desert, Samoya encounters Marcus, the battle-hardened centurion who will unearth the core of her desires and change the course of her destiny.

ISBN 0 352 32919 X

May '94

OUTLAW FANTASY
Saskia Hope

For Fee Cambridge, playing with fire had become a full time job. Helping her pirate lover to escape his lawless lifestyle had its rewards as well as its drawbacks. On the outer reaches of the 21st century metropolis the Amazenes are on the prowl; fierce warrior women who have some unfinished business with Fee's lover. Will she be able to stop him straying back to the wrong side of the tracks? This is the sequel to *Outlaw Lover*.

ISBN 0 352 32920 3

May '94

Three special, longer length Black Lace summer sizzlers to be published in June 1994.

THE SILKEN CAGE
Sophie Danson

When University lecturer, Maria Treharne, inherits her aunt's mansion in Cornwall, she finds herself the subject of strange and unexpected attention. Her new dwelling resides on much-prized land; sacred, some would say. Anthony Pendorran has waited a long time for the mistress to arrive at Brackwater Tor. Now she's here, his lust can be quenched as their longing for each other has a hunger beyond the realm of the physical. Using the craft of goddess worship and sexual magnetism, Maria finds allies and foes in this savage and beautiful landscape.

ISBN 0 352 32928 9

RIVER OF SECRETS
Saskia Hope & Georgia Angelis

When intrepid female reporter Sydney Johnson takes over someone else's assignment up the Amazon river, the planned exploration seems straightforward enough. But the crew's photographer seems to be keeping some very shady company and the handsome botanist is proving to be a distraction with a difference. Sydney soon realises this mission to find a lost Inca city has a hidden agenda. Everyone is behaving so strangely, so sexually, and the tropical humidity is reaching fever pitch as if a mysterious force is working its magic over the expedition. Echoing with primeval sounds, the jungle holds both dangers and delights for Sydney in this Indiana Jones-esque story of lust and adventure.

ISBN 0 352 32925 4

VELVET CLAWS
Cleo Cordell

It's the 19th century; a time of exploration and discovery and young, spirited Gwendoline Farnshawe is determined not to be left behind in the parlour when the handsome and celebrated anthropologist, Jonathan Kimberton, is planning his latest expedition to Africa. Rebelling against Victorian society's expectation of a young woman and lured by the mystery and exotic climate of this exciting continent, Gwendoline sets sail with her entourage bound for a land of unknown pleasures.

ISBN 0 352 32926 2

BLACK
lace

WE NEED YOUR HELP . . .
to plan the future of women's erotic fiction –

– and no stamp required!

Yours are the only opinions that matter.

Black Lace is a new and exciting venture: the first series of books devoted to erotic fiction by women for women.

We're going to do our best to provide the brightest, best-written, bonk-filled books you can buy. And we'd like your help in these early stages. Tell us what you want to read.

THE BLACK LACE QUESTIONNAIRE

SECTION ONE: ABOUT YOU

1.1 Sex (*we presume you are female, but so as not to discriminate*) are you?

Male ☐ Female ☐

1.2 Age

under 21 ☐ 21–30 ☐
31–40 ☐ 41–50 ☐
51–60 ☐ over 60 ☐

1.3 At what age did you leave full-time education?

still in education ☐ 16 or younger ☐
17–19 ☐ 20 or older ☐

1.4 Occupation _____

1.5 Annual household income

      under £10,000 ☐   £10–£20,000 ☐

      £20–£30,000 ☐   £30–£40,000 ☐

      over £40,000 ☐

1.6 We are perfectly happy for you to remain anonymous; but if you would like us to send you a free booklist of Nexus books for men and Black Lace books for Women, please insert your name and address

_____

_____

_____

_____

SECTION TWO: ABOUT BUYING BLACK LACE BOOKS

2.1 How did you acquire this copy of *Moon of Desire*

    I bought it myself ☐   My partner bought it ☐

    I borrowed/found it ☐

2.2 How did you find out about Black Lace books?

    I saw them in a shop ☐

    I saw them advertised in a magazine ☐

    I saw the London Underground posters ☐

    I read about them in _____

    Other _____

2.3 Please tick the following statements you agree with:

    I would be less embarrassed about buying Black Lace books if the cover pictures were less explicit ☐

    I think that in general the pictures on Black Lace books are about right ☐

    I think Black Lace cover pictures should be as explicit as possible ☐

2.4 Would you read a Black Lace book in a public place – on a train for instance?

    Yes ☐   No ☐

SECTION THREE: ABOUT THIS BLACK LACE BOOK

3.1 Do you think the sex content in this book is:
   Too much ☐   About right ☐
   Not enough ☐

3.2 Do you think the writing style in this book is:
   Too unreal/escapist ☐   About right ☐
   Too down to earth ☐

3.3 Do you think the story in this book is:
   Too complicated ☐   About right ☐
   Too boring/simple ☐

3.4 Do you think the cover of this book is:
   Too explicit ☐   About right ☐
   Not explicit enough ☐

Here's a space for any other comments:

SECTION FOUR: ABOUT OTHER BLACK LACE BOOKS

4.1 How many Black Lace books have you read? ☐

4.2 If more than one, which one did you prefer?

4.3 Why?

SECTION FIVE: ABOUT YOUR IDEAL EROTIC NOVEL

We want to publish the books you want to read – so this is your chance to tell us exactly what your ideal erotic novel would be like.

5.1   Using a scale of 1 to 5 (1 = no interest at all, 5 = your ideal), please rate the following possible settings for an erotic novel:

Medieval/barbarian/sword 'n' sorcery   ☐
Renaissance/Elizabethan/Restoration   ☐
Victorian/Edwardian   ☐
1920s & 1930s – the Jazz Age   ☐
Present day   ☐
Future/Science Fiction   ☐

5.2   Using the same scale of 1 to 5, please rate the following themes you may find in an erotic novel:

Submissive male/dominant female   ☐
Submissive female/dominant male   ☐
Lesbianism   ☐
Bondage/fetishism   ☐
Romantic love   ☐
Experimental sex e.g. anal/watersports/sex toys   ☐
Gay male sex   ☐
Group sex   ☐

Using the same scale of 1 to 5, please rate the following styles in which an erotic novel could be written:

Realistic, down to earth, set in real life   ☐
Escapist fantasy, but just about believable   ☐
Completely unreal, impressionistic, dreamlike   ☐

5.3   Would you prefer your ideal erotic novel to be written from the viewpoint of the main male characters or the main female characters?

Male   ☐   Female   ☐
Both   ☐

5.4 What would your ideal Black Lace heroine be like? Tick as many as you like:

Dominant	☐	Glamorous	☐
Extroverted	☐	Contemporary	☐
Independent	☐	Bisexual	☐
Adventurous	☐	Naive	☐
Intellectual	☐	Introverted	☐
Professional	☐	Kinky	☐
Submissive	☐	Anything else?	☐
Ordinary	☐	_____	

5.5 What would your ideal male lead character be like? Again, tick as many as you like:

Rugged	☐		
Athletic	☐	Caring	☐
Sophisticated	☐	Cruel	☐
Retiring	☐	Debonair	☐
Outdoor-type	☐	Naive	☐
Executive-type	☐	Intellectual	☐
Ordinary	☐	Professional	☐
Kinky	☐	Romantic	☐
Hunky	☐		
Sexually dominant	☐	Anything else?	☐
Sexually submissive	☐	_____	

5.6 Is there one particular setting or subject matter that your ideal erotic novel would contain?

_____

SECTION SIX: LAST WORDS

6.1 What do you like best about Black Lace books?

_____

6.2 What do you most dislike about Black Lace books?

_____

6.3 In what way, if any, would you like to change Black Lace covers?

_____

6.4 Here's a space for any other comments!

_____

_____

_____

_____

Thank you for completing this questionnaire. Now tear it out of the book – carefully! – put it in an envelope and send it to:

Black Lace
FREEPOST
London
W10 5BR

No stamp is required!

1
BLAZE

Blaze Werla buried Ortman before breakfast. It was the fifth of July, and already the day was white hot. Blaze peeled off his T-shirt and tossed it on the hard ground. He shoveled quickly and furtively, making a small, neat hole the size of a basketball. When the digging was through, Blaze knelt, and using both arms and cupped hands, filled the hole back up, covering Ortman forever. There was something fierce about the manner in which Blaze worked—the determined line of his mouth, the tension that rippled across his back. Dirt stuck to Blaze's sweaty body like bread crumbs; his damp red hair clung to his forehead in ringlets. Blaze slapped the ground flat with the palms of his hands, making a thudding sound and remembering all the other burials, glancing at the nearby stones that marked them.

Burials. There had been four others before Ortman. (Not counting his mother's.) The small graves formed a partial ring around the huge black locust tree on the hill near the highway behind Blaze's house. First there had been Benny. Then Ajax. Next Ken. Then Harold. And now Ortman. Blaze wondered what he would do once the circle was complete. Where would he bury then? He was ten years old. Would he still need to do this when he was twelve? Fifteen? He hoped not. He was tired of being afraid.

Blaze stood and stamped the dirt over Ortman one last time. He picked up the stone he had chosen earlier that morning and held it for a few seconds, as if it were a large egg containing precious life. He had chosen the stone because of its markings: pale mossy blotches that looked like bull's-eyes. Blaze set the stone down firmly in place. "Goodbye, Ortman," he whispered. Blaze backed up, scratched the scars on his ankles with either foot, ran his dirty hand through his hair, and stared at the grave site until the crescent of stones blurred before him, becoming a broken pearl bracelet around the arm of a tree it bound.

□   □   □

On the way down the hill toward home, Blaze was already creating someone new in his mind to take Ortman's place. Someone who would be big. Someone who would be tall. Someone who would be fearless. Someone who would be everything Blaze was not.

2

Blaze was slight, with small feet and hands. He thought his fingers resembled birthday candles, especially compared to his father's ample, knuckly ones. At school, Blaze was the shortest student in his class. His identity with many kids from other grades hinged solely upon his size and his red hair. His hair was so distinctive, in fact, that passersby often turned their heads to take notice. His clear blue eyes had a similar effect on people. Freckles peppered Blaze's cheeks and the bridge of his nose. His eyelashes were full and as transparent as fishing line. And—he was fearful.

Blaze swatted at the leafy, waist-high weeds that surrounded him and thought, I am a contradiction—my name is Blaze and I'm afraid of fire. And fire was only the beginning of a long list of things that made Blaze's head prickle just thinking of them.

Fire. Large dogs. Wasps. The dark.

And then there were the other things. The more important things. The really frightening ones. Nightmares. The Ferris wheel at the fairgrounds. The Fourth of July.

Blaze fixed his attention on the drooping slate roof of his house in the near distance. "Come on . . . *Simon*," he said over his shoulder into the warm breeze. "Let's go eat."

◻   ◻   ◻

"Morning, Blaze," Nova called pleasantly when she heard the screen door open and gently close.

"Morning, Grandma," Blaze said, entering the

kitchen. He walked to the sink and began washing his hands methodically with liquid dish soap, making a thick lather that worked its way up his arms. Ortman's dead, he said matter-of-factly in his head, watching a tiny pinkish blue bubble rise from his hands. Now I've got Simon.

Blaze didn't believe in imaginary friends the way he truly had when he was younger. He didn't set places for them at the table or make himself as small as possible in bed to leave room for them. He didn't talk to them out loud when anyone might hear. But every July he formed a new one. It was habit as much as anything else.

In a way, he compared it to Nova's practice of saying "Rabbit, rabbit, rabbit" for good luck on the first day of each month. It had to be her first words spoken or else it didn't work. Nova was far from superstitious, and yet, if she forgot to say it, she seemed annoyed with herself all morning.

Blaze also compared it to the relationship his father had with God. Although he had told Blaze many times that he didn't really know what he believed, Glenn said that he prayed every now and then. He talked to God when no one else was around.

Glenn had his version of God. Nova had "Rabbit, rabbit, rabbit." And Blaze had Simon.

"Well, what can I get you for breakfast?" Nova asked mildly.

Blaze had been looking out the window toward the hill. He turned and faced his grandmother. "Scrambled eggs, please," he said. And Nova hummed while she

4

made them. At the stove, with her back to Blaze, Nova's wispy moth-colored hair looked just like a dandelion right before you make a wish and blow it. But nothing else about Nova was wispy. She was generous in both size and spirit.

Breakfast was Blaze's favorite meal of the day, and the kitchen was his favorite room in the house. Towels, pots, pans, and various other cooking utensils hung on hooks from the walls and ceiling, reminding Blaze of the buy-and-sell shop in town. Four wide windows let in enough sunlight to balance the clutter. In the early morning, the dramatic shadows of the suspended spatulas and ladles spilled down the flowered wallpaper like stalactites. Or were they stalagmites? Blaze could never keep them straight. He had confused them on his final science test of the school year only last month.

During the summer, Blaze always ate breakfast with Nova, just the two of them at the thick, round oak table. Nova unerringly sensed Blaze's moods; she knew when he wanted to talk and when quiet seemed to be what was needed. If Nova wasn't asking Blaze questions or maintaining a peaceful, necessary silence, she was humming (as she was now); that meant she was deep in thought. Blaze was certain that Nova's low murmuring that morning was due to the cucumber beetles she had been battling in her squash patch. Books and magazines on organic gardening were stacked on the counter by the sink like dirty dishes.

Humming. Then silence. Then only the sound of silverware playing against china.

"I don't know how you do it—getting up at this hour when you don't have to," Glenn said, suddenly appearing in the kitchen doorway.

"Hi, Dad," Blaze said with a start, surprised by Glenn's unusually early jump on the day. His eyes skated up to meet his father's. Ordinarily breakfast was long finished by the time Glenn made it out of bed.

"Morning, Glenn. Eggs today?" Nova asked.

"Just coffee." He padded barefooted across the cracking linoleum and reached for a mug from the cupboard. Glenn was tall and big-boned. His straight blond hair fell into his eyes and barely grazed his shoulders, hiding the ringed birthmark on the back of his neck. It was purple and looked like Saturn. When Blaze was mad at his father, he pretended that the birthmark meant that Glenn was really an alien from outer space. "So what's on the agenda for you two today?" Glenn asked, filling his mug. He sat at the table precisely halfway between Blaze and Nova.

"Cucumber beetles," Nova said. "I'm going to try to lick them with a mixture of vanilla and water. It's a trick I read about in one of my magazines," she added, working her fingers as if she held a spray bottle.

"And you?" Glenn said, looking at Blaze.

Blaze shrugged. "Nothing really."

Glenn rubbed his steel gray eyes and yawned, his wide

6

unshaven jaw opening and closing like a machine. "Want a ride into town? You could call someone from school."

"Nah," Blaze replied, wrinkling his nose and shaking his head.

"I'll take you to the lake or the park. Anywhere you want to go."

"The moon?" Blaze joked.

Glenn yawned and chuckled at the same time.

"I think I'll just mess around here," Blaze told him.

After rubbing his eyes again, Glenn massaged the space between his eyebrows. "Just don't think too much," he said slowly, turning his mug on the table and winking. "It's not good for you." He rose with his coffee and headed toward the back door. He stopped at the sink and leaned against it momentarily. "Oh, by the way . . ." he said. He thrust his hand deep into his pocket and pulled out something small. He flung it gently across the tabletop. It was an old rusty skeleton key. It stopped right beside Blaze's plate, kissing his fork. "I found it yesterday," Glenn said. "For your collection."

"Thanks," Blaze answered. He watched Glenn disappear down the hallway, the key floating on the fringe of his vision. His ankles itched. Blaze knew that Glenn wouldn't give him keys if he knew why he saved them.

But here was a new one. Right before him. An ancient thing. It might be my best one yet, Blaze thought. The key's sharp metallic scent tickled Blaze's nostrils. He scooped it up and fingered it, and it seemed to burn in

7

his hand. Blaze wondered who it had once belonged to, what lock it would release, whose door it might open.

◻   ◻   ◻

It would be a typical July day. Glenn would spend it in the sagging garage that he had converted into a studio, emerging at dinnertime flecked with paint of all colors. Then he'd return and work again until very late, maybe until dawn. Unlike most fathers, Glenn was home all day in the summer. He was a high-school art teacher who devoted his entire vacation to painting large canvases that Blaze liked, but didn't quite understand. Nova would bustle about the kitchen and her garden—concocting, canning, weeding, pruning, and trying to exterminate cucumber beetles for all time. And Blaze would wander throughout the house and around the hill, occasionally talking to someone that no one else could see.

And it would be a typical July night for Blaze. In bed, he would will himself not to dream. Or, at least, not to remember his dreams when he awoke. He would take the library book from his nightstand, open it halfway, and place it beside him to look as if he had been reading. His mason jar filled with his lost key collection would be on the floor within reach. Then, his lamp still on, Blaze would settle in among his nest of four pillows, wishing and waiting for morning light.

2
BLAZE

When Blaze woke up the next morning his chest ached with strangeness. He had been dreaming. It was a dream he had had before. In it a maze of black snakes burst into flames at his feet while he struggled to open a door. The door was held tightly closed by a series of locks. His mother's voice came from behind the door. Sometimes in the dream he would have a key. But even when he did, it would never work.

Don't think about it, Blaze told himself.

His dreams were always so vivid during the summer. He might not remember having a dream for months, but come July they would return. It was peculiar the way that worked.

Blaze blinked and looked around. His room focused about him, becoming familiar and touchable. The library book from the night before was now closed and neatly placed on his nightstand, his bedside lamp turned off. Although he had never actually seen Nova or Glenn do these things, he had often sensed a presence—passing as a shadow, removing the book, turning off the light, tugging the bedclothes up under his chin, touching his forehead, pulling the door closed.

Blaze sat up and swung his legs out from under the sheet. It was dawn. A gust of wind caused the loose window screen to flutter and the faded plaid curtains to balloon and collapse. The curtains had worn thin in many places and were at least as old as Blaze. So was the large, multicolored oval rug that covered most of the floor. But nearly everything else was relatively new in comparison. The bookshelf, the bed, the nightstand, the dresser. Blaze could still remember the old blue-striped wallpaper, but now the walls were white. He had picked the paint himself. Snowflake, it was called on the paint chart.

It was several summers earlier that Glenn had urged Blaze to redecorate his room. "I could paint the solar system on your ceiling," Glenn had suggested. "And we could buy some of those neat glow-in-the-dark stars to stick on." Glenn paused, tapping his fingers on his chin. "We could redo the walls, too. This wallpaper's not the greatest. We'd have to clean this place out first, though. Get rid of some of this old baby stuff." As he spoke,

10

Glenn gestured vaguely toward the toys, knickknacks, and books that crowded Blaze's shelves, drawers, closet, and the dusty space under his bed. Things he had long outgrown. "What do you think?"

Blaze was looking at his prized possession—a plastic Noah's ark replica—perched atop the low overstuffed bookcase. "Okay," he answered reluctantly, not wanting to disappoint Glenn.

"Great!"

"But can I keep my ark?" Blaze's voice was urgent.

Glenn hugged him. "Of course," he said into his son's red hair.

Blaze picked the ark off the shelf and clutched it tightly. "And can we just paint the walls and ceiling white? No solar system?"

"You bet," said Glenn.

Blaze figured that the lighter the walls and ceiling were, the lighter his room would be at night.

Blaze still had the ark. He kept it tucked safely under his bed. Out of sight if a friend from school came over. Now he pulled it out and brought it to the window. Resting one end of it on the sill, he held it in place with his stomach and drew open the curtains to glance at the hill. He did this every morning. But that morning there was something different. Something very strange. Something so strange that Blaze stepped back from the window in surprise, causing his ark to fall. It cracked in half at his feet, little animals scattering across the floor like the pieces of a shattered glass.

11

◻   ◻   ◻

A chill hit Blaze in the small of his back and spread to his neck. Written with stones on the broad, mowed stretch of the hillside was the word REENA. Blaze felt hazy and anxious. His heart rattled. He closed his eyes and counted to ten before opening them again. Nothing had changed. Squinting, Blaze leaned on the windowsill, his nose pressed to the screen, then pulled back. The word was still there. It seemed to fill the window. The window seemed to fill the room. Blaze was smaller than ever.

REENA.

"Who did this, Simon?" Blaze whispered. His first thought was to wake Glenn, but something deep and instinctive led him in another direction. Temporarily forgetting about his ark, Blaze slipped into some shorts, a T-shirt, and shoes. His hands shook, fumbling with his laces and getting tangled in the folds of his shirt. But, once dressed, he managed to move quickly and quietly so as not to wake anyone—melting down the stairs, tiptoeing throughout the house, and then pushing up the hill with all his might.

When Blaze stopped, he was gasping for air. He doubled over—hands on knees—and tried to breathe evenly. His breath felt warm on his skin. He lifted his head. The letters were enormous up so close. Impulsively, Blaze shoved stone after stone aside with his feet, scrambling them so no one else could read the word. A few he heaved with his hands; they tumbled down the slope. A round and smooth stone with green rings on it caught his attention. It looked exactly like the stone he had chosen to mark Ortman's grave. He examined it closely. Recognized it.

"Oh, no," Blaze said, stunned all over again. The sky and the grass changed places in his vision as he raced for the black locust tree. After stumbling twice, he used his hands in an animal-like fashion to help him move without falling.

He wanted to cry. His stones were missing. All five of them. Whoever had written REENA had used them to help construct the letters. Blaze circled the tree a number of times, raising a cloud of dust. Then he sat resting against it, thinking. Waiting. Without the slightest idea of what to do next. A group of crows swooped down nearby. They strutted in a chaotic formation, their calls long and raucous. In a sudden beating of glossy black wings, they took off again. Up, up, up they flew, and Blaze watched, feeling as if he were sinking.

3

BLAZE

Blaze spent the morning in his bedroom, feeling unconnected. He was fixing his ark with Elmer's Glue. While he waited for the glue to dry, he gathered the small animals he had dropped earlier and played with them—first grouping them by color, then lining them up in a row. He held a memory of doing this with his mother, Reena. He remembered placing the pairs of animals—elephants, giraffes, bears, sheep—on one of the inner braided coils of the rug in his room, following the rug's contour, curving the line of the procession until it formed an oval. Reena and Blaze in the middle. Now there was only one of each plastic animal. When Blaze was five and Reena died, he took one animal from each pair and smashed them with a brick behind the house. Because the ark was his favorite toy and he wanted to punish himself somehow. Because a pair of anything didn't seem right.

Periodically, Blaze peered out the window, turning his gaze from left to right, checking for another message in stone. He was continually relieved when he found only the remains of the first, still strewn haphazardly across the hill like popcorn on a theater floor. Who did it? He kept asking himself that question. And he kept coming up with no answer. Although Blaze knew in his heart that neither Nova nor Glenn had done it, he toyed with the possibility.

Nova. She rarely left the house or garden, except to go grocery shopping. It was unusual for her to complain, but Blaze knew that by the end of the day her thick legs were puffy and sore. She often had to elevate them with pillows. Once, she said she had the legs of a ninety-year-old woman, even though she was only sixty. Her legs reminded Blaze of maps—bumpy blue veins connecting feet to knees like crooked highways. When he was younger, Blaze had found comfort in running his fingers over the bulging veins. Compared to them, the scars on his ankles seemed insignificant. The pinkish skin on his ankles was rippled, as if tiny worms were trapped underneath. It was as if twisting snakes were trapped under Nova's skin. Her legs didn't stop her from cooking and gardening with a passion, but trudging up the hill and

rolling stones around to spell the name of her dead
daughter was surely the last thing she would do.

And Glenn? It wasn't his style. Glenn was a private
person. And anyway, it was hard enough to coax him
from his studio for dinner or a telephone call on a summer day. Blaze knew he wouldn't take time away from
his painting to do something like this.

Who then?

Not his classmates. None of them lived this far out in
the country. (Blaze was the first one picked up and the
last one dropped off by the bus each school day.) And
although Blaze didn't have a best friend, he was treated
with genuine fondness by students and teachers alike.
He was smart, but not the smartest. Shy, but not the
most shy. He was ninth fastest in his class. And he was
considered by some to be the best artist in the entire
school. He could draw nearly any popular cartoon character upon request.

There were only two fellow classmates that Blaze
didn't like—Teddy Burman and Chelsea Kurz—but they
both liked him, so they were out of the question. Teddy
was a tiresome braggart and Chelsea was a tireless
brown-noser.

At Alan B. Shepard Elementary, Blaze was often
called Big Red (a nickname that didn't bother him at
all), even by Mr. Wiebe, the principal, who'd always try
to ruffle Blaze's hair if he spotted him among the noisy
throng that paraded past his office on the way to and
from recess.

Floy Stark was a possibility, but a vague one. She lived alone on the other side of the hill in a tidy, boxlike house the color of celery. She was about Nova's age, maybe younger. Sometimes Blaze lay on the hill and watched the Stark house. Nothing interesting ever happened. Floy did ordinary things like hang laundry on the clothesline, wash windows, cut the grass, and play fetch with a terrifying German shepherd she called Gary (who was, thank goodness, usually chained safely to the garage). That was about it.

Blaze couldn't think of anyone else. "Help me, Simon," Blaze said, flopping onto his bed like a fish. Pressed into his hand was a tiny plastic bird, wings outstretched, anticipating flight. He lay on his back, staring at the ceiling, trying to weave a plan. And remembering.

□   □   □

Soon after Reena died, Blaze, Nova, and Glenn went to a therapist together. Blaze couldn't remember how many sessions they had gone to, but he would never forget how uncomfortable he felt at them. "She looks at me like I'm an ant on a stick," Blaze told Glenn and Nova meekly, after what turned out to be their last session. They were walking across the parking lot toward their car. Blaze inhaled deeply, so happy to be out of Dr. Zondag's office. He sniffed his sleeve; the lemony smell of the office still lingered and he waved his shirttail in the air.

Glenn and Nova shared a long glance.

"It's really important to talk about things, you know," Glenn said cautiously, leaning against the car, jingling his keys.

Blaze nodded. He waited for Glenn to unlock the door, then crawled into the backseat. The late afternoon sun spilled into the car, creating sharp-edged shadows. Blaze moved his hand in and out of the warm light.

They stopped at a drive-in restaurant on the way home. Before they ordered, Glenn turned in his seat and leaned over toward Blaze. His head was touching the roof of the car, pulling his hair to one side as if he had slept on it funny. "We don't have to go back," Glenn said slowly. "But you have to promise that you'll always ask me anything you want to. Even if you think it's silly or stupid. I want you to always be able to talk to me." Glenn ran his hand along the back of Blaze's neck and rested it on his shoulder. "Mom would want it that way."

Semis and cars rolled by on the highway while they had dinner. Blaze ate nearly half of his hamburger and he almost finished his junior chocolate shake—something he had never done before. He slurped his shake so quickly he got a headache. The pain thrilled him and he tried it again, egged on by his sense of relief.

As they pulled out of the driveway and threaded into the stream of traffic to go home, Glenn said, "Nothing's too big or too small to tell me or ask me. You know that."

18

□   □   □

Blaze *did* know that. And yet he couldn't bring himself to tell Glenn about what he had seen on the hill that morning. For several reasons.

First, he was beginning to wonder if he had only imagined it or dreamed it. (That's what he wanted to think.)

Second, if it hadn't been a dream, would Glenn believe him anyway? Considering that Blaze had already jumbled the stones so that the hill looked as it always did?

Third, he was still shy when it came to talking about Reena with Glenn sometimes, even though he knew that he shouldn't be. Sometimes his unspoken words were almost tangible, he was so close to talking. Sometimes he stopped himself because he didn't want to take a chance on making Glenn sad. Blaze had seen Glenn cry once when Reena was ill. It had made Blaze feel as small as a dot and completely afraid. Now and then Blaze heard Glenn and Nova talk about Reena in what Blaze thought were sad, hushed voices. Of course, Glenn said things about Reena to Blaze, remembered things with him, but Glenn always initiated the conversations. That was the difference. Blaze didn't want to ask or say something about Reena if he couldn't be absolutely certain that the time was perfect and that Glenn would want to talk about her. Even at school if Blaze didn't understand something, he'd often try to figure it out by himself rather than raise his hand and ask a question.

And then there was the other reason. The eerie thought he was trying to suppress. The thought that his mother was somehow responsible for writing her name on the hill outside his bedroom window.

It was then that Blaze decided to handle this thing on his own. (With Simon, of course.) Maybe he hadn't been able to ride the Ferris wheel on the Fourth of July. Again. But this was surely a way to prove his bravery. He would get to the bottom of this. Blaze didn't want to be afraid anymore.

4
JOSELLE

Joselle Stark dried her eyes with the back of her hand. "No, I'm *not* crying," she called fiercely. She was crouched on the ivory wicker clothes hamper in her grandmother's narrow bathroom. She wound her arms tightly around her knees and rocked back and forth. The hamper creaked and sagged in rhythm.

"Joselle? What are you doing in there?"

"I'm coming, Grammy!" Joselle scooted down and looked at herself in the mirror on the back of the door. I'm a mess, she thought, sniffling. Her dark brown hair hung in tangled strands around her face, one untamed clump falling over her right eye. "I wish my hair would cover my *mouth*," she muttered, flipping her hair back.

21

Joselle's teeth were perfectly shaped, but they were sizes too big for her mouth. In fact, her teeth were so big, it took a conscious effort on Joselle's part to keep her mouth closed. Piano keys, she called them. And she had the nervous habit of bringing her hand up to her mouth, pretending to play a tune on her teeth, humming as she did.

Joselle wasn't fat, but her knees and elbows were dimpled like a baby's, and her arms and legs looked meaty. She was wearing an extra-large raspberry sweatshirt with the sleeves cut off; it hung to her thighs. The circles under her eyes matched her clothing in color. Joselle knew that her grandmother's eyesight wasn't terrific, but she knew that her grandmother wasn't blind, either. She hoped her grandmother wouldn't be able to tell that her eyes were bloodshot. Joselle stuck her tongue out at herself in the mirror. She flushed the toilet for effect, unlocked the door, and marched into the hallway, her red rubber thongs slapping crisply against her feet.

"What were you doing in there, sweetie?" Floy asked.

"Grammy, you're old enough to know what goes on in a bathroom," Joselle replied, walking away, an agonized look on her face.

"I'm also old enough to know when someone's been crying." Floy grabbed Joselle by the shoulders and spun her around. Floy was strong, despite her petite size, her grip unflinching. "You *were* crying." She drew Joselle against her chest. They were so close, Joselle could feel two heartbeats.

Joselle started to cry again. "I hate and despise my mother," she sobbed into her grandmother's sleeveless lavender shift.

"I know, I know," Floy soothed. "Come to the sofa. Let me do your eyelids."

Floy settled into the low end of the worn velour sofa and Joselle lay down, her head on her grandmother's lap, her eyes closed firmly. Although their visits were seldom and sporadic, the instant Floy touched Joselle's eyelids it was as if they had never been apart. "I've done this for you since you were a baby," Floy said.

"Since forever," Joselle whispered.

"Relax," Floy said, as she gently stroked Joselle's eyelids over and over. "Your eyelids are the color of my needlepoint lilacs."

Joselle couldn't have cared less about lilacs. Or needlepoint. Her mother had abandoned her. The Beautiful Vicki had taken off with her boyfriend Rick to "get away to try to be happy for a while without any interruptions." The more Joselle thought about it, the more upset she became. Her body shook; tears slid down her cheeks.

Her mother had done stupid, impulsive things before, but this was by far the worst. And the stupid, impulsive things usually had to do with men. Life would be going along just fine until The Beautiful Vicki became interested in someone new. As her interest escalated, so would her time away from Joselle and so would her rash behavior. Before Rick, Vicki had been involved with a man named Bert. This was late last summer. Bert had come into the restaurant where Vicki worked and charmed her completely. Bert was all she could talk about. It wasn't long before he moved in.

Before Bert, Vicki and Joselle had watched "The Mary Tyler Moore Show" in reruns every weekday night after the ten o'clock news. Since it was summer, Vicki didn't mind if Joselle stayed up so late. It became ritual. Every night "Mary Tyler Moore." Every night cream soda. Every night microwave popcorn sprinkled with Parmesan cheese. Every night Vicki and Joselle sprawled on the futon, the little electric fan turning side to side, cooling them off as they licked their cheesy fingers clean and laughed at Mary Richards and Rhoda Morgenstern. Every night the hypnotic light of the television flashing across the walls of the dark, dark room like a fire in a cave.

"This is my all-time favorite show," Vicki would say.

"We could watch it all night," Joselle would add, scooching closer to her mother. "If it was on all night."

But as soon as Bert came, everything changed. No more "Mary Tyler Moore" (he preferred "M*A*S*H" and Vicki let him watch it). No more microwave popcorn with Parmesan cheese and cream soda alone with Vicki. No more comfortable routine.

"He helps pay for the groceries and the electric bills," Vicki would tell Joselle. "And besides, he makes me happy."

"He doesn't make *me* happy," Joselle would counter. "And you hardly spend any time with me anymore."

"I've spent more time with you than with any-one—nearly my whole life."

"What about 'Mary Tyler Moore'? You even said it was your favorite show."

"So I changed my mind." Vicki sighed, exhaling frus-tration, losing patience quickly. "'M*A*S*H' is real. Watch it—you might learn something."

Joselle was ecstatic when Bert finally moved out about four months later. In a matter of weeks, things settled back to the way they had been, and Joselle and Vicki's spats were few and far between. But then Rick entered their lives, and the cycle began repeating itself.

A small part of Joselle seemed to understand what made Vicki change from being the mother she loved to being the mother she didn't. But she was always unpre-pared when it happened. Joselle brought her hand up to her mouth and began playing "Strangers in the Night" on her teeth.

"Listen, it won't be so bad," Floy said, competing with the melody. "I'm sure your mother will be back soon. You'll like it here. And anyway, it could be worse—that little Werla boy from around the hill doesn't even *have* a mother."

Suddenly Joselle stopped humming and crying and trembling. She sat up and stared at Floy with great as-tonished eyes. "You mean that skinny redhead I saw sit-ting on the hill this morning doesn't have a mother."

Floy nodded.

"Tell me, tell me," Joselle demanded, snatching her

25

grandmother's hands and squeezing them like sponges. She hoped that the skinny redhead's life story would be worse than hers. She hoped that it would be absolutely dreadful.

□   □   □

Joselle listened hungrily. She hung on Floy's every word until even the smallest incident blossomed into full tragedy in her mind. And there was tragedy enough, with or without the aid of Joselle's imagination.

The boy's name was Blaze Werla. And his mother had died when he was just five years old. Of cancer. "Her name was Reena," Floy said, doing Joselle's eyelids again. "She was so young."

Reena. Joselle liked the sound of the name. She thought it was kind of exotic and sexy. She repeated it softly, drawing out the long E sound like a bird call. *Reeeeena.*

"She died in the middle of the summer," Floy continued, "when it was hot and muggy. She had long, thick red hair, and I remember thinking how sad it was when she lost it."

"Lost her hair?" Joselle said, her eyes widening.

"From the treatment. Chemotherapy, it's called," Floy explained. "It made her hair fall out. She wore pretty scarves then. Bright ones. The last time I saw her, she was resting on a lawn chair in their yard wearing a chartreuse scarf that was knotted at the top of her head."

26

Joselle imagined the scene: The exotic and sexy Reena was so thin you could practically see every bone in her body. Blaze, her tiny son, was weeping hysterically, picking clumps of her hair off the ground and stuffing them into his pockets. The confused husband (who Joselle knew *nothing* about) was hiding behind a nearby bush staring into space like a lawn ornament.

Floy sighed deeply, regaining Joselle's attention.

"Go on, Grammy," Joselle ordered.

"Oh, sweetie, let's talk about something else. Let's talk about something happy."

"If we did that, I wouldn't have anything to say."

"Oh, Joselle!"

"At least tell me more about the boy," Joselle said in her best supplicating voice.

"Well," Floy said, shrugging, "he's quiet and small and he's about your age. He looks a lot like his mother to me. I remember about a year after Reena died, there was an accident at the fairgrounds. A fire. He burned his legs on the Fourth of July and spent the rest of that summer wrapped in bandages up to his waist. Poor little thing. Of course, he's fine now. I don't really know him, but I see him alone up on the hill a lot. From my window. He must like it up there. So you see," Floy added, "you're not the only one with a complicated life."

"What's that mean? Complicated?"

"Oh, I don't know. Confusing, I guess. Mixed up." Floy took her glasses off and cleaned them in her dress. "But enough of him. Let's talk about you."

27

"No way," Joselle replied quickly, getting up and clapping her hands. She was thinking about the word *complicated*.

"Well, then, why don't we unpack your bags and get your things organized?" Floy suggested cheerfully. "I'm just so glad you're here with me."

Joselle wanted more details (What about the funeral? What about the father? Did he remarry? What did Blaze's legs look like when they were burned? What did they smell like? What did they look like now?), but she figured that she'd work them out of Floy eventually. And the things that Floy wouldn't reveal or had forgotten or didn't know, Joselle would simply have to make up. And they would be the most awful things of all.

5

JOSELLE

Joselle paced about Floy's small house, surveying every corner like a cat. Since she was going to be staying here for a while, she needed to reacquaint herself with the way things looked, smelled, and felt. Joselle moved from room to room, shoving chairs and floor lamps an inch or two in random directions, leaving her mark. She rearranged Floy's Hummel figurines, turning some so that the backs of the children's heads with their odd peaks of hair faced outward.

"Just be careful with those," Floy warned, hovering over Joselle's shoulder, referring to the Hummels. "They're worth money."

Joselle discovered Floy's nail polish, and they took

29

turns painting each other's fingernails and toenails. Joselle was intrigued by the names of the colors: Rambling Rose, Cherub Frost, Iceberry. She wanted each nail to be a different color, but Floy didn't have that many bottles and some were empty.

"You look racy, Grammy," Joselle said, having a giggle fit.

When their hands and feet had dried, Floy made popcorn and Joselle strung the kernels with a needle and thread, making necklaces. The necklaces reminded Joselle of Hawaiian leis, and the popcorn reminded her of her mother. Joselle laced the garlands around her neck and did a rhythmic hula dance for Floy. Floy found it humorous until Joselle carried the joke to extremes, bumping her rear end into the furniture as part of her dance. Joselle gyrated until she became dizzy, falling into an end table. One of Floy's Hummels—a round-faced girl gazing dreamily at a book—wobbled and nearly fell.

"That's enough," Floy scolded. "And those popcorn necklaces are making grease stains on your shirt."

Joselle blushed with shame. "Leave me alone," she snapped, her eyes pinpoints of anger. She tramped to the front window and rolled herself into the drape. She stared blankly out the window, twizzling a strand of her hair.

After dinner, at the window again, Joselle noticed movement on the hill. It was the red-haired boy. Blaze Werla. Joselle watched him intensely until the window turned blue with the onset of night.

□   □   □

Later, on the sofa that was her bed now, Joselle regretted the meanness that she had shown Floy. At that moment she loved Floy more than anyone. "I'm sorry, Grammy," she whispered into the lonely night. The only one who heard her was Gary, Floy's German shepherd. He trotted over to Joselle from the kitchen, his tail wagging like a wind-up toy. He rested his head on her pillow, and she kissed him between the eyes. After a reciprocal lick, Gary folded himself up into a knobby sack on the floor beside her.

Gary's hairy body and pointy ears made Joselle think of her mother's boyfriend Rick. She wondered where the two of them were. How far they had driven. How long it would take before they wrote or called.

It had only been a few days since The Beautiful Vicki had informed Joselle that she needed a vacation. And Joselle would never forget that fateful day. Joselle had taken a felt-tip marking pen and drawn black stripes along the edges of her teeth to make them look even more like a real piano keyboard. "Look, Vicki," she had said to her mother excitedly. "You know, the black keys." Joselle pointed to her mouth and opened wide to reveal her handiwork.

"God, Joselle," Vicki had replied, throwing down her magazine in exasperation and grabbing Joselle's wrist. "It's things like this that make me—"

Joselle could fill in the blank many ways—crazy, want to send you away forever, regret being a mother.

Vicki pulled Joselle into the bathroom and brushed her teeth for her until her gums bled. "It's not a permanent marker," Joselle tried to explain.

But all Vicki kept saying was, "I could scream. I could just scream!" It was then that Vicki announced that she and Rick were going to take a trip. By themselves.

Joselle stayed in the bathroom, alone, crying, rocking on the toilet. There was greenish gray spittle all over the mirror and on the sink. Joselle knew she would always hate that color. Minty greenish gray.

□   □   □

It wasn't easy getting comfortable on Floy's old sofa with so much to consider. Joselle played her tongue against her teeth and gums and tried to focus on something stupid and safe. The sofa. Joselle imagined that it had been handsome when it was new—red and firm and plush. Now the dye had faded to a dirty wine color. It was soft, but lumpy. And the patchy raised pattern that was supposed to be roses reminded Joselle of bald mutant camels that were more hump than anything else. But soon the pattern resembled the fabric of one of Vicki's skirts. And then it resembled the uphols ry in Rick's car. It took a while, but Joselle finally nestled deep into the cushions, wrapped in a thin blue blanket, tight as a parcel. Tomorrow I will show Grammy how much I love her, Joselle thought. And I will complicate the life of Blaze Werla.

6
JOSELLE

"Thank you, Joselle," Floy said, smiling. "That was a wonderful breakfast. Where did you learn to cook so well?"

"Omelets are easy," Joselle said triumphantly, as she wiped the table with a dishcloth. "And I cook a lot at home. If I didn't, I'd starve to death."

Floy leaned back in her chair, saying nothing, the veins in her neck pulsing. The conversation seemed to have ended.

Floy looked older to Joselle that morning, and her face and neck had a bluish cast to them as though her skin had turned translucent and light were shining through. Floy had always been thin, but the older Joselle became, the thinner Floy appeared to be. Almost breakable, like blown glass.

"It's true," Joselle said finally. "I *would* starve. Especially since Rick and The Beautiful Vicki took a class at the community college on developing your ESP potential. They lounge around on the futon for hours—which is hardly unusual—and they go into trances to explore other countries. The trances really freak me out. I used to sit and watch them, wondering if they'd be home in time to fix me dinner. Now I just fix it myself. I've gotten good at it." Joselle was playing with crumbs in her hand, and only then did she notice that her hands were still dirty from her secret prebreakfast task. Little crescent moons of dirt shone through the places on Joselle's fingernails where her nail polish had chipped away.

"Well, you can cook for me anytime," Floy said, working at a spot on the tabletop with her thumb.

"I know The Beautiful Vicki's your daughter," Joselle said, glancing at Floy nervously. "And I—" she said, then hesitated a moment, deciding to change the direction in which her comment was headed. "And I was just wondering what I could make you for lunch."

"We've got all morning to decide," Floy said. She rose from the table and reknotted the ties of her bathrobe. "Just tell me one thing—why do you call her The Beautiful Vicki?"

"Because that's her name. And she is."

Floy turned around to face the sink, and her entire body began to move as if small waves rippled under her robe. Joselle was certain that Floy was crying, and her heart dropped as she pulled Floy toward her. But as their eyes met, Joselle's heart became weightless; Floy had been holding back laughter. "The Beautiful Vicki—that takes the cake," Floy managed to say between shrieks. "Well, I always thought she should be a beautician. Lord knows she spends enough money on cosmetics." Floy poked Joselle with her elbow and howled. They pressed together in hysterics.

While Floy went off to shower and dress, Joselle stayed in the kitchen. She opened the silverware drawer and pulled out every teaspoon and tablespoon. She looked at her face in each one. On the back of the spoons, her face was thin and long and right side up. On the other side, her face was wide and upside down. She moved the spoons at varying distances, distorting her face. She was amazed that each time it worked the same—upside down on the inside, right side up on the outside. Vicki had shown her this trick years ago, and Joselle still tested it wherever she went.

Joselle licked a spoon. My mother is smart, she thought.

They had been eating ice cream at the kitchen table right before bed the night that Vicki had presented Joselle with this minor marvel.

"It's magic!" Joselle had said.

"Try another spoon," Vicki suggested.

Joselle tried every spoon in the house, wide-eyed and mystified.

"Does it only work with chocolate ice cream?" Joselle asked.

Vicki opened the refrigerator. "Let's see," she said.

Laughing, they tried jam, cold leftover tomato soup, and maple syrup. They tried milk and orange juice, spooning them out of bowls. They tried peanut butter straight from the jar and sugar right out of the sugar bowl.

"*Every* spoon is magic," Joselle told Vicki, her voice cracking with excitement. "No matter what you're eating with it. Every spoon in the *world*."

They did the dishes together that night, the radio blaring. They played with the suds and serenaded one another using the spoons as pretend microphones. It was after midnight when Vicki finally kissed Joselle goodnight and tucked her in.

"I love being a single girl with you," Vicki whispered.

"Me, too," said Joselle. She had closed her eyes, lulled by Vicki's voice. She was asleep in minutes.

Joselle put the last spoon in its proper place and closed Floy's kitchen drawer. She wondered how her mother could be so perfect sometimes, and other times be as far from perfect as possible.

□   □   □

Joselle was pleased. She had accomplished everything she had set out to do for the entire day, and it wasn't even 9:00 A.M. Not only had she shown Floy how much she loved her by making her breakfast, Joselle had also

36

made Floy laugh harder than she had ever seen anyone laugh. But more importantly, Joselle had done something daring and original. Something that she thought could shake up someone's life. She wasn't exactly sure why she had done it—except she sensed that if she could make someone else more confused than she was, the weight of her own emotions might be lifted. It was worth a try. "Misery loves company," Vicki often said. The idea had begun during the night as a tiny seed that kept growing inside her until she was consumed by it and there was absolutely no way to fight it.

It was amazing how everything had come together so easily. Floy had said that he spent a lot of time on the hill. She knew his mother was dead. And she remembered that there were rocks and stones on the hill. In the weak light before breakfast, Joselle had done something that she hoped would complicate the life of Blaze Werla. She knew that if the situation were reversed, it would surely complicate hers. Joselle giggled with delight. She played the themes from "The Brady Bunch" and "The Mary Tyler Moore Show" on her teeth.

She was in the bathroom with the door locked, sitting on the clothes hamper. When she had finished her tunes, Joselle began decorating her thighs with ball-point-pen tattoos. At first she was going to put them on her arm, but she didn't want anyone to see them. So she settled on her thighs—so far up that they would only be visible if she were naked. And no one ever got a glimpse of her in that condition.

REENA was the first tattoo she gave herself. She was using her four-color pen and chose blue ink, pressing so hard that it hurt. Beneath it, she drew a rose in red ink and a leaf and thorns in green. It looked professional. She admired it. REENA.

This was the second time she had written the word *Reena* that morning. She wanted to write something else with stones on the hillside in a day or two. She practiced on her thighs. In black ink she wrote FIRE! And then in red she wrote YOU'RE ON FIRE, encasing the letters with jagged flames.

Just then Floy pounded on the door. "Joselle, are you upset in there again?" she asked.

Joselle hopped off the hamper, made sure her tattoos were concealed, unlocked the door, and greeted her grandmother holding her pen as if it were a cigarette. "I've never felt better, Grammy," Joselle said, grinning. She waltzed down the hallway blowing pretend smoke haughtily. "By the way," Joselle said, stopping and turning toward Floy, "what do you think is the worst way to die?"

38

7

BLAZE

The air was dizzy with insects. And Blaze was dizzy under the black locust tree. He had been twirling himself about, his arms outstretched like a propeller, until he was too unsteady to stand. He fell to the ground, and everything continued to whirl.

He had been talking to Simon in his head. About his mother. One piece of information for each full turn. Making a game of it.

She died when I was five and a half. *Turn around*. The last thing we did together was to ride the Ferris wheel at the fairgrounds. *Around*. She was already very sick. *And around*. It's my last memory of her. *Faster*. She was wearing a pink scarf. *Faster*. And there were blue rings under her eyes. *Faster, faster, faster . . . stop*.

Blaze looked straight up. Things were slowing down. He was shielded by a gigantic green canopy that shimmered as the wind blew, throwing shadows across his body. The pieces of sun that filtered through were so bright they hurt his eyes. For a couple of weeks in the spring, the canopy was white and fragrant. And on a clear moonlit night with a breeze, the canopy was silvery, as if made of stars rather than leaves or blossoms. He never thought you could love a tree, but he did. The black locust was perfect—except for the thorns that spun out from the branches like teeth, making it nearly impossible to climb. Blaze took a deep breath. Summer afternoons on the hill smelled of heat and dirt and grass and weeds and laziness. And—lately—of vigilance, caution, suspense. Blaze felt like an alarm clock just waiting to go off.

It had been two days since Reena's name appeared on the hill. Blaze had reconstructed his semicircle of stones around the tree, each marker in its proper place. The other stones he left dotting the hillside here and there. Everything looked exactly as it should, and yet there was a peculiar feeling in the air, as if someone or something strange were lurking nearby. Blaze circled the tree several times, then glided down the hill toward home in a zigzag fashion, his legs scissoring the sunlight.

He waved to Nova, who was bending over in her garden. She stood tall and waved back, calling out his name from beneath her wide-brimmed straw hat. Blaze turned and cut across the lawn, angling toward Glenn's studio.

Blaze often peeked in one of the huge windows to see what his father was working on. He tried to be invisible and quiet, careful not to disturb Glenn.

Glenn painted large canvases crammed with a multitude of figures and objects that were out of proportion in reference to one another. A man might be holding a plum swollen to the size of a basketball, or a woman might be walking a dog that was as large as a horse. Dragonflies and airplanes with the same dimensions flew side by side. Everyone in Glenn's paintings seemed detached, lost in a cool, claustrophobic dreamworld. There was often a red-haired woman in Glenn's paintings; Blaze knew that she was Reena. Sometimes Blaze spotted himself in his father's work—a pale, reedy boy hiding in the background among trees or floating in the air like a cloud. He liked that. It made him feel proud.

At the end of the school year Glenn would build wooden frames and stretch enough canvas to last the summer. Blaze would help. Blaze's favorite part was attaching the canvas to the wooden frames with Glenn's silver staple gun. It was heavy, and Blaze had to concentrate and push hard to get the staples into the frames as deeply as possible. The staple gun had a nasty little kick that jolted Blaze's arm, and it made a whooshing noise that reminded Blaze of getting a vaccination. Sometimes Glenn had to remove the staples and Blaze had to try again. Blaze noticed that it became easier each summer. He was growing stronger.

After the canvases were stretched, they had to be gessoed. Blaze helped with this, too. He had his own brush. Father and son would work together in the hot studio, perspiration beading above their lips like mustaches, first brushing the gesso in one direction, letting it dry, sanding it, then brushing it in the opposite direction, letting it dry, sanding it, brushing again, repeating, repeating, repeating. Canvas after canvas after canvas.

After a couple days of work, the studio was filled with about a dozen taut, white rectangles of various sizes, just waiting to be painted.

"This is either promising and exciting, or scary as hell. It all depends on how you look at it." Glenn would always say something like that as he stared at the empty fields of white laid out flat on the studio floor like perfect rugs. It would often take him a few days to actually begin. And then he would work passionately, as though painting were as important as eating.

Earlier that summer, their annual ritual completed, Glenn gave Blaze one of the canvases. "It's about time you had a real canvas to work on."

Blaze was dumbstruck. He loved to draw and paint, but he usually worked with colored pencils on newsprint tablets, or with watercolors on the back of heavy, dimpled paper that Glenn had done studies on. Most often, he drew television cartoon characters from memory, or he copied panels from comic books. "I don't know what to paint on it," Blaze said. Cartoon characters didn't seem important enough for a real stretched canvas.

"I'll let you use my paints and brushes when you think you're ready," Glenn said. "Do some sketches first."

The canvas was hidden away, leaning against the wall in Blaze's closet. He was waiting for a good idea. Something worthy enough.

Glenn worked in oils, and Blaze liked the way the combination of turpentine, linseed oil, and varnish smelled. When he reached the open window, Blaze inhaled deeply.

He heard laughter and froze. Glenn and a woman Blaze had never seen before were standing face-to-face in front of Glenn's easel. They were both barefooted. The woman had long grayish blond hair that fell to her waist. She was wearing a thick shiny band around her upper arm and an orange sleeveless dress that moved like water in the breeze that swept through the studio. Blaze watched them kiss. He considered closing his eyes, but intensified his gaze instead. Now Glenn stood behind the woman and coiled her hair into a nest on top of her head. He pulled a pencil out from behind his ear and positioned it in the woman's hair so that the bun stayed in place. Blaze had to catch his breath.

□   □   □

Glenn had dated other women before. A few—particularly a nurse named Carol—Blaze had liked. She talked openly and comfortably with him, and she gave him small gifts—shells, pens, and candy bars. She wasn't afraid to touch Blaze's arm or lightly rest her hand on his shoulder, but she never hugged or kissed him as if she were trying to be his mother. Carol didn't come around very long, however; maybe two months after Blaze had met her. And Blaze never asked why.

Some of the women Glenn introduced to Blaze made him feel squirmy and shy. They often looked at him with wide pitiful doll's eyes and their voices dripped with a sweetness that said, Oh, you poor motherless boy. His self-consciousness grew in their presence.

Blaze stared at this new woman. There was something different about her. He sensed that she would be around for a long time. And he wasn't exactly certain how he felt about that.

8
BLAZE

It took some prodding, but Nova convinced Blaze to go.

"I think you'll be sorry if you don't," Nova said from the pantry. She entered the kitchen with a jar of her homemade pickles.

"But *you're* not going," Blaze replied, eyeing the picnic basket that sat on the kitchen table bulging with good things to eat.

"Too much walking. And I wasn't really invited anyway," Nova said as she reorganized the contents of the basket. "I think your father would love for this to be just the three of you." Jars, small bags, and plastic containers fit together like the pieces of a puzzle. "This Claire woman must be special. It's odd of him to want you to meet her so early on."

Blaze didn't exactly know what Nova meant by that comment. And Blaze didn't tell Nova that he'd already seen the woman.

Nova tucked some silverware and striped cloth napkins into the basket and nodded approvingly. "There's too much food for just your father and Claire," she said, wiping her hands on her faded gingham apron. "I really want you to go," she added, her eyes doing half the talking.

Blaze fingered through the basket, looking at the food again. He could see pickles, plums, potato chips, deviled eggs, brownies, iced tea, and chicken. "Okay," he said. "For you."

◻   ◻   ◻

During the drive to the lake it seemed to Blaze that Glenn and Claire were smiling every other minute. The smiles broke across their lips like bubbles, and, more often than not, erupted into laughter. Glenn and Claire already appeared to be comfortable and familiar with each other—which made perfect sense, because Claire worked at the high school with Glenn.

"Claire teaches Art Metals," Glenn had told Blaze that morning. "You know—rings and belt buckles. Things like that." They had been folding an old blanket to use on the picnic. Glenn and Blaze each held two corners, the blanket drooping between them. The piping

46

was coming loose in Blaze's fingers, threads giving way. They drew near to meet, and as Blaze handed his corners to Glenn, he noticed a slightly amused look in his father's eyes.

Glenn also told Blaze how much he admired Claire's artwork. She made jewelry, but her specialty was small ornate boxes of gold and silver, delicately clasped and lined with dark velvet. "Last year was her first year teaching here," Glenn had explained. "And I really want you to meet her, Blazer."

Glenn seldom called his son Blazer—only when he was wildly happy after completing a painting successfully, or on the rare occasion that he had had too much to drink. Neither was the case that morning.

Blaze shifted around in the backseat. He rolled the window up and down. He fussed with the collar of his shirt and pulled it higher around his neck. He fiddled with the handles of the picnic basket. Finally they arrived. Blaze was relieved to be out of the car and into the open air that was busy with a myriad of sounds—birds, insects, and the laughter and voices of other people.

They found a shady spot on the grass to spread the blanket, secluded a bit from the crowd on the beach. The sun sequined the lake and Blaze squinted when he looked at it.

"Isn't it beautiful?" Claire said to no one in particular. She had long legs and arms that she moved gracefully. When she sat down, the skirt she wore over her swimsuit billowed and fell like an umbrella opening and closing.

"You are," Glenn said softly, touching one finger to Claire's sandaled foot. "And you are, too," he said loudly, looking at Blaze. Glenn raised and lowered his eyebrows comically. Then he winked at him.

Blaze could feel himself blush. "Da-a-a-ad," he said.

Throughout lunch Blaze tried to steal glances at Claire. His eyes flitted quickly from one detail to another. Yellow-green eyes. Long streaky blond-gray hair that made him think of animal fur. Skin tanned dark as tea. There was so much to take in, Blaze had to remind himself to chew.

They talked about art and the high school and what a good gardener and cook Nova was. They talked about books and recipes and Blaze's teachers from last year. They talked long after they had finished eating. Claire told Blaze that she had grown up in Chicago and that she liked being in Wisconsin now. Then they talked about art again. Glenn said that he wished he could make enough money painting. He wished that he didn't have to teach. He couldn't think of anything better than the luxury of being able to paint every day without worrying about mortgage payments and bills. And Blaze thought of his own blank canvas.

Although Claire and Glenn tried to include Blaze in the conversation, he tended to nod a lot and give one-word answers and comments. He was busy observing and being shy. He found himself watching Claire's hands.

When they had picked up Claire at her apartment, Blaze had been surprised by the seriousness of her handshake. As Glenn introduced her to Blaze, she held his hand in hers for a long moment as though she really meant it. Her hand had been warm. His had been cold.

After a while they went swimming. Blaze was leery about going in water over his head, so when they did finally go in the deeper water, he rode on Glenn's back while Claire floated beside them. Periodically Claire would swim ahead and then somehow end up surfacing behind them. She'd pop up out of the water, dripping and blinking. Her eyelashes were beaded with water droplets and they sparkled. Her color was high, her movements quick and sure.

"Look at that," Blaze said to Glenn.

Blaze had spotted a wiry towheaded girl and a big bald man not far from where they were. The girl climbed onto the man's shoulders, then jumped off, making an enormous splash. She did it again and again, her laughter growing louder with each jump.

"Want to try it?" Glenn asked.

Blaze tensed, but said, "Yes." His response surprised him. And he even asked Claire to watch.

"We should go a little farther out," Glenn said.

Glenn crouched.

Claire watched.

And Blaze climbed onto Glenn's shoulders, holding on like a clamp. Glenn's birthmark was visible between strands of his hair, between Blaze's thumbs. Blaze hesitated. He took a deep breath, closed his eyes—and jumped.

Blaze's hands were in fists as he hit the water. Then they opened up. And so did his eyes. And so did his mouth. He took a breath under water.

When Blaze surfaced, he was coughing. He grabbed Glenn.

"Are you all right?" Glenn asked, carrying Blaze to shallow water.

Blaze shivered. "Yeah," he said. He coughed some more. "I just swallowed some water."

"That was some jump," said Claire.

Blaze didn't say anything for a moment, and then he told them quietly, "Maybe I'll just sit on the beach for a while." His throat and nose and eyes were burning. He shivered again.

"Want company?" Glenn asked.

Blaze shook his head no. He was embarrassed.

Blaze walked the length of the beach looking at stones. Then he sat at the water's edge, poking his toes at the bubbly fringe that lapped about him, wishing that he knew how to swim.

"Bored?" someone said.

Blaze turned with a start. It was Claire. She wrapped her towel around herself and sat down.

"Where's my dad?" Blaze asked, trying to cross his legs in a manner that would hide the scars on his ankles.

"Over there," Claire said, pointing.

Blaze watched Glenn with a combination of pride and envy. Glenn sliced through the water, his arms cutting perfect angles, his head turning rhythmically.

"He's good," Blaze said. "At swimming. You are, too," he added.

"I didn't know how to swim until I went to college," Claire said. "I could hardly float before that."

"Really?"

Claire nodded and narrowed her lips. "It was one of those things I always wanted to do, and always put off. I still want to learn how to play the piano and speak French." She paused. "Is there anything you really want to learn how to do?"

Blaze was paralyzed by the question. There were so many things he wanted to be able to do. But they would seem so simple to anyone else: Go to sleep without the light on. Go out for the basketball team at school. Pet a big dog without shaking. Ride the Ferris wheel alone.

Sweat dripped down Blaze's face. He touched one corner of his mouth, then the other, with his tongue. "I'd like to fly," he managed to say. "I've never done it."

"In an airplane, or on your own like a bird?" Claire asked, smiling.

Blaze laughed, relieved a bit. "Like a bird," he said, relaxing.

"Me, too," said Claire. She closed her eyes and threw her head back, stretching. She hugged herself. "Wouldn't that be wonderful?"

Two children, holding hands, ran past Blaze and Claire, splashing them.

"You know, that jump you did out there was good," Claire said, her eyes following the children down the sand.

"Really?" Blaze thought it had been terribly clumsy, not to mention all his coughing.

"Good jump," Claire said. She ran her fingers through her hair. "Good jump," she repeated, her face slanted upward as though she were talking to the sun.

They stayed on the beach, side by side, silently. Without realizing it, Blaze had untucked his legs and begun rubbing his ankles. The blister-smooth skin was vivid in the sun, the rippled areas emphasized like tiny raised cursive writing. Suddenly, Blaze noticed that Claire had been watching him; he saw her looking at his ankles. When their eyes met, Claire didn't turn away; she just smiled naturally.

And then, for some reason, Blaze told her about the fire.

How he had been waiting in line to ride the Ferris

wheel on the Fourth of July after Reena died. How there had been a short circuit. How the electrical wires that lay at his feet sizzled and jumped like snakes on fire. He told her about the awful smell in the ambulance. Even about the paramedic who tried to comfort him by telling him that both his father and mother could ride with him to the hospital. And how—during a confusing minute—he asked for Reena, even though she was dead.

When Blaze finished he felt numb and weightless. He thought he might rise off the beach and drift above the lake like fog, the way he did in his father's paintings.

9
BLAZE

"Well, what do you think?" Glenn asked. They were driving home after dropping Claire off at her apartment.

Blaze shrugged. "I don't know," he said. "What do *you* think?"

"I like her," Glenn answered, lightly tapping out a rhythm on the steering wheel. "I like her a lot." Glenn looked sideways at Blaze. "Is that okay with you? I'd like it to be."

"I guess," Blaze replied. "She's pretty."

"She is, isn't she?" Glenn said, smiling. "And smart and artistic and nice . . ."

"Are you going to marry her?"

Glenn let out a quick laugh. "Not tonight," he said, joking.

"No, really, are you going to?"

Glenn lowered his voice. "It's too early to tell. But I know that we have a lot in common. We have a good time when we're together, too." He paused. "I've known Claire for a year at school now . . ." His voice trailed off. And he smiled a big smile again.

Blaze thought it was a goofy smile, like the smiles he drew with crayons when he was three. It made Blaze feel good to see Glenn so happy. And at the same time it was scary. What if Glenn *did* marry Claire Becker? What would their life be like? How would it change?

Blaze watched the passing clouds, searching for different shapes in them: a car; a cow; a wizened, bearded man. It had only been hours since he had told Claire about the fire, and already he regretted it. Why had he revealed so much to a near stranger? Claire was pretty; was that why? At least he hadn't told her everything. He hadn't told her about the skin grafting or how hard he had cried. And he hadn't told her *why* he had been waiting in line for the Ferris wheel.

"Do you mind if we stop at the grocery store?" Glenn asked. "I should pick up a few things."

"Okay," said Blaze.

Glenn hummed in the parking lot. He raced Blaze up and down the aisles. And, laughing musically, he plucked oranges from a display and tossed them to Blaze directly in front of a sullen-faced man who shook his head and clucked his tongue disapprovingly.

After grocery shopping they stopped for ice cream.

Sitting on the curb in the muggy afternoon air, spumoni dripping down his wrist, Blaze wished that he could see the future. He wished that he could see ahead to the end of summer, to Christmas, to the following summer. He wished that he could know for sure what would be happening to his family. He wished he knew what was happening now.

□   □   □

Blaze's mind was muzzy. He was thinking about his mother. He rolled over on his stomach and his bed squeaked. Sometimes he would forget exactly what his mother looked like, and he would have to study a photograph. Sometimes what he could remember was clouded. Sometimes he and Glenn would look at old photographs and mementos together, and it would make Blaze feel calm and edgy at the same time.

After a few minutes, Blaze flipped over on his back again. He thought of the fire and the Ferris wheel and Claire and what he *hadn't* told her. . . .

Reena rode the Ferris wheel with Blaze shortly before she died. It was the last thing they did together before Reena went to the hospital for the final time. They were at the fairgrounds on the Fourth of July. Glenn watched and waited while they rode. It was a small Ferris wheel, part of a small fair that came to town every July. There were rides and game booths and bright billowy tents where food was sold. Two weather-beaten wooden soldiers marked the entrance. They looked like the unwanted toys of a giant, dropped into the trees and forgotten.

The next year he wanted to do it by himself. For her. It was something he had to do. It was very important to him. He begged Glenn to let him try it. It was a small Ferris wheel, made for children, so Glenn said yes, bought him a ticket, and watched and waited again.

But Blaze needed the help of a friend. So he made one up. Benny was his name. Blaze whispered to Benny while he moved closer and closer to the man taking tickets. That was the year of the fire. Of course, he didn't go through with it *that* year. So he buried Benny. And then came Ajax.

Good-bye, Benny.

The following year Blaze had to ask to go to the fairgrounds. "Are you sure you want to go?" Glenn asked. Blaze was sure. "We can just walk around," said Glenn.

Blaze hadn't heard Glenn and Nova talk about insurance money and doctor bills for a long time. And Glenn told Blaze that a different company was running the fair now. The big wooden soldiers were gone, but there was still a Ferris wheel. It looked enough like the one he had ridden with Reena to count. It was small, with wire cages that spun gently as the wheel rotated.

"I want to try it," Blaze said.

"Okay," said Glenn. "Let's do it."

"I want to try it alone," said Blaze.

Glenn let him try.

But it was more difficult than he thought it would be. He worried about the Ferris wheel itself. He remembered the cords that had caught on fire. He thought about his mother. He couldn't do it. Ajax didn't help. "I changed my mind," he told Glenn. "Can we get something to eat?"

Good-bye, Ajax.

He tries every year. He doesn't want to be afraid.

Good-bye, Ken.

He stands in line, but turns away at the last minute. He goes on other rides.

Good-bye, Harold.

Now that he's old enough to go to the fairgrounds with some of his classmates, he sneaks off alone to the Ferris wheel. Unsuccessful every time. Or if his classmates want to ride the Ferris wheel, he says, "I have to go to the bathroom—do it without me." Or "I'm going back to the games for a while. Meet me there."

Good-bye, Ortman.

Every year that he can't ride the Ferris wheel, he buries his old friend and gets a new one.

Every year he tells no one.

Every year he digs another hole.

10
BLAZE

Blaze had a dream that didn't frighten him, but time and place and all other particulars escaped him. He stared listlessly at a spot on the ceiling in his bedroom, trying to make the dream come back. But he could only remember a foggy, pleasant feeling, and he tried to hold on to it, grabbing his chest as if the feeling were touchable and could be hugged like a pillow.

After looking out the window and checking the hill (no new words of stone), Blaze dressed and went down to the kitchen for breakfast. Nova made pancakes for him. She served them with butter, blueberries, and powdered sugar. Blaze played with the blueberries, forming a letter *C* with them on the top of his stack of pancakes.

"Do you like her?" Nova asked.

"Who?" Blaze said. He spread some of the blueberries to the edge of his plate.

"Claire, of course," Nova replied. "Who else would I mean?" She smiled at Blaze and her cheeks became a farmer's field of wrinkles.

"I'm not sure," Blaze answered, raising his fork, a blueberry speared on each tine. "But I think Dad's in love." The word sounded funny to Blaze: *love*. He wrinkled his nose.

"Love's not such a bad thing."

"I know, I know," Blaze said, tossing his head from side to side. He smiled at Nova. "You really wouldn't care if he got married again?"

"I'd love it, and I mean it, and you know it. We've talked about that before."

"Would you still live with us?"

Nova shook her head yes. "But don't you think you're jumping the gun? Slow down a bit. Eat your breakfast."

He ate and he thought. He thought that Nova was the most calm person he knew. And the smartest. And the nicest. He thought about going to rummage sales that afternoon with Glenn and Claire; Claire was looking for old furniture to fix up for her apartment. He thought about being short and wondered how tall he would be when he was fully grown. And he thought that he wanted to eat another pancake. And he did.

After finishing breakfast and helping Nova with the

dishes, Blaze walked up the hill to the black locust tree. He seemed drawn there as if by a magnet. It would be a hot day. Earlier there had been a milky haze on the hill that burned off, but the air was still heavy. Dew glittered on the tips of the grass. As he approached the crest of the hill, Blaze swung his arms back and forth, pretending to cut through the heat. When he reached the top, he stopped suddenly.

Within the border of the grave site were more messages. This time the words were formed with small stones and pebbles, each letter only a few inches tall at most. The stones spelled YOU'RE ON FIRE and FIRE! The words were written in an arc near the trunk of the black locust tree. The exclamation point that ended it was long and wiggly like a worm.

◻   ◻   ◻

"Come on," Glenn coaxed, slapping the upholstery beside him. "We're running late."

"I'm not going with you," Blaze said slowly, his eyes narrow because of the sun.

"What's up?" Glenn asked. He had been waiting in the car for Blaze, the motor idling. He was ready to pick up Claire and had been signaling Blaze by honking the horn.

Blaze shrugged. He didn't feel like talking. He knew the words would catch in his throat, possibly making him cry. He also knew that he never wanted to see Claire

Becker again. Now there was no doubt in his mind who was responsible for the words of stone. Claire Becker. A swift internal pull convinced him this was the truth. He had told Claire about the fire, and she had used the information for a cruel joke.

Glenn turned off the ignition. "Are you okay?"

"I think I ate too much for breakfast," Blaze said, holding his stomach. "It's not a big deal, but I think I should stay home."

"Would you rather I stayed home, too? I can call Claire."

"No," Blaze said. "You should go."

"Okay," Glenn said, almost like a question. "I hope you feel better." He started the car again. "See you later," he called.

Blaze waved. He had figured out who had written the words of stone. But what would he do now?

11

JOSELLE

Joselle was examining a scab on her knee when the phone rang. She jumped up to get it, but since the only phone in the house sat on the end table beside the rocking chair where Floy happened to be planted, her chances of answering it were next to none. After a pleasant hello, Floy's voice took on an icy edge. Joselle knew instantly that The Beautiful Vicki was on the line. Floy's face seemed to deflate and her lips pursed. Nearly everything about her became tight, and yet she cradled the phone against her shoulder and continued to work on her needlepoint. Her fingers moved like dancers, pushing and pulling, bringing a garden to life with thread. Lilacs, tulips, and daffodils bloomed between her hands.

Her silver needle glinted and Joselle thought of sparks. Even when Floy sighed heavily or rolled her eyes, her fingers continued to flow at the same rhythmic pace.

Joselle picked her scab while she listened. Then she drew her knee up to her mouth and bit off the scab. She swallowed hard and licked her wound.

"How can you afford that?" Floy asked. "What about your job at the restaurant?"

Joselle could feel her heartbeat quicken. She began playing "The Star-Spangled Banner" loudly on her teeth.

"Don't worry about Joselle," Floy said. "Good *heavens,* of course you should talk to her. Just a minute."

Floy handed the receiver to Joselle.

"Joselle?" Vicki said.

"Hi," Joselle answered reluctantly, flexing her toes inside her shoes.

"Sorry I didn't send you a postcard or call sooner. . . ." There was an awkward pause. "Uh, Rick and I decided we'd like to see the ocean—the Pacific Ocean. So we're going to be gone longer than we thought. It's a far way from Wisconsin, you know. But anyway, your grandmother's glad to have you there. And—don't worry—I checked it out with the restaurant. They'll give me my job back when I get home."

"Why can't I come with you?"

"Come on, Joselle. We're already on the road. And Rick doesn't want this to be a kid's vacation. We need a break. *I* need a break from *you*. You know how we get when we're together too long. This is good for you, too."

Joselle didn't want to pay attention any more. She tried to twirl the phone like a baton, but dropped it on the floor. She picked it up, hesitated a moment, then spoke into the receiver very clearly. "I might have blood poisoning," she said, curling her lip. "But if anything happens I'm sure someone will be able to locate you." Without waiting for a response, she gently hung up the phone.

Joselle and Floy looked at each other.

"I don't want to talk about it," Joselle said, turning her eyes away.

"Me neither," said Floy, placing her needlepoint on the end table and standing. She grabbed her sweater from the back of the chair and draped it over her shoulders. "The mall's open late tonight. Let's go shopping."

□   □   □

The air in the mall smelled stale—of popcorn, smoke, sweat, and perfume—but it was a hopeful smell; it carried with it the prospect of new things to take home. When Joselle shopped at malls with Vicki, they rarely bought anything. They purchased most of their clothes at resale shops. Vicki tried to convince Joselle that the clothes from Retro Fashions and Goldie's Oldies were more chic anyway, but Joselle knew that Vicki couldn't afford shopping at the other stores. And yet they went to them on a regular basis "just to look." Joselle disliked the whole routine because she often saw things that she wanted badly, knowing full well that she couldn't have them. She'd pout all the way home, bewildered by the injustice of it all. She referred to this practice as "visiting clothes." Last year for Mrs. Weynand's language arts class, Joselle wrote an essay about "visiting" a pair of tight, stone-washed jeans so many times that she became best friends with them. Mrs. Weynand said the essay showed a great deal of creativity but was lacking in other areas—namely grammar, spelling, and punctuation. She gave it a C-minus.

Joselle felt only slightly guilty that Floy was spending so much money on her. But Floy was the one pushing certain items, as though an extra pair of tights or some dangly rhinestone earrings could fill Joselle up until there was no room for unhappiness. When Joselle expressed an interest in a fuchsia tank top, Floy insisted that she have the black-and-white striped one, too. And Floy wouldn't take no for an answer when she saw the way Joselle's eyes widened as she stroked a peach cashmere sweater that had buttons like pearls.

"You'd look beautiful in that," Floy said, scooping it up and holding it in front of Joselle.

"Grammy, I was just looking," Joselle said, turning away. She had seen the price tag. She knew how expensive it was.

"It's got your name written all over it," Floy said. "Just think how envious your classmates will be next school year."

Joselle considered this and felt herself weakening. Even Sherry Gerke, who often made a point of criticizing Joselle's wardrobe in front of anyone who would listen in the girls' rest room, would have nothing but good things to say about *this* sweater. It was classy. Joselle cackled to herself.

"Okay, Grammy, you win," Joselle said, throwing up her hands. "I'll take it."

As they marched up to the checkout counter together, Joselle had to concentrate hard to keep her fingers from crawling onto Floy's arm and tugging the sweater away from her.

"Forget the bag," Joselle told the clerk. "I'm wearing it!"

Floy nodded approval.

"Thanks, Grammy!" Joselle shrieked. "Now you're sure this is okay?" she added in a very serious voice.

"Yes," Floy answered. "A good splurge every now and then does wonders."

But Joselle repeated the question over and over because she had noticed the way the corner of Floy's mouth had twitched upward, forming a thick indented comma deep in her cheek as she wrote out the check to pay for the sweater.

"If you ask me one more time, I'll start calling you a

broken record," Floy finally said, swatting Joselle softly on her behind. "Come on, we need to find some nail polish before the stores close."

On the drive home, the stars were brighter than Joselle had ever seen. And the evening smelled of grapes. Fireflies dotted either side of the highway as if there had been too many stars for the sky to hold and some had spilled downward. Joselle rubbed the buttons on her new sweater, pretending that they were tiny stars that had lost their light. And then, because she wanted the way she felt at that precise moment to last forever, she stuck her head out the window and gulped the air that rushed at her face, hoping that it would work some kind of magic inside her. Hoping that it would make her life perfect in every way.

12
J O S E L L E

Joselle woke up with a headache, and there was a pinching sensation behind her eyes. She blinked her eyes quickly and steadily, hoping the feeling would stop, but all it did was intensify the dull pain and make her see double for a minute. Gary heard her stir and raised his head. He slept on the floor alongside the sofa every night now. Right by Joselle. He nudged her hand with his nose until she petted him. Simultaneously, he wagged his tail and yawned twice, like an echo. Joselle covered her face with her arm. "I feel bad, but you smell worse," she told him.

Despite the heat, she had slept in her new sweater. It had transformed her ratty cotton nightgown into the ele-

gant party dress of a princess. Joselle slid off the sofa
and pirouetted to the kitchen, trying to work off the way
she felt. Gary snapped playfully at the frayed edge of
her nightgown as though her dance were a game created
especially for him.

Now, on top of having a headache, Joselle became
dizzy. After sitting at the table and counting to one hundred, she thought that food might help. She made a
three-minute egg, a piece of toast, and a cup of tea with
four spoonfuls of sugar and enough milk to turn the tea
pale and lukewarm.

After breakfast, Joselle felt better. Floy was still
asleep, so Joselle tried extra hard to be quiet. Joselle
wondered if Floy couldn't pull herself out of bed because
she regretted spending so much money on Joselle. Joselle pictured her grandmother flat in bed, lethargic as a
wet wool blanket, exhausted by the shopping spree and
clutching an overdrawn check book. The thought nagged
at her, and it just got worse when she retrieved all her
purchases from the closet and spread them out on the
sofa. There were two pairs of tights, two tank tops, a
bikini, earrings, socks, four bottles of nail polish, and,
of course, the sweater. Joselle knew that if The Beautiful
Vicki hadn't phoned about her prolonged trip the sofa
would be empty. Floy would never have permitted Joselle
to buy the bikini or the dangly earrings. They would have
been completely forbidden if Floy hadn't felt sorry for Joselle. Maybe she thinks she's partially responsible, Joselle
said to herself. After all, Vicki's her daughter.

Joselle had a fashion show. She tried on each new item and paraded around in front of Gary. He cocked his head, his ears alert, his tail sweeping the floor. But somehow the effect had worn off for Joselle. Last night, in the dressing rooms at the mall, she had been electric with anticipation. She had sniffed everything she tried on, intoxicated by the scent of newness. And on the ride home, buried beneath the shopping bags, her happiness had been a dazzling white spot. Now, sitting on the floor, picking Gary's wheat-colored hair off her rainbow-print bikini, Joselle was a brightly swirled, empty lump of self-pity. She could have gulped enough air last night to fill a hot-air balloon and it wouldn't have mattered. No magic had been worked. Her life would probably never be perfect.

With only her bikini on, Joselle's ball-point-pen tattoos were visible on her thigh. They had worn off a bit, so she took out her pen and wrote over them again, carefully tracing each letter. REENA. FIRE! YOU'RE ON FIRE. And then she added a new one: ORPHAN. And she wasn't entirely certain if she was referring to Blaze Werla or to herself.

◻   ◻   ◻

The distance between Joselle's house and the Pacific Ocean seemed endless. After the fashion show, Joselle discovered a road atlas on Floy's bookshelf, and her finger followed the red and blue lines that indicated highways, weaving across the country until they ended at

Route 101 on the coast. The number of miles that separated Wisconsin and the ocean was so staggering, her
finger quivered. On the map, the crisscrossed network
of roads looked like a maze—much too disorienting for
Vicki to negotiate. Joselle hoped that Rick was doing
most of the driving.

At least Rick was a good driver. In Joselle's opinion,
Rick's only other talent was turning his eyelids inside
out. It was one of the most disgusting things Joselle had
ever seen, but he was very good at it. Another disgusting
thing about Rick was his hair. The hair on the top of his
head was okay—short, brown, straight, thick. But the
hair on the rest of him wasn't okay. It sprouted from the
backs of his hands and from under his shirt collars like
twisty forests. The sight of it made Joselle want to throw
up. Rick was rangy and languid. He hunched his shoulders frequently, and a perfect pimple flourished on the
bridge of his nose. Vicki said that Rick was good at his
job; he was an electrician. But Joselle thought that he
was too absentminded and too interested in ESP to be
working with things as dangerous as power sources and
currents. She hoped that he would never rewire their
house.

Sadly, Joselle envisioned Rick and Vicki lost and
confused in Nebraska or stranded on some dirt road
in Wyoming. And yet, ironically, part of her wished
that the car *would* overheat, that they *would* run out
of gas, and that they *would* get flat tires. A minute

later, she wished them a speedy, safe trip, and she longed for Vicki so intensely that her eyes turned misty.

Joselle had never been out of southern Wisconsin, and she realized how small an area this was compared to the rest of the country, not to mention the world. She and Vicki lived in a small brick ranch house in Kenosha. Floy lived in the country outside of Madison. They were only a few hours apart by car, and yet they only saw each other two or three times a year. And it was nearly always Floy who did the visiting. If I ever make it out of the Midwest I'll probably faint, Joselle thought. Her father, who she had only seen once, supposedly lived in Texas. She never heard from him, and Vicki cringed whenever his name was mentioned, so Joselle didn't bother thinking about him very often. And she never asked Vicki to talk about him—that was hitting below the belt and she knew it. She could be awful, but not that awful. Joselle owned one photograph of him that she kept in the bottom of her sock drawer. The photograph was dog-eared and slightly out of focus, but Joselle could make out a man who she thought looked devastatingly handsome or evil as a snake, depending on her mood. His name was Jerry Hefko, and in the photo he was posing on a motorcycle wearing sunglasses and a red bandanna on his head. Dense black curls hung to his shoulders. Although neither Joselle nor Vicki had ever used Hefko as a last name, Joselle had secretly carved JOSELLE HEFKO on one leg of the kitchen table with a paring knife when she was seven and furious at her mother for something or other.

"Why do people live in certain places?" she asked Gary, staring at Texas.

Gary tipped his head and knitted his brow.

"I mean, why wasn't I born in New York or Miami? Someplace glamorous?"

"Planning a trip?" Floy asked in a voice thick and raspy with morning, startling Joselle. She shuffled across the floor in her fuzzy slippers.

"Nope," Joselle said, closing the atlas and replacing it on the shelf. "I was just killing time waiting for you to get up. Sleepyhead."

Between stretches and yawns, Floy banged around the kitchen making coffee.

"I checked on you five times, you know," Joselle said. "I wanted to make sure you were breathing."

Floy flicked her wrist and glanced at her watch. "It's only seven-fifteen. This is when I always get up. How long have you been awake?"

And only then did Joselle realize how early she had gotten up. She figured it had been hours since she awoke. "I don't know," is all she said.

Floy sipped her coffee, savoring every drop, as though it eased some discomfort. Her cup sounded like a tiny bell when it clinked against the saucer. "I thought I'd cut the grass today. If you're not too busy, I could use some help."

Joselle's chin crumpled. She hated yard work. "Well, actually," she said, "considering everything that's been happening to me lately I think I might need time alone today to contemplate my future."

Floy only nodded and looked away, her deep-set gray eyes focusing on the coffeepot.

"I'm probably helping you by *not* helping you," Joselle offered, her voice confident and round. "I'm usually much more trouble than I'm worth."

□   □   □

The lawn mower roared in Joselle's ears, but she walked right past Floy and toward the hill undaunted. Sometimes she hated herself for the way she treated people, for her selfishness. And yet, she seemed to have no control over her behavior. It's not my fault I am the way I am, she thought.

The sky was the blue of a baby's blanket and the clouds looked like massive heads of cauliflower. Joselle slapped her thigh and whispered, "Orphan." She couldn't decide if she should write the new word with stones as she had done with the other words or try something different. She wondered how Blaze Werla had been reacting to her messages. She hoped he was going crazy with confusion. Maybe this time I should write the word and then hide behind a bush and wait till he appears, she thought. Maybe I could see him cry.

But as it turned out, Joselle's plan was not workable. She skipped to the top of the hill and stopped suddenly, frozen. Blaze Werla was crouching beside the big tree. And before Joselle could move, their eyes met. And locked together.

13
BLAZE

The first time Blaze saw her, the hair on the back of his neck prickled. Although the sun was shining, he swore that she had no shadow, and despite the fact that she stood perfectly still and there was no wind, her dangly rhinestone earrings jiggled, making thin music. Her eyes appeared to be entirely black—like hard, shiny pieces of licorice. They were so hypnotic, Blaze had to work at forcing his eyes to break contact with hers. When she came closer he noticed that she smelled dusty, like a ladybug. And then she smiled. Her smile did anything but put him at ease. Her smile was enormous and glassy and sharp.

"Big teeth," was all he managed to say, walking backward as if in a trance.

The girl thrust out her hand, her fingers grazing Blaze's chest. "I'm Joselle Stark," she announced grandly.

Blaze's fingers felt dwarfed and breakable in hers. She had the grip of a man.

"The old lady that lives over there is my grandmother," Joselle said, pointing toward Floy Stark's neat, square house. "I'm staying with her for a bit while my mother explores the Pacific Ocean. She's kind of a scientist—my mother. My grandmother's just a grandmother." While she spoke she tossed her head and flared her nostrils. "So," she said, "who are you?"

Blaze could barely speak. His words cracked and melted. "My name is Blaze," he finally offered in a scratchy whisper.

"That's an odd name."

Blaze shrugged and scuffed his shoes.

"You're so *little*, too," Joselle said in a thrilled voice, rumpling his hair. "And if it wasn't impossible, I'd swear you were shrinking right before my very eyes."

Looking down, Blaze scanned his entire body, checking to make sure that he wasn't, in fact, becoming smaller. And then, as though he had no control over what he was saying, words spilled out of his mouth like the beads of a breaking necklace: "I'm the smallest in my class. I am every year."

"No kidding," Joselle said sarcastically. "It wouldn't take a brain to figure that out. Unless you go to school with midgets."

Blaze only fidgeted, regretful.

"Well, who cares anyway?" Joselle said, marching in place. Then she strutted around the black locust tree like a queen. "All I can say is—just look at this view! I've never been up here before. It's tremendously fantastic." She cleared her throat. "I just arrived today, you know," she said, turning her head toward Blaze, her eyes thin as slits. Because she wasn't looking ahead, Joselle tripped over one of Blaze's stones. Dust rose, veiling her as she stumbled and fell. Her knees and hands were streaked with dirt.

"Are you okay?" Blaze asked shyly, lightly nudging the stone with his shoe.

"I'll live," Joselle answered, her face bunched. And then suddenly her mood swung and she smiled again. This time gleefully. "Hey, look, I'm injured," she said merrily, pushing her knee at Blaze. Marking the middle of her knee was a perfect drop of blood. "It's an enchanted liquid ruby," Joselle whispered. "I'll seize it like this," she said, wiping her knee with her finger. "I'll share it with you like this," she continued, smearing blood on Blaze's leg. "And then I'll seal the magic like this," she told him, licking her finger several times. "Now we're true friends. Forever."

Blaze pulled the edge of his T-shirt into his mouth and bit down, and because he was breathing so hard, his mouth sounded like the wind. "I'd better go," he said tentatively, moving away. In his mind, he was already home, lying on his bed with the door closed.

79

"Come back tomorrow," Joselle called. "You have to. Same time. Same place."

Blaze ran all the way down the hill. As he tore through the weeds and grass, his arms making huge loops in the air, he felt as though he were emerging from a terrible and wonderful spell.

□   □   □

Thoughts of the girl stayed with Blaze all afternoon like a film on his skin. She baffled him and intrigued him. His mind strayed to her even as he set the table for dinner. He saw her face in each plate and bowl. Her teeth and her eyes materialized vaguely on the china like the Cheshire cat.

The day had grown hotter and hotter, so they were going to have a big salad and gazpacho. "Too hot to use the oven today," Nova repeated as she moved around the kitchen. Her skin had taken on a sweaty sheen. When she turned from reaching for the large wooden salad bowl in the cupboard, her forehead glistened and Blaze noticed damp saggy half-moons under her arms on her thin housedress. The heat didn't bother him nearly as much as it did Nova.

Glenn was slicing hard-boiled eggs for the salad. It had been just over a week ago that he had introduced Claire to Blaze and Nova. Since then, he had been spending a considerable amount of time doing domestic things: helping to make dinner, washing dishes, shopping for groceries. He wasn't painting nearly as intensely as he usually did.

"I'm going to freshen up before Claire arrives," Nova said. She flapped her dress and sighed. "Too hot," she murmured on her way upstairs to change clothes.

"You seem quiet," Glenn said to Blaze.

"Not really."

"Well, then talk to me," Glenn said as he arranged the eggs on a ruffly bed of various lettuces from Nova's garden. "How are you?"

"I dunno," Blaze answered, and it was purely the truth. He didn't know. And if *he* didn't know, how could he give his feelings a name and discuss them? He had too much to think about. Claire. And now Joselle Stark.

"I understand how you might feel about Claire," Glenn said. "I do . . ." He smiled his assurance and squeezed the back of Blaze's neck.

"I know," Blaze replied, hoping that he sounded cheerful and cooperative. But Glenn couldn't understand. Blaze hadn't told him about the words of stone.

At first it had made perfect sense that Claire had been the one to write them. Blaze had told her about the fire, and the next morning the words appeared. But since then Claire had acted completely normal—whatever that meant for someone you hardly knew.

Although Blaze had tried to avoid Claire, she still treated him kindly, which puzzled him. Even if he had been ignoring her throughout an entire meal, she would present small gestures—a look, a grin, a compliment—that would cause Blaze to drop his silverware.

□   □   □

"I have something for you, Blaze," Claire said when she arrived. "Come to my car."

It occurred to Blaze that he could pretend not to have heard her. He could just walk past her into the kitchen to get something to nibble on while he waited for dinner. He followed her to her car.

"Your dad told me that he had given you a canvas to work on. I thought you might like to have your own paints." Claire opened the car door and pulled out a box the size of a portable TV. She placed the box on the ground and opened it up so Blaze could see inside. "I know you have watercolors, but these are acrylics. They're my old ones—I don't use them anymore."

There must have been thirty tubes of paint. Blaze could tell that some of the tubes had been used, but others looked brand new.

"I know your dad would let you use his oil paints in his studio, but this way you can paint in your own room if you like. Whenever you want. And you can clean up with water. They're easy."

"Thank you," said Blaze. He turned the tubes in his hand, reading the names of the colors.

"The brushes are in here," Claire told him, picking up

a long, thin manila envelope that was tucked in the side of the box. She took out one of the brushes and pretended to paint in the air. Her wrist moved gracefully, round and round. "Well, I'm going to see if Nova needs any help in the kitchen," Claire said, handing the brush to Blaze.

"Thank you," Blaze said again.

"You're welcome."

Blaze carried the box to the porch and sat down. The tubes of paint reminded him of party favors frozen in various stages. The kind that unroll as you blow into them, then collapse on themselves as the air escapes, curling up. Blaze was familiar with most of the colors because of Glenn: cadmium red, alizarine crimson, burnt umber, cobalt blue, yellow ocher. He pretended to paint in the air as Claire had done. He was beginning to get excited about starting his canvas.

His certainty that Claire was responsible for the words of stone had been a knot lodged inside his chest. The knot was gradually loosening. Blaze was glad that he had waited, that he hadn't said anything to Glenn.

"*Was* it my imagination, Simon?" Blaze asked. He wanted to convince himself of that. He told himself it wouldn't be surprising, given that it was July. His dreams were proof of the power of his imagination.

He would wait. He would push it out of his mind. After all, he had something new to concern himself with: Joselle Stark. She had said they were true friends—and yet they barely knew each other. If they *did* become true friends, maybe he could tell her about the words of stone. Maybe she'd know what to do.

A spider hanging motionless in its web caught his eye. The web was a perfect, intricate hexagon strung between two posts of the porch railing. Blaze didn't like spiders particularly, except from a distance. He pictured Joselle Stark approaching this spider easily and touching it with her finger. Blaze knew he would go to the hill tomorrow. He wondered if she would be there.

14
BLAZE

"For the first couple years of your life, you were probably no bigger than a salt shaker," Joselle told Blaze, cupping her hand and holding it out to indicate size. "In fact, it's probably a miracle you lived. I'll bet your parents have photographs from when you were three, but they tell you they were from the day you were born." Joselle brushed a tangle of hair away from her eyes. "Parents do things like that," she added crisply, snapping her fingers.

Blaze wondered exactly what Joselle meant. She confused him completely, but at the same time she spoke with such authority that he was compelled to accept as true everything she said. "I was little, but not *that* little," he mumbled at last, blushing a bit, opening and closing his fists.

"Believe what you have to," Joselle said, shaking her head.

It was only their second time together. They were sitting beneath the black locust tree, within the semicircle of Blaze's stones. He hoped that Joselle wouldn't ask about the stones, or worse, move them. Whenever Joselle poked at them with her foot or gazed at them for what seemed like a long time, Blaze felt a small tremor in his leg. He could never explain his stones to this curious girl who reminded him of wild, impish, confident children he had only known in books.

"Want some?" Joselle asked, lifting the necklace of popcorn she was wearing over her head and offering it to Blaze. "Popcorn. Fresh popcorn," she called, making her voice sound important.

"Thanks," said Blaze, pulling off a few kernels. Bewitched, he handed the necklace back. Each time he chewed and swallowed, his teeth creaked and his throat tickled.

"I always get the hulls stuck on my teeth. And always my tooth with the micro-dot," Joselle said.

"What's that?"

"It's this teensy-weensy thing printed on my tooth with my name, address, and birthday. You can't even see it with the naked eye. I used to think it was really neat until I realized it would only do any good if they found me dead. You know, to identify me."

Blaze tried to absorb this, but his mind kept stumbling

on the word dead. It made him shiver. And of course, he thought of his mother. He could see an image of her, memorized from a photograph, so clearly among the leaves above him that he thought he could make the image stay there forever. But the breeze fluttered, the leaves stirred, and she disappeared. "My mother is dead," he heard himself say.

For once, the girl seemed to be at a loss for words. Wrapped in absolute silence, Blaze watched her. Joselle twisted her popcorn necklace, then pushed and pulled pieces of popcorn as though she were moving counters on an abacus. She appeared to be so deep in thought that Blaze wondered if he could see what she was thinking in the air around her if he looked hard enough.

"Well, you're not the only one," she suddenly blurted out, one large tear sliding down her face. "My father is dead." She placed her necklace over Blaze's head, draping it crookedly across his shoulders. "Welcome to the orphans' club," she sniffed. "The saddest club of all." Then she kissed his cheek sharply and quickly before vanishing behind the slope of the hill.

15

BLAZE

"That's about all I know," said Nova. "But if you like her, it would be nice to have someone to play with. Someone so close." She moved her basket up a few feet and continued picking beans. The plants were heavy with pods that ranged in color from milky yellow to emerald. The sizes and shapes varied, too. Some beans were huge and so swollen they looked surreal. Others were narrow and small and straight as nails. "Is she here for a long visit, or a short one?"

"She didn't say exactly," Blaze answered. He was sitting in the row next to Nova eating a bean. Mist tickled his eyes when he snapped it. "Her father died," he said.

"I wasn't aware of that," Nova said. She really didn't

know much about Joselle Stark. Or her mother. "I'm not even too familiar with Floy," Nova told him. "We greet one another, but that's about it. I guess the hill is big enough and our houses are far enough apart to keep our lives separate." Nova took off her hat and fanned herself with it. "Would you like to have Joselle over for lunch?" she asked. "Egg salad sandwiches? With home-grown beans and homegrown lettuce?"

"Not today. But maybe sometime." Would Joselle say yes if he asked her? Possibly. After all, she had kissed him. Blaze had never been kissed by a girl before. Just thinking about it made his heart anxious. And he thought about it a lot. No one had ever been so interest-ing to him before. And to have Joselle confide in him about her father bonded them.

When Nova finished picking her row, she pointed to the tomato plants. "I've got more tomato plants this year than ever. If they all ripen, we'll have enough tomato sauce and chili relish and salsa for the entire town," she said. She heaved her basket of beans into her arms and sighed. "I'm going inside to start blanching these. And I'm hoping that my legs don't fall off first. Bad circula-tion," she added matter-of-factly.

Blaze watched Nova trudge through the garden and across the lawn. Her thick, corded veins seemed to pulse with each step. Blaze wandered over to his favorite cor-ner of the garden, glancing over his shoulder at Nova until the back door shut behind her. In the corner, a stand of sunflowers formed a wall. Slivers of blue, blue sky shone through the lattice of leaves and huge drooping yellow flowers. When the wind hastened, Blaze could smell the basil, which was planted in a raised bed near the sunflowers. Sometimes he'd pick some of the basil leaves and rub them on a small patch of his arm near his wrist, tinting it green. Then, periodically throughout the day, he'd bring his arm up to his face and inhale deeply. Last year, he had hung a big bunch of basil from the doorknob in his room; the room smelled wonderful for nearly a week. It was amazing to Blaze that everything that was so alive and leafy and aromatic and productive in Nova's garden had begun as tiny seeds. The whole process was one of the most hopeful things he knew. Thinking about Joselle Stark was hopeful, too. Blaze wondered how long she would be staying with her grandmother. He hoped she'd at least stay until school started in the fall.

Blaze wanted to do something special for Joselle because he felt so badly about her father. He wanted to give her some kind of gift. He lay down under the sunflowers, trying to think of something appropriate. It wasn't long before he fell asleep, dreaming, as the morning crept away slowly without him.

□   □   □

The only things of value that Blaze had to offer Joselle were his lost key collection and his Noah's ark. He didn't think he could bear to part with the ark—and besides, he could picture Joselle commenting on how infantile it was—so he gladly put that thought out of his mind. The key collection would also be hard to give up, but not having it around would be something he would just have to get used to. At any rate, the lost key collection wasn't serving its purpose. Blaze had collected the keys and kept them near his bed while he slept with the secret hope that they might open the locked doors that often appeared in his dreams. Usually Reena's voice came from behind the doors, calling him. It was a stupid idea anyway, Blaze thought. A real key can't open something in a dream.

He looked at each key carefully, trying to remember where it had been found or who had given it to him. When he placed the mason jar that held the keys in a box and sealed it, he had a premonition that he would wake up in the middle of the night, panicked and needing the keys. "I hope I'm doing the right thing, Simon," he whispered. Regretfully, he wrapped the box in the comics from the previous Sunday's newspaper, tied a limp bow on top with red yarn, and held it tightly on his lap until he knew he was ready to meet Joselle on the hill.

□   □   □

As she opened the box, Blaze detected first amusement, then baffled uncertainty in Joselle's look. After a moment she shrieked lustily and said, "Oh, I get it—you think you have the key to my heart." She batted her eyelids and preened herself, obviously enjoying her remark.

"It's not a joke. It's a present."

"Oh, piffle, piddle," she said airily. "Don't be so serious all the time."

Blaze tried to explain his feelings about Joselle's father, but only got frustrated.

"Let's play a game," said Joselle, barely allowing Blaze a word. "It's called Personal Scent. It'll just take me a minute to get ready."

Blaze watched Joselle. She unrolled the top of a brown paper sack from the local grocery store and opened it up. The bag was soft and crumpled from use, from being held by sweaty hands. One by one, Joselle took out small glass bottles of various sizes filled with different colored liquids. She lined them up between them like a tiny fence.

"Like I said, the game is called Personal Scent. And I, Joselle Stark, am Keeper of the Scents." She shook the mason jar, rattling the keys. The sound was grating. "The game will now begin!" she announced. She placed the mason jar in the bag and moved it aside.

With a dainty flick of her wrist, Joselle chose one of the small bottles. She unscrewed the tarnished metal top and rubbed a generous amount of some of the clear golden liquid on her arm. She replaced the bottle and chose another one. This one was filled with a cloudy liquid tinted a suspiciously bright blue color. Joselle leaned over toward Blaze and splashed his shirt with it. She was so close that Blaze could practically taste the perfume she was wearing. It was overpowering and sweet.

"Now smell yourself," Joselle instructed.

Blaze did as he was told.

"That is your personal scent. Now you have to become a different person—someone who would smell like that."

Blaze was confused. His face was blank. "I don't get it," he said, mindful of Joselle's delight and discouraged that he didn't understand.

"Watch and learn," Joselle said. She sniffed her arm. "This is a beautiful, flowery perfume," she commented, her eyes half closed. She sniffed her arm again, then inhaled and exhaled luxuriantly. "I am definitely a Veronica," she said, speaking with a lilting accent. "Veronica Marsdale. And I am someone's perfect mother. Picture me wearing a carnation pink dress and lipstick that's thick and cakey in a nice way." She leaned toward Blaze again and whispered into his ear. "Who are you?" she asked, still speaking as Veronica.

Now Blaze understood how to play, but it took him a minute to come up with something. He fidgeted with his hair while he thought. The bright blue liquid was a dreadfully spicy after-shave. "I am Bruno Slobkin," he finally said in his deepest voice, flexing his muscles. He smiled to himself at this notion.

"Ha!" Joselle screeched. "That's good! That is really good."

That afternoon, shaded beneath the black locust tree, Joselle, Keeper of the Scents, rubbed and sprayed Blaze and herself with various perfumes, colognes, and after-shaves. They even used leaves, dirt, and berries. And depending on the particular mixture of smells, they became different people: famous movie stars, characters from books, or simply people they made up themselves.

Blaze laughed until his side ached and he had to massage it. He could not remember when he had laughed so hard.

Periodically throughout their game, Joselle—hand in mouth—would hum theme songs from television programs and make Blaze guess what they were.

"Why are you pretending to play music on your teeth?" Blaze asked, after successfully naming a tune.

"Because my teeth are as big as piano keys," Joselle said. "And it's a special talent."

"How long have you been doing this?" he asked in his Bruno Slobkin voice.

"Since the very day I was born, sweetheart," she answered, speaking with a pronounced southern accent.

During a particularly quiet moment when Blaze was trying to come up with the name of a song, he almost told Joselle about the words of stone. But he stopped himself for some reason. He just couldn't force the words out.

After they had been playing for quite some time, Joselle asked suddenly, "Can I come over to your house?"

"I don't know," said Blaze. The growing effect of their concoctions was light-headedness. He experienced a fluttering in his stomach, too. "I'd have to ask my grandma first." He stared at his knees. "And my dad. Maybe tomorrow would be better, or something."

"Then come over to mine," said Joselle. "You can call your grandma to let her know where you are." She gathered her belongings into her paper sack, her little bottles falling together and clinking against the mason jar.

Blood beat in Blaze's ears. He watched her get up and start to walk away.

"Come on," said Joselle. "Are you part statue?"

"I can't go," he said.

"Why?"

The way she said it, and the way she looked at him, made him feel invisible. "I'm afraid of your grandma's dog," he admitted shyly.

"Gary?" Joselle's eyes widened and she stretched her mouth in an exaggerated fashion. *"Gary?"*

"He's so big. And sometimes at night I can hear him bark all the way over at my house."

Joselle approached him and grabbed his arm as if she were going to pull him down the hill behind her. She clucked her tongue. "Silly," she said. Then she looked right at him, and as she did, Blaze saw something register in her eyes, and he felt something change in her grip. "You're *really* afraid of him, aren't you?" she asked, her voice serious and quiet.

Blaze nodded.

"Don't worry. Gary's just a pussycat. I'll introduce you properly and teach you to like each other. He smells awful, but that's his only bad point. And we don't smell so great, either. He'll like you."

"Really?"

"I promise," she said, waving him along. "What are friends for?"

16

JOSELLE

Something was shifting and changing inside Joselle. It didn't happen all of a sudden, but gradually, over the course of long, hot summer days. It was a feeling she couldn't exactly describe, except to say that it was private and dense and tight. She felt as if she owned something wonderful that no one else in the whole world knew about. She first became aware of the feeling the afternoon she taught Blaze how to pet Gary.

"I can't do this," Blaze had said, backing away.

"Yes, you can," Joselle told him.

Gary romped forward, pulling his chain taut, his tail wagging fast and hard.

Joselle petted Gary and commanded him to sit. Then

she stood behind Blaze and slowly pushed him toward Gary. She could feel him shake. "Stay," she said to Gary. "Now give me your hand, Blaze." She guided his hand, gently forcing it along the back of Gary's coarse head, again and again.

Blaze made a small sound in his throat.

"See, it's easy."

"Kind of," Blaze said.

Joselle suspected that it wasn't easy at all for Blaze, and she moved her hand with his like a shadow, nudging it along when he hesitated. And as she did, something occurred to her. He needs me, she thought. Blaze Werla needs me.

The following day the feeling washed over her again. She was showing Blaze the spoon trick. They were on the hill.

"I don't believe it," Blaze said, excited.

"It works every time," said Joselle. "Really, truly. Give it a try."

Blaze took the spoon from Joselle and moved it in front of his face. Closer, closer, farther away. Then he turned the spoon over and moved it again. "I'm always upside down on the inside," he commented. "And right side up on the outside."

Joselle nodded thoughtfully. "I told you. It's one of the small wonders of the world." And that's when the feeling struck. Watching the expression on Blaze's face, Joselle thought she knew how teachers must feel after they've successfully explained the mystery of long division.

A few days later, Joselle experienced the feeling under completely different circumstances. She wasn't helping anyone; she was being waited on by Blaze and Nova. She had been invited to Blaze's house for lunch. She was so impressed by the smells of fresh-baked bread and homemade cookies, by the matching towels with rickrack trim, by the flowers in coffee tins lined up on the counter, that afterward she couldn't even remember what day it was, and she actually danced around the table and offered to wash the dishes.

Perhaps it was Nova's bread that had done Joselle in. It was absolutely wonderful. Vicki and Floy were both partial to store-bought bread, the bleached white kind that is so puffed up with air and preservatives that it looks and smells like something kindergarteners are given to express themselves creatively. Occasionally Joselle would form little balls with her bread, and using the dull, knobby ends of the silverware, shoot them around the kitchen table billiard-style.

"You elevate the concept of playing with your food to new heights," one of Vicki's boyfriends had commented once.

"It's better than eating it," Joselle had replied, striking a cereal bowl with a small grayish wad.

One afternoon after she had eaten several meals and snacks at Blaze's house, Joselle asked Nova, "When was the last time you bought bread at a store?"

"I can't remember," Nova answered. "Baking bread is a cinch—and it's one of life's greatest pleasures," she added, smiling.

"I help with the kneading sometimes," Blaze said.

"You don't buy frozen or canned vegetables, either, do you?" Joselle asked.

"Not usually," Nova replied. "I freeze and can myself. Why?"

"Just checking," Joselle said, spreading butter on a slice of warm whole wheat. She licked her fingers, feeling drunk.

The feeling came back to Joselle even when she didn't expect it, even when she was alone. She wondered if she was falling in love with Blaze and his family. Was that possible?

She still experienced what she called "the hollow feeling" or "the Sunday afternoon feeling," but it seemed to come less often. She associated the feeling with The Beautiful Vicki.

Joselle used to think that she would end up alone. A spinster. Not a timid, frail woman with blue hair and lacy dresses, but a feisty woman who wore young, stylish clothes. A woman who could take care of herself. But now she wasn't so certain. Maybe living in a family could really work.

Sometimes Joselle tried to see herself through Blaze's eyes. Depending on her mood, she would see a fat, loud girl who, strangely, played music on her teeth. Or a strong, beautiful girl capable of mesmerizing boys and their families.

□   □   □

Each morning Joselle awaited the arrival of the mail. And each morning she was disappointed. She'd run to the mailbox at the edge of the road as soon as the red, white, and blue truck puttered away. With her eyes closed, she'd open the mailbox and reach into the dark space greedily. Without fail, her hope quickly disappeared; there was never anything addressed to her. After slamming the mailbox shut, she'd kick dirt all the way back to the house, and then toss the bills, letters, and advertisements for Floy carelessly on the kitchen table. She cursed her mother under her breath. The Beautiful Vicki hadn't sent even one postcard. She hadn't telephoned again, either. If Joselle thought about her mother long enough, she became so worked up she was convinced that her bones would twist out of their sockets and snap into sharp pieces.

"I didn't get anything from her either," said Floy one morning when Joselle looked especially disappointed.

"Well, you're not her daughter," Joselle said testily, pulling her chin.

"I'm her mother."

"That's different," Joselle said. She made a paper airplane out of a ShopKo circular. The lines of her folds and creases were precise as cut glass. "Maybe it's your fault she is the way she is," Joselle said, giving Floy a challenging look. Joselle sent the plane toward the garbage pail in a perfect arc, but it careened off course at the last minute and landed in Gary's water dish. Joselle pretended that the plane was an arrow and that the water dish was her mother's black heart.

"Try not to worry about your mother too much," Floy said softly, drumming her fingers on the counter. "She has the annoying habit of being happiest when those who love her the most are upset."

Floy's words confused Joselle, and she tried to make sense of them as she ran over to Blaze's house. She knocked fiercely on the door.

"Hi," said Blaze through the screen, looking gauzy. "What do you want to do today?"

Joselle pulled the door open a crack and squeezed inside. "It doesn't matter," she replied.

And it didn't. She just wanted to be there.

□   □   □

They began spending more and more time together. And when they parted at dusk, Joselle eagerly awaited morning when they would join one another again—usually on the hill.

Sometimes Joselle called him The Boy with the Apricot Hair. And sometimes she called him Blazey. But mostly she called him Blaze.

Sometimes Joselle wanted to tell Blaze everything about her life. But she didn't. She held back. What if he didn't like what he heard? What if he found out that she had written the words on the hill with stones? She had no idea how he had reacted to them—except that someone had always dismantled them. Would he still want to be her friend?

Sometimes Joselle wanted to know everything about Blaze's life. But she decided not to ask too many questions. She fabricated what she didn't know. And the history and circumstances she invented for him were exactly what she wanted them to be.

Sometimes Joselle liked to be alone with Blaze on the hill—playing with the hot, hot sun beating down on them, or sitting quietly against the black locust tree like bookends in the cool shade. And sometimes she liked to be with his entire family at their sturdy, round kitchen table. Blaze and Nova and Glenn and Claire.

Sometimes Joselle wished she could live with them. Sometimes she wished she were Blaze.

17

J O S E L L E

"**H**a!" Joselle shouted, storming into Blaze's bedroom, taking him by surprise. She was struck enough by Blaze's expression to add, "It's okay. I didn't mean to scare you." She joined him on the braided rug, plopping down so heavily that the walls seemed to vibrate. Although Joselle had spent a fair amount of time at Blaze's house, she had never been in his room before. She looked around, collecting details and storing them away. "Your grandma let me in. She told me I could come up here. Second door on the right."

Blaze seemed particularly quiet. His cheeks reddened

as he abruptly scooped up the toy he was playing with. "Let me just put this away," he said, talking so fast that Joselle had to decode his words, taking a few moments to understand him.

"What have you got?" Joselle asked, reaching around Blaze's arm and picking up a handful of small plastic animals. A camel, a swan, a goat.

"It's this stupid old toy I used to play with," Blaze replied. "I was just looking at it."

"It's a Noah's ark," Joselle announced. Without asking, she grabbed the toy out of Blaze's hands and scrutinized it. "I hate to tell you this, but it's defective—there are supposed to be two of every animal and you've just got one."

Blaze only nodded.

"Well, it fits, doesn't it? It's a Noah's ark for orphans." Joselle broke down completely with spasms of laughter, holding her belly with both hands. She quieted down quickly, however, since Blaze only averted his eyes and remained silent. Not even a flicker of a smile touched his lips. "I was trying to be funny, but I guess I'm about as funny as a big fat cinder block." She handed the ark back to Blaze and began picking at the cuticle of her thumb. "Sorry. Really," she said as gently as possible, offering the words as a gift.

Today is turning out to be a bad day, Joselle thought. First, no postcard from The Beautiful Vicki. Again. Then, I took it out on Grammy. Again. And now Blaze thinks I'm a dope. I shouldn't have joked about being an orphan. And I never should have lied about my father being dead in the first place.

She was sorry about that, but in a sense he *was* dead. At least to her. If she told Blaze the truth now, he'd hate her for sure. And that wasn't what she wanted at all. She wanted to be friends with Blaze Werla. Very best friends.

How many lies had she told Blaze? It was hard to keep track of them all. She had lied about her father. Lied about her mother being a scientist. She had lied about when she had arrived at her grandmother's house, so that Blaze wouldn't think she had had anything to do with the words of stone. And the words of stone were a kind of lie, too. She wished she had never written them.

Blaze had been the perfect candidate for deceit, and Joselle had gladly taken advantage of his innocence. Pinpricks of regret ran up and down her legs. No more lies, she told herself. No more words of stone. Joselle made a promise to herself never to lie again. She vowed to be honest in every way until the day she died, or as long as she possibly could. Which wasn't very long. Because as soon as Blaze's back was turned, Joselle sneaked the tiny plastic fox that Blaze had overlooked from beside his dresser and slipped it into her pocket. She couldn't stop herself. *This* is the last dishonest thing I will ever do, she said to herself. Ever, ever, ever.

After shoving the ark under his bed, Blaze pulled his

bedspread down until it touched the floor, hiding the ark entirely. He appeared to be more relaxed now. "I can't play with you today," he said. "I've got to go with my dad and Claire."

"Where?"

"Claire is selling her artwork at a fair. My dad and I are going to help her."

"Can I come, too? Please? If I'm there it'll be more fun."

Blaze seemed to blossom. "Let's ask," he said, already out the door and in the hallway.

The stairs sounded hollow as Joselle pounded down them. She caught up to Blaze and nearly knocked him over, she was moving so fast. She extended her left arm, placing her hand on his shoulder to stop herself. Her right hand was in her front pocket, her fingers wound tightly around the tiny fox. The fox was nearly weightless, but felt heavy against her leg.

◻　◻　◻

From the instant Joselle slid into the van with Glenn, Claire, and Blaze, she pretended that they were her father, mother, and brother. Buckled safely into her seat, she watched them fondly. She studied Glenn first, deciding quickly that she approved of every part that formed her new father. Longish blond hair, big hands, thick wrists, scratchy voice. How are you supposed to feel about a father? she wondered. Or a brother, for that matter?

She knew a bit more about mothers. But Claire seemed very different from Vicki. Vicki was surely beautiful; she worked hard at it with lipstick and eyeliner and curlers and manicures and hair spray. Claire didn't appear to be wearing any makeup, and her hair was simply pulled back into a ponytail with a red rubber band. But she looked beautiful, too. Her features were larger than Vicki's, but more stately, as though she belonged in a painting hanging in a museum in Paris. The Beautiful Vicki would be more at home on the cover of *Cosmopolitan*.

Joselle loosened her seat belt slightly and leaned forward, her chin resting against the front seat. This is my perfect family, she said to herself. When Joselle closed her eyes, she saw them (herself included) etched onto the backs of her eyelids. An aerial view. The four of them formed a rectangle that crept along the highway slowly and silently like a small toy. She basked in her newfound feeling of belonging all the way to the art fair.

Claire had rented the van because she needed room for her artwork and her display booth. Neither her car nor Glenn's would suffice. The van was silvery gray, and Joselle imagined that it was a sleek limousine taking them to a very important private party.

Claire was driving, but Glenn helped to check for traffic as they veered into the parking lot. When he turned his head from side to side, Joselle noticed the circular birthmark on the back of his neck. "One world," she said aloud, wanting to touch the birthmark with her finger.

"What?" asked Blaze.

"Oh, nothing," said Joselle, blushing. "I was just talking to myself."

Joselle and Blaze helped Claire and Glenn set up the display. Glenn and Claire did most of the work. Joselle tried to look busy, but she couldn't keep herself from holding her head high and gazing about loftily at the people who passed by. They all just assume that we're a family, she thought happily.

Joselle didn't know very much about art, but in her opinion Claire's work was exquisite. Claire was selling pins, barrettes, and a few of her boxes. Everything was gold, silver, bronze—and glinting. Claire's work made Joselle think of royalty and perfection and miniature heirlooms people tuck away in secret places that aren't found until years later.

A particular barrette shaped like a fleur-de-lis caught Joselle's attention. She looked at it longingly. She pictured her hair swept back off her face and fastened by the shiny golden swirls. She pictured strangers stopping to get a better look, transfixed by her beauty.

"Come on," Blaze said, tugging on Joselle's sleeve. "Let's go spend the money my dad gave us for lunch."

There was so much to choose from. They bought hot

dogs, soda, popcorn, and—best of all—cotton candy, whipped and spun onto paper cones like fancy pink hairdos. Joselle loved how cotton candy melted when it touched her tongue. She ate hers and nearly half of Blaze's. Her teeth ached from all the sugar.

"This is fun," Blaze said.

"Yeah," said Joselle. "But I think I ate too much."

They were seated at a picnic table, among many, under a large yellow tent. The sunlight shone through the tent, casting a jaundiced look onto everything.

"Want to walk around?" Blaze asked.

"Let's just sit a while longer," Joselle said. "We can watch people."

"Okay."

Joselle played with the soggy paper cone from her cotton candy. "Did you ever wish you were someone else?" she asked.

Blaze shrugged. "Not really."

"I do, sometimes." Joselle waited for Blaze to ask: who? But when he didn't, she continued. "Is there anything about yourself you'd change if you could? Is there anything you don't like?"

Blaze shrugged again.

"I'd get rid of these awful teeth, if I could." Joselle said, pointing to her mouth. "And I'd like to be smaller. Like you."

"I wish I was *bigger*," Blaze said. "And I don't like my scars. From the fire."

Joselle played dumb. "What scars?"

110

Blaze got off the bench and walked over to Joselle's side of the picnic table. "These," he said, turning his ankles and nodding. "I was in a fire one Fourth of July. I got burned—so did three other kids. It wasn't *that* bad. They did some skin grafting. I think they could do more if I really wanted them to. . . ."

Joselle leaned over and touched Blaze's right ankle. "They're tiny," she said. "I'd take your scars over my teeth any day. I always wanted a scar. They make you look brave."

"Really?"

Joselle nodded. "Yeah."

"You wouldn't lie to me?" said Blaze.

"Never," Joselle replied, feeling her cheeks turn pink as polished apples. "Let's go," she said, rising abruptly from the bench and running toward the crowd.

"Wait up," Blaze called.

They wove in and out of the artists' booths. Sometimes Joselle ran ahead and hid behind a tree or a group of people, then rushed out in front of Blaze. Small red flags flapped in the breeze.

"Look!" Joselle said suddenly, bending over. "A lucky penny."

"Let's see," said Blaze.

Joselle handed the penny to Blaze. "It's yours," she said, "on one condition. You have to tell me your wish."

Blaze's little fingers curled and uncurled around the penny. "Right now?"

"Think about it and let me know. But if you don't

tell me, it won't come true. True, true, true," Joselle called, running ahead again, dodging in and out of the crowd.

▫   ▫   ▫

Throughout the afternoon, Joselle was content to sit and observe. She watched Claire interact with the shoppers and browsers. And she watched Glenn holding Claire's money box, making change when he needed to. But when she and Blaze went back to the refreshment stand to get something for Glenn and Claire to eat, Joselle did more than observe. When a boisterous man cut ahead of Blaze in line, Joselle elbowed him. "Excuse me!" she said crisply. "My friend was here first." She felt very protective.

It wasn't until they were driving home at sunset that Joselle remembered that she had taken the fox from Blaze's room. And it dawned on her why she had done it. With the fox in her possession, she might have a kind of power over Blaze. It might add strength to her wishes concerning him. Unlike the key collection he had given her, the fox's whereabouts were unknown to him; that's why it was powerful. The fox represented her secret life with Blaze's family, the life that played out in her head.

There were occasional periods of silence as they rode. But they weren't awkward. They were breaks in the conversation in which time stood still, in which everything was suspended except Joselle's watchful eye. Even so, the ride was going much too quickly for Joselle. She wanted this day to last.

It was Blaze who broke a particularly long silence as they neared Floy's house. "Here," Blaze whispered, his voice as quiet as insects' wings. "You found this. It really belongs to you." He gave Joselle the lucky penny. "And you don't even have to tell me what your wish is."

The penny floated on the sweaty creases of Joselle's palm. She was touched. She pushed the penny into her pocket with the fox. Then she opened her mouth and tapped out "When You Wish Upon a Star." Her fingers smelled metallic.

Blaze joined in on his own teeth. They played it together, smiling, until the van pulled up to Floy's front porch.

18

JOSELLE

"**H**ow was your day?" Floy asked, head poised, waiting. She had been leafing through a magazine. It lay open on her lap.

"It was the best day of my life," Joselle said. She flung herself onto the sofa, her arms spread out over her head like a giant V. She sighed dreamily.

"I'm glad you had a good time," Floy said. "Tell me about it."

Joselle lay motionless on the sofa. She couldn't tell Floy. If she did, wouldn't Floy feel terrible? Wouldn't it bother her that her granddaughter could have more fun with someone else's family than she ever could with her own? "I can't exactly explain it," Joselle said finally. "I

114

mean, it wasn't *that* great. It was okay." Her lip flickered. She forced a laugh and got up to go to the bathroom. "I've had better days. For sure."

Floy closed her magazine. "I can't keep up with your thoughts," she said.

□   □   □

In Joselle's dream the moon was blue. And then it became a penny. And then it vanished. She sat up in the middle of the night with Blaze's words on the tip of her tongue: "You wouldn't lie to me?" And her answer haunted her: "Never."

She rose from the sofa and walked to the front window. There was no moon. It was raining. Water streamed down the window as though she were under the sea. She felt regretful. Joselle pulled her purse out from beneath the sofa. She searched for her four-color pen.

While the slow steady rain tap-tap-tapped against the house, Joselle darkened the ball-point-pen tattoos on her thigh. When they faded, she would darken them again. She would keep them as a reminder. She would keep them until she told Blaze the truth.

About everything.

The words of stone.

Her father.

Her mother.

The tiny fox.

Joselle placed the lucky penny under her pillow. She wished that when she told Blaze the truth, he would forgive her. She wished that she had a million lucky pennies; she felt she needed that much luck.

□   □   □

When Joselle woke up again, it was still raining. She put on her bikini and ran up and down the front sidewalk several times. The rain chilled her, and goose bumps sprouted on her arms and legs. But she felt much better, exhilarated.

She came inside, toweled off, and wrapped herself around a steaming cup of tea. Floy's door was still closed to the morning, so Joselle was very quiet. She wanted to get out of the house before Floy got up. She pulled her extra-large white T-shirt on over her damp bikini. The shirt fell to her knees, covering the tattoos easily. She wore her new sweater, her dangly rhinestone earrings, her red rubber thongs. She brushed her hair back into a ponytail as Claire had done yesterday. Joselle's ponytail wasn't nearly as long as Claire's, but she thought it looked smart, and with her hair away from her face, her earrings were more visible. She left a note for Floy by the coffeepot.

Puddles dotted Floy's lawn like scattered mirrors. But Joselle didn't mind. She hopped off the porch and skipped across the soggy yard toward Blaze's house, her feet sliding in and out of her thongs. Floy's umbrella shielded her like an enormous lavender flower.

She didn't feel brave enough today to tell the truth. She just wanted to see her friend.

19
BLAZE

The steely smell of rain was in the morning air. Blaze liked rainy days. "That's the artist in you," Nova said time and time again. "Most creative people like gray weather." Blaze didn't know if that was true, but he knew that Glenn also liked dark, stormy days. And according to Glenn, Reena had felt exactly the same way.

Reena hadn't been a painter, but a writer. She had majored in English in college. Before Blaze was born, she had taken a job with the local newspaper, writing book reviews. After Blaze was born, she stayed home with him, hoping to write a novel one day. Glenn said that Reena was never satisfied with her attempts at a novel and therefore had never kept any of them. Sometimes Blaze pretended that his mother *had* written a book. A book that could be checked out at the library. A book with secret references to him.

Blaze's train of thought was broken by a series of loud knocks on the door.

It was Joselle. She smiled radiantly and waved at Blaze, then flew off the porch into the rain. Instead of holding her umbrella above her, she swung it around, turning circles with it, dancing. She raced about like a top—spinning, twirling, laughing.

"Come out!" she yelled, waving. "It's fun!"

Blaze opened the door and stepped onto the porch. It was pouring. He could see that Joselle was soaked already. He could see her bathing suit beneath her T-shirt and sweater.

"Come on!" she shouted.

Blaze hesitated, thinking. It was only a summer shower. Nova wouldn't mind. He took off his shoes and sprang from the porch, cringing from the shivery rain. He joined Joselle in a large muddy puddle.

Joselle put her umbrella down and grabbed Blaze's hands, pulling him into her dance. "I'm drenched," she said, giggling, kicking her leg out playfully.

And then he saw it. His mother's name written on Joselle's thigh. He could see it through her wet, wet T-shirt which was plastered against her skin. And he could see parts of other words. All the words of stone curving around her leg in ink of various colors.

Blaze jerked his hands out of hers harshly. They stood face to face.

"What's wrong?" Joselle asked.

"I want my key collection back," Blaze said between quick, shallow breaths, his voice shaking with anger. It was all he could think of to say.

Joselle didn't answer, her face uncomprehending. Blaze could feel the silence in his belly.

Holding his breath, Blaze tried to calm himself. He squinted and concentrated, his eyelashes becoming veils that filtered things and blurred them. But it did little good; he just kept seeing the words of stone as they had appeared on the hill. He felt ashamed for being such an easy target, someone so easily tricked.

"You wrote the messages on the hill, didn't you?" he asked. "You wrote my mother's name."

"Oh!" Joselle said, glancing down at her transparent shirt, understanding. She covered the words with her hands and pulled her legs together. "No. I mean . . . yes." She looked away. "I'm sorry," she said. "It was just a joke. I didn't mean anything bad by it. And I stopped doing it once I got to know you." She knitted her fingers nervously. "Really."

"I thought you were my friend," Blaze said. His voice cracked. His fingers were extended on both hands like the points of stars. They whirled around his legs as he spoke. "Just get out of here." He gave her a hard mean look.

"You don't like me anymore," Joselle whispered, turning sideways, hiding her face. "I'm *sorry*," she reminded him, turning back, flipping a loose piece of hair out of her eyes. She still didn't look at him directly. "Please, don't hate me."

For a fraction of a second everything became razor sharp to Blaze. The pores on Joselle's face, the liquid of her eyes, each strand of hair, each drop of rain. Everything was so clearly defined that it hurt Blaze's eyes to rest them on anything.

In that instant, Blaze rushed toward Joselle and pushed her down as hard as he could. He hit her once across her shoulders. "Get out of here," he said. "Just get out of here." And then he grabbed one of the round buttons on her sweater and pulled it off, thread trailing behind it like a fine tail.

He didn't see her face again. He watched as she rose from the ground, picked up her umbrella, and scrambled across the driveway toward Floy's house without looking back. And that's when he started to cry.

□   □   □

By early afternoon the rain had passed and the sun was shining. Birds chirped and skittered through the ribbons of water in Nova's garden. Barefooted and shirtless, Blaze spent the rest of the day tagging along behind his grandmother while she weeded, or sitting by

121

himself in small spaces: his closet, under the porch, between a pile of bricks and the outside wall of Glenn's studio.

"You seem to be miles from here," Nova said, cocking her head so Blaze could hear her. "Are you feeling all right?"

"I'm fine," Blaze replied, gazing at a clump of nasturtiums until it became the sun.

Alone, resting against Glenn's studio wall, it occurred to Blaze that he had never pushed anyone the way he had pushed Joselle. He had never hit anyone, either. Or purposely ruined something that belonged to someone else. The button from Joselle's sweater reminded him of what he had done. Perhaps it always would.

But no one had ever made him feel so stupid before. No one had ever humiliated him the way Joselle had. No one had ever been so mean. He couldn't believe she had done it. And he couldn't believe that he had accused Claire in his mind.

He wished that he hadn't shown Joselle his scars. And he shuddered to think that he had nearly confided in her about the words of stone.

Now he felt as though he should have known. But how could he have known? Joselle had lied about when she had arrived at her grandmother's house. And when he had met her on the hill, she had told him that she had never been on the hill before. She'd probably lied a million times, he thought.

Or was there a part of him that suspected Joselle all along? If there had been, he just kept pushing it deeper and deeper inside himself until it virtually vanished. He had wanted to like her so much.

During the past couple weeks, Blaze had started to feel as though he had been friends with Joselle forever, but now he didn't know what was true. He didn't know what to believe.

Sitting alone, Blaze realized something else: he hadn't thought of Simon in days. Had Joselle taken his place?

Between his fingers, the button was as smooth as candy. He put it in his mouth and sucked on it.

20

JOSELLE

"I hate you," Joselle said to her reflection in the living room window. "I hate you, I hate you, I hate you." When she turned off the lamp on the end table, her reflection disappeared and everything was dark. Joselle remained by the window; it was past midnight, but she knew it was useless to try to fall asleep. By now she was beyond the point of crying. After dinner, in the bathtub, she had cried so much that her eyes were swollen and raw. So was her thigh. She had scrubbed the ball-point-pen tattoos with a vengeance so that the few remaining lines were as faint as thin spidery veins. "I hate you," she repeated. Joselle pinched her arm right above her wrist until she couldn't stand it any longer and there were red dents from her fingernails in her skin.

She felt the way she did at school when she hadn't prepared for a test, only much worse. An overwhelming sense of panic and frustration would fill her head like a storm, making it nearly impossible to sit still at her desk. What was the best thing to do? she'd always wonder. Guess, and most likely answer the questions incorrectly? Or leave the lined answer spaces empty? She'd weigh the odds in her mind, nearly always opting for leaving the test completely blank except for her name—which she would spend most of the period working on, carefully printing each letter with decorative touches. That made things for her teachers more complex, more baffling. Most of her teachers regarded her with suspicion and wrinkled noses, as if she were some kind of specimen that was hard to categorize.

Once, when she had completely forgotten about a vocabulary test for Mrs. Weynand's language arts class, Joselle felt compelled to approach Mrs. Weynand with a sincere hug and explain how awful she felt. But she knew that that would never work; there was too much history between them for Mrs. Weynand ever to think of Joselle as anything but trouble. A constant inconvenience.

But this wasn't a test in school. This was more important.

Joselle needed someone to talk to. She hadn't told Floy about what had happened at Blaze's house, because Floy's patience was wearing thin. Upon seeing the wet, dirtied cashmere sweater—twigs and weeds sprouting from the sleeves—Floy threw her arms up in exasperation. Her eyeballs rolled back and her mouth popped open like a fish when she noticed the missing button. "You'll never be able to match that pretty button," she said, yanking the sweater toward her to get a better look and releasing it with a snap, as though a mannequin were wearing it, not a person. "I'm not even going to ask what you've been up to. Just get yourself showered and cleaned and dried. And give me the sweater," Floy added. "I'll try to fix it up." Then she sighed heavily and shook her head. Joselle knew that she was fast becoming the same person in her grandmother's eyes that she was in the eyes of her teachers. Anyway, Floy was surely asleep by now. And Gary was little consolation.

Joselle needed her mother.

On the end table, resting against the lamp, stood a framed photograph of Joselle, Vicki, Floy, and Floy's mother, Alice. The photo was taken in the hospital on the day that Joselle was born. "Four Generations of Women," Joselle had called the photograph once. "I'd call it 'Four Generations of Fighting and Headaches,'" Vicki had retorted. Joselle thought it was odd that she had such a vivid memory when it came to Vicki's hurtful comments. She shrugged to herself.

Although Joselle's great-grandmother Alice died before Joselle had formed a memory of her, Joselle sensed a strong connection to her. In the photograph Alice's heart-shaped face was a lacework of grooves; Vicki's was flushed and young. Floy appeared stern and uneasy, and Joselle was a chubby bundle the color of a bruise. It was too dark to see the photograph clearly, but Joselle knew it like she knew the image of George Washington on a dollar bill.

The only information that Joselle had about her great-grandmother was from photographs and from stories Vicki and Floy had told her. When she was younger, Joselle had thought of Alice as a guardian angel, a bent, wrinkled woman who lived inside the crack in Joselle's bedroom ceiling. Someone who was able to see and know all things. Someone who would emerge upon request to rescue and comfort Joselle. As routine, Joselle used to say good-night and good morning to the crack every day. It didn't take Joselle very long, however, to come to the conclusion that the crack was only damaged plaster and that her great-grandmother could never, ever truly help her.

Once, when Joselle lost one of Vicki's favorite earrings and was sent to her room as punishment, Joselle called for Alice. "Here, Alice! Here, Old Grammy!" she cried. At first she waited patiently, sitting cross-legged on her bed, her head tilted upward. When Alice failed to respond, Joselle climbed onto her dresser and removed the curtain rod from the window frame. Using the curtain rod as a tool, she chipped away at the ceiling until bits of plaster dusted her bedspread like snow and she knew in the very bottom of her heart that what she was doing was not only pointless, but would only get her into more trouble.

□   □   □

In the moonlight Joselle wandered. From room to room she roamed without purpose. After she had walked through every room (except Floy's bedroom) several times, Joselle found herself back in the living room beside Floy's rocking chair, staring down at the telephone. With the telephone cord spiraled around her, Joselle dialed her own number. She wanted Vicki to magically answer the phone and say: "Hello, sweetie! Of course it's me. I'm having all the calls forwarded to me in California. Whatever it is you want, I'll do. I'll be on the next plane home if you need me." But all she heard was the faraway sound of a dull bell in an empty house. Joselle let the phone ring and ring and ring. She pictured her mother and Rick running along the beach, the orange-and-pink sun dropping into the Pacific Ocean behind them. She pulled the cord across her face, placed it in her mouth, wove it between her fingers. She was all set to hang up, when suddenly she heard a sleepy, but familiar, voice bark, "Hello? *Hello?* Who *is* this?"

Joselle hung up the phone without saying anything. She fell into the rocking chair. After the initial shock passed, she cried in rhythm with the movement. Back, forth. Whimper, sniffle. She cried quietly at first, like someone at a movie. But then she began to rock faster and cry louder. When she thought that she might completely lose control, she sprang from the chair and barged into Floy's room.

"Grammy," she sobbed. "Grammy, help."

21
JOSELLE

While Floy talked on the telephone, Joselle sat on the floor behind the sofa. The longer Floy talked, the louder her voice grew. "I don't care if it *is* one o'clock in the morning," Floy said. "What are *you* doing home? Your daughter and I were led to believe that you and your friend were somewhere out west."

Twisting this way and that way, Joselle tried to hear better, tried not to hear, tried to see Floy's expression, tried to hide her own eyes so she couldn't see a thing. Joselle heard Floy say, "What do you *mean,* you've been home all along?" and "I don't care what you call it, I call it lying," and "Too bad the word responsibility isn't in your vocabulary," and "You'll never change," and "Nothing's ever your fault, is it?"

By the time Floy slammed the receiver down, she was shouting. Her "Good-bye!" made Joselle cringe.

"Well," said Floy, her face pinched with anger, "The Beautiful Vicki strikes again. She thinks her wishes are more important than your needs."

Joselle hated talk like this; it meant nothing. She wanted facts. She gave Floy a searching look. "What are we doing?" she cried. "What's *happening*?"

"I'm taking you home where you belong."

"Right now?"

"Right now. I won't be able to sleep. You won't be able to sleep. We might as well." Floy bent down and kissed Joselle on each cheek. "She was home the entire time. The Pacific Ocean thing was just one of her stories." Floy inhaled deeply. So deeply that Joselle thought that Floy might suck in the whole living room. She let out the breath slowly and steadily. "Come here, Joselle," Floy said, her voice changing, turning lighter, almost airy. "Let me do your eyelids one last time."

□ □ □

Within minutes after having her eyelids done, Joselle was packed and they were on the road. Floy was in such a hurry that she and Joselle kept their nightgowns on. Joselle wore a sweatshirt over hers.

Joselle's sweater was lying on a towel on the backseat. It was still wet. Earlier that afternoon, Floy had washed it by hand and sewn on a flat, mismatched, dove-colored button. "It's the best I can do," Floy had told Joselle.

When they passed a street lamp, Joselle turned in the car to look at the sweater. It was no longer a perfect thing. It was limp and dull. *Now it truly belongs to me,* she thought regretfully.

The night was thick and black and full of motion. The white painted lines on the highway slashed through the darkness as if they had been cut with a monstrous knife. There were only a few cars on the road, and when Joselle spotted one she wondered where it was going. She was going home. It may not have been under the best of circumstances, but Joselle Stark was going home.

Joselle's bags were in the trunk, but she kept her purse and her knapsack on the floor between her feet. In the knapsack were her new clothes, the lucky penny, Blaze's key collection, and the fox she had taken from his Noah's ark.

Blaze Werla.

What could she do about him now? Would he ever forgive her? How could she have been so stupid? Why had she danced in the rain?

A small part inside her wanted to forget him—put him out of her life completely, throw his things into the trash when she got home. But she knew that wasn't possible. She had already added him to her life. Most people she trusted ended up breaking her heart into a million pieces. Blaze was different. Why did she have to go and ruin everything?

"I've got something for you," Floy said, interrupting Joselle's thoughts. "Grab the wheel a minute. Traffic's light."

Joselle leaned over and clutched the steering wheel. She turned it ever so slightly, testing it, feeling the power. Floy had never let her do this before and it surprised Joselle. The highway curved gradually and Joselle maneuvered the car expertly.

Floy fished under the seat for a minute and came up with a small, flat bag. "Here it is," she said. She slid the bag onto Joselle's lap and grabbed the wheel, pushing Joselle's hands away. "I bought this the night we went shopping at the mall. I paid for it while you were in the dressing room. I thought I'd keep it and give it to you when you needed it most." Floy flipped the overhead light on.

It was a scarf. A beautiful scarf. It was black, bordered with a network of birds of all kinds, printed in gorgeously bright colors. Every color Joselle knew. And even some she couldn't identify by name.

"Thanks, Grammy. I love it." Joselle stroked one of the birds. "I love you," she told Floy.

"I thought it would look nice with your new sweater. Jazz it up a bit."

A lump formed in Joselle's throat. She wanted to say more to Floy. Apologize for getting the sweater dirty. Thank her again for the scarf. She started to cry.

"I know you don't understand everything your mother does," Floy said. "I don't understand, either. But I know she loves you." Floy rubbed Joselle's knee. "Let's just drive," she said. "Let's just drive and think."

Joselle had a lot to think about. The Beautiful Vicki

topped her list. But if Joselle thought about her mother too long, she was overcome with sadness. She tried to keep the sadness moving. Joselle pictured the inside of her body as a pinball machine. And she willed the sadness—the little steel ball—to stay in motion, moving around and around throughout her. Never stopping. If it stopped, she might explode.

Her mind drifted back to Blaze. He may have been the best friend she ever had. If nothing else, she knew that she had to return the key collection and the tiny fox. It was just a matter of time. Joselle remembered so clearly the night that she had thought of the words of stone, how impressed she had been by her own brilliance. And when she had first looked at Reena's name on the hillside, she had felt so elated that her toes tingled. Thinking about it all now caused her stomach to sink. She had set out to complicate someone else's life, and ended up complicating her own.

And that's when she took her pen from her purse and hiked up her nightgown. I'M SORRY, Joselle wrote on her thigh. And—I'M BACK. And she knew that she would be back. She was counting on it.

Floy glanced over, clicked her tongue, and flicked off the overhead light. "Just drive and think," she said again, softly.

After putting her pen away and readjusting her nightgown, Joselle folded and unfolded the scarf on her lap. Then she wound it loosely around her neck and knotted it above her heart, tossing the ends casually off to the side. Even in the darkness, the birds on the scarf were so colorful, so vivid, that for a brief moment Joselle was certain that she heard them sing. A wild throaty song.

22
BLAZE

The bedroom simmered with stale heat. Joselle was standing at Blaze's window, looking out toward the hill. She was wearing a skirt that reminded Blaze of a tulip, upside down. The skirt changed color constantly—green to blue to gray. And everything wavered. She was intent, her body firmly fixed to the window frame like a statue. Blaze wanted to see what she was seeing. Was there a message on the hill? He tried to run toward her, but could only move in slow motion, as if he were moving through deep water. By the time he reached the window, Joselle had leaped out. He leaned over the sill, but she was nowhere to be seen. She had disappeared into a blinding yellow light. But her voice came from all around—above, below, and from within. "I'm every-where," her voice said, echoing in his head like a bell, making his ears ache. "I'm everywhere."

When Blaze woke up, his sheet was pulled over his head, and his room was sizzling with the summer sun.

□   □   □

For days after the incident in the rain, Blaze didn't see Joselle at all. But then he hadn't gone up to the hill since then, and he wasn't exactly sure if he wanted to see her anyway.

He spent a good portion of each day preparing to paint the canvas that Glenn had given him at the start of the summer.

Blaze had decided to try to paint in a manner similar to Glenn's. He would paint a surreal landscape. Blaze knew that people rendered realistically weren't his spe-cialty, so he thought he would choose different objects to represent people he knew. He would have the objects floating in a night sky, stars all around. Anything was possible in the darkest part of the night.

Lying on his bed, Blaze made a list of the people he wanted to include and the objects that might represent them.

> DAD—a paintbrush, his birthmark
> GRANDMA—a cucumber beetle, green
> beans, tomatoes, a flower
> MOM—my ark, the Ferris wheel

Should I include Joselle? he wondered. Or Claire? Or myself?

He added to the list.

> JOSELLE (maybe)—a spoon, the button,
> stones
> CLAIRE (maybe)—*long* hair *(not red)*, a
> silver barrette
> ME (maybe)—my key collection, my ark, the
> Ferris wheel

Some things could stand for more than one person, Blaze realized. A paintbrush could stand for Glenn or himself. Or even Claire, seeing as there were brushes in the box of paints she had given him. His ark and the Ferris wheel could stand for Reena or himself. His key collection also symbolized Joselle, since she had it now. And Joselle's button represented both of them, too; it was hers, but it was in his possession. We're all linked in certain ways, he thought.

He sketched on paper first. While he worked, Blaze remembered the day he had told Joselle that he wanted to be an artist when he was older.

"A famous one?" she asked.

"I don't know," he replied, shrugging. "Just an artist."

"*I'm* going to be famous," Joselle told him, smiling.

"At what?" Blaze asked.

"At whatever I want," Joselle answered. "Currently I plan on being a famous doctor, or at least a surgeon of the heart or brain."

Even though Joselle was on his mind, he decided to concentrate on Glenn and Nova and Reena. Soon, a large paintbrush, green beans, and a tomato circled a full moon. And so did an ark with animals spilling out across the sky.

When Blaze sketched the ark, he set the real one on the floor in front of him. That's when he discovered that his tiny fox was missing. He looked for it under his bed, in his closet, and in all his drawers. I'll find it later, he said to himself.

He worked and reworked his ideas until he was satisfied. Then he smeared charcoal on the back of his drawing, taped it to his canvas, and traced over the drawing. Now the image was on the canvas. He left enough space for other objects he might include later.

With his paints like a box of candy before him, Blaze sat in his room waiting to begin. "Beginning is the hardest part," Glenn always said. Blaze surely felt that now. He waited and waited and waited. He wasn't yet ready to make a mark on the canvas with paint.

◻   ◻   ◻

The next day Glenn asked Blaze, "Where's Joselle? I haven't seen her around lately."

"I'm not sure," Blaze answered, trying to be as vague as possible.

"Maybe she'd like to come for dinner, too?"

"Oh, not tonight," Blaze said.

"Okay," said Glenn, absently. He was poking at the

fire in the outdoor grill with tongs. Claire was coming
for dinner. They were going to have bratwurst.

Blaze was wary of the fire. He stood at a distance and
squinted his eyes. He could feel the heat and smell the
lighter fluid. Blaze crossed his arms, rubbing his elbows
tentatively. His ankles felt itchy. The air above the
flames rolled and flickered as though he were looking
through waves. It was mesmerizing.

Blaze had asked to invite Claire. It was his way of trying
to make up for the times that he had ignored her. Glenn's
eyes had glinted when Blaze had suggested it. "Good
idea, Blazer," he had said, placing his hand on the back of
Blaze's neck and holding it there for a moment.

□   □   □

After dinner, Blaze found a few minutes when he and
Claire were alone.

"I wanted you to come for dinner," Blaze told Claire
softly. The kitchen table stood between them, a flat
brown space. They had already cleared the table of dirty
dishes and rinsed them. Water dribbled down Blaze's
arm. He wiped it on his pants. "It was my idea."

"I know." Claire's mouth was a perfect circle when
she finished saying the word know. And her expression
was so bright his head spun.

□   □   □

Before Claire left, she came to Blaze's room to say
good-night. The door was open, but she knocked and
waited in the hallway.

"You can come in," Blaze said, sitting up. He had been lying on his bed. His Noah's ark was on its side, capsized atop a rumpled mess of bedspread waves. The animals were scattered, adrift among the creases of the sheets. He had been wondering (as he often did) about what happened to all the animals that were left behind, all the animals that weren't allowed into the ark. Did they all drown? And how many animals *had* been left? Hundreds? Thousands? Millions? The waters of the great flood must have stunk, he reasoned. And what about the *people* left behind? That was the worst part about the story of Noah's ark. The part they never really tell you about. What happened to all the people?

"I just wanted to thank you for inviting me tonight," Claire said.

"That's okay," Blaze replied. His cheeks turned hot. "This was my favorite toy when my mother died," he said, picking up the ark and offering it to Claire. Their fingers touched in the exchange.

"It's nice," Claire said. Nodding toward an animal, she said, "May I?"

"Sure." Blaze handed her the tiger. "I had twelve kinds of animals, but just yesterday I realized that my fox is missing. I keep this in the ark to take its place. Until I find the fox." He held up the round, lustrous button from Joselle's sweater.

"No foxes." Claire looked quietly, then gently placed the ark and the tiger at the foot of Blaze's bed. "Well, I should go, but I just wanted to thank you. It was nice to see you again. And thank you for letting me look at your ark. It's an interesting story, don't you think? Mysterious."

Blaze could only nod in agreement. Mysterious was right. He almost pulled his canvas out of his closet to show Claire, but changed his mind.

"Good-night, Blaze," Claire said from the doorway. Her face was in shadow, but her long, ringed fingers waved in the light, catching it and sending it back like miniature comets.

"'Night," he answered. He listened to her oddly rhythmic footsteps pattering down the hallway. She's skipping, he thought, thrilled by the sound and thrilled by the picture it created in his head: a tall adult doing what he had only seen little children and his kindergarten teacher do. Blaze fluffed his pillows and wedged them behind his back. "See you soon," he whispered.

23
BLAZE

Because he knew he would have to face Joselle sooner or later, Blaze walked up and over the hill to Floy's house and rang the bell. Gary charged for the window and barked so fiercely Blaze shuddered. After a long minute Floy answered the door, opening it just a crack and blocking Gary with her spindly legs.

"Hello, Blaze," she said, her bespectacled nose protruding through the small gap between the door and the doorjamb.

"Hi," he said shyly, trying to keep an eye on Gary. "Can I talk to Joselle?" he asked, twiddling his fingers nervously. "Please?"

"She went back home," Floy replied. "It's been a few

days now. I don't know what Joselle told you, but she was only here for a short visit. For all I know, she told you she moved in here."

Suddenly Blaze felt lonely. "She didn't say good-bye." The boldness of his voice surprised himself.

The door opened wider as Gary quieted down. Blaze could see Floy entirely now. She was wearing a sleeveless white housedress patterned with deep red roses, and she held a magazine in her hand. Her pockets were overflowing with tissues.

Gary slipped past Floy and trotted out onto the porch. He rubbed against Blaze. Blaze scratched Gary behind his ears, trying to remain calm, trying to remember everything Joselle had taught him about dogs. After circling Blaze twice, Gary made himself comfortable in the shady corner of the porch.

"Well, to be truthful," Floy said, "I ended up taking Joselle home in the middle of the night. It was a sudden departure."

"Is Joselle okay?" Blaze had carried the button with him. He felt for it in his pocket and pressed it into his leg. He looked at Floy intensely, seeking an answer.

"Oh, sure. I didn't mean to mislead you. Don't worry about Joselle. She's fine. Joselle's Joselle." Floy swatted at a fly with her magazine. "Listen," she said, "do you want something to eat?" She stepped aside and gestured for Blaze to enter the house. The sweep of her arm pushed the door open all the way. "I think I've got some cookies. Store bought."

144

"No, thank you," Blaze said politely, moving slowly off the porch. He backed up to the railing and leaned against it. "But—but is she coming back?"

"Oh, she'll be back. As a matter of fact, she ran off at the mouth about you to her mother. She told her mother that she wanted to live here, she liked you so much. Her only true friend in the world, she called you."

Blaze blushed completely and uncontrollably.

"It'd put me away for sure," Floy said. "Having her live with me." She sighed and rolled her eyes. Then her eyes welled. "You know Joselle. She's a handful. But a sweetheart, despite all her troubles." She laughed, and it seemed to Blaze that it wasn't exactly a joyful laugh.

Blaze cleared his throat.

Gary stretched and yawned. A long wheezy yawn followed by heavy panting.

"She really likes you," Floy continued. She was blinking her eyes quickly, as though she had something in them, irritating them. "It's the only time I've ever seen her so interested in another child."

Looking down, Blaze played with his feet, waggling his toes; his shoes seemed sizes too small. "If you talk to her, will you tell her I said hi?"

"I sure will. And you say hello to your father and your grandmother for me. Funny, we live so close and never see each other."

Blaze said that he would. Then he went up to Gary

and petted him, cooing to him as he stroked his sides, the way Joselle had shown him. Gary's tail wagged briskly, and Blaze hopped off the porch.

"You're a nice young man," Floy called. "I'd like Joselle to be around you more. Thank you. Thanks a lot."

"Bye," Blaze said, turning back toward Floy for a moment before running home, his heart booming.

He had gone to Floy's with the intention of demanding the return of his key collection, and now he didn't even care about it; he only missed Joselle. He had thought and thought about how he could ever forgive her, and already it was done.

◻   ◻   ◻

Several mornings later Blaze rose to discover a small wrapped box outside his bedroom door. A note was attached. It said, *I made these for your ark. Love, Claire.*

Blaze opened the package and found a pair of shiny bronze foxes, no larger than an inch in any direction. Blaze picked them up. He hadn't told Claire that he owned only one of each animal. Of course she'd assume there'd be two. The foxes sat on Blaze's palm, heads low, tails curled slightly sidewise. He moved his hand, examining the foxes from every angle. The details fascinated him: delicate lines to indicate fur, the holes that served as eyes, the teensy upturned peaks that formed the pointy noses. The foxes were more sturdy and heavy than Blaze's plastic animals. More beautiful, too.

He looked at the foxes for so long that they became huge. So huge that there was barely enough room in the world for anything else.

□ □ □

Something wasn't right.

Blaze peered at the drawing on his canvas from various distances, tilting his head this way and that way. He still had not begun to paint. He thought of asking Glenn for help, but he wanted to do this all on his own. To make it work.

Blaze had considered adding objects to represent Claire and Joselle to the painting right from the start. And that's exactly what he decided to do.

Claire would be easy. He drew two foxes as expertly as he could, looking carefully at the statues from Claire. He drew them on the underside of the full moon, flying, reaching out and up and toward the ark. The only pair of animals on the canvas.

Joselle was more difficult. But after about an hour of thinking and sketching, it became obvious; with only a few changes, the large, round full moon could also serve as Joselle's button.

It seemed right. Everything circled the button-moon the way Blaze's summer seemed to revolve around Joselle.

He knew it wasn't perfect, but he felt as ready as he would ever be. And so he began to paint.

24

BLAZE

It was August. School would be starting soon. Blaze and Nova were at the cemetery, tending the flowers beside Reena's grave. Glenn had been working with them, but decided to go for a walk. "I'll wait for you by the car," he told them. It was parked at the side of the highway.

"Dad doesn't like it here, does he?" Blaze said. He was pulling handfuls of weeds and piling them into Nova's basket.

"I think he was just ready to leave," Nova said. "It *is* taking me longer than I thought it would, but I wanted to cut all the roses back."

"Sometimes it's scary here," Blaze told her as he watched withering rose petals flutter to the ground.

148

"Sometimes."

"And sometimes it's just quiet."

"I think you're right."

While Nova finished working with her clippers, Blaze ran his hand over his mother's name. REENA PREHN WERLA. No matter how hot it was outside, the stone felt icy to his touch. The chiseled edges of the letters numbed his fingers. Sometimes he'd press his hand against the stone until an impression was left on his skin. He'd watch it vanish like breath on a window.

When he was in the second grade, Blaze had found a picture of a cemetery in a big book at the school library. He couldn't remember the name of the book, and although he had looked for it again several times, he never found it. The picture was of four boys sitting on tombstones, riding them as if they were horses. The boys were wearing hats and blowing trumpets, as Blaze recalled it. The picture frightened him the day he saw it, and he always thought of it when he came to the cemetery. He could never do what the boys in the picture were doing. But he could imagine Joselle doing it. He saw her clearly. Joselle—hopping onto a gravestone, clicking her heels and whooping, wearing a loopy grin on her face and an outrageous hat on her head. It didn't seem wrong for Joselle.

Blaze took Joselle's button out of his pocket and rolled it along Reena's gravestone. When it fell onto the ground, Blaze picked it up, wiped it off on his shirt, and tucked it into his sock. Sometimes he kept it there, sometimes in his wallet, sometimes in a pocket. But he always carried it with him now, wherever he went.

"We'd better go," Nova said. She leaned on Blaze as she got up.

"It looks nice," Blaze remarked, helping his grandmother gather her things. He felt sleepy all of a sudden, and yawned.

"Give me your hand, Blaze," Nova said. She held it until they reached the car.

◻   ◻   ◻

Being at the cemetery had given him the idea to go to the hill. He walked around the black locust tree, weaving in and out of the stones.

Blaze thought about the burials he had been responsible for: Benny's, Ajax's, Ken's, Harold's, Ortman's. And everything went fuzzy for a moment. In some ways the whole idea seemed childish to him. Had it always? Or was this some new feeling? He wondered how changes take place in people. He wondered if people knew when things changed in their minds any more than they could feel their bones or hair growing.

Blaze took the five stones, added one for Simon, and formed a letter *J* with them as best he could near the black locust tree.

He hadn't seen Joselle since the morning in the rain. He wondered if he'd ever see her again.

150

□   □   □

When Blaze painted, hours could pass without his knowing, and he could vacillate between complete satisfaction with his work and total disappointment within that time over and over again.

It had taken Blaze weeks to finish the canvas. He had gotten to the point where he just couldn't do anything else to it. And yet, he didn't want to show it to Glenn or Nova or Claire. He didn't want to explain what anything meant.

Blaze signed his name in the lower right-hand corner of the canvas, using little white dots of paint to form the letters.

□   □   □

On the last Saturday in August, Blaze woke up feeling exceptionally buoyant. He and Glenn and Claire were going to the county fair. They would be leaving early and making a day of it. Blaze was out of bed and dressed in minutes. He went to the window and threw open the curtains. The morning was shiny with rain from the night, the air breathtakingly clear. Above the hill, the sky was a radiant blue, and beneath the black locust tree on the slope of the hill were stones. The stones were white moons that bled together. They spelled: I'M SORRY.

Blaze stared at them until all the sounds of the morning quieted to nothing—the birds, the clock, the wind.

Then he pinched himself to verify that he was, in fact, awake and alive, and bounded down the hallway to Glenn's room.

He'd have to explain some things to Glenn, but Blaze felt that he could handle that. There was a lot of telling to do, but he'd only say as much as he needed to for now. Blaze had simply told Glenn and Nova that Joselle had gone home. He hadn't told anyone about the words of stone. Maybe he'd even show Glenn the painting.

Blaze's footsteps were much too loud for early morning, but he didn't seem to notice. He reached Glenn's bedroom and stopped, loosely holding the doorknob. He didn't know where to begin. He thought for a minute, then slowly opened the door.

"Dad," he whispered excitedly, "get up. I want you to look at the hill."

It was a good place to start.